PLAYING FOR KEEPS

DON SPEARS

Copyright © 2002 By Don Spears

Printed and Bound in the United States of America

Published and Distributed by:
Milligan Books
an imprint of Professional Business Consultants
1425 W. Manchester, Suite C,
Los Angeles, California 90047
(323) 750-3592

Word Processing by Pamela D. Hunter, Shawishi St. Julien, and K.L. Flick
Cover by Alexandra W. Baker, DNA Illustrations, Inc.

First Printing, February 2002
10 9 8 7 6 5 4 3 2 1

ISBN: 1-881524-52-3

Publisher's note
This is a work of fiction. Names, characters, places, and incidents either are product of the author's imagination or are used fictitiously, and any resemblance to actual persons, living or dead, events, or locales is entirely coincidental.

All rights reserved. No part of this book may be reproduced in whole or in part, in any form or by any means, electronic or mechanical, including photocopying, recording or by any information storage and retrieval system, without permission in writing from the author.

ABOUT THE AUTHOR

DON SPEARS, is an engaging artist, educator, publisher, playwrite, and Screenwriter. He is the author of the compelling National Best Seller "IN SEARCH OF GOODPUSSY." He has appeared on numerous television and radio show and resides in New Orleans.

PLAYING FOR KEEPS

Dedicated to my mother, Ruth Spears, my sisters Juanita Lynn Spears and Brenda Spears Guinn, my grandmother Creasia Price, my godmother Getrude LeBlanc, my father Julius D. Spears Sr., and my son Patrick Shannon Spears

Acknowledgments: To all those who believed in my first book "In Search Of Goodpussy," who continue to support me, Keith Douglas, Stephanie Clark, Brittney Nicole Spears, Julius and Arlyn Spears, Arnold Spears, Gerrick and Janel Spears, Willie "Pine" Spears, Brenda Dupre Williams, Rhonda Vaughn, Michael Radford, Sam Greenlee, Velma Benjamin, Bonita Blakely, Alvin and Sandy Meekins, Andre Laborde, Barry Mayeux, Noah and Karin Hopkins (MIRG), Debra and Wayne Arnold, Hiram Cooke, Inspector Wendell Watkins, Georgr "Tex" Stephens, Spencer Coudray Sr., Chief Arnasta Taylor, Raymond Lewis, C.J. Blanche, June Gardner, Robert "Skeet" Jones, Selena Casey, Kurte Pellerin, Dr. Kirby Green, Dr. Luther Glenn Williams, Frederick Dent and countless others.

Special thanks to Dr. Rosie Milligan for her enduring support and encouragement.

PLAYING FOR KEEPS

PART I

PROLOGUE

New Orleans, Louisiana 2000, 1:30 A.M.

The windows of the 22-year-old MG roadster started to fog as Debbie and Ray snuggled in front of her uptown home on Audubon Place. Debbie not only felt warm and secure in Ray's arms, she was also relaxed, knowing her parents' palatial home was in a gated, exclusive community and her neighborhood was safe at night. In fact, Ray felt so confident that he didn't even bother to lock the car doors whenever he took her home from a date.

"Debbie, it's almost two," Ray whispered between kisses. He cupped her face gently as though she were a delicate porcelain peach, then kissed her nose.

"I know, I know..." Debbie murmured. With her eyes shut, she almost thought she heard the sound of the surf, but then she realized it was the pounding of her own blood crashing in her ears.

Without a word, they both knew that two o'clock was Debbie's self-imposed curfew. Ray had never been late, sometimes overruling her when she was tempted to stay longer at a party or just hang out with friends, especially in New Orleans.

Tonight was different, though. If she wanted to, she could stay out. Earlier that evening, she and Ray had attended a banquet being given in her father's honor, then partied at the Alpha Phi Alpha house on Broadway, Ray's fraternity. Her parents were still not home.

Debbie held Ray tighter and slipped her tongue into his ear.

"Brakes!" Ray said, gently releasing Debbie from his

embrace.

"Debbie's lips pouted into a sulk, but she caught herself. "Thanks, Babe. That's why I love you."

A second-year graduate student at Loyola University, Ray was majoring in law. As a martial arts enthusiast, he neither drank nor smoked—excellent credentials for Mayor Samuel Jammison, Jr. and his wife, the former Morrow LeBlanc, Debbie's overprotective mother and father. The tall young man was studious, soft-spoken, and well-mannered. Unlike her previous beaux, he was also firm and unmoving when he had made up his mind about something—even when it came to her.

Although an independent-thinking young woman like Debbie would never admit it, she admired the fact that she could not wind Ray around her little finger as she had so many others. Mainly, she admired his views on premarital sex. He never pressured her to give in. He was a Christian and he wanted to wait until they were married.

Ray smoothed the tendrils back from her pretty face. "Okay, one more kiss for the road," he said, taking her back into his arms.

* * *

Debbie and Ray were too busy kissing and petting to notice that Officer Hadley, the security guard, was not at his post, or that the lights outside the house had gone off momentarily. Deep in an embrace, neither one of them heard the late model Cadillac that had followed Ray's MG from the fraternity house a few blocks away.

The Cadillac eased up quietly and parked just behind the cozy, foggy-windowed sports car.

Two bulky men inside the Cadillac slipped on stocking masks, checked their weapons and silently slid out of the car, the interior lights coming on for brief seconds. A third man, also wearing a stocking mask, approached from the driveway. A nine-millimeter Beretta with a four-inch silence suppressor hung by his side, still smoking.

Without warning, the first man flung open the unlocked car door and thrust a long-barreled Colt revolver inches from Ray's face.

"Sit still, nigger, and you won't get hurt." His voice was low, deadly.

Debbie gasped. For a split second, Ray was so struck by surprise, he gulped air in amazement, then let out a shocked grunt. Quickly, gathering his wits, he instinctively chopped the gun out of the stranger's hand and sprung out of the car. With cobra-like precision, he gave the short pudgy man a stinging, closed-fist blow to his solar plexus. The downed man slumped to the ground, groaning in agony, as Ray dashed toward the other two men. He was propelled by Debbie's shrill screams, which pierced the somnolent night. The other two assailants had pulled her, kicking and swinging, from the car.

Ray lunged at the second man, then pulled him away from Debbie. In a swift flurry of motion, he dropped him with a spinning kick.

While Ray's back was turned, the third gunman regained his footing. He came up behind Ray and reached Debbie first. In one final coup, he smacked Debbie on the head with his gun butt, knocking her out. He pushed her limp body to the ground.

Pivoting around, Ray took in what had just happened. He leaped up in an attempt to give Debbie's attacker a frontal kick, but something hot and sharp stopped him in mid-air.

With the trained precision of a hit man, the corpulent stranger pumped two bullets into Ray's chest. The young man dropped to the ground. The muzzle flashed again when he fired a third shot into the dying boy's head as he lay helpless in the driveway, warm blood pouring from the open wounds and spilling on the ground in a puddle.

The gunman looked down at the young corpse. He calmly slid the black and gold Beretta back into the shoulder rig beneath his coat.

Turning back to his partners, he spat at them in disgust. "Come on, you fucking punks, let's go. Let a damn kid take you out!"

"Shit, why didn't somebody tell us the sonofabitch was into karate or judo or whatever the fuck that was?" said the stocky one. "Broke my goddamn nose. This is fucked up."

"Wouldn't have made any difference with you two," said the tall, well-dressed man, the obvious leader of the three. "Without your pieces, you're fuckin' pussies anyway! Come on. Let's get this little bitch outta here."

He lifted Debbie's limp body with ease and placed her into the back seat of the Cadillac. The trio then entered the car and drove away down the deserted avenue unseen, except for a woman peeking discreetly through partially open blinds from the large white house across the street.

CHAPTER 1

New Orleans, Louisiana 1948

    Indian summer made the still autumn air thick and damp without the usual gusty breeze from the northeast, which created small debris-laden whirlwinds in the cloistered neighborhoods of the inner city. The rains that normally cleared the area of people had ended hours before, yet the streets remained dismal and deserted.
    On that rain-muggy night there was only one lit storefront, the small grocery store owned by Samuel Jammison Sr. and his wife, "Miz Genny." Much like mom and pop groceries throughout the ghettoes of America, there was a storeroom and small toilet in the back rooms, and the front was filled with canned goods, produce, and staples.
    During the cold winter months, the men would gather around the searing hot pot-bellied stove in the center of the floor to lie and signify, tell tall tales from Southern folklore, create newer ones, and laugh away the pain of relentless slights in the segregated South. During the summer, they would drift up in the cool of the evening and gather on the oak bench out front that Samuel had made with his own hands shortly after opening his grocery. Good-natured friends spent many hours boasting and telling exaggerated lies of

their imagined success with women, or become embroiled in heated arguments about political issues.

Samuel and Genevieve Octave Guilmette had done well for themselves, raising their only son, Samuel Jr., and watching him grow into responsible manhood, buying their own home eventually on Seventh Street. They gave generously to Bethel Baptist Church where Samuel had faithfully served as Head Deacon for more than fifteen years.

Samuel and Genevieve had moved south from Chicago years before to avoid the icy winds that roared off Lake Michigan, mercilessly attacking Genevieve's chronic arthritis. Chicago had given them a good life, shielding them from the ravages of racism within the thriving ghetto that colored people in Chicago had affectionately named "Bronzeville." New Orleans had proved a godsend until confronted by Theo Brazzi's relentless greed.

Although raised in the gentle ways of a small Baptist church in a rural area of northern Louisiana, near Clinton, Samuel had been a carouser in his younger days, drinking corn liquor by the gallon, chasing women by the pound. Moving to Chicago for a short time after World War I, he had been an amateur and professional boxer during his early twenties and a barroom brawler until he joined Greater Bethesda Baptist Church on Fifty-Third and South Michigan, on Chicago's South Side. It was there that he met Miz Genny, visiting one Sunday during a revival, and eventually he mended his ways.

Because of his own checkered past, the elder Jammison recognized the seed right away in young Samuel Jr. when he saw him going his own way as a wild youth. One afternoon, he sent Miz Genny away for a couple of hours, took his fifteen-year-old son into the back yard and laced on the gloves to show him that there was always a better man with his fists and a better way than to fight, except in self-defense. Constantly, the elder Jammison impressed upon his young son the virtues of honesty, fairness, integrity and having a good name.

After a tour of duty in Europe during World War II, Samuel Jammison, Jr. had started college at Dillard University on Gentilly Boulevard. That same year, to his parents' delight, he had married his college sweetheart, Morrow LeBlanc. The two had met at the party after the traditional football game between Dillard and Xavier. A sophomore at the time, Morrow had been a cheerleader for the losing Xavier side. It was love at first sight.

* * *

Samuel Jammison, Sr. sat in the pale yellow light from a lamp that rested near the end of his freshly shellacked counter, the large old-fashioned pendulum clock ticking steadily, the only noise except for the soft sounds of the night birds and insects filtering through the screen door. It was seven twenty-five, five minutes before closing time.

Samuel sat motionless, head cupped in his hands, brow furrowed in deep thought. He sat quietly reflecting on all the hardships he remembered having overheard his parents and grandparents whisper about as a child—the kidnappings, the brutal rapes of colored women and young colored girls by white men and their sons, the beatings, the lynchings, the brandings, the castrations, the ears and feet cut off, being buried alive, cooked alive, or even being boiled alive over a slow fire. Once his mother, Creasia, had talked to him about her own childhood and growing up on the Alford Plantation in Wall, Louisiana. She told him about having to hide in the sugar cane fields from Mr. Alford and his sons on their horses, and how the Alfords had had sex with all of her playmates, except her. How much colored people had been forced to endure. He sat wondering what would they have done to a nigger like him one hundred years ago?

Jammison's grocery store had been riddled with bullets before, but no one was injured. Publicly Samuel Jammison held a number of dangerously unpopular views that left him sitting on a powder keg. Among them, he believed that colored people should have the same rights and privileges white people did, including the right to go wherever they wanted to, whenever they wanted to, and the right to vote. Every time the old telephone on the wall next to the storeroom rang it could have been another threatening call.

He was a tall, wiry man, dark brown skin, prematurely gray, short-cropped kinky hair, his horn-rimmed glasses resting down low on his pug, wide nose. His eyes were red from fatigue—his face marked with deep wrinkles that did not hide the laugh lines on both sides of his mouth. A quiet man, he enjoyed a good joke, and would sit on a stool at his counter, a bottle of Dr. Pepper at hand, while his friends and customers passed a jug. Although he no longer smoked or drank, he respected those men who did. He had only one rule: if they could not hold their liquor, they were not welcome in his store or around his family.

He wore a short-sleeved blue cotton shirt that had been handmade by his wife as a Christmas gift the year before, neatly pressed trousers and a clean butcher's apron—one of two that he rotated on a daily basis, carefully washed, ironed, and starched each night.

The Jammisons were considered well off by most of their neighbors, but they believed in being thrifty. They bought few gifts, preferring to make things with their own hands rather than buy a cold, impersonal manufactured item for their friends and relatives. One year Samuel had spent nearly two months hand carving a lamp for his wife from an old mahogany log.

Located in the heart of the district, the air outside of Jammison's Grocery smelled of stale beer and whiskey, and burgers or liver and onions cooking on a grill. There was another smell, too, a strange mix of blood, burned chicken feathers, grain and chicken droppings coming from the chicken coop out back. When the customer bought a chicken, live, the grocer would wring its neck and chop the head off, then drop the bloody, headless chicken, spinning and kicking violently, into a large, ashy, smoky black barrel.

Dr. Daddio, George "Tex" Stephens and especially O.C.W. Taylor, a popular local political activist, could be heard over the radio that was usually playing inside.

Samuel Jammison, a staunch defender of negro rights, often held small meetings where community leaders and other colored businessmen openly voiced their opposition to Jim Crow and segregation. Samuel Jammison hated the way colored people were treated, and he made no secret of it.

* * *

Three armed men waited silently in the dark storeroom to his rear. Typically, they wore shabby clothes, work boots, bib overalls, and dark plaid shirts. In the corner sat Malcom, the twenty-three-year-old son of the neighborhood carpenter. A two-barreled, twelve-gauge shotgun lay across his knees. Next to him sat Larry Shannon, age twenty-two, whose parents were high school teachers. He had a captured nine-millimeter German Luger. In the far corner was Samuel Jr., twenty years old, holding an Army Colt 0.45 automatic.

The three young men were ready to defend the Jammison grocery. Several other boys and men hid in the shadows to the front and rear of the store, all waiting with that quiet patience that marked black people in general, and those of the South in particular.

CHAPTER 2

New Orleans, Louisiana 1948

One Friday evening during a routine sweep, the police had picked up Samuel Jr. He was spotted walking in the eighteen hundred block of Dryades Street.

"Hey you, nigger! Nigger! Nigger!" one of them yelled, leaning out the window of the black van and waving his billy in the air. Samuel Jr. kept walking, ignoring the two policemen, but he could see their reflections in the storefront windows. The cops sped up and cut him off at the corner.

"Nigger, didn't you hear us talkin' to you, boy?" the officer who had been waving the billy shouted. His face twisted in a snarl as he jumped out of the vehicle.

"You been to jail before, boy?" asked the driver. "'Cause if you ain't, you goin' today."

"But why?" Samuel Jr. raised his hands imploringly. "What are you arresting me for? I haven't done anything."

"'Cause you a nigger, that's why!" The driver, stepping up to Samuel Jr.'s face, bared his teeth like a rabid dog and tapped the billy against the side of his leg.

Samuel Jr.'s heart sank. He knew that whenever the cops stopped a colored man or a colored boy, there was no escape, no way out. Scared to death, he understood clearly that he did not know how far they would go with this or even if they would kill him. He tried hard not to imagine himself as a bloody, battered punching bag, beaten to death.

They ordered him to get into the black mariah, a police paddy wagon. He complied. It held so many men they were sitting on each other. At the precinct on Annunciation Street, things were no better. The cells were overflowing. Some of the men, their faces swollen and bleeding, had been beaten up already. There was nowhere to sit down. Samuel Jr. had almost ended up with a hickey himself when his back was to the iron bars and the guard passed, knocking people in the head with a large, heavy ring of jailer's keys and a wooden billy club he was carrying.

Another boy was thrown into the cell, bloodied and smeared with feces. The toilets were always full. If you refused to confess or tell the cops what they wanted to know, they had ways to make you talk. One of the cops would put on long rubber gloves, swirl newspaper around in the filth, then rub it all over your face.

A favorite trick if they could not get somebody to talk was to take them out to the lakefront. If a beating didn't work, they would jack the police car up, pull your pants down, then race the engine while the driving wheel, the right rear wheel, tore the skin off your behind.

One Saturday night, Samuel Jr. had seen some policemen drive up and park in front of a bar at the corner of Phillip and Danneel Streets. "Get inside, niggers!" they shouted. "The captain said you niggers are gettin' outta line and he gave us orders to kill as many of you niggers as we could." The policemen went inside the bar and when they came out drunk, they beat up every colored man they could find.

Gimp Leg Louie was one of the meanest. He would beat any old colored man in the back until the man's nose bled, then spit chewing tobacco juice in his face. When another policeman, the Russian Bear, walked the beat with his gun and billy club, even the most ferocious negroes would actually run and hide.

Samuel Jr. had been to jail once before, picked up during the sweep. Most of the boys in the neighborhood had jobs in the evening making deliveries for the drugstores and the markets. He and his friend, Harry, who was a few years older, had heard about an abandoned house where they could find some stolen bicycles and maybe get some parts for their own bikes. He needed another kickstand and Harry needed handlebars, so they went to the house, but ended up getting caught.

There were two cops in the police car with them. One of them, a younger man, was driving, while the older man was in the back seat sitting next to Harry. The old cop casually raised his arm, pretending to be rubbing his forehead, and elbowed Harry hard in the face.

At the precinct Samuel Jr. was terrified because they were about to beat him, too, until the captain realized that he was only a minor and put him into a separate cell, saying that beating a juvenile up could get them into a lot of trouble. From the other cell, he could see that they had surrounded Harry and were taking turns punching and kicking him to a pulp.

No one could find Harry, not even his mother. The cops had hidden him somewhere for a month until the swelling went down. Samuel Jr. remembered that he was only thirteen then. He had hated cops ever since, especially Irish cops.

He could hear black prostitutes on the other side of the wall shouting, "Not like that. I'll do it the other way!" as the jailers demanded oral and anal sex.

"Any of you niggers got any money at the desk?" a red-faced sergeant asked. "My wife needs market money. If you wanna get outta here, you don't have no money at the desk. You know what I mean."

The so-called sweep or investigation was just an excuse to pick colored men up on Friday after they had been paid, and quietly steal their wages for the week. The police would take the money, give you your watch and your belt, then let you go, as long as you had not offended any white women, and that meant not even a smile.

Samuel Jr. recalled to himself that another thing that saved him from getting his head banged that night like the others was the fact that one of the policemen recognized him. Lieutenant O'Donahue, a precinct cop, remembered seeing him as a small boy playing around outside a speakeasy owned by his father's baby sister, his aunt Zina. He had watched him grow up in the neighborhood over the years.

Aunt Zina was well known. Her speakeasy had been located on Dryades Street near Melpomene. It was only a few blocks away from the Page Hotel, the colored hotel where celebrities like the Kansas City Monarchs, one of the popular baseball teams, stayed when they were in town.

They were called speakeasies because they were so noisy, especially with loud piano playing. The policemen who were on the take would stop by and say, "Don't make so much noise because the captain's gonna pass soon. You better speak easy." Of course, the captain who was on the take already knew what was going on, but during Prohibition, the FBI was looking for bootleggers, and there were still a few honest cops around.

Aunt Zina was one fine colored woman. She was built like "a brick shithouse." She had beautiful jet-black skin with high cheekbones and sculptured features, long coal black hair, a tiny 21-inch waistline, and flowing hips.

Zina was running with a man called Overhaul Bill, an informant for the state and federal police, which gave her added clout. One

PLAYING FOR KEEPS

day when the cops drove up, Sam Jr. and some of his friends were playing dice. Overhaul Bill, who saw what was about to happen, told the boys to leave the dice and the money on the ground and stand by the wall. The cops talked to Bill, then laughed and drove off, saying, "If y'all had started running, that money was gonna be ours."

Her piano player, like just about everybody else, was in love with her. His name was Paul Duplain, and he was a handsome creole man who had played briefly with King Oliver—that was, until he saw Zina. She would give him 150-proof homemade white lightning and Paul would play all night. At her speakeasy, she also served red beans and pig tails or back bones or pork chops.

After they found out young Samuel Jr. was kin to Zina, he was released. As he was walking out, Lieutenant O'Donahue told him to tell his Aunt Zina that he wanted some red beans and ham hocks, and make sure that colored woman named Hattie was there waiting for him.

* * *

Most of the cops were Irish thugs and some of them could not even read. They disliked the Italian immigrants almost as much as they did the negroes. For many of them, their sole reason for being on the police force was to brutalize colored people.

This part of town had been widen open—good-time joints, illegal lotteries, graft and bingo halls everywhere. Colored businesses, like white ones, thrived from the income, both legal and illegal. Negroes always played the numbers, and it only cost a nickel. Gambling was everywhere, and so were the pawnshops. In the unofficial colored red light district, people like Mama Lucy ran pitty-pat and kotch card games. The undisputed, most notorious place for gambling was Al's House, at 300 South Rampart Street.

At Carnival time, members of the Zulu Social Aid and Pleasure Club would beg white people for money, then parade from barroom to barroom. Getting costumes from pawnshops and borrowing police uniforms, the men dressed up like cops and made fun of white people. The Zulus put the money they collected aside and used it to bury brothers who had died and to help their surviving wives and families.

Like the Zulus, the Mardi Gras Indians paraded, too, with one big difference. Watching white folks on the screen at the Gallo Theater or the Lincoln Theater killing Indians, once they put their costumes on, the negroes actually thought that they had become real Indians. Following chiefs and witch doctors, they got drunk and marched down Rampart Street fighting and actually killing each other in black Indian wars.

Whenever a white man was beaten up or killed by a colored man, whether he deserved it or not, white people went crazy. Any negro man getting off the bus at Canal Street on his way to work could be beaten unmercifully by an angry white mob. Mr. Patterson, a white man who owned a hardware store across Canal Street, said that he would arm his nigger drivers if the ruffians didn't stop beating them up.

Colored people still stepped aside when a white person approached, shuffling condescendingly, eyes pitifully downcast, never looking them in their often hate-filled faces. Eye contact with whites was tantamount to defiance, a dangerous pride. Eye contact with whites could get you killed and often did.

Many of the residents were dirt poor. Some lived in rundown shanties rented for as little as two dollars a week. Tin roofs leaked and there were wooden and in some cases dirt floors, with no indoor plumbing. Outside there were ill fitted, unpainted weatherboards with gaping holes. During the winter many residents had to dress warmly inside, to keep from freezing, and any furniture they had was old or secondhand. After the Civil War, many rag-tag poor former slaves had followed Union troops into the cities with little more than the clothes on their backs.

In some uptown neighborhoods near Magazine Street or Napoleon Avenue, negroes could not safely walk outside at night. Captain Smith, the huge, three hundred pound commander in the Second District Precinct, had arthritis so bad that he had to lean against the door in the police car. He would order his driver to pull up beside colored people, then heave large globs of spit on them, shouting, "Damn black nigger bastards!"

Samuel remembered, however, that as a young boy in the 1930s, there were many good white folks around, too. Some of them boisterously complained that too many colored women were alone, and that they did not have papas to help them get milk for their babies. T. C. Semmes Walmsley, the mayor, hatefully responded, "Let them niggers eat the babies!"

Now those same streets were all but deserted. Shops that had been filled with gaudy goods and gaudier clothes were gone; bars boarded and shuttered; grocery stores, shoe shine parlors, barber shops, beauty parlors, restaurants, all gone. Almost anything owned by negroes had disappeared.

Now this neighborhood was a ghost town. The bakery owned by Amos Jackson had been forced to close, as had the cleaners operated by Mr. and Mrs. Bibbs. Most of the owners had moved out—Mr. Burns, who had grown wealthy selling white folks' "secondhand" furniture to colored people, even the tough Marshall brothers, Cleo and Foster, who owned the hardware store.

Only Samuel Jammison and a handful of merchants remained, as well as a few storefront churches and tiny, rundown working class bars. One of the more popular ones was "The Blue Eagle" on Felicity Street at Loyola, which was owned and ruled with an iron fist by Mr. Dave Brown, the so-called Mayor of South

Rampart Street. Serving hot fried fish and delicious home-cooked southern fried chicken, or chicken with dumplings, with live music by Sam Cook or possibly Lloyd Price, business couldn't have been better. Mayor Brown was also a man who was not easily intimidated.

In 1948 Dryades Street was the second largest shopping district in New Orleans, and for very good reason. Even though many of the stores like Kaufman's Department Store, the A&P Supermarket, Levitan's Furniture Store, and Autolec Auto Parts on Felicity and Dryades were owned by whites, most of their customers were negroes who did not shop downtown on Canal Street because of segregation. For colored people, Dryades Street was downtown. They could make purchases in stores like Stevens Apparel on Carondelet, Marks Isaacs Company or Krauss Department Store on Canal Street, but they could not try anything on, not even a dress or a hat. No, Samuel knew he couldn't give this store up.

Samuel Jammison's fight had been uphill in his marriage, too, but his bullheaded stubbornness had prevailed. Almond colored, hazel-eyed Genevieve Guilmette, with long curly black locks and a gentrified creole heritage, was hardly a match for a dark-skinned negro whose family had been farmers and sharecroppers. No matter how many times Genevieve's family would turn him away, he would still come back for more. And Genevieve's determination to marry the man she loved matched Sam's obstinacy.

Before the Civil War, the Guilmette family had owned slaves, too, and many of Genevieve's wealthy cousins had fought for the Confederacy in the Colored Native Guard. These Catholic gens de couleur libres, free people of color, considered themselves neither black nor white. Their customs and language were French, and like the Guilmettes they were often indistinguishable from white settlers, possessing great wealth with no visible slave heritage. Many had private tutors or were educated in France, like Genevieve's great-grandfather, Etienne, a creole businessman and plantation owner with a passion for the sport of fencing. Both black and white people in New Orleans owned slaves or "blacks," and so did Etienne. His grandparents had come to Louisiana in 1807 from Saint Domingue to escape the resentment of former slaves after the murderous slave uprising.

Some seven hundred and fifty black creole families owned about twenty-five hundred slaves, with assets of about fifteen million dollars. They were politicians, businessmen, bankers and teachers, before the Civil War and during Reconstruction, but after the war they found themselves for the first time, not much better off than slaves themselves. Thousands of light skinned Creoles decided then to go west to California where many started passing for white, or to the midwest and Chicago, like Genevieve's grandparents, Pierre and Estella.

Brazzi had issued his final threat to Samuel Sr. "Sell or die." The showdown was imminent. Samuel Jammison would fight, risking his life, before he would let the Brazzis of this world simply take what he and his wife and child had worked so hard to build. There was a time to take low and a time to fight; this night was the time to fight.

Brazzi did not bluff. One by one, defiant store owners had either surrendered to his demands or died. Mr. Green's house had been dynamited as his family slept. He, his wife and their daughter died in the explosion. Bird Robertson, who owned the radio repair shop, had been machine gunned in his own building one night after refusing to surrender half his weekly receipts to Brazzi. After that, one by one, the other shops had closed, their owners leaving in the dead of night, defeated by measured terrorism.

Civic improvement, slum clearance, it all amounted to the same thing. When the rich and powerful wanted a particular part of town, the residents had to move. It was that way everywhere. Theo Brazzi, Mafioso renegade and self-styled "real estate developer," not yet rich and powerful, saw his chance to grab as much property as possible in what he believed would become a desirable neighborhood for rich and middle-class whites.

Cunning, ruthless, yet barely literate, Brazzi knew that Dryades, Rampart and the surrounding neighborhood would one day be crucial to the expansion of the downtown business district of booming New Orleans. One day, commercial property owned by colored people—broken-down shanty houses and seemingly worthless land covered with ugly warehouses near the Mississippi River—would be valuable.

Created by thousands of impoverished, first and second generation descendants of former slaves—poorly educated negroes who had moved to the big city from rural areas like Moss Point, Mississippi and Bayou Goula, Louisiana—this area, Brazzi knew, would one day be occupied by rich whites and the businesses that lived off their custom. When that time came, those rich whites anxious for a good deal would have to buy property from the newly affluent Theo Brazzi.

The Italian Mafia had come to New Orleans around 1878, the most infamous families being the Provenzanos, the Matrangas and the Stoppangherra, the murder society.

For the most part, the Italians were the best friends a colored man could have. If you wanted to go into business and you were a little bit short of cash, they would be the ones to help you out, as long as they got their cut. And they made sure of that. But the Italians also wanted to get close to colored women, and would take liberties in patting or slapping a man's wife or sister on the behind, and enticing them further.

CHAPTER 3

A dark blue Packard sedan moved slowly down the street toward the grocery store as a light misty rain fell steadily. In the back room, the men stirred, cocked their weapons.

The Packard stopped across the street from the building and parked in front of "Pete the Fish Fry King," a paint peeling building on the corner of South Rampart and Melpomene. Four white men, wearing wide-brimmed Borsolino hats, swaggered from the car, turned the collars up on their coats, checked their guns, paused briefly, then crossed the street almost in step, carefully moving toward the grocery store.

Samuel smelled the car's exhaust, heard the doors closing, and could hear the cocking of weapons. He steeled himself for what was certain to come.

One by one the white men entered, stationing themselves around the room. The last man closed the door, and one of them waited outside. A big burly heavyset man, weighing at least two hundred and fifty pounds, their leader, approached Samuel Jammison, cockily puffing on a large cigar, twisting it between his lips with his thumb and index finger, his disdain unconcealed.

"Here's the contract signin' your store over to me, nigger."

said Brazzi menacingly, towering over the store owner, his baritone Italian accent thick. "Just put your John Henry on it so's I can be on my way. I got other fish to fry." He slapped the document on the counter, turning to his friends with a broad grin. "You know, I think I'm gonna like this. I ain't never owned no grocery store before. Now I can buy groceries from myself." He laughed, then turned back to face the store owner. "I might even buy me one of dem little white aprons, or maybe I'll just keep yours."

Samuel slipped his glasses up his nose without looking up and began to read.

Brazzi blew a long puff of blue-gray smoke in Jammison's face. "You wastin' my time, jigaboo. Sign the fuckin' papers. I ain't got all night. You know, maybe you shoulda done like that monkey chaser up in Harlem said. What's his name, Garvey?" He grinned, looking toward the accomplice to his left. "And got your black nigger ass on one of dem boats back to Africa." The unassuming store owner was thinking to himself that the uninvited trespasser was clearly an evil man, the kind of man the world could do without. If Brazzi really had that big a problem with colored people in America, he could just as easily have taken a boat back to Sicily or wherever he had come from. If the old country was all that, then why had he and his ancestors hauled ass coming here?

But then, Samuel Jammison had never agreed with Marcus Garvey's plan either, to establish a nation in Africa so that negro people could have their own country. What was there in Africa for him? As a matter of fact, the thought of ever going there had never crossed his mind. Besides, Genevieve was not about to leave New Orleans, to go to Africa or anywhere else. He had always wondered what it was about white people that made them think that everything automatically belonged to them, or that whatever anybody else thought or felt was unimportant. He already had a country and he was here to stay.

PLAYING FOR KEEPS

Adrenalin fed the anger he was trying very hard to conceal as he remembered that this was hardly the first time somebody had tried to abuse him. Even during World War I, he and other negro soldiers had been victimized by different forms of Jim Crow—slander, discrimination and even violence at the hands of the military and white citizen alike.

He had volunteered to fight in World War I in 1918 when he was only seventeen. He served in the all-Negro 93rd Infantry Division stationed in France. The American commanders at that time did not want colored soldiers in their ranks, so he and the other members of the 93rd Infantry fought under the French flag, using French equipment, with some of the men in his platoon wearing French uniforms. The French and the British had already been fighting for two years when the Americans got involved, and the French, who were hurting from manpower shortages, were glad to have the colored troops. General Pershing, however, leader of the American forces, cautioned the French not to treat negro soldiers as equals, because they would expect the same thing once they got back home.

Devil Fighters From Hell was what the Germans called them, because they fought so ferociously. Seven hundred and fifty black soldiers were killed and more than five thousand wounded by mustard gas. On Bastille Day, July 14, 1919, when French and British troops marched down the Champs d'Elysees during the victory parade, Private Jammison and other black troops were visibly in their ranks, while not one negro soldier marched with the Americans.

Samuel Jammison had done his share of fighting, too, and had earned the Croix de Guerre, the French equivalent of the American Legion of Merit, to prove it. From the looks of it, he doubted that any of his uninvited guests had done the same.

After the war, there was a resurgence of the Ku Klux Klan

and even though he and the others had fought valiantly, there was no change in their status back home. In fact, white racists who had seen pictures of French women hugging negro soldiers might beat up a black man in uniform if they got the chance, as a reminder that he couldn't get away with something like that back here. Sheriffs would agitate them, saying, "You think you're gonna lay up here like you did with the whores in France."

Why shouldn't he be able to buy a house anywhere he wanted to live or send his children to a good school if he could afford it? Jammison was thinking, quietly mumbling, "no way."

He agreed with Garvey about one thing, that "a Beggar-Race would never be respected." That was why he had opened his little storefront in the first place. As a good Christian, Jammison truly believed that the Lord helped those who helped themselves. He always made sure he did his part and more.

Marcus Garvey said that good white folks were paying negro leaders to tell bedtime stories, lulling colored people to sleep like children, telling them that their problems would go away as the years went by. He said that being collectively slothful, colored people accept the easy way out. Maybe that was true, too, Samuel thought, but he had never been one of those colored people.

Samuel silently continued to read.

"I believe the coon's hard of hearin'," said Brazzi to his men, frowning and bristling impatiently. No one made a sound as the burly Italian turned around, slowly pulled a long-barreled Smith & Wesson revolver from his shoulder rig, pointed it toward the ceiling, then fired. "Hear that, nigger?" he said with a smile. "The next bullet goes through your thick black skull. Figlio di puttana." He raised the revolver to shoulder height and aimed it straight at Samuel.

The store owner's heart hammered in his chest as his eyes slowly drifted up from the paper. He very calmly looked deep into

PLAYING FOR KEEPS

Brazzi's dark eyes.

"What kind of a fool do you take me for? My store is worth ten times this," said Samuel in a voice that was soft but stern, staring defiantly at the mobster.

"I ain't tellin' you again, Sambo," Brazzi snarled, frustrated, tension in his gruff voice, his face turning redder by the second. "Sign the fuckin' papers!" He cocked the weapon as his companions drew their own—a sawed-off shotgun and two automatic pistols.

"Boy, you don't know who you're playin' with, do you? You fuckin' nappy head coon. Burn this sonofabitch down!"

Brazzi gave the order and his men began to wreck the store, knocking and pulling goods from the shelves, breaking and flinging them to the floor, glass and debris everywhere. The man standing near the front door picked up a kerosene lantern, struck a match and lit it. There was one thing that Brazzi and his companions understood only too well. Like any other white man, they could easily kill any nigger without fear of being arrested. Even when niggers killed other niggers, little was made of it.

Without warning, deafening gunshots erupted from the storeroom and the street. Hot blood gushed from the wound and was running down his face when Brazzi was hit between the eyes, a .45 caliber slug exploding in his face. His heavy body collapsed on the countertop, then dropped with a loud thump on the wooden floor. The man with the lantern was struck back and front, the lamp bursting into flames when it hit the floor. The third man crashed through the storefront window screaming and firing wildly as the glass splintered. He had been hit by rifle, pistol and shotgun fire, slinging his twisted body back through the broken window. The fourth man, outside, spinning around and shooting aimlessly in the direction the shots came from, was mowed down by crossfire as gunshots flashed in the shadows, painfully burning hot holes in his body.

In less than a minute the shooting had ended, the smell of cordite, smoke and blood rising, white bodies sprawled in the reddish-orange glow of the flames. The first man stepping from the shadows, the muzzle of his machine gun still hot and reeking gray smoke, was South Rampart Street Mayor, Dave Brown.

CHAPTER 4

With the shoot-out at Samuel's store, what was to be called the Rampart Street War began; the Brazzi mob retaliating, the community fighting back while white policemen looked the other way. Encouraged by the stand taken by the tiny band at Samuel's store, many of the men of the neighborhood came out of hiding, but the body count mounted.

Things had backfired for Brazzi's mob. Even downtrodden black people who normally licked the white man's boots, bowed and scraped, or turned the other cheek, were fuming and so angry that they refused to be pushed around any more.

Sam's and Miss Genny's lives took center stage again when a carload of men firebombed his house, using Molotov cocktails stuffed with rags, opening fire with shotguns and machine guns. Both Jammison Sr. and Jr. fired back with carbines and handguns, and the family survived.

Veterans of World War I and World War II lent their combat expertise in setting up roadblocks and ambushes. Forty millimeter antipersonnel hand grenades came out of storage, captured weapons were dismantled, cleaned and oiled, then reassembled. Four Browning automatic rifles, Springfield 1903 military rifles, several bolt action .30 caliber rifles, two German Army issue

Mauser rifles, one .45 caliber Thompson submachine gun, three other Tommy guns captured from the Brazzi mob, and assorted hunting rifles and shotguns were their arsenal, and these rural negro men, most of them raised on hunting game since childhood, knew how to use them.

Violence against negroes even in the inner cities was not an isolated phenomenon. In a colored district in Wilmington, North Carolina, four hundred white men chased hundreds of colored people out of town, killing some and wounding others. Similar riots took place in cities like St. Louis and in Memphis, where forty-six black men, women and children were murdered. A negro postmaster in Lake City, South Carolina was burned to death in his home, as well, and his family shot to death while trying to escape.

On "Black Wall Street" the thriving business district in Tulsa, Oklahoma, whites were resentful because negroes were the ones flourishing. Jim Crow laws worked in their favor. Because there were strict curfew laws and it was illegal for a colored person to go into another section of the city except to work for a white business or a white family, the money they made stayed in their own community.

Wealthy entrepreneurs owned banks, bus lines, airplanes, and even movie theaters and a school. The Ku Klux Klan and the white Camellia were furious, believing that a message should be sent to other niggers to stay in their place.

During the Tulsa race riots in 1921, three thousand colored citizens died when their stores and homes were bombed from the air, burned down and bulldozed, then buried under tons of dirt.

It was in Chicago during a hot summer in July 1919 that the race riots ended, Samuel remembered, until the aftermath of World War II. Race relations were a sonofabitch in Chicago the ten years he lived there.

A brutal heat wave had forced thousands of both negroes and

PLAYING FOR KEEPS

whites to the Lake Michigan beaches. On Thirty-First Street Beach, a chain link fence plus a series of buoys marked the demarcation between the white and colored sections of both the beach and the water in which thousands of Chicagoans of both colors swam—de facto rather than de jure segregation.

A teenage boy swam beyond his depth and, exhausted, clung to a buoy marking the line between the white and colored sections of the same lake. Enraged whites, many of them drunk, began to stone the boy in plain sight of the astounded blacks. The teenager drowned under the onslaught and an enraged black mob skirted and climbed the fence to attack the white mob.

A free-for-all ensued, and the blacks, reinforced by men and women from the nearby ghetto, engaged in a pitched battle with the white mob that was eventually joined by the police. Overwhelmed by the enraged blacks, the police and whites retreated. Blacks throughout the ghetto took up hand-to-hand combat with roving white gangs and an almost lily-white police force.

Sparked by World War I veterans returning from Europe, blacks broke into the National Guard armory on Thirty-First and Shields Avenue, and with confiscated military weapons set up strong points throughout the ghetto, engaging first the police, and later the state militia.

The battle raged for the better part of the week, ending in stalemate and a negotiated settlement. The Chicago riots of 1919 marked the first time that American blacks had gone on the offensive and ended wholesale attacks on colored neighborhoods for more than three decades, with the exception of the Rampart Street war.

Violence against negroes was not new in New Orleans, either. During the New Orleans Riots after Reconstruction, an uncontrolled mob of southern sympathizers, the Ku Klux Klan and the White Camellia, had run wild for three days as well, murdering, robbing and viciously assaulting negroes. Nearly a century later, it was the Brazzi mob making their move, but unexpectedly they had met their match. New Orleans was not to become another Tulsa City.

Out of the blue the Rampart Street warriors got the break they needed most when they least expected it. From Jonesboro, in northern Louisiana and another little town called Bogalusa, across Lake Pontchartrain, came fifty black men in a caravan of cars and pick-up trucks.

Heavily armed with pistols, carbines, shotguns and more hand grenades, they were not just taking a drive to pass the time. Facing the same kinds of attacks in their own communities—colored citizens being assaulted in public, in Jonesboro and in Bogalusa by both the Ku Klux Klan and by the police, being dragged out of cars and clubbed, and even being beaten in the back of police cars by white officers who were supposed to be protecting them—these men were more than ready for another fight.

One of the men, Willie Lewis Jr., was a young man about Samuel Jr.'s age. Everybody called him Williejunior. He was dark brown with wavy processed hair and one of the first colored men Samuel Jr. had ever seen who did what he called "pumpin' iron," to build himself up. He had huge, rippling muscles and a body as solid as a concrete wall. Williejunior was quiet and thoughtful, but he hated white folks with a passion. He hated all white people.

Whenever Williejunior talked to anybody, which was rare, he spoke of an uncle of his, Sam Holt, who had been burned alive at the stake in Newman, Georgia one Sunday evening in front of two thousand white people, including church men and church women. He told how several newspapers, including the Kissimmee Valley Gazette and the Springfield Weekly Republican, had written about it, saying that, "As the flames rise about the victim, the people watched the quiverings of the flesh and the writhings of the frame, and shouted back descriptions to the jostling, cheering hundreds on the outskirts of the ring." Williejunior had committed the words to memory.

Sam Holt had been accused of murdering a white man named Alfred Cranford with an ax, then raping his wife in the man's own blood. An angry mob had found Holt in a little cabin that belonged to his mother and brought him to jail. After waiting for two weeks for Mrs. Cranford, who was sick in bed, to identify his uncle as the man who had attacked her and murdered her husband, Sheriff Brown, was forced to turn his prisoner over to the crowd to avoid assault on the jail and the possibility of bloodshed. Many of the men had pistols and clubs in their hands. They marched him to Mrs. Cranford's mother's house and she and her daughter made the identification even though they did not witness the crime.

Williejunior told how eyewitnesses reported that a line of buggies and vehicles of all kinds followed the procession led by the prisoner himself, their drivers fighting for position in line. Stones and other missiles were thrown, blood streaming from his head, face and body as he was struck with clubs, sticks and whips. They found a strong pine tree near the side of the road. The mob tore his clothes off, in sight of the women and children, put his back to the tree and wrapped a heavy chain around his body. Before pouring kerosene on him and lighting the fire, they piled dry brush and wood around him. Pulling out sharp knives, they cut off his uncle's ears, fingers and genitals. Fiendishly tortured, after the first flames licked at his feet he was temporarily removed from the tree. It was then that he was said to have confessed, allegedly stating that he had been paid twenty dollars to do it by "Lige" Strickland, a negro preacher. The fire was deadened while he was chained back to the tree.

According to an old newspaper clipping Williejunior guarded like a prized possession, "Holt went to the stake with as much

courage as anyone could possibly have possessed on such an occasion, and the only murmur that issued from his lips was when angry knives plunged into his flesh and his life's blood sizzled in the fire before his eyes."
    Then he cried, "Oh my God! Oh, Jesus."
    "Prayin' ain't gon' do you no good now," somebody in the crowd was supposed to have yelled. Holt's head dropped to his chest and as soon as it looked like he was dead, before his remains had even cooled, there was a mad struggle as people fought over the smoldering flesh. His body was mutilated and cut to pieces. Even the charred bones were crushed into small bits and sold as mementos and souvenirs for twenty-five cents. His heart and liver were cut into several pieces and some of the white men were selling a bit, crisply cooked, for twenty-five cents. One of the men took the head as men, women and children got on special trains coming from Atlanta to see the fun. They pinned a sign on a nearby tree. "We Must Protect Our Southern Women." Later that evening, small children poked with sticks as they played with the ashes.
    Reverend Strickland was seized in the dead of night and taken from his cabin in the woods, his wife and children left weeping. Major Thomas, the sturdy old man who owned the plantation, followed the lynchers in the buggy, then explained that Lige Strickland did not have twenty dollars. The lynching party strung the preacher up at least three times, trying to get him to confess. Each time he protested his innocence, once saying, "I have told you all I know, gentlemen. You can kill me if you wish, but I know nothing to tell." Finally, they cut his ears and fingers off, too, and left him dangling from a persimmon tree. Pinned to his chest was a bloodstained paper. One side read: "We must protect our ladies." The other side cautioned: "Beware all darkies! You will be treated the same way."

PLAYING FOR KEEPS

That Monday afternoon at the coroner's jury inquest, the usual verdict was rendered—death at the hands of parties unknown, even though nobody had bothered to wear a mask.

Usually before the victims were dead, while they were still hanging or burning, their bodies were riddled with bullets. Samuel Jr. had an uncle himself who lived in South Carolina who was shot and killed by white men. His fifty-year-old aunt and the couple's two daughters were taken outside, stripped and severely flogged, and told to leave town.

Years later on Rampart street everyone who could joined in, determined to fight to the finish. Colored servants in white neighborhoods proved an excellent source of military intelligence, and the community was usually forewarned of impending attack. Like the old days of the Civil War, cooks and housekeepers playing dumb would overhear white folks' plans and pass the word on. Dark cars would race through the streets, guns blazing from within, to meet returning fire and encounter a roadblock at the end of the street, only to face a withering crossfire.

One mobster's French Quarter cottage on Dauphine Street was blown apart on the day that his staff of colored servants became mysteriously ill. Another white man was garroted in his sleep by his negro valet.

A slumbering black giant had awakened, and whites lived in fear throughout New Orleans. Negro preachers denounced violence from the pulpit on Sunday mornings, called for peace, and often joined the community's defenders under cover of night. Samuel's pastor, Reverend Mills, who had served at the front as a chaplain with the 369th Infantry regiment during World War I, became an underground combat leader.

A number of women fought shoulder to shoulder with the men. Others operated a canteen to serve food and coffee; several nurses established a field hospital, with community doctors rotating their services.

The women organized cake bakes, sewing bees, and social teas to raise funds for ammunition and supplies under the supervision of Miz Genny, assisted by her youthful daughter-in-law, Morrow, and Samuel's sister, Zina.

Samuel's own unit of fighters fought almost nightly and never had a man either killed or wounded, due to Samuel's innate caution: he never fought unless he had superior numbers or firepower. If not, they ran to fight another day. At first he had to restrain his rash, young fighters until they saw the wisdom of his guerrilla tactics, naming themselves the Nat Turner Brigade. They fought until the winter rains came, when the Brazzi mob finally broke off their attacks and peace reigned in the neighborhood.

Samuel and Miz Genny quietly returned to running their small business, and a stranger would have never known that this peaceful and devout couple had once been determined guerrillas. Samuel Jr. and Morrow returned to their studies, graduated, then moved to Washington, D.C., where she became an elementary school teacher and he pursued his law degree. When asked what they had been doing in New Orleans, they said simply that they had been studying and helping Samuel's father with his store.

CHAPTER 5

New Orleans, Louisiana 2000
(Earlier that night, around 6:30 p.m.)

"Why so pensive, honey?" asked Morrow. "Worried about the police strike?"

She turned from the gilded mirror in their bedroom suite, clipped on a diamond earring, and studied her husband.

Rubbing his palms up and down the arms of his rose damask Louis XVI chair, Samuel Jammison answered with an enigmatic smile. His wife had always known how to read him. But something else was running through his mind. He wondered if women knew how good they looked putting on an earring, the way they tilted their heads just so, the angle they held their arms while their breasts sloped gently forward like ripe melons. Of course they did, he thought; they always know. After almost fifty years together, he knew he was never tired of looking at his own wife from any angle. And he knew she enjoyed his scrutiny, dressed for him, undressed for him in ways that seemed forever fresh.

Morrow Jammison, at five-six, weighed one hundred and eighteen pounds and kept slim by intelligent diet and exercise.

During the summer, she played squash and tennis. Without fail, she swam in the family's indoor pool every week. Her short-cropped black hair, with a touch of gray at the temples, embraced her like a crown, and her green eyes picked up the color of the emerald brooch she wore. Her skin still held the color of a light persimmon. Samuel was grateful she was not getting any darker with age, as sometimes happened with creole women.

The envy of the Black elite, the Jammisons made a striking couple. Sam was six-two, one eighty-five, only a few pounds heavier than he was at Dillard University decades ago. His hair was salt and pepper, gray at the temples, slightly curly. He had a ruggedly handsome face, a slightly broken nose giving it a manly aura. He was just good-looking enough to appeal to women—yet not too pretty to turn off men. Sam's gray eyes complemented his color, a quality inherited from his mother.

Morrow was a true New Orleans creole beauty, light enough to pass—a thing she'd never thought of doing. It wasn't that she couldn't. She had relatives darker than herself who had moved to Los Angeles and Chicago, and done exactly that—miraculously become white.

Finally Samuel responded. "What else," he sighed wearily. "I was sitting here thinking about the old days, what they still call the Rampart Street War. How much simpler things were then. It was us against them, gun against gun."

Peering into the mirror, Morrow smiled at her reflection, as she smoothed the bodice of her form-fitting, floor-length black Armani gown.

Out of the corner of his eyes, Samuel noticed that she still had a stunning decolletage for a woman her age. He beamed with pride. He had always admired her impeccable taste in clothes.

"I suppose those were the good old days." Morrow continued to primp and preen, checking her sheer hose for runs.

PLAYING FOR KEEPS

Samuel crossed his legs, then rubbed his eyelids with his index fingers, as if even thinking caused eyestrain. "I'm not so sure about the good old days, but they were definitely some dangerous ones. Nowadays, the same kind of people we fought back then hide behind attorneys, committees, and bought-and-paid-for politicians."

Morrow took a deep breath and nodded. She turned away from the mirror. "Do you remember the Jonesboro Deacons and the Deacons for Justice and Defense, of course they weren't the Deacons back then, and CORE?" She spoke in the gentle, slurring voice of a true Louisianan.

Samuel's eyes lit up. Relaxing, he loosened the belt on his silk paisley smoking jacket.

"That old two-story building at 2209 Dryades Street during the 60s. How could I ever forget it? Jackson and Dryades... And Collins, Douglas and Elie, CD and E and all the telephone calls we made from that old phone on the corner at Jackson Avenue because we were afraid that J. Edgar Hoover had the FBI tap the one at LCDC headquarters."

"You know, those were three brave young lawyers back then," Morrow continued, her eyes warmly meeting her husband's. "Getting mixed up in the civil rights movement the way they did... risking their lives."

The mahogany grandfather clock in the marble foyer downstairs chimed seven o'clock. Absently, Samuel looked down at his watch. He went on. "Yes, Bob called it 'ghetto practice.' There were less than a dozen black laywers in town and they were only getting divorce cases and traffic tickets. He said they had to take whatever they could get in the beginning because middle-class blacks and black merchants used white lawyers. The judges even humiliated them in court...."

Samuel paused, before going on. "And what would have

happened if the Deacons hadn't shown up during the Rampart Street War?"

Morrow walked over to Samuel and began massaging his shoulders. He felt some of the tension flowing out of his spine into his limbs. He stretched his toes and flexed his left pinkie finger, which boasted a diamond ring.

"They were the brave ones," Sam continued, "taking on KKK nightriders and the police right there in the middle of Klan country. The same Klan that had beaten up the first two black deputies in town, killing one of them. They sure pulled our asses out of the fire, didn't they?"

Morrow walked around behind his chair and slid her trim frame into his lap. He caught her perfume, "Obsession." Samuel liked the fragrance. He wondered how she seemed to know everything he liked.

"Enough of this reminiscing," Morrow interrupted with a broad grin. "We've got a party to go to." In a coquettish voice, she teased, "Don't tell me you want to go out and shoot somebody, Sam? We've come a long way from that time. What do the kids say, chill out?"

"Have we? It's still the Sicilians behind it all. Call it the Mafia, the Mob, the Syndicate, whatever."

"That's a stereotype, honey."

"Like fun it is. No, it's still Brazzi's people. They just don't wear wide-brimmed Borsolinos anymore. Nowadays, it's tailor-made Armani and they send their kids to Harvard or Notre Dame, but it's the same bastards we fought to a standstill in forty-eight."

Samuel wrinkled his brow as he rubbed Morrow's back. "They still fight just as dirty. It's the same old game. But these days they use the system, twist it, distort it to their own advantage. I guess the only difference is that there wasn't any system back then to manipulate."

Morrow placed her head against his and they were silent for awhile, listening to the soft music: Clifford Brown with Strings. Once again, he wondered what Clifford Brown might have become if he hadn't died so tragically young in an automobile accident on his way to a gig at the Beehive Lounge on Chicago's South Side. What year, he wondered. Fifty-six, fifty-seven?

"You know most of the cops are on your side, Sam, even some of the white ones."

"It's not the cops, baby," he replied. "It's the damn union and the mob controls it."

"What's the real problem, sweetheart? You can live with a union; you've been a liberal all your life."

"I'm not challenging unionism, Morrow. You know that. If the mob controls this particular union, the gates to the dope trade coming through here from the Caribbean and South America are going to be wide open."

"How about Mexico?"

"Forget about Mexico. It's bad enough that we've already got crooked cops distributing heroin and cocaine and protecting dealers."

"Stop being so hard on yourself, Sam. Everybody knows that cleaning up political corruption and the Police Department is one of your top priorities. You're doing everything you can."

"Sure," he agreed, "but we've still got six different Police Departments in a city the size of New Orleans, and now the Levee Police want to muscle in on city jurisdiction. Your guess is as good as mine what that's all about. That goddamn Levee Board president, Tranchina, acts like the city belongs to him—Mafioso. I can smell it."

Morrow rose smoothly and walked to a small refrigerator in the corner. "Drink, honey?" she asked.

"Yeah. White wine. I want my head clear for the banquet

tonight."

"Any preference?"

"Baby, you know you're the expert on wines. Remember, I grew up drinking corn liquor out of Mason jars."

"Sam, save that 'good ol' boy pulled himself up by the bootstraps' stuff for your constituency, okay? You have a better nose for wine than I do. As good as my father."

He laughed. "Well, your father taught me, didn't he? And he tasted his way clear through the Sorbonne."

She glided back in that graceful way she had and handed him his glass. He took a sip. The soft ceiling lights shimmered and cast a rosy glow over the wainscoting of the room. If they hadn't had to leave, this would have been a perfect romantic evening.

"Hmm, Chardonnay? California?" Samuel grimaced in mock condescension.

She laughed. "Give me a break! You know damn well that's a vintage Montrachet."

"Baby, did you ever think we'd be drinking vintage wine back in those days in southwest Washington, when we had to save up for a jug of Gallo?"

"I never thought about it. I guess I was just having too much fun being in love with you. You were so ambitious, so intense. Now look at you, Mr. Mayor."

"Yeah, a mayor with his back against the wall."

"Isn't that when you fight best?"

"Daddy! What are you doing sitting there in your robe sipping wine?" said their twenty-six-year-old daughter, Debbie, rushing into the room in that long-leg way she had. "You'll be late for your own banquet."

"Nag, nag, nag," said Sam.

"Well, somebody has to keep you in line around here, you and your overindulgent wife. It's a good thing for you two I'm back home."

"Overindulgent?" Morrow smiled.

"Just kidding, Mom. We both know how hardheaded Daddy is, don't we?"

"And have you ever known him to be on time for anything?" Morrow added.

"Well, for meals. Sometimes."

"Sometimes is right."

"Debbie, will you get off my case?" said Sam. "Can't you see I'm chillin'?"

"Chillin'," Debbie answered, her eyebrows raised and a broad smile on her face, sliding into her father's lap. "Gimme a sip. Uh-huh. Montrachet, right?"

"How did you know that? Just how much booze have you been sipping in Atlanta, young lady?"

"I'm cheating. I heard Mom when I came in." They all laughed.

Morrow began to fix her thick black hair in the mirror. As vain as she was, Samuel was surprised that she had refused to dye it.

"Stand up and let me see your new gown," said her father.

Debbie rose and struck an exaggerated model's pose.

"Gucci?" her father asked.

"No, daddy. Pucci! You'll never learn about women's clothes, will you?"

"I know how much they cost," Sam replied playfully.

Debbie had been a late child, born when they were in their forties, and the Jammisons doted on her, spoiled her to the core. Even so, she was a vibrant, generous young woman, a graduate student at Xavier, her mother's alma mater.

She's every bit the looker her mother was, Samuel was thinking to himself. He marveled at having two such beautiful females spoiling him rotten. They had a way, each of them, of taking his mind off matters of state within minutes of his return from a long ten- to twelve-hour day at City Hall.

Morrow stood smiling her girlish smile at her blossoming young daughter as she walked toward the dresser and raised the lid on a small rhinestone-encrusted, pastel blue jewelry box. She removed a one-half-inch jade bracelet with a thin rim of gold running along each side.

You're probably looking for this," Morrow said, in her usual easygoing way. "I wore it with my green Donna Karan suit to the A.K.A. luncheon yesterday at Roje's. I didn't think you would mind."

"I'm glad I didn't have to go," Debbie winced. "I hate those things. They're so stuffy. Everybody pretending to be something they're not."

Morrow's head tilted slightly to the side as her eyebrows rose simultaneously.

"Actually, it was a lot of fun, because of the Carnival season, I guess."

"Well, I'm still glad I didn't have to be there. What about the police, Daddy? Do you think they're gonna strike?" asked Debbie in the direct way she'd inherited from her father.

"Not if we give them Fort Knox and everything in it. I'm not going to let them blackmail me," he said firmly, as he picked at a never-healing blemish near the base of the right side of his neck. They can go to hell first."

"I'm sorry, but I still can't see how a black policeman could strike against you," Debbie blurted quickly, her disappointment obvious. "You're the best mayor New Orleans has ever had. Everybody knows that."

"Not everybody, sweetheart," responded Samuel proudly. "Your mother and I were just discussing that when you walked in.

There are a lot of good cops, both black and white, on my side. It's not the cops. It's the union and the men behind it. Greedy, corrupt men trying to break my back!"

"Calm down, honey," said Morrow, turning abruptly to face him. "Remember your high blood pressure."

"I can't help it, Morrow. There are two things that make my blood boil—a thief and a con, and you know that's exactly what this is. A damn crooked ass power play."

"Mama's right, Daddy," said Debbie, holding his large hand between her own small ones. "It's not worth it. Getting yourself upset like this."

"Your father thinks it's the syndicate."

"It wouldn't be the first time," responded Samuel. "I've seen it happen before. And this wouldn't be the first police department that's been bought with dirty money."

"But won't the police lose, too? If they strike during Mardi Gras, everybody loses," said Debbie. "Business, working people, even the cops would lose all that overtime pay."

"Short-term only, honey," her mother said, sitting down and picking up her wine glass. "It's all about the future. In the long run, if the people who control the union force your father into the concessions they demand, then they literally control the city and he's no more than a puppet."

"Being mayor won't mean anything," her father added. "I might as well be selling Lucky Dogs on Bourbon Street. These people don't mind losing a little now, as long as they get what they want down the road."

"What is that?" Debbie lifted her eyebrow.

"Power... Power is more important than money. If you have power, the money is automatic, sweetheart. Not all the rich are powerful, but all the powerful are rich."

"If they control New Orleans, Debbie," said her mother, "the rest of the Gulf follows."

"Like a stack of dominoes," Sam added. "First New Orleans, then Jefferson, Chalmette, and St. Bernard will be easy. That's why it's so important that I don't give in. That's why I've got to stand my ground."

"The people behind the strike don't play, Debbie" said her mother. "They control drugs, the riverboat casinos, so why not their own dummy police force?"

"Over my dead body!"

"Sam, don't talk like that!" Morrow shuddered. "They've killed before. Who knows that any better than we do?"

"Daddy, please be careful."

"Don't worry about me, baby," he said reassuringly. "I'll be fine. It's my problem. I'll handle it. I always do, don't I?" Jammison put his powerful arm around his daughter's neck, pulling her close so that their cheeks touched.

"Don't fuss over me so much. Besides, you know how good my security detail is. You just have a good time tonight."

"Well, I still don't like it," responded Morrow, obviously disgusted.

Debbie began to relax. Time after time, she really had watched her father take care of everything, always being there to fix things or make the pain go away.

Samuel Jammison could sense that the two most important people in his life were very happy. Since his mother Genevieve had died and his father shortly afterwards, Debbie and Morrow were all that he truly loved. He thought about how long and hard he had worked to give them happiness and security.

Morrow looked at her watch. "Sam, get dressed," she said firmly. "Or we really will be late."

When his wife spoke in that particular tone of voice, Sam had learned to do as told. Without a word, he rose and went into his dressing room to slip into his tuxedo.

Debbie and her mother smiled at one another, silently acknowledging their mutual love and admiration for Sam, the man at the center of their lives.

CHAPTER 6

New Orleans 2000, 8:30 p.m.

Samuel Jammison and his wife, Morrow, sat expectantly in the luxurious stretch Lincoln limousine as it glided silently down St. Charles Avenue, past stately turn-of-the-century colonial mansions. "Easy Listening," softly played on 102.9, filled the limo. Holding hands, they eagerly anticipated the night's festivities. Sam had waited almost eight years for this moment, and now it was here.

An aging man dressed in a black suit, with tight, kinky gray hair visible below his chauffeur's cap, smiled as he glanced into his rearview mirror. Calvin Wilkerson was thinking about how much his life had changed from thirty years of work as a streetcar operator, rain or sunshine, sick or healthy. As his arthritic hands expertly maneuvered the car behind two motorcycle escorts, he found himself admiring the subtle beauty of the lazy majestic oak-lined boulevard that he had never really noticed before, and the colorful New Orleans skyline in the distance. Officer Boyd, the mayor's bodyguard, sat beside him.

As they drove past Confederate general Robert E. Lee's statue at Lee Circle, facing north, the mayor's expression quickly turned sour. There they were again, rowdy young bohemians with

PLAYING FOR KEEPS

camping bags and tents, in town for Mardi Gras. With mohawks dyed red, orange or green; lips, nipples and navels pierced, they were white, middle class, often bright, politically militant, and homeless by choice. Tattooed, wearing studded dog collars, many of them not over 21, hundreds of young rebels—gutter punks—hitch-hiked, caught rides or hopped freight trains, drifting into the city to live on the streets.

Some of them caught rides from Greyhound bus lines, taking advantage of free or reduced fares offered to runaways heading home. Of course, it was only a scam to get somewhere else. Home was what the rebellious young outcasts were escaping from.

Gutter punks hated Samuel Jammison, Jr. Because of complaints from Warehouse District residents, French Quarter merchants, and politicians about public urination, fighting, and drunkenness, the mayor ordered the police department to crack down, sweeping the punks from the streets. In addition to being a public nuisance they were a health hazard, but he would handle that first thing in the morning.

It was interesting, too, the mayor thought, that Lee Circle, the center of the new Arts District, was one of the gutter punk hot spots. Ironically, the circle and Robert E. Lee's statue were less than six blocks away from the National D Day Museum on Higgins Boulevard, honoring World War II veterans who had fought so that all Americans could be free, including the punks. What Jammison did not need, however, was affluent Warehouse District voters angry with him.

But Mardi Gras was not the only party punks crashed. During a family vacation in 1991, Sam had seen them at Disneyland in Anaheim, California. Hundreds of ghoulishly dressed teenagers bought ninety-nine dollar annual passes so they could hang out on weekend nights, turning the area into a free-for-all, drinking, camping out, using spray paint, and heckling tourists.

After their parents dropped them off in their unassuming street clothes, they would change into their punk-like extreme attire, hogging benches in Tomorrowland, listening to rock bands, and dancing. Others smoked joints or roamed the parking lots, committing acts of vandalism, petty theft, selling methamphetamine, LSD, speed, and various forms of cocaine. But there was one big difference. Disneyland had a private security force with a zero tolerance policy.

"We should be there in about ten minutes," said Wilkerson.

Samuel Jammison squeezed his wife's hand, his expression saying it all as he looked into her eyes. What an amazing life, he thought, glancing at his Rolex President—almost nine. College, a law degree from Howard University, two terms as councilman-at-large, and almost two terms as mayor. If things went the way he hoped, he might become the first black governor of Louisiana since P.B.S. Pinchback during Reconstruction.

He remembered civil rights demonstrations, sit-ins and freedom marches for equal justice for black Americans in the '50's and '60's with Reverend A. L. Davis, Jr., whose nickname was Jack, and the Southern Christian Leadership Conference meetings in 1957 at New Zion Baptist Church on Third Street. Good old Jack became New Orleans' first black city councilman, but he paid dearly for the priviledge, including threats on his life and warnings about bombing his house on Second Street and his church.

Reverend Ralph Abernathy and young Martin Luther King, Jr. were also there. The charismatic Reverend King, only twenty-eight at the time, had graduated from Morehouse in Atlanta in 1948, the same year Sam and his father were fighting the Italians. Another old friend, Reverend Avery Alexander, had become immortalized in a photograph—being dragged by the legs by white policemen during a sit-in at the all-white lunch counter in City Hall, where blacks had always been denied service.

He thought about the Montgomery, Alabama bus boycott in

PLAYING FOR KEEPS

1955 that ended segregated seating on that city's buses. In cities in both the north and south, Sam and his friends were jailed, sometimes beaten with billies, or sprayed with fire hoses, but finally the Civil Rights Act was passed and then the Voting Rights Act.

In 1963 he was there marching with Martin Luther King Jr. in Washington, D.C., and standing less than ten feet away from him when he made his heartstopping, "I Have a Dream" speech. He was with him again, marching in Birmingham, when Sheriff Bull Connor's dogs attacked them, a horrific scene that was played over and over again on national television. The policemen, who were outlaws themselves, would stand by watching picketers being clubbed and beaten with bullwhips, then arrest them for trespassing.

Sam remembered that day in Memphis in 1968 when his friend Martin was assassinated at the Lorraine Motel by James Earl Ray. Another day, in the same year, Bobby Kennedy, the energetic young Attorney General whom he had met in Washington, was murdered in Los Angeles by twenty-four-year-old Arab immigrant Sirhan Sirhan. His mind raced back to one of the most shocking moments in his life, the day President Kennedy was assassinated in Dallas, struck by two rifle shots fired from the sixth floor of the Texas School Book Depository by a former Marine, Lee Harvey Oswald. They were all gone, but he was still hanging in there.

"Still think you should have gone to medical school instead of law school?" Morrow teased, using her hand to brush a few lint particles from Samuel's lapel.

"Maybe law school wasn't such a bad choice after all," Samuel smiled. "I just hope I know what I want to be by the time I grow up." He raised her right hand to his lips, then gently kissed it.

Canal Street was a dazzling vision of color beneath clear skies—bumper to bumper traffic and a virtually impenetrable sea of beaming headlights and honking horns. Flashing blue lights from the police motorcycle escort were now complemented by the high-pitched shrill of police sirens. New Orleans' Finest, crowd control superstars, with orchestrated precision, stopped a car here and a car there moving toward their destination.

"Glad these guys aren't on strike yet," Samuel teased, "or we would be walking by now."

"Nervous?" asked Morrow.

"I'd be lying if I said I wasn't. Besides, you know me too well for that. You could always tell when I was lying about something."

"Oh, so you admit that you lie to me."

"No, sweetheart," he kidded. "I just mean that if I ever did lie to you, you would know it." He gave her an affectionate peck on the lips as she nodded and grinned teasingly.

Samuel thought for a minute about his great good fortune, about his mother and father and how proud they would have been, especially after some of the mistakes he had made as a boy. Fifty years ago, they were only trying to stay alive on Rampart Street, and now he could stop traffic on Canal Street, one of the oldest and most famous streets in the world with one simple telephone call.

He nodded his head and smiled, thinking about the irony. Here he was, a black mayor on a street called Canal, which had never really been a canal. Even stranger was the neutral grounds down the center of the street, called a median everywhere else, that had separated Americans in Faubourg St. Mary from the Creoles they hated in Old Town. Once again, he remembered that as a boy, he couldn't even use a restroom down here or set foot inside a white school. Yes, Sam and Miss Genny would have gotten a big laugh out of that one, too.

Yellow Rollins cabs and beautifully decorated horse-drawn carriages with formally dressed riders were breast to breast, all heading to the Marriott Hotel. Blue spotlights, courtesy of Sky

PLAYING FOR KEEPS

Search, crisscrossed the starry sky like a Hollywood premiere, as a steady procession of limousines dispatched cheerful revelers.

"You've come a long way," Morrow said proudly.

"We've come a long way," Samuel responded. "Not sorry you married a poor colored store owner's son, are you?"

"I'll let you in on a little secret," she said. "The first time I saw you, I knew I was going to marry you." She kissed him.

When the entourage pulled in front of the hotel, an exuberant crowd had worked itself up into a furor and was impatiently waving blue and white signs that read, RE-ELECT SAMUEL JAMMISON, MAYOR #3, with a recent picture of the third term mayor-to-be. A thirty-foot banner with the same inscription framed the front of the building as The Big Easy Jazz Band, dressed in black military hats, black ties, black trousers, and white dress shirts struck up "When the Saints Go Marching In."

"Well, this is it," Samuel said, leaning forward to get a better look.

"Showtime."

He kissed his wife firmly on the lips, giving her a big hug.

"We want Jammison! We want Jammison!" the enthusiastic crowd yelled, when the mayor and his first lady exited the car. Amidst frenzied handshakes, noise, and commotion, Gene Kennedy, the mayor's friend, shook Samuel's hand and kissed Morrow on the cheek.

As the mayor's keen eyes scanned the crowd, he too beamed with excitement. There was unbridled passion from his supporters and detractors alike. Disgruntled picketers, including third term opponents and off-duty policemen that he recognized, were yelling and screaming, but there was another group, too, one Sam did not expect to see, shouting just as loud—gutter punks.

Gothics, wearing pale makeup, black blush, black eyeliner,

black lipstick, and velvet capes were the spookiest of all punks. A couple of girls wearing long black velvet dresses, white pancake makeup, and blood-red lipstick were with them. Standing near the gutter punks was another riotous group, Neo-Nazi skinheads, sporting skull and bones, swastikas, and their own contagious breed of hate.

Kennedy led the mayor and his wife into the crowded lobby, escorted by ceremonially dressed black Mardi Gras Indians in colorful, beautifully feathered costumes as partygoers danced the second line, waving white handkerchiefs wildly over their heads.

Officer Boyd, plainclothes detectives, and uniformed N.O.P.D. officers formed a perimeter around Samuel and Morrow as flashbulbs went off and network cameras rolled for the ten o'clock news on Channel 4, Channel 6, and the Fox Network.

"Mayor Jammison, do you think there's any chance the city and the police will reach a settlement before their present contract expires?" shouted an anxious reporter.

"Will the firemen and the Sanitation Department go out with the police officers?" yelled another.

"I have no comment to make at this time," said Samuel, moving briskly.

"It's Carnival time! Laissez les bon temps roule! Let the good times roll!"

"We want Jammison! We want Jammison!" shouted the jubilant crowd as a thousand blue and silver mylar balloons ascended to the ceiling accompanied by tumultuous handclapping. A pretty young girl approached, putting bright purple, gold, and green Mardi Gras beads around the couple's necks.

Sam Jammison beamed, surveying the scene, holding Morrow's hand attentively, looking up and seeing his entry captured on a twenty-foot screen on the stage at the front of the hall. Kennedy led them to their seats in a reserved section of the ballroom, still flanked by vigilant security.

Meticulously organized, Kennedy's appearance attested to his eye for detail. Forty-five, with stringy blonde hair, steel gray eyes and a rubber band-tight physique from daily two-hour workouts in his home gym, he did not look a day over thirty-five.

A political insider, he had been Sam's campaign manager through three tough but successful elections. From old money, but not related to the John F. Kennedy family, Gene Kennedy had never worked a day of his life at a real job. His last position had been going to Europe twice a year to check on his family's extensive financial holdings in Brussels and Vienna.

Power was his game, and this Boston University graduate loved every minute of it. Kennedy's motto was never a king, but a kingmaker, and he thrived on being with a winner. He made sure the Jammisons were comfortably seated, then excused himself to welcome other guests.

Sitting to Samuel Jammison's left was Chauncey Williams, conducting business as usual by being in the right place at the right time. Unwaveringly dedicated, he was also one of Jammison's staunchest allies, as well as his aide. Handsome, Williams resembled a younger version of the elder statesman. Their complexions and facial features were typical of most creole men, only Williams' hair was blacker and wavier. The two men briefly discussed the huge turnout as Jammison surveyed the room.

City councilmen loyal to the mayor, the Chief of Police and his rank, the Fire Chief and his rank, aides to the Governor, state representatives and state senators, oil company executives, the Superintendent of Schools and school board members, casino investors, real estate developers and, of course, beautiful hispanic, black, creole and white women eager for a good time and a chance to meet the right man—they all had come. Samuel could also see Lawrence Daniels, his only real competition, Elder Elliot Parsons, flamboyant leader of New Orleans' largest black church, and lovely Inga Sorenson, his banker.

Kennedy moved up front and as the band finished playing "Such a Night," an old New Orleans favorite, he took the mike and center stage. Kennedy raised his arm and started ringing an old-fashioned brass school bell as he called for order.

"May I have your attention, please! May I have your attention, please!"

It took about five minutes before he could get the merrymakers quiet enough to propose a toast. Finally, everyone stood, raising their glasses in salutation as the high-spirited eating, drinking and dancing resumed.

CHAPTER 7

New Orleans 2000 2:00 a.m.

Across the street from the crime scene, Miss Peabody found herself caught on the horns of a dilemma. Her horoscope had been clear. "Beware of the movement of others and avoid unnecessary involvement." She knew that she should call the police to report what she had just witnessed, but the horoscope.... She lifted a silver voodoo amulet concealed between her breasts beneath her dress, studied it carefully, then returned it.

Miss Peabody slowly walked to the table where the telephone was, reached for it, then turned away. She then hurriedly walked back to the window, looked through gold-plated theater glasses once more, and returned to the telephone.

Without further hesitation, she lifted the receiver from its cradle and timidly dialed Ragule, her guru and personal spiritual guide. Ragule answered on the third ring.

"Mr. Ragule, sir. Oh, I'm so glad you're in. Forgive me for troubling you, but I have a rather serious problem."

"Who is this?" Mr. Ragule sounded irritated.

"I'm sorry," she apologized. "This is Miss Florence Peabody."

"Yes, Miss Peabody? How may I help you?"

"I have just witnessed a murder and kidnapping. I know that I should telephone the police. However, sir, my horoscope said 'no involvement.' I just don't know.... And I'm so sorry I disturbed you at this late hour."

"Miss Peabody. Yes. I remember it, but think about what your horoscope actually said," replied Ragule, his East Indian accent craggy. "Your horoscope said no unnecessary involvement," he continued. "It is obviously necessary that you call the police immediately! As an eyewitness, by necessity, you are already involved. You should notify the authorities at once."

"Yes, I see. Certainly. Thank you, Mr. Ragule. And again, I apologize for disturbing you."

For a moment after Miss Peabody hung up, Ragule kept the phone cradled between his neck and his shoulder, while he fished around for a Salem cigarette. After he hung up the receiver, he poured himself a snifter of twenty-year-old Quinta Noval port. Shaking his head, Ragule wondered if the old lady had suddenly gone senile. He took a quick drag from the cigarette. He smiled as he took his first sip. Not that one, he thought. Her mind was as clear as a bell, and she was as tough as leather. Although there had been a slight tremble to her voice, she was calm and in complete control. If she said she had seen a murder and kidnapping, that is exactly what she had seen.

For a moment Ragule wondered if he might expect a visit from the police; then he relaxed. She would not mention his name. Miss Peabody cherished her privacy, and she wished that no one know that she had a Voodoo priest as advisor.

Miss Peabody rang off and dialed 911. "I wish to report a murder and kidnapping, please. My name is Florence Peabody." She gave her address and phone number and was switched to Homicide. In the meantime, the Cadillac pulled further away from the neighborhood.

"Homicide, Detective Clark speaking."

"I wish to report a shooting," said Miss Peabody. Clark switched on his tape recorder, took out his notepad, and started writing.

"Miss Florence Peabody, on Audubon Place." Again, she gave her address and phone number.

"Tell me about this alleged shooting, please, Miss Peabody."

"Alleged?" she snorted. "Dead, I'd say, and they took the poor girl."

"I see," said Clark. "Do you know who was shot?"

"Yes. Raymond Deveraux. He's dead, lying on the lawn across the street."

"Are you certain he's dead?"

"Three shots, two in the body, one to the head. Yes, he's dead all right."

"This girl, the one they took. Do you know who she is?"

"Of course I do. She was here for tea just yesterday. Debbie Jammison, the mayor's daughter."

Clark was suddenly alert. He'd have to check this out himself, no matter how farfetched it sounded.

"I'll be right over, Miss Peabody. Just stay put."

"Where would I go, Detective? But please hurry."

"Yes, ma'am." He rang off.

"Burke, we need to get a prowl car to the mayor's house, pronto! Signals thirty and forty-five," his expression disturbing as he called to his partner.

Detective Burke growled orders into his phone, watching Clark with growing interest as he took his H&K nine millimeter with a four inch barrel from his locked desk, checked its load and slid it into his shoulder holster. Burke was already wearing his Beretta nine millimeter with a two inch barrel under his arm.

As he hung up the phone, Burke asked, "So what's up, Al?"

The detective jumped to his feet. "Looks like someone snatched the mayor's daughter, shot her boyfriend." They grabbed their briefcases, portable radios, and suit jackets and hurried from the office.

CHAPTER 8

"The coffee will be ready in just a minute, Detective, Clark, is it?"

"Yes, ma'am. Thank you."

It would not do to rush things, even though they were police. This woman was a bourbon aristocrat, and social protocol was as important to her as religion. For many of them protocol was their only religion. First, they would serve you something, if no more than a cold glass of water—sweet spring water, without a hint of chlorine or chemicals—or coffee or tea, or a small glass of brandy or sherry. Next, a modicum of small talk. Then on to the business at hand. If he tried to rush things or showed even a hint of bad manners, she would shut him out as a clam does a starfish, but with a great deal more success. It didn't matter that it was after two a.m.

"Are you related to Mr. Byron Clark, the Johnsons' majordomo?"

"My father, Miss Peabody. But he's retired now. Spends all his time these days fishing. Doesn't hit a lick at a snake."

"Yes, I thought so. I can see the resemblance. And, Officer Burke, are you related to the Burke family from the Irish Channel?"

"Yes, ma'am. That's where I grew up, on Race Street."

"Do you know that we here in the Garden District owe a great deal to you Irish, Detective Burke? Quite by accident, however."

"How is that, Miss Peabody?"

"Why, if your Irish roustabouts hadn't been stampeding their cattle and trampling our azaleas and rose bushes on their way to the slaughterhouses, we never would have started using our beautiful iron fences. I believe they referred to our homes as Prairie Palaces in those days."

Detective Burke silently registered Miss Peabody's remarks. Many wealthy Garden District "nouveaux riche" Anglos had looked down on penniless Irish immigrants who had come by the boatload in the 1840's and 1850's, with little more then the clothes on their backs, fleeing persecution and the potato famine in Ireland.

Sure, Burke was thinking to himself, Irishmen were rowdy, hardworking, hot-tempered and considered carriers of the plague, and because they competed with blacks for labor jobs like stevedores, collecting trash, and digging ditches, they gained little respect. Many of his relatives died during the yellow fever epidemic. Because of the slaughterhouses, the Irish Channel smelled constantly, and when it flooded in New Orleans, which was often, children swam in the ditches. It was a miracle that any of them survived at all.

Miss Peabody was right about something else, too, Burke reflected. The Irish were tough. Strangers were often bricked, and it was definitely not safe for outsiders to enter the Channel after dark. The St. Mary's Market Gang, the Crowbar Gang and characters like Rat Tooth Flynn hung out in riverfront saloons like the Bucket of Blood, the Bull's Head Tavern, and Mike Noud's Ocean Home Saloon on Adele Street. The Irish and the second largest immigrant group, the Germans, would often fight as well, especially the group from Little Saxony. His grandfather Daniel had told him the same stories over and over and over.

And yes, Irishmen had been quick to fight. They had to to

survive. The first official prizefight in New Orleans had been between two Irishmen, James Burke, one of his own relatives, and Sam O'Rourke back in May of 1836. John L. Sullivan had even fought Jim Corbett in New Orleans at the Olympic Club on Royal Street, he remembered fondly. His great-grandfather Sean had been a fighter, too, and a "screwman," packing cotton in boats on the wharf for five dollars a day.

Miss Peabody's maid came in with the coffee, an antique sterling silver service on an ornate tray. Awakened from a deep sleep, the rotund woman was less than cordial.

"Thank you, Edna," she said. "Cream and sugar? However, you both look like black coffee men." They nodded. "Double strength Colombian, dark roast. Perhaps you'd like a pinch of chicory, Officer Burke?"

"Yes, please. Thank you, ma'am."

The two exchanged looks. Miss Peabody sat slim and erect, her liver-spotted hands deft at the pouring and the passing of cups that bespoke the select finishing schools she had attended—Sacre Coeur Academy in New Orleans and in Paris. She wore a flowered dress of Egyptian cotton, her straight blonde hair, now graying, held in a bun. Still beautiful, she must have been a knockout years ago, the dark-skinned detective was thinking.

As a small boy, he remembered seeing rich white women like Miss Peabody, from uptown, riding the St. Charles or Carrollton Avenue streetcar or being driven by their black chauffeurs to Canal Street. Clannishly self-centered, they appeared to be numb to the suffering masses around them. Going shopping on Canal Street was a very special outing during those days, and the crème de la crème always wore fancy hats with matching shoes and handbags dangling from their arms and expensive white gloves on their hands, probably so they wouldn't actually touch any dirt, Clark thought—then smiled. Then it was on to Galatoire's on Bourbon

Street for lunch, laughing and talking with that exaggerated Southern antebellum drawl.

"Now, Detective, I know you have questions," she said, looking serenely at Al Clark.

Outside, across the street, lights from the prowl cars and ambulance flashed as uniformed police officers cordoned off the street and began moving house to house canvassing and questioning the neighbors. Clark and Burke had visited the scene briefly before crossing the street to Miss Peabody's elegant, Queen Ann Garden District mansion. Burke had pulled out his pad and started taking notes.

When the two detectives arrived on the scene, it was just as the caller had described. A marked unit with flashers on was already there from the Second District. One body lay beside an MG in front of the house. A police officer's body had been discovered near the rear of the house, also murdered.

"Can you describe the men, Miss Peabody?"

The mayor's house was floodlit, thought Clark, and she must have had a good look at the scene from her present seat, a wing chair near large bay windows, probably an original Chippendale. His father had taught him about the good things during his career as retainer.

"Three white men with stocking caps pulled over their faces."

"What makes you think they were white?" Clark gently asked.

"The way they moved, not loose and feline the way colored people walk. Stiff, like white men. I'm sorry, does 'colored' offend you? It's hard to know what's correct these days."

"No, ma'am. Can you describe them further?"

"One, the driver, was short and rather awkward. Raymond subdued him first. Another was bulkier, average height, but wide. The third, the murderer, was tall, broad-shouldered. He wasn't in the car. He just appeared in the driveway after the lights came back on. The one who shot Ray."

"So you mean the lights were off?" asked Clark.

"Yes, for about two or three minutes," responded Miss Peabody.

Clark turned to Burke. "That explains why they found Officer Hadley's body by the fuse box."

She took a sip of coffee, eyeing Clark with interest over the rim. Miss Peabody looked him invitingly in the eye, lust curiously ill-concealed.

Damn, thought Clark, she's still hot to trot even at her age. She must have really been something years ago. He wondered how many dark-skinned men had lain between her firm alabaster thighs. She hardly glanced at Burke. "The blacker the berry..." thought mahogany-colored Clark.

"Can you describe the car they drove?"

"Ninety-three to ninety-six Cadillac Fleetwood. Same as my own in the garage. Black, or dark blue. Louisiana plates. I only caught the first three letters: DOE," she said.

This old woman doesn't miss anything, thought Clark. Probably guessing the size of my dick. As if reading his mind, Miss Peabody gave Clark a slight, seductive smile. Clark looked down at his notes, found himself blushing. Shit, he thought, I'm damn near tempted. He wondered how old the chauffeur was, and if he was a black man, too.

"The tall one, apparently the leader, used a long-barreled automatic pistol: possibly a Browning or Beretta."

Clark and Burke exchanged looks. Burke carefully drew his own weapon. "Like this?"

"Yes. That's a Beretta, I believe."

Burke nodded.

"The bulky one carried a Walther P-38, often confused with

the Luger. The driver had the larger weapon, in compensation for his short stature, of course: a frontier model Colt with an eight-inch barrel, I'd guess."

"You know handguns, Miss Peabody?" Burke asked curiously.

"My father was national skeet shooting champion three years running. I fired my first .22 carbine at the age of ten; owned my own Purdy over-and-under shotgun at fifteen. Perhaps you'd care to see Daddy's gun collection?"

"No, thanks, ma'am. Thank you," said the chastened Burke. Miss Peabody turned her sapphire eyes back onto Clark, toying with him. For a moment, he felt himself stirring. Shit, he thought, this classy old grand dame is beginning to turn me on. He was wondering what other tricks she had up her sleeve.

"Anything else?" asked Clark.

"Yes, now that you mention it. The tall one walked with a slight limp. He's very strong. Lifted Debbie as if she were nothing, and I know she's a solid one-thirty or so."

"What about your housekeeper? Do you think she might have heard or seen something?"

"I'm afraid not," Miss Peabody answered. "Her quarters are in the west wing and she sleeps like a bear. As a matter of fact, it was I who woke her."

"And what time was that, Miss Peabody?" Burke inquired.

"It was one thirty. I had just looked at the clock. I'm on a new medication; I'm sure it's too strong. Edna thought it was the stew, but I just know it's those darn capsules. There's nobody but Edna and me," she continued, with a very pronounced Southern drawl, somewhat reminiscent of T.V. Sheriff Bill Gillespie's in 'In the Heat of the Night.' So if I wake up during the night, I have a habit of checking the house. Well, I looked out the window, and that's when I saw it happen. It was just horrible, I tell you."

"And you're sure you could see all that from this window?"

asked Clark, still not absolutely sure about Miss Peabody's account, rising to look for himself.

"I can see a gnat on a horse's ass at two hundred yards with these," she answered, holding out the theater glasses.

"If you think of anything else, please call me at this number, at any time," said Clark, handing her his card.

"Colored and Irish working together. I'm impressed. Progress at last. Daddy would be pleased. Do you know that Mr. Booker T. Washington sat in your very chair, and his personal secretary, Mr. Scott, where you sit, officer Burke? I'd offer you some libation, but you're on duty, as they always say on television. I detest those abominable talk shows. Beauregard Peabody would be turning over in his grave. It's just disgraceful! I tell you, disgraceful."

She rose as they did, extending her hand, giving Clark's an extra squeeze, smiling that sensual smile.

"Do give your daddy my regards. I believe he might remember me. And please let me know if you find out anything about Debbie."

I'll bet he would, thought Clark. Wonder if Daddy ever tapped Miss Hot Ass, here. Maybe one of those nights that the Johnsons unexpectedly needed him to work late. Glancing at Miss Peabody, he smiled to himself. I'll just bet daddy really did have to work late sometimes, and hard, too.

They said their good-byes and crossed to the scene of the crime to put out an APB. Burke pulled out his pad again, writing down each person's name who had been at the scene.

Clark's mind raced as he approached the body lying beside the car. The lab technicians were taking their customary photos, from full length to close-ups, and collecting what evidence the bodies provided. There would be a ransom call from the kidnappers soon.

CHAPTER 9

Samuel Jammison, Jr. had been called into the manager's office at the Marriott Hotel where he received an urgent telephone call. Refusing to give any specifics, the police informed him of an emergency, insisting that he return home immediately. Walking briskly, Jammison gave instructions to Kennedy.

"Something's happened at the house. The police want Morrow and me to come home right away."

"I don't understand," said Kennedy. "Why wouldn't they tell you what's wrong? At least give you some idea."

"A Detective Clark, that's what he said his name was. He just said that it would be best if he didn't say anything over the telephone, and that Morrow and I should come straight home," Jammison told Kennedy, who was almost running to keep up. People were constantly trying to stop the mayor for conversation.

"You stay behind and cover for us. Keep things moving."

Always cool and composed, even Kennedy was unnerved. What could be so urgent that the mayor had to be called away in the middle of a thousand-dollar-a-plate fund-raiser for his third term announcement? A thing like that was unheard of.

"Could be a practical joke or a prank, you know," said Kennedy, grabbing at straws.

"I thought about that, too," Jammison responded. "That some sicko just might want to ruin this night for me. Sounded too urgent. I'll get Morrow, you grab our coats."

Samuel Jammison, Jr. maneuvered his way through the crowd, finally reaching Morrow, who was laughing, talking to several elegantly dressed ladies. As he bent over and whispered into her ear, her expression quickly turned to despair and confusion. When they reached the lobby Kennedy was already there waiting with their coats. He helped Morrow into her black ranch mink, then escorted the anxious couple to their waiting limousine.

Silently they each wondered what could have been so terrible, turning the possibilities over and over in their minds. Had something happened to Debbie? Why all the secrecy? They sat close on the back seat, Jammison still holding his wife's hand.

How could anyone dare not to give the mayor or any other city administrator information he demanded, Samuel wondered. But then he remembered that this was not just some other city; it was New Orleans, one of the world's most unique cities with some of its most idiosyncratic people.

A European rather than British settlement, French and Spanish influence made Louisianians more laid back, less formal and rigid, than in places like Atlanta or Houston or Dallas. Plus this was the Deep South, he reminded himself, and public officials were generally regarded as "one of us" instead of "one of them."

"Can't we go any faster? It seems like it's taking forever to get home," Morrow lamented.

"Not if we want to get there in one piece," Samuel answered blankly.

"What if something's happened to Debbie? Maybe she and Ray had some kind of accident in that little old car of his."

"Why don't you stop jumping to conclusions, sweetheart? All you're going to do is make yourself more miserable and worried than you already are," he said, attempting to console her, concealing his own distress.

"Well, I can't help it, Sam. I've never been as strong as you are. I never will be. I'm sorry," Morrow wailed, beginning to cry softly. "They call us away from the banquet, tell us to come home right away, and you expect me to be calm and gracious when we know something terrible must have happened."

Samuel Jammison pulled his wife closer, wrapped his arm around her, and kissed her gently on the forehead.

"No, I don't expect you to be calm and gracious, Morrow. I just want you to try to hold yourself together until we find out what happened, that's all. We'll be home in a few minutes."

The limousine and its escorts turned onto Audubon Place. The anxious couple surveyed all the activity in front of their magnificent, one-hundred-year-old home: police cars, emergency units, photographers, television camera trucks, and a small crowd of mostly pajama-wearing spectators. Leaning forward, Samuel Jammison could see that everything seemed to center around Ray's car, parked in the circular driveway directly in front of the door. When their limousine stopped, it was immediately encircled by defensive police officers trying to contain newspaper reporters and photographers who had breached the cordon. Emerging, the Jammisons could see that one of the photographers was taking snapshots of a human figure lying beside the MG. It was Ray.

"Debbie! Debbie! Oh, my God!" Morrow Jammison cried hysterically, her voice trembling, her knees buckling.

"Where's my daughter? What in God's name has happened here?" Samuel Jammison asked, holding his wife close.

"Detective Clark is in charge, sir," said a young officer nearest them. "Here he comes now," he continued, pointing in Clark's direction.

"Officer, where's my daughter? What the hell's going on?"

Jammison passionately demanded.

"It appears that your daughter has been kidnapped, sir. I'm sorry. There's a young man's body over there. He's been shot several times at close range. According to his identification, his name is Raymonde Deveraux."

"Oh! Where's my child? No! No! This can't be happening! It just can't be happening! Poor Ray!"

"Is there any word on my daughter?" The mayor's voice almost broke, his face contorted, showing signs of strain. "Does anybody know what happened?"

Clark's mind raced, trying to find an easy way to talk to the Jammisons. As a homicide detective, he had faced situations like this many times before. Each time, it was just as hard to find the words to explain such a senseless tragedy. But now it was even more difficult. This time, he had to try to explain it to one of the few men he admired, to someone everybody loved. He had to explain it to the man who was also his boss.

"I want to know where my daughter is, Detective!" repeated Jammison insistently, the bones in his jaw tightening. "And I want to know now!"

"One of your neighbors across the street saw the whole thing. We have an all-points bulletin out for three men, probably Caucasian, in a dark blue or black Cadillac."

"Did they hurt her?"

Clark quickly thought about all the answers he might give. He could try to soften the blow, to say something like, "We're sure she hasn't been harmed," but he understood Samuel Jammison, Jr. He knew that the mayor was a man who always wanted to know what the bottom line was.

"Not that we know of," Clark responded empathetically. "According to the witness, they put her into the car and drove away."

"There was a witness? Someone saw what happened here,

what happened to Debbie and Ray! Who? Who is it?"

"It was your neighbor across the street, sir. Miss Peabody."

"Miss Peabody," the mayor repeated, taken by surprise. "Miss Peabody," he repeated again. "What did she say? I've got to talk to her!"

"Mayor Jammison, with all due respect, right now I think it would be a good idea to take Mrs. Jammison inside. I'm sure this three-ring circus isn't helping matters any. As soon as things settle down a little out here, I'll come inside and tell you everything we've learned."

"Detective Clark, we've got to know what's happened to our daughter," Jammison insisted.

"Sir, I can understand that," Clark responded convincingly, obviously disturbed himself. "You can count on me. I'll keep you posted. Every detail... every detail."

"And if anything comes up, you'll let me know immediately?"

"Immediately," said Clark, sympathetically gripping the mayor's arm. "As soon as we know something."

Samuel Jammison entered the house and was helping Morrow to a seat when the telephone rang.

"Debbie! Debbie, where are you?" Jammison exclaimed excitedly, snatching up the receiver.

"Sam, it's me, Gene," answered the voice at the other end of the telephone call. "What's going on? What happened?"

"Gene, you'd better get right over here. Ray's dead, Debbie's been kidnapped."

"What?" said Kennedy, astonished. "I'll be right there. I'll be right there!" he unconsciously repeated again.

"Hurry up, buddy," Jammison responded, sounding vulnerable for the first time since Kennedy had known him. "We really need you."

"I'm on my way."

CHAPTER 10

Debbie lay on the bunk, bound and gagged. She knew that she was on a boat. She could smell the water, hear it moving past the hull. There was no salt in the smell; the boat must be on a bayou or in a channel.

The boat slowed to a halt, engines off, only the hum of the generator sounding in the sudden silence as it rocked from side to side.

Tears trickled down her cheeks as she thought about Ray, her hysterical crying muffled by the white linen cloth tied over her mouth. Starting to hyperventilate, she found herself gasping for breath.

"RAY IS DEAD! RAY IS DEAD!" echoed over and over in her mind. It was all she could think about.

"WHY? WHY DID THEY HAVE TO KILL HIM?" What were they going to do with her? What about her parents? She longed desperately to see them again and to know that Ray was still alive, to wake up and discover that it was all just a horrible nightmare.

Seconds later, she realized that a bell was ringing steadily. A foghorn sounded twice, the engine caught again and the boat moved slowly forward. She began to count again: "one thousand one... one thousand two... one thousand three..."

Minutes later, she heard another bell, the foghorn sounded twice; then a pause, and the horn sounded twice again.

The boat slowed and bumped against the side as it docked. She could hear voices above, then footsteps moving in her direction. She closed her eyes, pretending to still be unconscious.

She was tied with a rope so tightly that it was cutting into her wrists. Squinting for a brief fraction of a second, she saw two men enter noisily—one stocky, wearing a cowboy hat, and the other short with long sideburns.

"You like that, huh, Mario?" said the man wearing the cowboy hat, laughing and scratching his pubic area. He moved closer to Debbie, lifted her dress, then gripped her face so tightly with his large, rough hand that she could not move. She could feel that his little finger was missing from just above the knuckle, flinching as the nub touched her cheek. She jerked involuntarily when he twisted her face, squeezing it until it felt like her jaw would break.

"Can't do shit with her yet, but maybe the boss'll let us have her when he gets what he wants," he said. "I'll tell you what: we flip a coin. Heads, you win. Tails, she's mine."

"No dice, you fuckin' pencil dick coon ass," replied the other man. "I only bet on a sure thing, and I ain't takin' no chances on losin' a sweet piece of ass like this. Eatin' pussy. I tell you what. I'll buy your half, five hundred cash."

"Fuck you, you fuckin' dago," said the man wearing the hat, unzipping his pants, pulling out his penis, then shaking it at the other man. "I'm gonna fuck her first, then you can lick her sweet, black eatin' pussy off my fuckin' dick."

CHAPTER 11

The blue souped-up Trans Am Firebird pulled smoothly to the curb, parking just outside the police cordon, its motor purring softly.

Nick Shannon got out and paused to survey the chaotic scene, his experienced eyes making sense of what looked like an anthill of activity; there were bodies in motion everywhere, but each man with a definite purpose.

Shannon was a well-built, chiseled-faced, olive-complexioned man, wearing a black Brioni leather jacket, white turtleneck pullover, tailored jeans and black handmade Ferragamo boots. He moved toward the cordon with athletic ease, pausing to talk to a uniformed officer at its perimeter.

"How's it going, Jake?"

"Looks pretty grim, Nick. Not to mention freezing my nuts off out here. How's the private eye business?"

"Better than the city was paying me," Shannon answered.

"I hear you," said Jake. "My wife's on me to go into business with her old man and her brother. Can you see me selling life insurance to some poor slob?"

Shannon looked at the big cop, the shoes he was wearing easily a size twelve, then answered with a grin. "Not hardly. You and me, we have to be where the action is."

"Yeah, you're right. And tonight X marks the spot. Guess

you heard somebody snatched the mayor's daughter?"

"Yeah. Any ideas?"

"Who tells me anything? I got word to let you through."

The big cop started laughing. "You haven't started digging through trash cans like the rest of those guys yet, have you?"

Nick Shannon nodded, "Not yet," and laughed, too.

Jake held up the yellow plastic tape that cordoned off the area. Shannon slid deftly underneath.

When Nick Shannon entered the large, plush room, Gene Kennedy and four other men were there with the frustrated mayor, who was painfully addressing a captive audience. "I don't give a damn! How many men are we talking about?" There was a deafening, almost numbing tension inside the warmly-appointed study.

"What are you doing here, Shannon?" asked Clark sharply.

"It's all right, Detective. I asked him to come. We're old friends. Sit down, Nick. Drink?"

"Thanks. Scotch and water. How's Morrow holding up?"

The mayor motioned to Kennedy, who began pouring the drink.

"Right now she's under sedation. She'll be all right. Tough stock. Chauncey is upstairs sitting with her. Good old Chauncey. Always there."

"And you?"

"I'll make it. I can't believe any of this is happening. Nick, this is Special Agent Callahan, from the FBI. I think you know everybody else." They shook hands. Callahan was medium height, broad shouldered, stocky build, his dark blonde hair in a crew cut. There was a Marine Corps ring on the third finger of his right hand. He wore the uniform of FBI agents—dark suit, white shirt, tie.

Shannon accepted the single malt whiskey and took a sip. He surveyed the room. In addition to Agent Callahan and Clark he saw Detective Burke and Lawrence Daniels, head of one of the city's most powerful political organizations.

"Any leads, Detective?" Shannon asked Clark, who looked toward Sam Jammison. For a moment there was a strained silence as the mayor shot the detective a warning glance.

"I can see that you two don't like each other, Detective Clark, but that's a personal problem. So let's leave it at that. We're all here for the same reason, and that's to get my daughter back unharmed. Is that clear?" The detective lowered his eyes as Shannon walked across the room toward a large easy chair.

Clark nodded and cleared his throat, looking from the mayor back to the PI. "Not much, Shannon," he continued. "Three armed men in a late model Cadillac killed the boyfriend and one of the mayor's bodyguards, drove off with the girl. We have an APB out, but they've probably gone underground by now. Next move is theirs."

"Phone taps?"

"Latest and best equipment," Callahan replied. "We're hooking it up right now."

"Any witnesses?"

"Miss Florence Peabody, across the street. Saw the whole thing. Thinks they were white men," answered Clark.

"What do you think?"

"Probably were white; kidnapping is seldom a black thing, I'd say. We don't get many signal forty-fives down here, but you already know that." Clark looked toward Callahan, who confirmed his statement with an affirmative nod.

"It looks like a professional job," Callahan added. "They were in and out in a matter of minutes. The young man never stood a chance. They had to shoot to stop him. Took on all three. Karate."

"That took a lot of nerve," Shannon answered. "Things might get rough."

"We'll try to keep a lid on it," said Daniels. "If we don't get some answers soon, who knows what might happen?"

With a deep sigh and a look of frustration on his otherwise expressionless face, the agent addressed everyone in the room.

"Every year," he said, "in January around the time of Martin Luther King Jr.'s birthday, things start to heat up again. You may not read about it or see it on television, but it's still going on. Racist domestic terrorists—the KKK, neo-Nazi skinheads and white supremacy militia groups—set fires and firebomb black churches. There were nine in 1999 within the first week, and small fires at black colleges, including Florida A&M. Besides being a scare tactic, it is their way of protesting the celebration."

"But that's crazy," Lawrence Daniels interrupted. "That goes against everything Dr. King stood for."

"It works, though," Shannon added. "If people don't feel safe in church, especially black people whose entire lives revolve around church, what else is left?"

"I saw some skinheads tonight," the mayor said. "Outside the hotel."

"We're already on it," concluded the agent, clicking a ballpoint pen in his right hand repeatedly as he spoke. "Any lead we can get."

"It might be there. It might not," Clark answered confidently, his eyes circling the room. "We're checking everything."

"I'm making a statement on the morning news," Sam added. "Asking the people to remain calm. The last thing we need right now is a race riot. That won't get Debbie back, and it might be exactly what these people want. Divide and conquer. Especially at election time."

"You think this was politically motivated?" asked Shannon.

"Anything's possible, Nick. We're fairly well off, but not rich by any means, and the kidnappers must know that, too. Graft's never been my thing," said the mayor, taking a sip of brandy from a large snifter.

"What about the Union or the Teamsters?" posed Callahan as diplomatically as possible, turning toward Clark and Burke, then back to the mayor. "Do you think the police strike could have anything to do with your daughter's abduction?"

"I can't believe that," Jammison rebutted, surprised himself that anything so outrageous would even be mentioned. "An illegal strike, that's one thing. But murder and kidnapping? Besides, all that ended with Jimmy Hoffa, didn't it?"

"I'm just trying to cover all the bases, playing devil's advocate."

"Sure. We've got some trash and a few racists in the department, like anywhere else, but I can't believe even they would stoop to something like this."

Special Agent Callahan was sympathetic to the mayor's response, but he still appeared to be uncomfortable with the answer.

"Fear and anger can make people do some crazy things sometimes. Nothing surprises me anymore."

"But what could the Union or the Teamsters possibly hope to gain by kidnapping Debbie?"

"I'll nose around, hit my contacts, see what I can find out," Shannon said to the mayor. "We'll get her back."

"I appreciate your help, Nick. I knew I could count on you."

Shannon shook hands with everyone except Clark and Burke, who nodded calmly as he left.

This is a tough one, Shannon thought, driving off into the dark night.

CHAPTER 12

Shannon drove down sleepy St. Charles Avenue, listening to the muted trumpet sound of a Miles Davis tape playing "Round Midnight." Miles always had a soothing effect on Shannon, and he needed a cool head to do what he had to do. He'd known Debbie since she was about five years old, and the idea that she was alone and frightened somewhere tightened his jaws, sent waves of rage through his body. He forced himself to concentrate on the music coming from the custom speakers in the car, watched the water on the hood, beaded from a recent rain, run rivulets down the windows.

His first custom Pioneer sound system had been stolen. Shannon hunted down the junkie thief and broke both his kneecaps. The junkie now hobbled on two canes, visible advertisement not to rip off Nick Shannon. Since that time, he no longer bothered to lock his car, not even in the toughest neighborhoods.

Shannon drove down St. Charles to Washington Avenue, the streets virtually deserted, a bit past four a.m. A cold wind blew in across the Mississippi River; the few people on the streets huddled deep into their upturned collars; hands buried in the pockets of their overcoats; heads down, watery eyes regarding the damp sidewalks, eager for the St. Charles Avenue streetcar to arrive.

Making an illegal left turn, expensive Garden District mansions quickly faded in the distance. Heading west on Washington past unpainted shanties, huge flophouses, and tenement buildings of graying, peeling, once-white paint, only a few blocks later he had already reached the low-rent district.

In city after city across America it was always the same: Memphis, Charlotte, Detroit—fine homes owned by rich whites, rundown shacks a few blocks away generally owned or rented by their domestics.

Only a handful of shivering black people stood at the Freret bus stop at Washington and LaSalle; the night and day shifts would not begin to change for at least two more hours. But this was New Orleans, like New York, one of those cities that never sleeps; and even at this hour, cars were lined up in front of Club Fifty-Seven. Outside, Shannon could hear the low muffled hum of moving traffic and horns honking as a red 500 series Mercedes sporting A.B.S. rims streaked across the light and came to a smooth stop, double parking in front of the club. A tall, hard-looking black man emerged wearing a beige cashmere overcoat and disappeared into the building, leaving his emergency flashers on and a female companion in the car. The light changed and Shannon was moving again, nodding his head as he thought about how much money was tied up in a rig like that, and what type of business the hurried driver was really up to. He drove past A. L. Davis Park and stopped in front of an alley next to the Camero Lounge, music still blasting from within. Fats Domino was singing "I'm Walking to New Orleans."

Across the street stood the dismal Magnolia Housing Project, looming like the urban prison it was, most of its inhabitants trapped there for a nonjudicial life sentence.

During the summer months, the streets would be swarming with people, moving, jostling, laughing; most of them going nowhere at all. They would be sitting outside on their steps watching a constant stream of shabbily dressed children and cocky-walking adults making their way from the dilapidated projects with cracked windows and missing doors to the One-Stop Record Shop, or they might go to any one of three grubby bars, or to the Claiborne Shopping Center, especially around the first and the fifteenth of the month, when the food stamps and assistance checks came.

Shannon was thinking about Maya Angelou's poem "Black On A Saturday Night," thinking that there should have been a sequel, "Black on the First and the Fifteenth." Everybody in the 'hood was happy and shelling out cash, flaunting their wares. Sixteen and seventeen-year-old girls would spend time with eighty-year-old men, giving them sex, most often oral sex, for money to get their nails and their hair done, to buy drugs or whatever else they wanted. Three days later, everybody was broke again.

Shannon checked the loads in his weapon, a .38 caliber Smith & Wesson on a .45 frame. He jacked a round into the chamber, set the safety, slid the weapon into his waist holster, and got out of the car.

He stood there for a moment, his head turning like some jungle cat checking for danger, then entered the alley cautiously. The wind whistled and howled in the narrow canyon, landscaped by trash-filled boxes and overrun garbage cans. As he walked deeper into the darkness, the absolute stillness and his intuition told him that he wasn't alone. Not even a dog or cat looking for food, only the occasional squeak of a mouse and the rip of paper being torn.

The scrape of shoe leather on the concrete alerted him, and when two junkies pounced upon him wielding blows to his head and midsection, Shannon was ready. Grabbed from behind, he downed the first attacker with a karate kick to the chest. The second assailant received a not-so-friendly elbow to the stomach, a judo chop to the Adam's apple, then Shannon twisted his arm and rammed him into a stack of trash-filled wooden produce cases.

Stepping back, he drew his piece in the same motion, the click of the safety coming off sounding loud in the alley.

Alarmed by the commotion, a door opened several feet away, and half a dozen seedy characters emerged—silhouetted by the light from within. Shannon held his gun along his leg, his finger pressed against the trigger ready to fire. One figure moved ahead of the rest, the street light from beyond Shannon reflecting off his dark glasses, the fiery red tip of his cigarette glowing as he took a long, slow draw. The music resumed.

"Be cool, my brothers," the man said. I'm sure Mr. Shannon don't mean us no harm. Do you, Mr. Shannon?" There was an icy sneer in his voice and not a hint of fear.

"Not unless you fuck with me, Billy. Then I got seven friends in this piece to help me out," said Shannon in a soft and deadly voice that matched Billy's.

"Big mouth mothafucka, ain't he?" the man standing to Billy's right said. "Maybe we oughta shut it up for him. Teach him some mothafuckin' manners."

"No need," said Billy. "Shannon just blows hard like the winter wind. He ain't no trouble at all. Whadafuck you want, Shannon?" Billy was big and black, with a thin mustache and a clean-shaven head. He was as dangerous as he looked.

"Know anything about the Debbie Jammison snatch?" asked Shannon, his gun still hanging casually at his side.

"The line is dead, and this ain't no four one one," Billy answered, his deep voice as rough as sandpaper. "What makes you think I'd tell you anything, even if I did know somethin'?"

The alley was silent again, except for the sound of someone in the background rapping something solid in the palm of his hand. Shannon knew that he was taking a big chance showing up alone at night. He also knew that time was not on his side.

"I'll tell you one thing, Shannon. You got a lotta fuckin' nerve waltzin' your ass down here, especially after what happened last time."

"I could have busted you when I was on the force. You owe me, Billy," Shannon rebutted. "We grew up together."

"Don't owe you a mothafuckin' thing!" Billy snapped. "Grew up together? Don't mean shit, except once we were in the same ditch at the same time. You went your way, I went mine."

"We make choices, Billy."

"Didn't have no fuckin' choice, man!" Billy snarled defensively. "Besides, in my business I can't afford none of that mothafuckin' sentimental bullshit." He paused for a moment to gather his thoughts, then spoke again.

"You know sometime I see my mother on the street. She thinks I'm trash and acts like she don't even see me. But she does, and I know it, and she does, too. That's a good go-to-church-every-Sunday Christian for ya."

"She's still your mother, Billy," said Shannon, trying to reach him.

"Yeah. So what? I used to speak to her, but after a while I just said fuck it. You know. Fuck her, too. She had me. Raised my ass in this goddamn cesspool, then put me down for doin' what I had to do. She might be my old lady, but she ain't no better than me. Tell you what. I'm gonna do you a favor, Shannon, for the old days and shit. I'm gonna let you leave outta here in one piece."

The music pulsed from the bar. An occasional passing car briefly lit the dark alley. Shannon holstered his piece, turned his back on them, and walked toward his parked car.

"Hey, Shannon!" called Billy. Shannon stopped and turned around. "Know Gino Provenzano?"

"All American linebacker, out of LSU?" asked Shannon.

"You got it, baby. Down here almost every night. Likes the music, likes dark meat. Real smooth white boy. Don't take no shit, don't give none."

"So?"

"Connected, you know what I mean."

"Yeah?" said Shannon.

"Wasn't down here tonight. Hasn't been around for days, and he always makes it on weekends. We got strippers. Might wanna check it out."

"Thanks, Billy," said Shannon.

"Ain't about you. Just don't need no more heat down here. It's bad for business." He turned and led his men back inside. Shannon stared into the gloom where the door had closed on the light.

At about four-thirty a.m., Shannon merged into traffic that was steadily moving on Carrollton Avenue. When he reached Tulane Avenue, he eased his car over to the newsstand in front of the Bayou Vista Hotel, and watched the newspaper vendor approach. Pete was wearing a weatherbeaten brown overcoat with holes at both elbows, a greasy nine-year-old gold New Orleans Saints baseball cap, grimy jeans, and shoes so old that the heels on both were worn to the point that he was nearly walking on the sides. Even before the window went down, Nick was already remembering the foul stench that was about to assail him.

"How're you doing, Pete?" said Shannon to the grubby seventy-year-old man, whose frizzy hair and yellow teeth were now only inches away, as he leaned against the car to talk, his arm resting on the cold roof.

"I'm still around, Nick," Pete replied enthusiastically, sensing that a reward was in the making. "I'm doin' my thing, just like the mailman. Tryin' to pay the bills." He grinned insincerely, revealing at least fifty years of acute dental abuse, front teeth missing and the rest green, brown, and yellow with rotten cavities and tobacco stains. He handed over a newspaper through the open window.

"Have you heard anything about Debbie Jammison?" Shannon

asked, passing the vendor a twenty-dollar bill. Pete scratched his scrubby two-week-old beard, then spat on the sidewalk, his putrid saliva forming a small, slimy puddle where it landed.

"No, I ain't heard nothin', yet," Pete responded. "But I'll keep my eyes open."

"If you do, you know where to reach me," said Shannon, leaning toward the newsman to get his point across. Pete nodded affirmatively as Shannon checked his rearview mirror and swung back into the traffic flow.

Making regular stops along the way, checking with snitches and sources, Shannon drove across town to Florida and Desire, crossing the small bridge separating the Desire Housing Projects from the rest of the world.

"Desire." Desire was a world in itself, Shannon thought, remembering that nearly ten thousand poor black people lived, raised families, and died within its boundaries. He remembered the story of two policemen friends who had taken fifty children from Desire to a McDonald's restaurant, and that it was the first time that some of them had ever even seen the inside of a McDonald's or tasted a Big Mac.

The signs of poverty were everywhere, trash blowing, junked cars, graffiti like "Melvin loves Tanya," and, of course, "Fuck you," "Suck my dick," "Pussy," "Fuck this and fuck that."

Shannon walked up a poorly lit stairway to the third floor, to a door with sixty-nine scratched where the original number had been. Hearing bellowing moans and groans, he entered without knocking. A large, well-proportioned, two hundred pound woman lay in a bed that banged against the wall, a trick busy between her legs, his clothes hanging from a chair. Ignoring Shannon's entrance, the scrubby-looking man never missed a stroke.

"Close the door, mothafucka. You grow up in a barn?" the woman growled.

"Yeah," Shannon answered evenly, his eyes scanning the room as he pulled the door to, "and every time I see a big fat cow, I think I'm back home."

The woman threw back her head in laughter, almost bucking the man out of her, but he grabbed her ample behind with both hands and kept on stroking.

"One, two, three, four," counted Shannon, snapping his fingers to the cadence, as the unmistakable smell of sex filled his nostrils. "Molly, Molly," he said, moving toward the bed, "you can do better than that, can't you? You're off beat. Give the man his money's worth."

"Fuck you," Molly grunted, as the man increased his pace, Shannon wondered if the bed would collapse under the strain.

"You kinky sonofabitch," she snapped, her breathing hampered by the weight of the man on top of her. "This how you get your rocks off these days?"

"I wish I had my camera," Shannon answered. Molly spread her big thighs even wider and kicked both legs in the air. "I'd almost pay to watch this. Heard anything about the Jammisons' snatch?"

"Ain't... uh... heard... uh... nuthin'," she gasped, gripping the tarnished gold headboard. "I heard about it," gasp, "but that's all I know." As she stretched her legs even wider, Shannon thought she looked like she was going to split herself in two, as the muscles in her john's behind tightened. Becoming almost violent, their breathing turned to growling and Shannon knew it was time to leave. He took one last disbelieving glance, wondering how a woman Molly's size could do things like that with her body, and closed the door behind him as the shouting and groaning of orgasm began.

* * *

Shannon drove to the Atlantis, a large building of high-rent apartments for singles in Metairie, adjacent to Interstate 10. He parked his car between a Jaguar and an Audi, took the elevator to the second floor, and walked to Apartment 207. Loud party noises were coming from inside.

After ringing the doorbell and pounding on the door to no avail, he tried the knob and let himself in.

The sweet smell of marijuana poured into his nostrils as soon as he stepped inside the crowded room. Someone handed him a pipe; he took two deep hits, and passed it back, holding the smoke in his lungs until the pot bit in.

He looked around, nodding greetings through the noisy dance music and smoke. Shannon knew most of the faces because this was a weekly floating party.

The pot smokers were in the front room; the cokeheads would be in the kitchen. Several people were dancing; others sat on the couch or on the floor, their backs against the wall. Some held wine-filled water pipes. One man held a large bong of bamboo.

Danny B., disc jockey, pimp, dope pusher and all-around hustler, sat between two ladies of the evening from his stable. Dressed in his Canali with at least two one-karat diamonds on each hand, his "I know I'm the man" attitude was coming on even stronger than the weed. Word had it that a straitlaced nurse at Baptist Hospital had opened his nose, and dumped him when she found out what he really was. He had been strung out on cocaine and too many other drugs to count since she had ditched him. Her name was Brenda and he had met her at a hospital picnic. The streetwise hustler fell for her like a concrete cinder block, but when her brother, a policeman, found them together, Danny B.'s charade was completely exposed. Shannon waved and Danny B. smiled a greeting through drug-fogged eyes.

A slim woman approached, handed Shannon a drink, and kissed him on the cheek. "Hey, lover, glad you could make it," she said, putting her arm around his waist, her raspy voice as deep as his.

"Hey, Butch," said Shannon. "How are things? Your new lady?"

"Not too bad," she answered, pointing. "Madalyn's here, she's over there in the corner. We got married last week."

"Congratulations. What's this, three or four?"

"Third, but who's counting? Besides, this is the real thing. You know, she couldn't understand why she'd been through four marriages before I got my head between her legs. We're having a party to celebrate next week. You're invited."

Shannon nodded to her friend seated across the room as she smiled and waved; as fine in her own way as was Butch. "Good luck, you two."

"I'd have invited you to the wedding, Nick, but it was an all-girl thing, you know? But I want you at the party. Bring Sue, all right? I like her. Doesn't seem to get uptight around gay people. Like you."

"Do your own thing. That's my motto."

"Never even been curious?" asked Butch, her ruby red lips pouting, blowing Shannon a kiss.

"Nope."

"Me, neither. I knew what I was by the time I was ten. Got turned out by my gym teacher at thirteen. Been women ever since. Oh, I've met men from time to time, even been fun sometimes; but women are my thing. I guess I just love pussy too much. Miss Thang over there claims to be bisexual. Shee-it. Far as I'm concerned, a bisexual is somebody who can't make up their mind. "Don't forget to bring Sue next Saturday," said Butch. "Good thing you met her before I did."

"Funny, I was thinking the same thing about your old lady," rebutted Shannon, with a smile.

Butch laughed and winked as she crossed the room, sat next to her friend and kissed her full on the mouth.

Stepping over smokers, Shannon moved toward the kitchen, but he was only looking for one man.

"Where's Junior?"

Coughing and choking, the man couldn't speak, but pointed to a small door in the hallway. Shannon inched his way through the congestion to the door and pushed it open, almost falling in. Junior, a dark-skinned Rastafarian, sat there on the toilet, long graying dreadlocks dangling in front of his face, a joint in his mouth.

"Hey, yo', what it tis, mon?" responded the strange-looking figure wearing dark glasses and a huge mudcloth hat. He took another draw on his reefer.

"Round and round and round I go; where I'm gonna stop, nobody knows," he said with a distinct Jamaican accent.

"Mind if I come in? What's going on, Junior?" asked Shannon.

"Don't you know, mon," Junior replied. "My mind is clean. My body is clean. I am God."

"Sure, man, sure. Anything you say," Shannon agreed.

"You just don't dig it, do you?"

Shannon's eyes and expression must have mirrored what he was thinking. "I'll have to try it sometime," he said, humoring Junior. "Know anything about the mayor's kid?"

"No, mon," Junior responded, taking another hit of pot. "All I know is Jack took her up the hill, and she ain't been seen since. Who knows, maybe it got good to her."

"And that's all you know?" repeated Shannon.

"Her old mon's a good dude, I know that. He didn't change color when he made it. Not like the rest of 'em," Junior replied passionately. "Good brother. I'd go to the front for him myself. I'm tellin' you, mon, I ain't heard nothin'."

Shannon finally had to put a handkerchief over his nose to cut the odor.

"If you do, give me a call, huh, Junior?"

"Sure thing, ma main mon," responded Junior. "Hey, Shannon, do me a favor—Hand me some toilet paper."

Shannon threw him a roll from the cabinet behind him and left, truly amazed at this point. First Pete, now this. Maybe it was time to try another line of work.

Lighting a Camel, Shannon carefully made his way to a vacant corner and leaned against the wall. Belting out "I Have Nothing," Whitney Houston really had the room floating. Shannon took a long drag, feeling somewhat alone, but relieved at the same time, because he was probably the only truly sane person there. One especially dizzy bitch, Daphine, was making her way around the room, flitting like a butterfly and throwing her too-firm-to-be-real boobs in anybody's face who would stand still long enough.

Shannon took another deep gulp of the Crown Royal Butch had given him. As the alcohol flowed warmly through his system, he thought about Susan, his girlfriend, and her son Kevin. She was the first woman he thought he had ever really been in love with since Paula, his first wife, had died of kidney failure in nineteen eighty-nine. Filling in as a dad for seven-year-old Kevin meant a lot to Shannon, too, giving him a chance to do some of the things he might have done if he had had a son of his own. A boy needed to have a man around, and even though Sue was a wonderful mother, there was only so much she could do. How he wished he could have been with them right then.

Shannon motioned to Danny B. with his head. Danny followed him outside onto the balcony.

"You're looking good."

"You, too," Danny responded. "It's all good."

"Heard anything about the Jammison snatch, Danny?" asked

Shannon.

Danny pulled the collar of his jacket up and crossed his arms against the cold. No one would have believed that Danny had once been a competitive bodybuilder. His skin was pulled tight over his face, giving him a skeleton-like look. His clothes hung loosely on his gaunt frame. Coke will keep you thin; anorexic models knew it, too.

"Nothing yet, and you know bad news travels quick. One thing, though; everybody's bent, been keeping a low profile in the 'hood for about a week. White dudes, I mean, connected." Danny sniffed and wiped his nose. "Shit, even good blow is hard to find. Good thing I had a stash."

Danny took a small vial from his pocket, did a quick two on two using a gold-plated coke spoon hanging from a chain around his neck, and offered the vial to Shannon. Shannon hesitated, then did a two on two, also. The coke would keep him awake and alert for several hours more. He had things to do.

"Think the mob might be involved, Danny?"

"Good chance," he answered, sniffing twice to round off his hit. "I'll ask around."

"No, don't ask. Just keep your eyes and ears open, okay?"

Danny lit a cigarette with shaking hands. "Seen Brenda around, Nick?"

"Last week. Around lunch time, up by the hospital. She looks great. I don't know how you let that one get away, man."

"Asked about me?"

"No."

"Think I can get her back, man? She's in my guts."

Shannon hunched his shoulders. "Never say never."

"How? How, Nick?"

"Kick that shit first." Shannon looked Danny in the eye. "You can't handle it anymore."

"Sure. Tomorrow—uh, maybe.... Maybe next week."

"Yeah, sure." Shannon turned to go back inside.

"No, wait," Danny pleaded. "Suppose I do kick it, then what?"

"Change your show from do-wops to gospel, start showing up at her church after you've been clean for a month or two. Then, when she gives you a soft look, testify."

"Testify?"

"The way George Wallace won black people over. Get up in front of the congregation and confess your sins. Promise to do better." Shannon nodded his head. "Promise the Lord and the congregation. Say you're on the road back because of the love of Jesus and the good woman you love. And stay off the shit."

"Think she'll come back?"

"If she doesn't, should get to half the women in the congregation."

"Think I'll try it," Danny B. answered, shivering uncontrollably.

"Don't try. Do it," said Shannon. "Man, I hate to see you strung out like this."

"I will, Nick. I will. I promise, man. You got my word."

As Shannon re-entered the living room, he heard Danny B. snorting more cocaine.

Shannon made his round of the party, but no one else had a clue regarding Debbie's whereabouts. Two tips on the mob, he thought. Where there's smoke, there might be fire.

Shannon finished his drink, then slid out into the cold dawn, closing the door behind him. He walked about thirty feet to a stairway at the end of the balcony, then down a narrow set of concrete steps leading from the second story to the ground floor. Looking over the rooftops of other parked vehicles, he walked across the deserted parking lot to his own car. He patted his jacket, listening for the familiar jingle of his keys, then took them out of his left pocket and opened the door.

Comfortably settled inside the warm Trans Am, he turned the ignition key and started the engine, then reached over and switched the radio on. He gripped the gearshift lever, checked the rearview mirror, then backed out of the parking space. There was a slight amount of tension in the female announcer's voice as she delivered a breaking news story. "At this moment firefighters are battling a four-alarm fire at the Second Mount Pilgrim Baptist Church, located at 2929 Marengo Street. The fire, which broke out just before five o'clock this morning, started out as a two-alarm but quickly escalated to a three-alarm. The building, reported to be unoccupied, is suffering heavy damage and will probably be completely destroyed. Authorities say that they will be investigating to determine the cause of that fire. Elsewhere in the news, authorities say that they still have no leads in the kidnapping of Debbie Jammison, daughter of Mayor Samuel Jammison, abducted early this morning."

Looking into the rearview mirror again, he started breaking south, toward the Mississippi River. A soft, misty rain began floating down; although it seemed to be warming up and there were breaks in the overcast sky through which a full moon peaked from time to time. In the distance, a reddish-orange glow outlined the horizon.

CHAPTER 13

In east New Orleans, dawn's weak light reflected off shimmering green waves and showed through the window of a white Le Courbusier-style mansion. The large room on the second floor overlooked the pristine rose garden below.

"The kid's all right?" asked Sal Cintenni.

"Except for a bump on her head, yes," answered Gino, "she's good. Why didn't we know her boyfriend was a martial artist? We thought he was some soft, high-society punk. It didn't go down smooth, Sal."

"That fuck we got on the string in the mayor's office, I'd like to cut his balls off and feed 'em to him. Like I always say, only thing you can count on a snitch to do is fuck up."

Sal swiveled his leather armchair around and stared out into his garden toward Lake Borgne, barely visible beyond his high-walled fence.

They sat in the large study on the second floor, next door to his bedroom. He took a sip of wine and turned back to Gino.

"It's all right, Gino. I appreciate you wanting things neat and clean, but this will work for us. Terror fucks up the mind. Now that fuckin' cunt mayor knows we mean business."

Gino nodded. Nevertheless, he was sorry he had to ice the

kid. The fucking pretty boy had shown balls of brass, taking on three armed men without a blink. Must have been crazy about the little bitch, he thought. Didn't blame him, though, because she really was a prime piece of black ass.

Almost as if reading Gino's mind, Sal said, "Nobody harms the girl, got it? If we send her back as damaged goods, then all bets are off."

Gino nodded his agreement. If they returned the mayor's daughter abused, her father would come at them like a crazed maniac. Both men were clear about that.

"Right, Sal. We know Jammison's no pushover."

"Not by a long shot. He'd do the same thing I would if somebody harmed anyone in my family. Besides, we're not fuckin' animals like the Colombians. Fuckin' dog shit. It's a matter of honor. The mob never harms the family. Families are sacro—sacro—"

"Sacrosanct," Gino finished. As a member of the notorious Provenzano family, the word sacrosanct was one that he understood long before he had ever heard it.

"Right. Good to have a college boy like you around, Gino. Gives us some real class. Lotta the wise guys think an Italian-made suit and gold cufflinks make the man, but real class always shows. How's the knee?"

"All right. Bothers me when it rains. In fact, I walk around with a weather bureau down there. Two days before rain, it starts hurting. Probably have rain again tonight."

"How'd you feel, blowin' it out in the Sugar Bowl in front of eighty thousand people? You woulda been a first-round draft choice. A sure thing, if I ever saw one. And believe me, you were one of the best. No bullshit. Made me proud."

Gino shrugged. "Injury's always in the back of your mind," he replied. "Sure, it would have been great to have had a pro career. Find out just how good you are against the best of the best. But I had the family to fall back on. I was lucky."

"Lucky my ass. I promised your old man I'd look out for you if anything ever happened to him. I gave him my word. You know, you're even better than he was, already? When it came to family business, he was one cold-blooded sonofabitch. If I fucked up, I think he woulda even had my ass whacked. You both got that cool head when everybody else is goin' fuckin' nuts. The both of you, you never lose sight of the real objective."

"Thanks, Sal."

"Thanks, whaddaya mean thanks? I knew you'd do all right. Tony Provenzano's son? If he was still alive, I'd be sittin' where you are, takin' orders, and Tony'd be givin' 'em," Sal laughed. "When I retire, you'll be sittin' over here. C'mon in the greenhouse. I always think better when I'm workin' on my orchids. Bring the Chianti with you."

Sal shook his head. "Who'd ever thought that Salvador Cintenni, a shrimp fisherman's son raised on Dago red, would be drinking vintage Chianti? Sure, I got better table manners, nowadays. I can even speak pretty good English when I hafta.' But I got no illusions... naw, I mean delusions. I'm just the son of a simple fisherman with a lotta dough and a lotta clout. Clout, power, that's where it's at. Don't never forget it, Gino. Like that Tuscan sonofabitch, Machiavelli. He knew. You keep readin' to me outta The Prince, you hear? Way back then, he knew about power and how to use it. Like you always say, if the fuckin' Medicis had been listenin' to him, they'd be rulin' the world today. Everybody would be speakin' fuckin' Italian."

They walked the short distance to the greenhouse that occupied one end of the balcony at the rear of the house.

Gino took off his suit jacket, carefully folded it, put it over a nearby chair and loosened his tie. The greenhouse was kept at a regular, humid eighty-eight degrees, year round. Unlike most of the wise guys, Gino was not into Italian suits, favoring a tailor and shoemaker on Saville Row in London.

Sal began to spray a white orchid. "You know, most people think orchids are delicate, but they're not. In the wild, they're tough as weeds. Go out in the bayou, they're everywhere. It's when you try and bring 'em inside, they die. Like some guys. On the street, tough as nails. Put 'em in the joint, they die slow. Your father, now, he was no orchid. He was a cactus. Did two years hard time in Angola like he was standin' on his head. You'd be the same way. Stoic, you two. Me, I'm an emotional guinea. Put me away, I don't know. Only thing I'm afraid of, doing time."

"You'd do all right," said Gino.

"Think so? I dunno. Being locked up, told what to do. Scares the fuck outta me."

"Sal, you'd be running the joint in a week." Sal shook his head, unconvinced.

"Made the ransom demand yet?"

"Tomorrow night, Sal. We want them to sweat a little, first. And we make it look like a simple kidnapping, right?"

"Right," Cintenni replied. "So's nobody knows what we're really after. Not even that dumbfuck Mayor."

"He's probably already guessed. Jammison's no fool," said Gino, taking out a nail clip and removing dirt from beneath one of his nails.

"Ya really think so? I just can't get used to the idea of a really smart nigger. Know what I mean?"

"They're usually smart enough not to let you know how smart they really are," answered Gino.

"Yeah, guess you got to really know them porch-monkeys pretty good, playin' football with 'em and all. They really got some smart ones, huh?"

"Some smarter than us, and the mayor's one smart cookie.

Don't underestimate him, Sal. Machiavelli would have spotted him in a minute."

"Well, the fuckin' mayor outsmarted himself this time. Imagine that bastard tryin' to put one over on me, Sal Cintenni." He continued spraying the orchids, touching them lovingly from time to time.

"He almost got away with it," Gino replied evenly, taking a sip of the good wine.

"You know, you're right. If we didn't have a man inside, we woulda wound up on the outside lookin' in. But I got him by the short hairs, now. He dotes on that daughter of his. If he cooperates, she goes back untouched. If not, we send her back in pieces. Nobody harms the kid. Got that? Not till I say so."

"Got it, Sal."

CHAPTER 14

"Let's see the tape," Sal motioned, after returning to the study, taking a sip of chianti from a large snifter. Gino rose, crossed the room and inserted a video tape into the VCR. He pressed a button, and Debbie's image came on the screen.

"Daddy, I'm told to say that I will not be harmed as long as the ransom demands are met. The men holding me are always masked. For my own protection, they say. Please take care of Sicky. Daddy, I'm scared, and poor Don." She then burst into tears.

"Great. I like the tears. You tell her to do that?"

"No, did it on her own. She's really scared."

"Sicky?"

"Her dog. Checks out. Heard him inside barking when the deal went down."

"Good touch. It'll play well on the networks. Copy of the tape goes to the television stations today, right?"

"Right after it's delivered to the mayor. I dropped them off in the UPS box on my way here."

"Phone call?"

Sal took a Havana Corona from a humidor on his desk, taking his time in the ritual of cutting and lighting it.

"We make the call from a fishing boat by portable phone out in the Gulf, throw it overboard when we're through. It's been subscribed under a fictitious name. Every time we call, it's from a different phone and a different boat. The first call comes from the Gulf, the second one from Lake Pontchartrain. We make two calls, three tops. First one to demand the money, the next one to give instructions for delivery. Third to tell them where to pick the girl up," said Gino.

"Yeah, sounds good. Killin' the kid and the cop might fuck things up for a minute or two, but you had no choice. Nobody will know what we really want except the Sambo mayor. When he agrees, he gets the kid back. Meanwhile, everybody else is left in the dark. How much you askin' for?"

"Two mil."

"Good figure. The mayor can raise it, and it looks like small-time hoods think that's big money. Two million. Shit, fuckin' chump change. I could drop that one night on the tables at the casino and never miss it. If I gambled. Never gamble, Gino. Always run the game. The house never loses in the long run. Know what I mean? Only suckers gamble, and there's one born every minute, like Barnum said. Wonder if he was Sicilian?"

"You know, that Peabody woman was a bonus," Gino told Sal. "Imagine her claiming the kidnapping had been done by white men. Otherwise, we'd have had to put that out another way. You pay good money to plant a leak like that. This one was a freebie."

"Right," said Sal, lighting the large cigar. "And the chance of race riots puts more pressure on that fuckin' mayor. They probably think the fuckin' KKK did it. We gotta keep a cool head about this, Gino, because every time I think about that fuckin' Jammison, I wanna waste the bastard. Tryin' to pull a fast one on me. For two bucks I'd cut his fuckin' balls off and throw 'em in the bayou. Give the catfish somethin' to do. They'd probably choke on 'em," he grinned.

"Can't afford that, Sal, the stakes are too high."

"You're right. Keep remindin' me of that. Know what I mean? You're sure the kid's okay?"

"She's fine, Sal."

"What about that cajun fuck, Boutte? He'd fuck a snake if you held it by the head."

"I can control Boutte."

"I never trust Cajuns. Keep your eye on that fuck. Fuckin' crazy-ass Frenchman."

"Okay, Sal. Whatever you say.."

Gino slid into the leather chair in front of Sal's massive desk. He had his suit jacket back on because the air conditioner was going full blast even at this time of year. The only place in the house that was warm was the greenhouse. Sal said it was because of his childhood days, sleeping with four brothers in a tiny room in a seaside shanty, roasting in the summertime heat. Ever since that time, his surroundings were always cold. Whenever Sal went to his favorite restaurants, the air conditioner was turned up an hour before he arrived, and he would rush through the warm, humid New Orleans air from his air-conditioned Mercedes into the freezing interior of one of several restaurants he owned or controlled. Even on the "Scoundrel," his forty-foot Hatteras yacht, he seldom came aboveboard, preferring to stay below in the frigid air of his huge bedroom in the stern, or the large stateroom. Perhaps Sal was right about prison, Gino thought; perhaps it wasn't the confinement he feared, but a lack of cold air in a small cell about the size of the room he'd shared with his brothers years ago.

"I'd better get back to the safe house and check on the girl. She's probably a perfect candidate for Stockholm syndrome," Gino told Cintenni.

"Good. Keep her calm. We want her lookin' good when she

goes back home to papa. Know what I mean? I'll have the cook make up some food for her. Find out what she likes to eat. Maybe she likes cornbread, collard greens. You know, nigger food. Corn bread!" Cintenni snorted.

"Come on, Sal. You mean you never ate polenta?"

"Hell, yeah. Like it was comin' outta my ears as a kid. That's why I hate the shit so much. Why I got restaurants of my own, so I can eat whatever I want. I might still be a peasant in most ways, but I'm an aristocrat when it comes to eatin' good. Polenta! Fuckin' corn mush. Pig food. Coon food."

Gino laughed. "Maybe you ought to try peacock tongues like the Medicis."

"Think so?" Cintenni mused, then he saw the look on Gino's face and they both laughed. "Go on, get outta here, you fuckin' dago," said Sal affectionately. "Keep me posted."

Sal stood in the window overlooking the driveway until Gino emerged and drove away in his black BMW. He walked into the bedroom and let his eyes roam over the slim figure reclining there. He began to slowly undress, feeling himself stiffen as his eyes roamed over the sun-bronzed body.

"Miss me, baby? Well, I'm back. Now, suck my big, beautiful cock, bitch. Then I want you to beat me with a wet towel and fuck my ass. Hear me, you beautiful cunt?"

"Of course, sweetheart. I'm all yours," declared the boyish looking young man, as he took the swollen member into his mouth.

"Suck it! Suck it!" Cintenni ordered, as he threw back his head and groaned.

CHAPTER 15

Shannon headed back uptown on Magnolia Street to the Community Health Services headquarters where Train, one of his best snitches, worked as a driver. With eight paramedics on at all times, they handled everything from epileptic seizures and strokes to shootings, beatings and stabbings. Inside, Shannon was surprised to find all eight men present. Train, a heavyset black man about five seven, two hundred thirty pounds, in his mid-forties, was seated at a six-foot folding table playing poker with three other men, while a fourth looked over their shoulders. Two men slept on metal cots, while another sat in a corner under a lamp reading from a Bible. Before Shannon could speak, the alarm went off and Train and his partner Westley were on their feet. Shannon followed close behind, climbing into the orange and white van, speeding away with the siren screaming and lights flashing. Outside, several poorly dressed adults looked on curiously.

Their destination was an old building on Calliope Street. On the second floor, they found an elderly woman, about seventy or seventy-five, unconscious and literally wedged in the floor. Two small children, no more than four or five, dressed only in clothes fit for rags, told how the flooring had given way under her weight and how their grandmother had cried because her leg hurt so much, until they thought she was dead.

The building looked as though it should have been condemned years ago. Plaster hung from the walls and ceiling, window panes were broken, the wooden floor sagged, and there were boards loose on the stairs.

"How is she?" Shannon asked, after comforting the children and moving them to safety.

"Her leg's broke," Train replied emphatically. "And she's in shock, but I think she'll be all right once we get her to the hospital. It's a goddamn shame the way the city lets some of these landlords get away with shit like this," he growled, as they carefully lifted the old woman onto the stretcher. They had gotten her out and set her leg in a matter of minutes, making their way down the rotting stairway.

Headed back to headquarters from the hospital, they got another emergency call over the radio and were told to proceed to an address in the St. Thomas Project. Two young girls, both pregnant by the same boy, had gotten into an argument which resulted in a knife fight. Both girls were bleeding and refused to be loaded into the same ambulance.

"If you put me in there with that fuckin' ho' I'm gon' kill her mothafuckin' ass," shouted one girl.

Train was firm and authoritative, very calmly explaining to the girls that either they would go together or they both could stay there and bleed to death. They agreed to a temporary truce, but before the unit could leave the scene, there was gunfire from another apartment. It seemed that one of the mothers had spotted the so-called Phantom Lover and opened fire on him.

"Damn! What the hell's going on around here? It's like a war zone."

"Man, don't even sweat it," Train answered. "That bitch is crazy." He pointed to one of the girls. "That's the little thin chick's old lady. Three months ago, we got a call on her. She was in the middle of labor doin' herself with a coat hanger, talkin' about she didn't know nothing. That whore had twelve kids already, she was going to get rid of that child. That's what she was tryin' to do."

"Shit," Shannon responded, the lines in his face hardening.

"Look, Nick. This ain't nothin'. I could write a bestseller on the stuff I've seen black people do to each other since I've been on the job."

"You could always do something else."

"Don't get me wrong," Train interrupted. "I like the job because I like helpin' people, but half the time I'm so messed up by the time I get home I ain't even got no appetite."

"It happens to the best of us," Shannon added, remembering his own trials.

Train continued to talk. "We got a code three over the radio one time, but while we were answering it, we got a cancel. Well, we turned off the lights and the siren and we figured we'd drive by, you know, just to check it out."

"So what happened?" Shannon asked, his curiosity building.

"We pulled up to a place called the "Yellow Door" on Orleans Avenue, where there were about fifty niggers standing outside. The cops were already there, but we went in anyway. Would you believe there was this dude propped in a chair with a straw hat on and two bullet holes pumped in him. When we came out, some of the niggers standing around wanted to know if he was dead or not. I told 'em, 'yeah, the dude's as dead as he can get,' and I heard one of 'em tell the others, 'What did I tell you? Now pay up, mothafuckas.' Those junkies had shot the man, then put money on his head."

Shannon's expression mirrored the deep respect and pain he felt for Train, one of the few men he actually liked.

"Half the shit that goes down never even gets called in," Train continued. "Another thing is there's too much fuckin' prejudice in the world today. Some of the calls we get are from some real assholes. You could be dying, and if you're white, your family wants only white paramedics, or if you're black, your people want only black people to help you. Whether you live or not is irrelevant. It's fucked up, I'm tellin' you."

"Well, that's kind of why I came looking for you," Shannon said. "I'm trying to get a lead on Debbie Jammison."

"Sorry, Nick," Train offered sadly. "Not even a rumble yet. I cruised by there tonight. They didn't have to kill that boy, or that cop. I don't think some of these bastards deserve capital punishment. It's too easy. I think they oughtta be tortured a little."

"My sentiments exactly," Nick agreed. "You can let me out here. What about the KKK or skinheads?" he said, half joking.

"What, around here? You got to be kiddin'. Let me tell you somethin'," Train went on. "If I get shot or somethin' and end up maybe paralyzed, and I know who did it, no court in the world is gonna save his life. Wherever I am, in a hospital or at home in a wheelchair, I'm gonna make sure that motherfucker gets his."

Just then another call came over the radio. Train nodded, his heart sinking, a disturbing grin on his face.

"It's gonna be a long day."

"I'll get a cab back to my car," Shannon said as the van pulled to the curb. "You can let me out here."

"Sure. You can bet I'll call you."

Shannon stepped out, slamming the door behind him. The ambulance sped away.

CHAPTER 16

Just before seven o'clock on Sunday morning, Nick Shannon lay sprawled on his girlfriend's white leather Broyhill sofa recliner. Exhausted, he had not slept for nearly thirty hours. After a long hot shower, he enjoyed Sue's gentle touch as she massaged his feet. Shannon managed a slight smile, thinking about how lucky he was that a woman like Sue could love a renegade like him.

Even though she had been sleeping before he arrived, she still looked great. Her firm breasts teased the top of the black silk teddy she wore; her large round nipples were silhouetted by the delicate fabric. She lifted his foot, kissed it gently, then caressed his big toe with her tongue.

"Baby, please. Please don't do this to me," he said. "I can't take it."

"Can't take what?" Sue cajoled, as she drew his big toe deeper into her warm mouth. "You really must be tired."

"Today was one of those days from hell," said Shannon, running his fingers gently through her silky brown hair. "It's been a real killer. I've gone from one end of this town to the other. Nothing. Nobody knows a goddamn thing, at least not enough to help me. Alleys, flophouses, I can't go another step."

"Do you think she's all right?"

"I guess so," replied Shannon, somewhat removed. "If they intended to harm her, she would have been killed on the spot. She's probably safe, at least for now," he said, rubbing his tired eyes and stretching.

"You need to get some rest, Nick. Why don't you try to relax? I'll go in the kitchen and fix you a snack."

Sue gently kissed Shannon on the lips.

When she returned with a ham omelet and fresh-squeezed orange juice, Shannon was already fast asleep.

An hour later, he awakened from one of his "power naps" to find that Sue had covered him with a light cotton spread and placed a pillow under his head. Again, Shannon thought about his good fortune. Life had taught him not to trust or love anyone; then he met Sue, Susan Melancon.

A military widow, she was quite attractive, but not the usual glamorous type a man-about-town was accustomed to. There was just something about the way she had looked at him—kindly, but without any inkling of personal attraction. Sue made sense when they talked, and she could always make him laugh. But most of all, Shannon admired her devotion as a mother.

He closed his eyes again briefly. When he opened them, a small boy dressed in green shorts and a white Power Rangers tee shirt was standing over him. He closed his eyes again and rolled over on his right side, turning his back to the youngster. The boy did not move but stood patiently looking down on Shannon.

A few moments later, hearing Sue singing in the kitchen, he turned back over and rapped the youngster, Kevin, over the head playfully with the pillow. Shannon and the boy looked each other in the eye, then began to count. "One... two... three," and raising their hands quickly, aimed and went "Bang! Bang!" Grabbing one another, they toppled playfully to the floor, and Sue entered with breakfast: grits, scrambled eggs, country ham, and the freshly squeezed orange juice.

"Okay, you two. That's enough of that."

"Aw, Mom, you never let us have any fun," Kevin argued, getting up, leaving Shannon on the floor. "I was winning."

"Well, you'll have to take a rain check," she said authoritatively, but in her usual pleasant manner.

"Breakfast is ready. You two go and wash up."

Shannon scooped Kevin up and carried him on his back out of the room. When they returned, the three of them sat down to eat. Kevin's eyes gleamed as he cheerfully gulped down his food.

"Kevin, don't eat so fast. You'll choke."

"But, Mom, the faster you eat, the better it tastes."

"I'm sure it does, if you say so, but slow it down anyway."

"Nick, my softball team is having a father-son little league game in two weeks. I told the coach you would come," said Kevin confidently.

"And it's a good thing for you that you did," Shannon teased.

Kevin appeared to be thinking very hard about something before he spoke again.

"Mom said that when my dad was alive, he was the greatest player ever. I have a picture of him in his baseball uniform in my drawer. I'll show it to you later, okay?"

"Your father was quite a guy," Sue explained sentimentally. "I want you to always remember that. But now Nick is your pal, and maybe someday when he gets ready, thanks to you, he'll make some little boy a great dad, too."

Sue and Shannon exchanged affectionate glances across the table as Kevin polished off his meal.

"Mom, I'm finished. May I be excused?"

"All right. You can go to your room and play for a little while, but keep it quiet. It's still early."

Kevin excused himself and left the table.

"Oh, I almost forget, I've got something for you," Shannon said. "I fell asleep before I could give it to you."

Shannon reached into his pocket and came up with a tiny black velvet box that he handed to her. Sue opened it slowly. Tears began to trickle from her eyes as she beheld a one and one-half karat marquis diamond ring. Nick removed the ring from the box and gently slipped it on her finger.

"If this fits, it's yours. It was on sale. You know me and a bargain," he told her, leaning over to kiss her tears.

"I love you," he said. "I know I'm no prize. I know that. It's up to you. I'm yours if you want me."

With tears streaming from her eyes, Sue embraced Shannon, throwing herself into his arms.

"Oh, Nick," she said, squeezing him so tight that he could hardly move.

"Kevin is going to be so happy." Sue paused, thinking for a minute. "But Nick, you've been by yourself so long. Are you sure this is what you want?"

Shannon took Sue's hand into his. He had been thinking about this for a long time. He knew better than anyone else how wild his life had been. Marriage was a commitment, but he had thought about it. It was time to do something with his life. Yes, he was ready.

"Perfect fit," said Shannon tenderly. "Just like everything else about us."

CHAPTER 17

At seven o'clock, the hallways at Central Lockup on Perdido Street were buzzing with activity as men and women wearing blue shirts and dark trousers with pistols strapped to their sides, walked with cups of steaming hot coffee. A cadre of others moved about hurriedly, intense faces, all appearing to have some distinct purpose.

Some of them were just getting a clear picture about Debbie Jammison's kidnapping and were still in shock. They wondered about the Mayor's daughter, but they were also worried about their jobs. In addition to the possibility of a police strike during Mardi Gras, there was also friction between P.A.N.O., the Policemen's Association of New Orleans, and BPA, the Black Patrolmen's Association, most of whom supported the mayor.

Most P.A.N.O. members were white, and many lived in other parishes, some as far away as Houma, Louisiana. Comfortable with the status quo and the seniority they enjoyed because of hiring practices instituted before civil rights legislation, many became furious when the mayor had proposed a residency requirement, making it necessary that all city employees live within the city limits, and a road use tax for anyone who lived somewhere else but worked in New Orleans. Their choices were simple: either move into the city, or find work elsewhere.

Tension was high as black officers and white officers picked sides. Black officers would sympathize with the mayor, but many disgruntled white policemen and policewomen would vindictively believe that Samuel Jammison, Jr. was getting exactly what he deserved.

His position had been clear. If the City pays your salary or if you use its services, you put something back into the kitty. Traffic coming into New Orleans in the morning and leaving the city in the evening was always nightmarish as white suburbanites rushed back to manicured, green lawns in crime-free neighborhoods, leaving behind the decay, dirt and filth they so despised. They were satisfied accepting city checks as long as they could spend the money, pay for services, and pay taxes somewhere else. Many whites hated Samuel Jammison and considered him an arrogant tyrant and a racist for threatening their comfortable way of life. Jammison argued that he was a conservationist, and his job was to take care of the city and all of its citizens. Whether they liked him or not, one thing everybody knew about the mayor was that he loved New Orleans and its people, all of them.

* * *

"Al, we went over those grounds with a fine-tooth comb," said the homely-looking little man, the hair on his balding head pulled to the front to cover his receding hairline. "Not a thing. Nothing that could help us. We haven't given up, but it doesn't look too promising."

Chet Henry was the picture of conservatism; starched snow-white, knee-length lab coat, freshly creased navy blue pants, spit-polished brown penny loafers and a wide brown and blue spotted bow tie. His suit coat hung beside the neatly folded brown paper bag containing his lunch, a peanut butter and jelly sandwich.

"Maybe you overlooked something," grumbled Clark offensively, his pot belly beginning to bulge like a heavy sack over his belt buckle.

"Al, I've been doing my job for thirty years," snapped the meek little man defensively. "I believe in being efficient. If there was anything to find, I would have found it."

"We just left the postmortem," Clark answered sadly, looking at the technician, disappointed. The boy's autopsy revealed three entry wounds, contact wounds, powder burns. Hadley was shot once, right through the heart, at close range.

"I'm sorry, Chet," Clark apologized. "I know you're the best in the business. Sorry I went off like that, but this case means a lot to me. And I've got Nick Shannon and the FBI to worry about."

"Well, I guess that's that," Burke answered, turning to face Clark.

"Thanks, Chet. Come on, Tim," Clark said to his partner as they turned and left the crime lab.

The hallways were clean and well lit, more like a hospital than a police station, part of Samuel Jammison, Jr.'s revitalization program. But Clark hadn't really noticed that it was unusually crowded for that time of morning, especially for a Sunday. It wasn't normally like this until nine, when people began showing up for court during the weekdays. It was the reporters, Clark realized, seeing several men with cameras and press cards. They were looking for anyone who might give them a story. There were Louisiana State Troopers, too, and police officers Clark did not recognize wearing different uniforms, probably sent from surrounding parishes and precincts in case there was trouble.

"Not a clue," said Clark, as he and Burke stepped to the side to let two officers pass with a handcuffed prisoner.

They walked on, nearing several reporters who rushed toward them, throwing questions from all angles at once—the kidnapping, the strike, Mardi Gras, white officers against black officers. Clark managed to answer several of them with the same authoritative "no comment."

The newsmen followed persistently, yelling questions, until Clark and Burke were safe behind closed doors in Clark's office.

"Reporters are a pain in the ass," Clark complained, disgusted. "They want us to solve cases and tell fairy tales at the same time. Then if we do have a problem, they're the first ones to come down on us."

Clark plopped down in his swivel chair, then leaned back, turning from side to side.

"But they're not going to get us on this one. We're gonna bust this case."

Clark kicked his dirty faded shoes on top of his crowded desk and crossed his legs, his hands clenched in his lap.

"What about Shannon?" asked Burke. "He knows what he's doing, and he doesn't have to be tied down by red tape."

"Tim, I said this was our case. If Nick Shannon gets in the way, we'll deal with him, too."

Clark stood behind his desk, walked over to some four-foot metal file cabinets, and started looking through the S's. He pulled out a dossier on Shannon, leaned his elbow on the cabinet top as he glanced through the file folder, then threw it on the desk in front of Burke. Clark returned to his seat and propped his feet on the desk top again while his partner scanned the file.

"Do you really think there's going to be trouble?" asked Burke, his face expressionless.

"The way people feel about Sam Jammison, what do you think? Especially if it's a hate crime. The KKK in New Orleans. All hell would break loose."

Clark reached into his top coat pocket and took out a half-smoked cigar butt. He sniffed it, then chewed on the frazzled end several times before lighting up.

"Everybody in the country is going to be watching this case. We'll be famous," smiled Clark. "With all that exposure, I could finally get out of this shithole and start my own agency."

"You're right about Shannon, though. We'll just stick with him as long as we need him. If he shits, we'll be there to wipe his ass."

CHAPTER 18

Norman Riley, a black television anchorman, sat in the Channel Six studio looking very disturbed, which was not normal for Norman, a seasoned anchorman and former White House correspondent. All the visuals were the same: the neat closely tapered haircut, the trimmed mustache, the coordinated blazer and tie, but something about Norman was different today. Norman Riley understood the news, but more importantly, he understood the power of the media. He knew what he had to do, but he also understood what the consequences might be if he did not do his job well. MAYOR'S DAUGHTER KIDNAPPED would be an even bigger headliner than BLACK CHURCH BURNED, but he had to remember the ramifications. Too much hype and the results could be devastating.

He understood full well that in reporting the news, the bottom line was still ratings and profit, but his integrity had never allowed him to sensationalize or "milk" an inflammatory story, not even during his early days in Washington before a national audience. He called it selling out or pimping the public, "P-P-ing," as he had seen so many other reporters and elected officials do time and time again.

The city was already on edge, and Norman did not want his

personal feelings for Samuel Jammison Jr. to come across too emotionally in front of half a million viewers.

"Locally, authorities report that there are still no leads on twenty-two-year-old Debbie Jammison, the daughter of Mayor Samuel Jammison, Jr. abducted early this morning, in front of the home where she resided with her parents. Murdered during the incident was Detective Phillip Hadley, a fifteen-year veteran of the New Orleans Police Department, and twenty-three-year-old Raymonde Deveraux, a graduate student at Loyola University and a close friend of Miss Jammison. We join the mayor live as he addresses the city."

The screen switched from Norman Riley to Samuel Jammison, Jr. and his wife Morrow, casually dressed, sitting on the silk brocade couch in their den, holding hands.

"Good morning," said Samuel somberly. "By now, you all know what has happened. There have been two murders, and my daughter, Debbie, has been kidnapped. My wife Morrow and I have come before you to plead for calm. There has been no contact made yet, no ransom note or kidnap demands. Our prayers go out to the families of the murder victims Raymonde Deveraux and Officer Phillip Hadley, and we pray that our daughter Debbie will be returned to us safely. At this time, our city is experiencing a great deal of unrest and the only way we can come through these difficulties successfully is together. We ask that you remember us in your prayers. And again, for our sake and the good sake of our beautiful city, my wife Morrow and I beseech you to set your differences aside and remember that New Orleans is not a democratic city or a republican city, or a white city or a black city. It's our city. It belongs to all of us. Pray for us, and for the safe return of our daughter, Debbie. And our prayers go out to you. Please, please help us. Thank you."

When they finished the taping, his friend, Lawrence Daniels, the thirty-five-year-old head of C.O.P.E., stepped forward. Once more, he offered his condolences and support. Compassionate, articulate and a consummate professional, the charismatic young man was nearly as popular as Mayor Jammison.

"Sam, Morrow, I'm going to have to be leaving, but if there's anything I can do, anything at all, you know where to find me."

"We know, Lawrence. Thanks," said Jammison, gripping the younger man's hand firmly.

"Any movement on the strike?" asked Daniels, searching the mayor's eyes.

"Nothing you don't already know," the mayor answered sadly. "They've given us until tomorrow at midnight to meet their demands."

"Have you reached any decision yet?"

"My hands are tied, Lawrence. You know that. Talks have broken off. I don't have the authority to submit to binding arbitration or grant a pay hike. That's up to civil service and the city council. But I've spoken to the governor. State Police and one thousand national guardsmen have been placed on standby. I've asked for an extension, and so has the governor. Just thirty days, but the union won't hear of it."

"If Mardi Gras is canceled, it will be a long time before the city recovers," said Daniels, much concerned.

"That would be disastrous," responded Jammison. "New Orleans would lose nearly a billion dollars, but I know for a fact that the city council's not going to budge. They are not going to surrender control of city government to a bunch of thugs."

"Things are bad, Sam. But I'm sure my people will sit tight until they hear from me."

Jammison's expression was intensely serious as he looked Daniels squarely in the eye.

"Lawrence, you know we're counting on you to help keep the

top on this pot. If this thing boils over, there will be no way of stopping it."

"You can count on us, Sam," Daniels replied, sincerity spelled out all over his face. "The people trust you, and they'll do what's right."

"Larry is right," Chauncey interrupted. "Chief, the people love you, and they will do what is best."

"And Lawrence, I'm glad you didn't decide to oppose my third term and run against me. Would have been a tough choice with everyone torn between which one of us to support."

"You're a great man, Sam," said Daniels with a warm smile. "It was you who inspired me, who gave me something to shoot for. I've got plenty of time. Besides, you're the best. You just keep doing what you're doing. I'll be busy learning the tricks of the trade."

"And Lawrence, I'm glad you didn't decide to oppose my charter change referendum for a third term to run against me. Would have been a tough choice with everyone torn between which one of us to support."

"You're a great man, Sam," said Daniels with a warm smile. "But more importantly you've done the impossible by turning this city around, the crime, the apathy. You deserve four more years: And don't forget it was you who inspired me, who gave me something to shoot for. You've been my role model ever since I was a teenager. I've got plenty of time. Besides, you're the best. You just keep doing what you're doing. I'll be busy learning the tricks of the trade."

CHAPTER 19

They had run the tape three times, but it offered no clue. Shot against a plain wall, good, clean lighting, a professional looking job, broadcast quality, and good enough for network television. It had already run that morning on Channel 4, Channel 6, and the Fox Network shortly after Samuel's press conference.

They were seated in the mayor's study: Shannon, FBI Agent Callahan, Clark, and Burke. It was ten a.m., the morning after the kidnapping. Earlier, the Mayor and Morrow had visited Miss Peabody.

"She seems in good shape," said Special Agent Callahan. "That's a fair indication that they really intend to return her. That, and the masks she spoke of. Pros will often kill the kidnap victim to keep from being identified—usually even before they get the ransom."

Callahan took a sip of coffee and lit a cigarette.

"Mayor Jammison, you've had a little while to think about it. Do you have any idea at all why someone would have a reason to do something like this?"

"Take your pick," Jammison quickly responded. "My policy has always been to help rather than hurt anyone, but everybody in this room knows there are a lot of people who hate my guts right now. I don't like admitting it, but half of them are police officers."

"You'll never win them all," Callahan replied in a very detached tone.

"Why haven't they made a ransom demand yet?" asked the mayor. He was seated behind his desk, apparently unruffled, neatly shaved, fresh, although he had not slept since the kidnapping.

"They want you to sweat," said Clark. "Break you down, make you easy to manipulate."

"Yes," Callahan added. "Standard procedure. We'll get a call any minute now. They'll want to take the money and run."

"Think we'll be able to trace the call?" asked the mayor, his eyes meeting the agent's.

"No doubt about it. Usually, it will take three minutes or more for a trace. Criminals know that and keep the calls short. However, the FBI has developed a computerized setup that will trace a call in a matter of seconds. We have it set up here and at your office."

"I've had my men check with their snitches," Clark huffed, slowly looking around the room. "Nothing so far. Anything on your end, Shannon?"

"Nothing solid. I've got a few hunches to play."

"Callahan?" asked the mayor, as he toyed with a letter opener.

"As you know, N.O.P.D. found the abandoned Cadillac in Westwego near the Huey P. Long Bridge. It was stolen, of course, and wiped clean, no prints. We did find some of Debbie's hair. Matches with hair from her brush. It's the getaway vehicle all right."

"Who's Sicky?" asked Clark.

"Her dog. Cocker spaniel. He died two years ago. We had him fifteen years. Debbie was crazy about him. We got another one right after that," replied the mayor.

"Why would she mention a dead dog?" asked Callahan. "She doesn't appear hysterical."

"I didn't even think about that," said the mayor with a puzzled look. "I guess I was just glad to see that she's still alive."

"What about your new dog?" Clark interrupted, sitting forward in his seat.

"Treasure," answered the mayor, "but Sicky was always her favorite."

"Maybe she's trying to tell us something. Would she have the presence of mind, Mr. Mayor?"

"Yes, I think she would, Detective. Now that you mention it, I've never known her to overreact. You see how she was on the tape, scared, but not panic-stricken."

"Mentioning Sicky had to mean something," Shannon responded, the wheels turning, "but what?"

Sam Jammison rose and began to pace. They regarded him in silence. He walked to the window, gazing at Miss Peabody's house across the street. Suddenly, he turned to the group assembled around his desk.

"Wait!" said the mayor, smiling like a light had just gone on inside his head. "We used to take him on boat trips with us on the weekends. He'd get seasick every time. That's why we called him Sicky."

"She's telling us she's somewhere around water. And the car was found across the river," Shannon added. "Might have had a boat at Bayou Segnette, my best bet would be Lafitte. It's close and it's still pretty isolated."

"Debbie loves Lafitte. Goes down there all the time. We would go to Lafitte on weekends to fish sometimes at a little camp owned by one of Morrow's cousins."

"That must be it," said the mayor, grasping at straws. "She's telling us she's in Lafitte."

"How would she know that?"

"Debbie has a very keen sense of direction, Detective. She

grew up playing Blind Man's Bluff in the back seat of our car, trying to figure out where she was."

"Doesn't matter," said Shannon. "It's all we have to go on. The APB didn't pick them up, so maybe they did make their getaway by boat. Maybe not Lafitte, but what else have we got?"

"I'm telling you, if my daughter is within fifty miles of here, she knows where she is. Lake Borne, Lake Catherine, the Rigolets—I'll bet on that."

"Maybe you're right," Callahan answered, throwing his hands up. "I've heard stranger things."

"Debbie has been going hunting and fishing with me since she was old enough to walk. She knows the woods and bayous around here like the back of her hand. My daughter could pick her way through a deer path in a hurricane. In fact, the Indians and Cajuns used to call her Little Swamp Fox," Jammison said proudly, momentarily forgetting his loss.

"Since Lafitte is relatively close to Westwego, where the car was found, I'll have my men concentrate their search there."

Clark stood up. "No," he snapped crisply, glancing briefly at the mayor. "FBI agents in Lafitte would stand out like coal on a snowbank. Better that my unit handles it. We'll check in with the local cops."

"And me," said Shannon.

"Could I keep you out?"

Shannon glanced casually at Clark but said nothing.

"As long as my team takes over once you locate the site, right?" Callahan insisted, rising and circling the room to make his point.

"No problem," replied Clark. "We pinpoint the location, pull back, and you FBI guys take charge. It's your party."

"Shannon?" asked Callahan, exchanging glances.

Clark remained standing. "Shannon's a loose cannon. It's

why he left the force. He'll do what he wants to do." The detective regarded Shannon with a mixture of contempt and respect.

Shannon sat silently, apparently in thought, then his deep brown eyes met Clark's and the two men seemed to be peering right through each other.

"Whatever it takes."

CHAPTER 20

Nick Shannon had remained behind to have a brief talk with his friend, Samuel Jammison, Jr. The mayor was still pensive, but much more relaxed than he had been earlier.

Larry Shannon, Nick's father, was one of Jammison's oldest and dearest friends, even before the Rampart Street War in the old days. From time to time after his father's death, Shannon had even felt like the son Sam never had.

"Look, Nick, you're going to have to help me," Jammison said in a deep and intensely serious tone. "You know how much I have riding on this proposition, but the most important thing is getting Debbie back safely."

"You were the only real friend my father ever had," Nick responded, his eyes riveted to the mayor.

"Yes, Larry and I were quite a pair," agreed Jammison sentimentally. "He was the closest thing I ever had to a brother. Your daddy was one crazy fool, but he was all man. We really tied one on the day you were born. The next morning, I found him passed out in the bathtub sleeping in his clothes, my old buddy," he laughed.

"And you were the one who caught his murderers," said Shannon, reflecting both obligation and gratitude.

"I just did what I had to do. Nick, I think there's more going on here than meets the eye."

Jammison's mood was beginning to change. The anger in his voice was becoming more obvious. The lines in his face were sharp and hard, his eyes cold and keenly alert. He walked slowly over to the well-stocked bar and mixed two drinks.

"I think that's the way you like it," sipping his own drink as he passed the other one to Nick.

"That's it," Shannon answered, savoring the taste.

"You don't forget anything, do you?"

"I try not to," Jammison said evenly. "In my line of work I can't afford to. Anything I forget to do can cause me problems later. Problems I don't need. I miss my daughter, Nick. If anything's happened to her..."

He breathed heavily, raised his glass, then slammed it on the bar top, shattering it. There was a strange, momentary silence except for Jammison's breathing, his jawbones flexing rigidly again beneath his skin.

"Nick, I've tried to be civilized about this. I'm fighting it, but it's not easy."

Samuel Jammison was trying hard to moderate his tone. The house was so quiet that Morrow would surely have heard any irregularity.

"I can remember when I would have killed someone for looking at me the wrong way, but now I'm supposed to just sit back and let somebody else solve my problems. And this isn't just another problem. This is my daughter's life we're talking about."

"Look, Sam, you're only human," Nick rebutted. "Nobody expects you to act like a robot. We know you, remember. We know how you do things. But this one you're going to have to play close to the vest."

Nick stood and walked over to Samuel.

"What's happened to you and Morrow is enough to make anybody go off. If I were in your place, I'd be tearing this town apart by now. When my dad was killed, you know what I went through. Nobody could tell me a damn thing." Shannon's fists were clenched tightly as he momentarily relived that time in his life, his eyes piercing Jammison's. Deep feelings burned in both men.

"Nick, I don't want any goddamn sob story from you or anybody else. I wanted you to stay because I thought you would help me, but it looks like I'm going to have to take care of this myself."

Sam Jammison was disappointed, even in his old friend.

"Don't be a fool, Sam. I never said I wouldn't help you. I just don't think you'd be going about it the right way if you open yourself up," argued Shannon, trying to convince Jammison to exercise patience.

"Any way I can get my daughter back safely is the right way!"

Jammison nervously unscrewed the cap on the container of one of his handmade imported Portofino cigars. He bit the end, lit it, then took a long, deep draw, slowly turning to Shannon.

"Maybe you're right, Nick. You're one helluva detective. Maybe we should try it your way," suggested Sam. "I'll do whatever it takes to get Debbie back, but I'm telling you now, if you don't come up with anything soon, I'm gonna do it my way. Agreed?" Jammison said, extending his hand.

"Agreed," Shannon answered, gripping Sam's hand firmly, then giving him a hug and a double pat on the back.

"The first thing we've got to figure out is how they knew when to hit. Either they were watching the house, or somebody's working both sides of the street."

Jammison was surprised. "Are you telling me that one of my people is selling me out?"

"I don't know," Shannon responded, "but I intend to find out. And we've got to keep your past in the past where it belongs. We don't need any conservatives changing their minds about you. But one thing's for sure, whoever pulled this off must have figured they didn't have anything to lose."

"Didn't have anything to lose," snapped Jammison, becoming emotional again. "If this were the old days, I'd show them, myself. But as you said, I can't afford to. As far as my past is concerned, it's dead and buried and we'll keep it that way."

"My dad told me how your gang used to rip off store owners who took advantage of black people, and the way you would deal with slum landlords."

"Yes, we got some justice," Jammison reflected. "Never could stand a cheat. Did Larry ever tell you about that scam we worked on Reverend Simpson?"

"I don't think so," Shannon answered, trying to remember. "What happened?"

"Well, you know how it is," Jammison explained. "Whenever black people have a problem, the first thing they do is go running to the preacher. Well, your daddy and I found out that Old Man Simpson had an apartment on Galvez Street where he was secretly entertaining some of the sisters. That was his business. He was human. But we found out that he was making some other deals, too, with some of the white city councilmen. They would tell him what they wanted the colored people to do, and he would very conveniently point us in that direction. He was being paid to sell us out. Nickel slick sonofabitch. Ripping off the people who trusted him, and who really needed his help."

"What did you do?" asked Shannon, both curious and amused.

"We set him up. What else? Then we blackmailed him. We told him if he didn't go along with us, we would expose him,"

Jammison smiled. "Pardon the pun. It was your daddy's idea. We used him to find out what the crooked politicians were up to, then we would feed phony information back to them. It worked like a charm for about two years, until they realized what he was up to. Needless to say, Reverend Simpson had to leave town in a big hurry, and I haven't seen or heard from him since."

Jammison moved back over to the bar and brushed the broken glass into a nearby trash can. He mixed himself another drink, raised it to his mouth, and quickly belted down a big gulp.

"I'm sorry I blew up, Nick. If you can't help me, who can? I don't care how you do it or what it takes, but I'm counting on you."

"I'll handle it, Sam. We'll get Debbie back."

"And after this is over, we still have some things we need to talk about," the mayor added. "I'll need your answer soon."

Shannon rose smoothly, embraced his friend again, then saw himself out.

Jammison walked to a nearby table and picked up a small silver frame containing a black and white family photograph. He and Morrow were smiling happily, and Debbie was only five years old in that picture. She was wearing a yellow and white dress. Sam Jammison remembered because yellow was always his daughter's favorite color.

Upstairs, the room where Morrow grieved was dark; the drapes had been pulled, and it was almost completely quiet, except for her faint weeping. For the first time in a long time, not since the Rampart Street War, had she felt such fear and hopelessness. Seated in an easy chair, her eyes swollen, she quivered and her hands were clenched so tight that they were beginning to turn white. Thoughts of Debbie ran through Morrow's mind as she numbly rocked back and forth.

CHAPTER 21

"You say that you're a private detective, Mr. Shannon?"

"Private investigator, Miss Peabody; although I spent several years on the New Orleans police force," replied Shannon. "I resigned as a homicide detective."

"How exciting. Private dick, as they say in mystery novels," she said with a smile just this side of lewd.

As flirtatious as Scarlett O'Hara, thought Shannon. But he had business on his mind and ignored the obvious invitation in her smile. At one time, he would have been sorely tempted. Even now, he could not help but admire her trim figure and almost blatant sexuality. "Once a freak, always a freak," was a slang that popped into his head.

"You're certain the kidnappers were white?" said Shannon, as his eyes continued to make contact with hers.

"Indeed, Mr. Shannon. As I told Detective Clark and his partner Detective Burke earlier, they definitely moved as white men do. One man, I assume he was the leader, appeared to have been an athlete of some sort—football, I would say from his size. He walked with a slight limp."

Shannon had taken her through several minutes of interrogation and found her surprisingly observant. Too bad, he thought, that most eyewitnesses lacked her skill.

"Is there anything else, anything at all you might have left out in your interview with Clark and Burke? What about the way they were dressed?" Shannon asked.

"Well," Miss Peabody went on, "the tall one, the leader, was dressed well: dark slacks, a dark crew-neck shirt and a sport jacket. One of the other men wore slacks and a jacket. The other one wore a jacket and blue jeans."

"So they weren't dressed like young thugs?"

"Oh, heavens, no," she laughed. "Young people live in faded blue jeans and two hundred dollar sneakers these days. No, they definitely weren't kids. I'm sure of that. I can assure you they were deliberate. They weren't amateurs. They knew exactly what they were doing."

She took a sip from her tiny tulip glass of brandy and Benedictine, leaned back holding the glass in well-tended, long fingers and closed her eyes. She sat forward after several moments.

"Boots, Mr. Shannon. Boots."

"Boots, Miss Peabody?"

"Yes. One of the men wore expensive-looking cowboy boots of reptile. Python, rather than the more common boa constrictor, I would say by their color. I have a pair of Parisian shoes almost exactly like them. It was he Ray downed with that spinning, leaping kick they favor in the movies. We were so busy talking about guns that I suppose I forgot all about that. But detectives Clark and Burke are such virile, handsome men, like yourself, Mr. Shannon. It's so seldom that I have company these days. Sam and Morrow stopped by this morning. It's so sad."

"Thank you, Miss Peabody. Anything else?" asked Shannon.

"Not that I can recall at the moment. However, don't hesitate to return if you wish. I have some knowledge of detective technique and anticipate several more visits from the police. I'm a devotee of detective fiction, you see. A habit I inherited from my dear departed father. Do you read detective fiction, Mr. Shannon?"

"Matter of fact, I do," smiled Shannon.

"Chandler, Hammet, the MacDonald Boys, Leonard, Parker? That new writer, Mr. Mosley. Excellent writer, wouldn't you say?"

"All of them and more. But you left out my all-time favorite."

Shannon was eager to move on, but to leave abruptly would be extremely rude. To a genteel Southern woman, good manners were almost a dedicated ritual.

"Who might that be, Mr. Shannon?"

"Chester Himes," replied Shannon.

"Of course, how thoughtless of me. A sheer master of the genre. 'Cotton Comes to Harlem?'"

"'Blind Man With a Pistol' would have to be my favorite."

"Indeed," replied Miss Peabody. "An excellent choice. However, I'm keeping you from the hunt. We old women do ramble. This was a real treat."

She rang a tiny silver bell sitting on the round coffee table of white carrera marble, and in a short time, her buxom servant appeared without a sound.

"Please show Mr. Shannon out, Edna. Until we meet again." She smiled and winked.

She held out her hand; Shannon took it gently into his and for a crazy moment almost kissed it. Miss Peabody had a way of taking someone into the Southern Gothic past of a Faulkner novel.

Shannon walked outside past the activity of the cordoned-off area and the policemen manning their posts. He entered his car and resumed his search.

CHAPTER 22

During the night the wind had shifted to the southwest, moving a warm front and high-pressure zone into the city. The warm air scooped from the Yucatan Peninsula, swept across the Gulf, and the temperature rose into the upper seventies, moving the air pollution northeast, away from the Mississippi River, turning the cloudless sky into an impossible blue.

Shannon cruised the Crescent City Connection thinking how much easier his trip would be now that the new span was built. The old bridge had been resurfaced and widened from two lanes to four. The Greater New Orleans Bridge had been renamed by a third grader during a contest years earlier. Before completion, traffic would sometimes be backed up for miles, and he might have been one of sixty-five or seventy thousand frustrated drivers stuck in an endless traffic jam of overheated cars.

The mighty Mississippi, mused Shannon. Mark Twain said that it was the crookedest river in the world, the river that had inspired "The Adventures of Huckleberry Finn." Once William Faulkner, who also loved the muddy Mississippi, had commented that if he ever came back to earth, he would want to come as a buzzard, because then nobody would ever threaten him and he could eat anything he liked. Faulkner had even declined President

Kennedy's invitation to dine at the White House, insisting that he was too old to travel so far to eat with strangers. Shannon thought, too, about all the pirates, murderers and buccaneers who had hidden treasures along the river and about all the secrets it held.

As he traveled the elevated expanse over the Harvey Canal, he could see a flurry of activity below—huge freighters, tugboats, container carriers, railroad yards, warehouses, tall cranes and other heavy equipment, a working city in itself. Shannon wondered if the busy canal might have been used by Debbie's kidnappers, too, as an escape route to reach the marshes and bayous on the west bank.

Turning left onto Barataria Boulevard, he drove past Madona Manor—several huge one-hundred-year-old faded white Spanish buildings that now served as a homeless family center.

At the Lafitte Larose Highway, he made another left turn and found himself driving on one of the smoothest roadways he had ever seen, as smooth as glass. Why had so much money been spent on a road leading basically to nothing but a couple of poor, tiny fishing villages, Shannon wondered.

As he crossed the road that led to Crown Point, he noticed that things were very busy at the Bayou Barn Restaurant and Cajun Tours. Children were playing around the water while their parents talked on the front porch.

Minutes later, he was crossing the Crown Point Intercoastal Bridge, glimmering in the sunlight. It had been at least two years since his last visit.

Another left onto LA 45 south, and the wide Crown Point Intercoastal Canal was now on his left. Glistening water flowed quickly as it was pushed by strong winds and framed by thick cypress, pine, spanish moss, and lush greenery on the other side. A few miles further and Shannon's questions were answered. Beautiful custom-built homes, some completed and already occupied, others in different stages of development, peeked behind tall trees. They appeared to be on at least an acre of land with large cabin cruisers and speedboats docked on the water behind them. Shrimp and fishing boats lined the banks of the bayou, statues of Jesus or Mary sat on front lawns along with crab traps.

Lafitte had been transformed into a Cajun paradise and Shannon had only been driving for half an hour, as long as it might take to get to overcrowded New Orleans East in heavy traffic. "The best of two worlds," he thought, "country living and city life in the blink of an eye."

He drove on past the Lafitte Assembly of God Church, the Cajun Propeller Shop, the Lafitte Harbor Marina and Boat Launch, and parked in front of the restaurant on the waterfront. Shannon walked to the covered verandah in the rear overlooking the water. Injun Joe Malveaux sat at a table to the right of the kitchen window, a sunbleached, battered White Sox cap on the back of his head, a bottle of brandy on the table, a heavy-bottomed old-fashioned glass half filled in front of him, smoking a corncob pipe.

"Joe," said Shannon, "how's it going?"

"Fine, Nick. Ain't seen you in a coon's age. Sit down, have a drink. Marie, bring another glass," said Joe over his shoulder.

"I thought I had made a wrong turn," said Shannon, settling comfortably into a wooden chair.

Joe smiled, looking around. "Place has changed a lot, huh? Don't feel bad. Sometimes I think I'm lost, too. Looks like you didn't get much sleep last night. Out tom-cattin'?"

"Working on a case. Got in a few hours' nap."

"Mayor's kid?"

"Yeah," replied Shannon.

Marie came through the back door, sat a glass before Shannon, then leaned over and kissed him on the cheek. Joe poured Shannon a drink. He took a sip, let the warm brandy go down slowly.

"Nick," she said, speaking with a broken French accent,

"comment ca va, ma cher? Bien?"

"Ca va bien, Marie," replied Shannon.

She moved to Malveaux's side. He put his arm around his wife's waist.

"How is that pretty girl I see you with?" asked Marie.

"Sue? She's fine, Marie."

"You two gonna marry?"

"C'mon, Marie," said Joe. "Can't teach an old dog new tricks."

"I taught you a few, you old goat," said Marie, smiling.

Joe was in his mid-seventies, looked to be in his fifties, tight body, flat stomach. His high cheeked bronze face was hairless, wrinkle-free and tempered by a lifetime of blistering sunfilled days, working and playing in the hot tropical climate. One long, thick braid hung below Joseph Littlejohn's weather-beaten cap. A white tee shirt inscribed 'EAT OYSTERS AND LOVE LONGER,' and faded freshly washed blue jeans hugged his massive frame, his black cowboy boots graying, as worn as his cap.

Marie was thirty years younger, one hundred and ten pounds when they met. Her pretty, youthful face had not changed, but forty pounds heavier, her plump figure told a story of contentment and eating her own homestyle cooking. She and Joe had been together since Marie was fifteen.

"Sure did," said Joe. He laughed.

"That's a good woman, Nick. I can tell," said Marie. "You marry her, time you settled down, have some children. Be good for you."

"Well, we've talked about it," replied Shannon, smiling at the thought of the ring he had already given to Sue.

"Don't talk, do it," said Marie, smiling. "Before somebody else snatch her away."

"You know, I just might take you up on that," smiled

Shannon.

"Bring us some food, woman," said Joe, slapping her playfully on her ample rear.

"Shut up," said Marie in mock anger. She moved away, hips swaying, giving Joe a look over her shoulder.

"We take a siesta, later on?" said Joe suggestively.

"Put être," said Marie, as she disappeared into the kitchen.

A few minutes later she returned carrying a tray laden with slices of French bread, butter, two small plates, and a thick slab of homemade hogshead cheese.

Shannon realized how hungry he was as he smelled the spread.

"You fishing in the usual place last night, Joe?" asked Shannon.

"South of here? Yeah."

"Anything unusual late last night?"

"Mebbe so. We eat first, I tell you."

Shannon put butter on the bread, added some spread.

"Bon appetit," said Joe, his broad face expressionless, twirling the brandy around in the glass.

"Bon appetit," Shannon replied. He took a bite of the bread and hogshead cheese, shut his eyes as he chewed.

Man, that woman can cook, Shannon thought, smiling to himself. Marie was country creole, from out in the bayou, and nobody could do what she could do with fish and wild game. Joe brought it in, Marie did the cooking.

The fish they didn't use in the restaurant Joe would sell to the fancy eating houses in the French Quarter—Antoine's, Olivier's. Joe wouldn't haggle, charged top dollar for his catch of the day. Once, a chef wanted to argue about the price. Joe dumped the fish on the sidewalk in front of the restaurant, smiling into the rearview mirror of his pickup as he drove away. The next week he charged them for the discarded fish and got the money. Thereafter, no one tried to haggle.

Shannon looked out toward Joe's fishing vessel, appropriately named the "Marie," as it gleamed in the sun, moored just thirty yards away, at the dock. It was spotless, nets waving in the gentle breeze as they dried in the sun. The last time he saw Joe they had gone alligator harvesting in the marshes around New Iberia. Hunting alligators was bloody and dangerous. In fact, one of Joe's dogs had actually ended up in a big gator's belly, but alligator hunting was great sport, too, and one helluva way for Joe to pick up some quick cash during the off season.

"How are the kids, Joe?"

"Fine, just fine. Michelle finishes Tulane medical school in June. Gonna do her residency at Grady Memorial in Atlanta." Joe spread paté on a large chunk of the homemade bread and took a bite, chewing slowly.

"Grady? Man, that's a tough one," said Shannon.

"It's okay. Michelle's tough like her mama. Says it will be good experience, but she really wants to join her boyfriend. He's doin' the last year of his residency there. They gonna get married next December. He's a good boy. Catholic, from Biloxi. They gonna move over there when Michelle finishes, set up a practice. His old man's a funeral director. Marie likes the idea they'll be so close. Wants some grandchildren."

"The twins?" Shannon said as he took a sip of brandy.

"Last year at Arizona State. I think Gerard's gonna make the bigs, got drafted last year by the White Sox."

"Your old team."

Joe nodded. "Gerald, I dunno. Can't hit the curve ball, but Gerard's like me. Got the arm, too, and the range. I think he's gonna be good as I was."

Joe had played the Negro League, broke in when he was sixteen, played for the Kansas City Monarchs, Birmingham Black

Barons, the Chicago American Giants, then three years with the Sox when he was well into his forties, as a pinch hitter.

They'd just finished the hogshead cheese when Marie brought out two steaming bowls of seafood gumbo filled with shrimp, oysters and blue crabs, followed by blackened red snapper, hush puppies, mustard greens and corn bread with fresh peach cobbler for dessert. She sat a bottle of raisin wine, that Joe had made himself, on the table between them.

"Now that's my idea of country cooking," said Shannon, as the two ate in silence.

Shannon loved Lafitte, as he was sure its namesake Jean Lafitte, the pirate, had. As boats passed and their skippers waved to Joe, Shannon wondered how many of them were twentieth century pirates, drug smugglers.

He had read somewhere that Jean Lafitte himself had started working these waters when he was twenty-four. Raiding Spanish ships in the Gulf, Lafitte then hid out in Barataria with his band of cutthroats and water rats like Gambi, who had murdered ten men with an ax. Unlike his contemporaries, however, Lafitte would share part of his bounty with merchants from New Orleans, who would be reluctant to turn him in.

Only a skilled boatsman could maneuver the hundreds of bayous that might begin as a stream, become a wide lake, and then narrow again; floating marsh, cheniera, with grass as tall as a man and huge oak trees. Shannon could imagine Lafitte with his mansion in the swamp, his fleet of barges and his one thousand men moving from Grand Isle to Grand Terre to Cheniera Cominda to the Gulf. In his own way, Shannon admired him, but he wasn't too fond of the fact that Lafitte's biggest commodity was black slaves who were sold once a week for eight hundred to one thousand dollars each.

Shannon loved history. He was always looking for a new book or an old one, or for someone who might know more than he did. His favorite source was old people. Maybe that's why he had become a detective.

Lafitte had chosen well, thought Shannon, and so had Debbie's abductors if they were here. Barataria stretched from the Mississippi River sixty miles south to the Gulf of Mexico and hundreds of men had never been seen again after entering the swamp... Debbie might not ever be found.

CHAPTER 23

They sat back sipping brandy and strong coffee flavored with chicory. Injun Joe Malveaux was puffing languidly on his pipe as they stared out over the water. Joe's copper colored Indian face was burnished by the sun to a rich mixture of browns, yellows, mostly red. His people had owned the land on which the restaurant sat back to the dawn of time, fishing the lake, fishing the Gulf, fishing the bayou. Joe would never sell this land.

Joe's big right hand, scarred by fishing lines and thick with calluses, dwarfed the pipe. He stood six two and looked even bigger because he was so thick. Massive shoulders, wide chest, thick waist, thighs like tree trunks. Joe weighed no more than a few pounds more than he did thirty years ago when Nick used to come out here as a young boy.

"Know who killed it?"

"Killed what?" asked Shannon.

"The Negro Leagues. Black baseball. Jackie and Branch Rickey, that's who," said Joe, as he carefully knocked the burnt tobacco from his pipe into the ashtray. "Can't really blame him, he did what he had to do. Once he went up to Brooklyn we couldn't draw flies down here. Rickey put him on a leash and it killed him. All that anger bottled up inside. He was a fighter and they wouldn't let him fight until it was too late. Turned him mean at the end—unleashed anger killed him young."

"You don't believe in integration?"

"Hell, naw, and neither do you. You like peckerwoods? Hell naw, you don't. I hate the motherfuckers. What they did to my people, to your people. Any Injun, anybody black say he loves white folks is either a damn fool or a liar.

"Choctaw ancestors fished these waters, lived in peace with the bayou. Fought the Creek, fought Chickasaw, fought the Cherokee, and when they came, they fought the Spanish, the British, and the so-called Americans—the worst of their kind. Killed black baseball, killed your people's spirit. Know why I don't like white folks?"

"No, why?" asked Shannon.

"'Cause white folks don't like me. Oh, yeah, they come here for Marie's cooking, shake my hand, talk baseball, but behind them phony smiles you can see the hate, smell it even. Can't stand the bastards."

Joe looked out over the water with narrowed eyes, like one of his ancestors lying in ambush in the bayou watching the white men come.

"Debbie's a good kid, not like her phony ass pappy," Joe continued. "The wife's all right, too, for a creole."

"Marie's creole," Shannon said gently.

"Marie's different. So is the mayor's wife. Remember what that fuckin' Jelly Roll used to say: 'I'm not a negro, I'm a creole.' Mayor's the same damn way, didn't want to know no black until he run for office."

"His old man wasn't creole," said Shannon.

"Makes no difference. Creoles like the mayor, who ain't but half creole, they the worst kind, like the mule spent all his time talkin' about the horse side of his family."

Shannon laughed, taking another sip of brandy.

"Now, Debbie couldn't give a damn about that kind of shit," said Joe. "You know, durin' the summer she does volunteer work up on Rampart Street. Bring the kids out here to mess around in the water, fishin' and crabbin', eat up Marie's food. Know what? Most of them never even seen Lake Pontchartrain, never get off Rampart Street until she bring 'em over here. They love her, them kids, and she love them. They go crazy in the water, runnin' up and down the bank, eatin' Marie's cookin'. Shit, most of them got crackhead mamas don't cook shit. Eat potato chips and hot dogs, think Mickey D's a damn feast."

"Little Swamp Fox and her boyfriend, that Ray he was all right, too. They was here a couple of months ago, sittin' out here on the porch over there laughin' and talkin' French with Marie."

Joe fell silent, his big hands clenching and unclenching as if thinking of what he might do to the people who had Debbie.

"Still just got two cops down here," Joe added. "That's why nobody ever sees anything. Biggest thing they do is lock people up for stealin' aluminum sidin' or bicycles. Last week, one of the local boys got busted for hacking one of his neighbor's pigs about thirty times. Family needed food. Boy had blood all over him."

Shannon nodded. "Times are getting tough, Joe, all over."

"It's them drug dealers," Joe continued. "Divin' up and down the street blastin' them damn radios. Hustlin' people and usin' kids for lookouts."

Gulls skimmed the still water, dipping to scoop up a fish. Higher overhead, the pelicans circled on the wind currents, their wings and tails barely moving as they worked the thermals, then tucking in their wings, descending like a bomb. They disappeared into the water with a splash, emerging with a fish trapped in their big beaks, the bottom pouch distended with fish and water, the water escaping in tiny streams through the small holes in the bottom of the pouch.

Got any idea who might have snatched her?" asked Shannon.

"The fuckin' Italians, that's who. Who else would it be?"

"Why would the mob do that? They haven't been into kidnapping since it became a Federal offense after the Lindberg case. And the mayor's daughter. What would they gain?"

"To keep the mayor in line. That's why."

"You think Sam Jammison's on the take? He was my dad's best friend."

"Times change, Nick. He's a politician, ain't he?" Joe snorted. "End of conversation."

Shannon waited as Joe carefully refilled the corncob pipe that he had carved and cured himself, as had his tribal ancestors for centuries. Joe got his pipe going, carefully puffing blue smoke. He turned and looked Shannon straight in the eye.

"Late last night, about three in the mornin', a boat pulled in down the way from where I was fishin'. I knew somethin' funny was goin' on because they came in slow to keep the sound of the motor down, had their runnin' lights off. Thought maybe it was just a dope run bringin' in some marijuana. Got no problem with pot, smoke a little myself now and again. That other shit... One of the reasons you see so many big houses here now. Ain't no business bigger than dope.

"Anyway, I put the night glasses on 'em. Got out armed, shotguns, automatic weapons. But they didn't unload no marijuana. No, they carried off a woman."

"Debbie?"

"Couldn't tell for sure. But it was a woman, all right. She was the right size. Could well be Debbie," said Joe, bending closer.

"Marie," Joe called over his shoulder. "More coffee, and

bring me the chart off the wall in my office."

"How many?" asked Shannon.

"Three on the boat, plus the man on the wheel. Short time later, three cars pulled up. Five more went inside loaded down with guns. That fuckin' scar face Cajun was with 'em on the boat. Him and his snakeskin boots, overpriced straw cowboy hat. Boutte. Hangs around down here with drug runners."

"Boutte?" asked Shannon.

"Yeah, that sonofabitch. Came in here drunk one time, raisin' hell. I threw him out in the parkin' lot, took his blade and beat him until he crawled. Wanted to kill him, but Marie wouldn't let me. You'll remember him when you see him. Drives a fancy red pickup."

Marie came out, refilled their cups, and left the small pewter pot on the table. She handed Joe the map, touched him lightly on his shoulder, and returned to the kitchen without a word.

Joe spread the map on an adjacent table, placed a gnarled finger on it.

"Right about here," said Joe, "down where they got them fancy, overpriced vacation and weekend homes. Nobody comes out during the winter. They're in there, though, with somebody. You can bet on it. Figured you'd be along. That's why I didn't call the cops. Knew they'd fuck things up, and maybe get the girl killed. I'm tellin' you, her paw ain't shit!"

They sat, stirred in milk and sugar, sipped the hot coffee.

"You goin' after her?"

"Yeah," said Shannon. "They found the getaway car in Westwego. It's easy to get from there to here by boat. Cops know it, too."

"When?" asked Joe, puffing on his pipe again.

"Tomorrow morning, just before dawn."

"When they're tired and sleepy."

"Right," answered Shannon. "But I've got some homework

to do first."

"You goin' in alone?"

"Too risky. They might have time to kill her before I get to her. I'll have to put a strike team together. And they're gonna have to be real pros on this one."

"How many?"

"Five or six, including me. Got a few ideas about who I want. Combat experience, good in a fight."

"Come in from the water?"

"Best way," Shannon answered, turning the combination of possibilities over in his mind.

Joe pointed to his boat, riding high, softly rocking on its anchor. "You got her," said Joe, kicking his boots up in one of the wooden chairs and resting his head against the wall. "Just tell me where you want to be picked up."

"A couple of miles down the bayou, in time for you to get to your usual spot, where you fish every night. We can't afford to change your routine."

"Four?"

"Right," said Shannon.

Joe put his finger on the map. "I'll pick you up here," he said. "There's a dock right behind the levee."

Shannon studied the map. "That's a thirty-minute drive from my house on Bancroft Drive. Let's synchronize our watches."

"Let's drink on it," said Joe. He refilled their brandy glasses; they raised them in toast.

"Clouds comin' up. Think it might rain."

CHAPTER 24

Shannon slowly cruised down the street, B.B. King singing from the speakers, and saw a man in a Hawaiian shirt—tall, curled-brim cowboy hat, wearing snakeskin boots—emerge from the house down the street to his right.

"Bingo," he said softly to himself. Joe was right. He did remember Boutte, a cold Cajun bastard, ice water in his veins. Boutte favored a knife, a dagger with a six-inch blade carried in a pouch in his right boot. He was equally skilled with a pistol, shotgun, rifle, carbine, or automatic weapon. Boutte had done time with the Twenty-Fifth Infantry Division in Viet Nam. He had almost been killed in the Mekong Delta one night on patrol, shortly after he'd called a young gang banger from Philly a nigger. He was awarded the Purple Heart for his wounds.

Shannon had spotted Clark's men on the other side of the bayou going house to house, although this was not their jurisdiction. Even in plain clothes they were as out of place as Black Muslims at a KKK rally. Might as well be the FBI, Nick thought to himself. Couldn't be any more conspicuous. Pretending to be conducting a survey, they probably wouldn't get over this far until tomorrow.

He cruised past and watched Boutte get into his highly waxed, candy apple red Ford pickup. When Boutte pulled away from the curb, Shannon waited for several cars to pass, then made a U-turn and followed at a distance, the gleaming pickup shining like a beacon ahead. It was common knowledge that he had a chop shop in Chalmette, and the truck was probably part of his contraband.

Boutte looked as if someone had put him through a meat grinder. Ray must have really caught him right, Shannon thought, frowning and shaking his head, remembering that two men had been killed already.

Boutte pulled into Diago's, a waterside fast food joint that specialized in seafood, and went inside. Shannon pulled ahead, made a U-turn, and parked two hundred yards down the street. He walked into Patin's grocery store to pick up some goodies—a bag of fresh fruit, a six-pack of Heineken, two ready-made ham and cheese sandwiches, and a can of peanuts, keeping his eyes on the pickup down the street.

He walked back outside, got in his Trans Am, turned on the motor and waited. What if Joe was right, he started thinking to himself. Every politician he had ever known was a liar and an opportunist, whether they started out that way or not.

He kept time on the steering wheel with his fingers. Bobby Blue Bland was singing now, B.B. playing his electric guitar, Lucille, behind him as only B.B. could.

In a short while Boutte came back outside carrying what looked like enough food for several men. He pulled off and Shannon followed. Shannon moved on past the pickup when Boutte parked in front of the house, carrying the food and beer. Most of the houses were summer homes, now boarded up, including the one directly across the street from the house Boutte had left a short time before. Boutte paused, looked around, then went inside the well-kept white frame house. Through the tall pine trees, Nick could see a mid-sized cruiser, twenty-six or twenty-seven feet, moored behind the house.

Shannon continued down the road and parked, then approached the house across the street from the woods to the rear. Windows were boarded up on the ground floor, burglar bars everywhere, but the ones on the second floor were unboarded.

Shannon took his portable phone, beer, and food, and walked to the back door, looking around carefully. He set his things on the ground next to the door, studied the locks briefly, pulled a set of picks from his pocket, and was inside in a matter of minutes.

Closing the door behind him, he allowed his eyes to adjust to the dim light. Shannon went to the light switch on the kitchen wall and tried it, to no avail. He wasn't likely to be disturbed.

He walked upstairs, jerked a sheet off an armchair, pulled it over to the window, and parted the drapes enough to look out. He had brought something else, too—one of his favorite toys, a fourteen hundred dollar, thirty-five millimeter Contax, the Rolls Royce of cameras, with auto zoom and auto focus.

In a few minutes, Boutte came back outside carrying the takeout food. Shannon counted five guards—one seated on the porch with a gym bag next to his chair. Probably got a machine pistol in the bag, thought Shannon, as he quickly snapped shots.

Two more guards were in the bushes on either side of the house. They'd had to reveal themselves when Boutte brought them their food. Shannon figured there was a fourth guard in the rear on the water side, as he watched the cajun carry the last of the food around the side of the house. He spotted the fifth in the second floor window when the sun glinted off his shades.

Shannon opened the peanuts and a can of beer, sat back, and did what cops did everywhere—waited, his eyes relentlessly scanning the area.

CHAPTER 25

"I'm not giving up the children!" she bellowed angrily.

She belched loudly, wiped her mouth with the back of her hand, smearing her lipstick, and took a drink of straight vodka. She reached to the half-filled fifth of Smirnoff on the cocktail table and, hands shaking, filled her glass. Clark watched her with disgust.

"You don't have any choice, Celeste," he said evenly, shaking his head. "The papers are with your lawyer. I know she's advised you to take the deal."

"No!" she repeated stubbornly.

"It's that, or I drag you through court and have you declared an unfit mother."

"Crap!" she said, taking another swig of Smirnoff, straight. "The courts always favor the mother."

"Not if the mother is a dysfunctional alcoholic."

"I'm not an alcoholic, damn you. I'm not an alcoholic!" she yelled.

"More than two fifths of booze a day! Look at this house, Celeste. It's a mess! This is no place for growing children," Clark pleaded.

The house was a mess. She'd gone through a half-dozen domestics; no one wanted to put up with an aggressive drunk.

There were three empty vodka bottles strewn about the living room. The carpet was stained and had not been vacuumed in weeks. One picture hung askew, a bra and panties lay in the corner, and a half-eaten box of Church's chicken sat on the cocktail table next to another Smirnoff bottle. The kitchen was even worse, littered with dirty dishes in the sink, pots uncovered and half-filled with rotting cooked food on a filthy built-in GE stove, several large New Orleans roaches crawling over everything, undisturbed.

"No, I said!"

"Look, I'll sweeten the alimony payments. You won't have to spend a dime on the kids. Be reasonable, Celeste. Listen to your attorney. It's best for the kids."

"What part of no don't you understand, Al?"

"But why?"

"Because that's what you want," she said slyly. "Don't you understand, you bastard? I hate your fuckin guts! You left me, dammit. Left me! I was Miss Louisiana runner-up. I had a film career until you knocked me up, you horny black bastard. I coulda been a star. A fucking movie star. The new Elizabeth Taylor. Everybody said I looked like her." She primped her unwashed hair, preening and posing as if she were still eighteen.

"All a goddamn black man wants is a high yellow piece of ass. You had a college degree. That's why I married you. We're trying to live on a measly forty thousand dollars a year! Miss Louisiana runner-up," she slobbered.

It was true, she had resembled a young Elizabeth Taylor when he'd met her. Just turned eighteen, she was breathtaking. He just had to have her, Clark remembered. But she couldn't act worth a damn: one expression for surprise, anger, horror—eyes wide, mouth agape, eyebrows raised. She'd done three local low-budget films intended for southern drive-ins. Tits and ass films, and she'd had that before she gained more than sixty pounds of booze-soaked fat. She'd spent most of the footage with her clothes off.

"I know what you're thinking. No negro female movie stars, right? Well, I coulda passed. Everybody thinks I'm white, anyway, you kinky head, black nigger bastard. Look at my mother, a blonde with blue eyes, and my father, black blow hair like me. I coulda been a star," she said piteously, looking into her drink as if the Academy Award might be in the bottom of the glass, her eyes starting to mist.

"Celeste," Clark answered sympathetically, "the kids are getting out of hand. You can't control them. Barbara is running with a wild bunch, and I found a bag of weed on Junior last week when they came out to the boat for the weekend. Do you even know that Barbara had an abortion late last year?"

"So what? I had three."

"When?"

"While we were married, stupid. Why do you think I stopped going to church? It was a mortal sin that I could never confess."

"But why?"

"Because I didn't want to have any more of your children, that's why. I couldn't use the pill, and you wouldn't leave me alone. Not that you could fuck worth a damn, anyway."

Every woman's ultimate insult, he thought. Did they really believe that every man measured his manhood in his jockey shorts?

"Either sign the papers, or I take you to court," he said, his face expressionless, rising to leave.

"Get out! Get out!"

She flung the glass at him, missing by a foot. As he looked back at the door, she was greedily drinking, directly from the bottle.

Al Clark had barely set foot in the cabin of his boat before the telephone started ringing. His caller ID confirmed his suspicions. It was Celeste. This was her usual MO after there had been an argument. But this time he needed a sedative himself. He

unplugged the telephone, then settled down with a glass, some ice, and a fifth of Jack Daniels.
    A call came in on his cell phone. "Clark here."
    "Detective Clark, get up to Felicity and Dryades right away. Looks like a riot's going to break!"
    "I'm on my way," said Clark.
    Belting down the remainder of his drink, Clark grabbed his coat, heading for the door. Outside, he entered his squad car, placed the portable magnetic light on the roof over his head, started the engine and pulled away from the curb, peeling rubber, siren howling, roof light flashing.

CHAPTER 26

Back in his stripped-down, unmarked white Ford Crown Victoria, Clark moved swiftly through traffic, cursing to himself. How did he ever wind up married to such a bitch, he thought. But he knew. The first time he'd seen her bursting out of a skimpy bikini, he knew what he wanted. What a body, he reminded himself again, remembering her long legs, her solid ass reflecting her African genes. And no matter what she was saying now, twenty years ago when they were young and in love, they both were fucking each other's brains out. Celeste couldn't get enough of his big black dick.

Now she was a fat slob of a drunk. She'd never been much of a mother or housekeeper, but she'd been dynamite in bed until the booze took over, one night she'd passed out while he was still in her, her booze-soaked breath making him nauseous, lying under him like a beached whale. He could never bring himself to touch her again after that.

Maybe that's when she began to hate me, he thought; but he knew that was a lie, because like many of her kind, she had a profound contempt for dark-skinned men already, except as bed partners or sugar daddies. At one time all he and Celeste had was sex; nowadays, nothing, not even that. He wanted a high yellow woman with good hair and now he was paying for it.

He barely made the next light, then slowed to time the lights from that point on, moving smoothly with the traffic, changing lanes to keep his pace.

He had to get the children away from her. They were good kids, and he saw them often, taking them out on the boat every weekend he was not on duty. After a few hours in the sun, on the sea, their tension seemed to disappear until they had to reluctantly return to the alcoholic squalor of what was no longer a home.

Clark had been living on his boat, a thirty-five foot Chris Craft with an inboard Chrysler marine engine, his pride and joy. Living on the boat so that he could save on rent, keep up the child support payments, take the kids out to movies, ball games. But they were growing up in the '90's like other teenagers, too fast, and he wasn't there full-time to keep them in line. He had to get them before it was too late.

He began to think about the two hundred and fifty thousand dollar insurance policy he had on her, double indemnity. With half a million, less taxes, he could work it out, make things right. He could put the girl into a good convent school, the boy into military school, visit them regularly, have them on off-duty weekends. It wasn't too late.

He swerved to avoid a car changing lanes, the driver hadn't bothered to use his turn signal.

"Dumb sonofabitch!" Clark murmured to himself.

It would be so easy. Make it look like a burglary, put her out of her misery, put a down payment on a three-room condo in east New Orleans near the levee and the marina where he docked his boat. He could hire a cook-housekeeper. He could save his kids.

He shook himself; this was dangerous thinking, an occupational hazard. You had to learn to think like a criminal, and some cops went over the line and became one. Now he was thinking of murder. There had to be another way. Had to be.

He pulled up to the uneasy crowd, cops in full riot gear standing by, talking, smoking, moving restlessly, adrenaline up, ready for anything. They moved the police barrier aside and he drove slowly down the street to what appeared to be the command post.

He got out, examined his surroundings, watching the people stirring anxiously, tension high, sullen, rabid looks on their faces. The news media was there catching it, too.

CHAPTER 27

Clark walked slowly through the crowd, testing their mood. They were angry, milling about, but not quite yet ready to explode. He reached the command post to find Captain Pat O'Malley, head of the Riot Control Squad, speaking into his radio microphone.

Usually in a situation like this, O'Malley would be dressed in full riot gear: flak jacket, riot stick, tear gas canisters attached to his waist, gas mask in a canvas bag slung across his shoulder, hard helmet with a plexiglas visor.

O'Malley was a beefy Irishman who stood well over six feet and weighed close to three hundred pounds. Often, his imposing presence alone could cool an unruly crowd.

O'Malley finished his conversation and turned to Clark.

"Detective Clark," said O'Malley, "sorry to call you off your investigation."

"It's all right. I have Burke on the case. How do things look so far?"

"This thing could blow any second, and you know this neighborhood better than anyone on the force."

"Yeah, I grew up down here," said Clark. "This was my first beat. In the old days black cops didn't have much of a choice. It was either black neighborhoods or the projects. The only Carnival parade they let us work was the Zulus, because they didn't want us to get into trouble trying to arrest drunk white folks."

"I know," said O'Malley, wiping his red face with a soggy handkerchief.

"I understand that the mayor's daughter does volunteer work down here, and the people seem to have a personal interest at stake," said the massive officer.

"Mayor Jammison grew up down here, too," said Clark.

"I didn't know that," O'Malley replied, surprised. "Right down here?"

"Yeah. His father had a grocery store not far from here. These people gave Mayor Jammison a ninety-eight percent plurality in the last election, and some of them were trying to find the 'traitors' belong to the other two percent," said Clark wryly.

O'Malley permitted himself a brief smile. "Tight-knit neighborhood, like where I grew up. Everything revolved around the church, teas, bingo, baseball. Everyone knew one another by their first names, like here. That might work to our advantage if we can get to the responsible people who are respected here," said O'Malley.

At the head of the crowd, Clark spotted Tyke and members of his gang—dope pushers, petty thieves, muggers, and all-around scum. They would lead the looters if a riot broke out. O'Malley noticed his look.

"Yeah, Tyke," said O'Malley with disgust. "Him and his scumbag flunkies have been stirring things up. Otherwise, I'd judge the crowd to be more concerned with the safety of Mayor Jammison's daughter than anything else."

The people watched the two cops closely, ready for anything. They'd faced the riot squad before, notorious head busters until O'Malley took over and instituted a more pacifistic approach with community policing. "Officer Friendlies," without riot gear, circulated through the crowd, speaking softly, calling people by their names.

Clark noticed Billy seated at a table outside his restaurant, next to the Camero Lounge, casual, at ease—missing absolutely nothing behind his sunglasses. Clark noticed that the doors to the club were closed, too.

"Did you order the bar closed, Captain?"

O'Malley heaved a sigh. "No, but thank the Lord that it is, because booze and an angry crowd don't mix. The liquor store down the street is closed, too, with the shutters down. Only alcohol available is beer or wine from the groceries."

Disembodied voices came from radios and bullhorns, and the whirling red and blue lights from the squad cars and ambulances cast a strange, flickering light on the people, who stood cautiously watching Clark and O'Malley.

Just past the barrier on the corner squatted the police armored personnel carrier, its driver leaning against the front fender, having a smoke, observing the scene. Ready.

For once, no music from automobile radios or boom boxes suffused the streets with their sounds.

"What do you want me to do, Captain?"

"Circulate through the crowd, assess their mood, and report back to me. I'm going to keep the riot squad out of the area until absolutely necessary. Pulling them in now, in full gear, might be a mistake."

"I agree," said Clark. "See you in a little while."

Clark began to move through the crowd, brushing Tyke back deliberately with his shoulder as he passed. Tyke sneered, but said nothing; he was more than a little afraid of the big black cop.

Clark moved slowly through the crowd, smiling at old friends, nodding to acquaintances, speaking softly to the people, calling them by their names.

"Any news on Debbie?" asked one old woman.

"Not yet, Mrs. Bennet," replied Clark, stopping for a moment. "So far, there is no evidence that she's been harmed. We're doing everything we can. In fact, I had to leave the investigation because of the activity over here."

"That's a shame," said Mrs. Bennet, shaking her gray head. "You ought to be out there looking for Debbie instead of fooling around with this mess."

"You know who got her," said one angry man. "The white folks hate the mayor and want him to drop out the race. That's what this is all about."

"We don't know that, Chuck," said someone near the center of the group.

"Sure we do," said a slim, dark-skinned woman dressed in blue jeans, her hair braided down the center of her head. "You know them white people hate the mayor because he won't kiss their ass."

"Right on," said another.

"Yeah," said a third.

"We don't know what they want yet, and we still don't know who did it," the detective answered evenly, moving up front. "We're waiting for a ransom demand right now. In the meantime, we're doing all we can to track down the rats who did this."

"And he can't do much while you fools is raising Cain," said Mrs. Bennet indignantly. "Why don't y'all go on home and turn on the television and let Officer Clark get back to work?"

Several other voices agreed.

"Y'all crazy? We oughta tear this town apart and let the people got Debbie know we mean business. You know it ain't 'bout no bread—that's just a scam. It's the ruling class behind it—peoples what own this city. White folks!" It was Tyke's voice from the fringe of the crowd.

"Got that right!" said one of Tyke's flunkies from the opposite side of the rapidly gathering crowd. "Three strikes you out, chain gangs, private prisons that put white folks to work watchin' niggers. Fuck all that!"

"Right on, brother," interrupted another. "We been bitin' ass too long and we ain't gon' take it no mo'. It's time to kick some ass. The only good honkie is a dead honkie. We got to git dem befo' dey git us! Just like burnin' dem churches. It ain't nobody but dem white folks and the KKK."

The angry crowd roared in agreement.

"Johnny right," yelled Mary from the rear. "We been fakin' 'n' bullshittin' too long, givin' us mothafuckin' welfare 'n' Medicaid. We don't need that shit! We can take what we need, wha's rightfully ours!"

"I ain't worked in three years," bellowed a man standing near Clark.

"It ain't our fault there ain't no jobs!" yelled someone else.

Johnny and Tyke could see that their plan was beginning to work. A few minutes more, and they would have the hostile crowd eating out of their hands. In one night, his gang could steal more than they could in six months.

"An' what about Debbee Jemason. We don' know what dem honkie freaks is doin' to huh right nah," Johnny continued. "As long as dere's a cracker 'live, none of our black sistas is gonna be safe. Dis is war!"

"Yeah," said another. "Let's get it on! Show the white folks we mean business! Slavery been over!" her shrill voice cutting the air.

Tyke's gang was spread through the crowd, but being widely despised as troublemakers and predators, they were working at a serious disadvantage. It would be when respected people got fed up that the riot would begin, thought Clark. Clark let them debate among themselves, let off steam.

"Yeah, monkey business, you little punk! We know what y'all want to do: steal, rob and loot so you can fill y'all's heads up with dope," said one large woman.

"Watch your mouth, woman," said Tyke, "less we..."

"Less y'all what? I ain't scared of you, you little mousy motherfucker. 'Scuse the French, Miz Bennet," the large woman apologized.

"That's all right, Selma," said Mrs. Bennet. "You go right ahead. Only kind of language these motherfuckers understand." The crowd roared with laughter.

"Later for you, bitch!" said Tyke from behind the safety of the crowd. Tyke was short and thin. He wore dirty shoulder-length dreadlocks, faded jeans and a long-sleeved shirt to hide his scrawny arms. A Rolex watch, too large for his skinny wrist, and expensive jewelry were fruits of his gang's rip-offs.

His rap sheet was three pages long, but the closest Tyke had come to doing any real time was for statutory rape and sodomy of a thirteen-year-old. The charges were suddenly dropped after the girl's father was mysteriously beaten up and nearly drowned.

Willie, Tyke's number two man, was following right along in big brother's footsteps. Much like a larger version of Tyke, Willie's face was scarred and his front teeth missing, a souvenir of a lead pipe that one of his enemies had used in a street fight. Ura, his common-law wife, stood at the rear of the crowd, her face battered and bruised, too, but by Willie's hands. Still, Ura claimed to love him.

Tyke was always armed with a razor-sharp switchblade knife of Solingen steel and a variety of automatic pistols. Several people in the neighborhood carried scars from his blade, and he was rumored to have murdered at least half a dozen men personally, and ordered the death of at least that many more. Today, because of the police, he'd left his firearm at home, but he had his blade.

"Call me bitch one more time, nigger, and I'll hit you so hard you'll be smelling beef for a week," said Selma, holding up her man-sized fist.

Selma was an outsized Amazon who stood over six feet and weighed well over two hundred pounds. She'd been known to down a grown man with one powerful punch. Tyke shut up as the crowd laughed and hooted in derision.

Laughter is good, though Clark, as he moved toward Billy. Music would be an even better sign that things were calming down. A Luther Vandross tune could cool out anybody.

Clark noticed that another group had quietly infiltrated the crowd—Sherif, Tyke's worst nightmare, with his Posse. The Posse was a self-proclaimed Black militia who followed many of Malcolm X's self-reliance principles. Unimposing but deadly. If Tyke started something, Sherif would be in the mix, too. Things would quiet down now.

CHAPTER 28

"Hello, Billy," said Clark to his old friend, after negotiating his way through the dense crowd and crossing Washington Avenue.

"What's happenin', Al. Sit down. Coffee?"

"Yeah," he sighed, as he seated himself next to Billy. "Don't mind if I do. I'm getting too old for this shit. Glad to see brother Sherif's still on the job."

"Selma," Billy said over his shoulder, "baby, bring us a pot of coffee, please."

They were sitting in front of Billy's restaurant. Four tables sat on the sidewalk outside. Inside, a long counter ran the length of the room to the kitchen in back, tables covered by white plastic tablecloths occupying the rest of the room. Fresh flowers in water glasses on the tables gave the room a festive air. A portrait of Malcolm X hung behind the counter and soft jazz music sounded from a tape recorder in the kitchen.

Billy's wife appeared carrying a tray with a pot of coffee, a container of cream, and several doughnuts. She was tall, slim, blue-black skin. She wore a tie-around ankle length shift of bright African print over a yellow leotard.

Large round earrings framed her almond-eyed, round, thick-lipped face. Selma wore a short Afro, and her white teeth gleamed as she smiled at Clark.

"Hello, Al. Long time no see," she said, as she put the food on the table.

"How are you doing, Selma? You're looking good."

"You're as bad as Billy."

"Where you think he learned it?" Clark smiled. "I taught him everything he knows, but not everything I know."

"What you know ain't much," Billy answered, and they all laughed. "You should've kept it for yourself."

"Will you join us?" asked Clark, smiling boyishly.

"No, thanks. I'll leave you two to your male bonding ceremonies. Next time don't stay away so long, Al."

"How could I live without your red beans and rice, and you looking so good, too."

"Flattery will get you everywhere. Shall I bring something to eat, Billy?"

"Yeah, baby," said Billy. "One of New Orleans' finest looks half-starved. Can't eat too good on cop's pay, I guess."

Selma walked back into the restaurant. Wynton Marsalis' trumpet wafted out the door.

"What do you think, Al?"

"Things might cool out, they might blow. On the razor's edge right now. Tyke and his punks are stirring it up pretty good."

"Yeah, I can see all that. I mean with the girl. Think they'll ice her?"

"I doubt it. Looks like a simple snatch for the money at this point. They promised a call for a ransom demand this evening. We'll know more then because they'll have to let Debbie speak so we know she's still unharmed."

"FBI on the case?" asked Billy, his voice full of contempt. Billy had an attitude about the FBI stemming from his days with the

PLAYING FOR KEEPS

Black Panther Party.

"Yeah. Kidnappings about the only thing they're really good at."

"Glad to know they're good at somethin'," said Billy. He poured coffee into two heavy, old-fashioned white mugs. They spooned cream into their cups, sat back and sipped the strong coffee, flavored with a hint of chicory.

"You really hate the feds, don't you?"

"Ever since they killed my cousin in Chicago, along with Fred Hampton and Mark Clark."

"I thought that was the Chicago cops," said Clark.

"Cointelpro set it up. Shot my cousin fifteen times while he was still asleep. He didn't stand a chance. Then had the nerve to call it a shoot-out when our side got off just one wild round."

"How come they didn't get you?"

"I'd just been transferred over on the south side to back up Bobby Rush. They hit Bobby's crib that same night, where I was stayin', but we were out in the streets. Had to go underground for a week after that."

"Well," said Clark, "at least it started a black voters' revolt, or Harold Washington would never have been elected mayor, otherwise."

"Tell that to my cousin and Fred's widow."

Selma returned with a tray and laid out the food: ham hocks, red beans and rice, corn bread and collard greens, two bottles of beer, and a small salad of sliced tomatoes, onion, green pepper, and lettuce.

Clark picked up the bottle of Louisiana hot sauce.

"Who do you think snatched her, Billy?" asked Clark, as the two men exchanged looks, the moon peeking behind the clouds.

"What makes you think I know anything, Al?" replied Billy. "That punk Shannon was down here asking me the same damn thing. Surprised me—that he'd come to me, that is."

"Because you know everything going down in this town, that's why. What did you tell him?"

"I think it's the Italians," Billy answered, his expression emotionless. "Cintenni. I'd bet my last dime on it. It smells like him. When you've been around as long as I have and lived to tell about it, that's something you don't soon forget."

"But why? They've been pretty low key since the casinos came in," said Clark, as he took a bite of cornbread.

"Because the mayor's on the take, just like the rest of 'em. He must be gettin' out of line. And don't forget the mafia took Hoffa out, even after he financed Vegas with all that Teamster money."

"You really believe that?"

"Don't you? Ever hear of an honest politician?" Billy snorted. "Jammison's about as ambitious as they come. That's just another way of sayin' he's greedy from where I'm sittin'. All that money and power, who wouldn't be tempted? He supported video poker, remember. He wanted that casino downtown. And when the D.A. came down on dockside gambling and said the riverboats had to sail or else, Jammison sided with the money. Saving jobs, bad weather, and crab traps was just a bunch of bullshit."

"I don't know, Billy. The mayor seems clean to me. You know, Burke and I were on his security team until I got switched over to homicide."

"He's slick, all right, but he's bent. Nothin' like his father, Mr. Jammison. Now, that was a good man."

"Have it your way," said Clark. "You still haven't told me why you suspect the mob."

Down the street the debate continued, loud voices cutting through the warm air. Let them vent their anger, thought Clark, let off steam.

"You know that ex-jock, Gino?"

"Provenzano? Yeah."

"Well, he's down here in the club next door almost every night, and when we got strippers, he's always here. Got jungle fever, dig?"

"So?"

"Well, he hasn't been here in over a week, not last night either. Works for Uncle Sal."

"That's not much to go on."

"I don't have to give hard evidence at a trial. That's your job. I told you, I just feel it," said Billy, as he took a long drink of Budweiser from the bottle.

"Could be," Clark answered curiously. "I'll check it out. But I still think Sam Jammison is straight. I'd bet the farm on that. Cintenni sounds plausible. But Sam Jammison, wrong ball park."

"Be my guest," said Billy. "But the dude didn't get black until he started runnin' for office. I just don't trust him. Same smell."

"Billy, you're prejudiced. You just don't like creoles."

"I don't like Sam Jammison," said Billy. "Ain't nobody better than me, especially no half-breed who's half white because some poor-ass cracker had sex with his fuckin' grandmother."

"What about the church fires?" Billy shook his head no, gritting his teeth.

"You know, Al, you've come a long way from hot wiring cars, picking locks and cracking combinations."

"We were just punk kids back then, Billy. Glad I cleaned up my act."

"You know what they say. Like riding a bike. Once you learn, you never forget."

"So I've heard," Clark answered blandly.

They finished their meal in silence, sensing the mood of the crowd. Clark knew that the shotgun was still leaning against the wall inside. If someone tried to loot Billy's restaurant, they were in for a big surprise.

CHAPTER 29

"I better get back to work," Clark said, draining his coffee mug, as Selma cleared the table. "Thanks, Selma, that was a great meal, as always." Clark did not insult his old friend by offering to pay.

"Anytime, " said Selma, walking away from the table with the dirty dishes and looking over her shoulder.

"Take care, Al. Maybe I can do somethin' to cool out the crowd, buy you some time. Don't want them burnin' down the neighborhood."

Clark looked down at Billy, sitting relaxed, and as deadly as a vicious black mamba whose swift bite was fatal. "I sure do hope so," said Clark. "I need to get back on my job, stop screwing around here."

Clark moved toward the command post.

Billy raised the beer to his mouth, downed it and rose. He walked the short distance to the crowd and stopped next to Tyke, who regarded him warily.

"Tyke, we need to talk."

Billy walked a short distance away, out of earshot of the crowd. Tyke followed carefully, looking over his shoulder to catch the eye of his main man, who nodded that he had Tyke's back.

Sherif was watching, too.

"What you want to talk about, Billy?" His face snarled and his eyes were hooded, tension obvious between the two dangerous men.

"About the looting once the deal goes down."

"Yeah? What deal?"

"Look, Tyke, no sense my boys and yours goin' head to head about who's gonna take what. We work it out ahead of time, right? Save us both some grief."

"We want the television store," snapped Tyke decisively, defiantly walking around Billy and eyeing him up and down.

"No problem, man. We'll take the hardware store." Dumb motherfucker, thought Billy to himself; nigger strugglin' down the street with a big ass television was a sitting duck. The power tools in the hardware were a much better bet: small, portable, and easy to sell for a good buck. Shit, everybody already had a damn TV.

"What about the rest of the stores?"

"Come on back to the restaurant, and we'll work it out. All right?"

"I thought you couldn't stand my guts," Tyke answered, still looking at Billy suspiciously.

"I can't. I think you're a fuckin' asshole, but we got to work together on this thing, dig? Do it right. Efficient. Then everybody maximizes their profits."

"Maximize the profits. Yeah," said Tyke. "Yeah, I like that."

"First, though, a little peace offering to let you know I'm down. Here's a little somethin' for your boys. They get high first, be some bad motherfuckers when the shit hits the fan."

Billy slipped several small coin envelopes of crack cocaine into Tyke's hand.

"Yeah, Billy. Thanks, man. They get high first, be rippin' off shit all fuckin' night!" laughed Tyke.

"You got it. Meet you at my place. All right?"

"Yeah, man. I think the shit's ready to jump off any minute now."

"Best thing for us, right?" said Billy.

"Right," said Tyke. "Gotta maximize the profits, ain't that right, Billy?"

"Got that right. See you in a few."

Billy turned and walked away as Tyke motioned to his main man.

Tyke walked over to the restaurant five minutes later. Before he could sit down, Billy rose.

"Come on in the alley, Tyke. Don't want people seeing us negotiating, and get stuck with a conspiracy rap later on, right?"

"Conspiracy. Naw. You right. Let's go negotiate, to maximize the profits, you know."

They walked into the alley between the restaurant and the Camero Lounge. Tyke looked at Billy's face over his shoulder, still not sure that the big man could be trusted. Without warning, Tyke whirled around and drew a switchblade, popping it open, eyes wide with fear and anger. Instead of holding the knife down low and in front, Tyke held it out and away, even with his ear, lips pulled back in a wicked snarl like a wild animal that had just been trapped.

Billy, realizing he'd given himself away with the look on his face, didn't hesitate. He lashed out with his heel, catching Tyke squarely on his kneecap, nearly breaking it. Tyke went down with a moan.

Billy picked up the knife and grabbed Tyke's shoulder-length dreadlocks.

"Don't kill me, Billy! Please! I'll do anything you say, man! Anything, anything!" He was crying in fear, and Billy could smell the urine as Tyke pissed on himself in terror. "Take it all, man! Take it all!"

"Ain't gonna kill you, bitch. You ain't worth it. These dreads come from the Rastas, righteous spiritual brothers in Jamaica. Too good for a rat like you, motherfucker."

Billy slashed away at the dreadlocks, cutting them off close to the scalp, leaving tufts of hair standing up, bald spots gleaming through the dirty residue on Tyke's head. He laid the blade against Tyke's throat.

"Listen good, punk, so I won't have to repeat myself. I want you to get the fuck out of New Orleans, you hear? Go back to that little jive ass Mississippi town you came from and don't even think about comin' back."

"Yeah, Billy, yeah. Anything, just don't kill me."

"You come back, I will kill you, motherfucker. You believe me?"

"Yeah, Billy, yeah, I believe you. I won't be back. Just don't kill me! Please, man! Please! Please don't kill me!"

Billy stood up, looking down at Tyke for a long time, wanting to waste him. Tyke could feel Billy's murderous rage and shuddered in fear. Billy closed the knife, stuck it in the pocket of his jeans.

Without another word, Billy turned on his heel, walked out of the alley, and motioned to Clark, who joined him in the middle of the crowded street.

"Al, you can stop worrying about Tyke. He had a little accident."

"Uh-huh," said Clark.

"And you can quietly pick his boys up for possession. They're all carryin'. Got a dime bag of rock on 'em."

"Wonder how that happened?" said Clark, poker-faced, peering through the restless throng.

"Wouldn't have the slightest idea," said Billy. "Anyway, I think things will be cool for now."

"I think so, too. Thanks, Billy."

"For what?" said Billy as he walked back toward his restaurant.

Clark walked back to the command post.

"Captain, have your men quietly pick up Tyke's boys. They're all carrying dope, and you might have to look for Tyke."

"Wonder how that happened?" said O'Malley, eyes twinkling as he turned to give orders to his men. O'Malley turned back briefly to Clark. "I think we can take over from here. Thanks."

CHAPTER 30

Back in New Orleans on Dumaine Street, a dark figure removed a two-gallon plastic container from the trunk of a 1999 Saab convertible, then proceeded down a long, dark alleyway. Forcing a cheap lock on the back door with a quick bump of the shoulder, the man slipped quickly inside a small room. Using a tiny flashlight gripped firmly between his teeth to get his bearings, he started dousing the room with gasoline.

Moving swiftly in the dim light, the intruder brushed past a stack of aluminum communion trays that fell to the floor with a loud clamor. Suddenly, a light came on under a doorway a few feet away. The intruder turned off the flashlight and scurried out of sight.

"Who's there? Somebody in here?" yelled the short, hunched-over figure silhouetted in the doorway, the voice weakened by age. The little man stepped forward, his head tilting slightly from side to side as he fumbled for the light switch on the wall beside the door.

Lunging forward, the intruder struck the man with the butt of a gun he carried in his jacket, knocking him to the floor unconscious. He emptied the can, pouring gas on the old man as well. He looked around again, and at the old man, then bent over to remove a wristwatch and money from the man's wallet. Tossing a match from the doorway, he closed the door snugly behind him, leaving the container inside. He took a can of spray paint out of his jacket pocket and started spraying a nearby wall.

The smell of freshly burned wood and ashes filled the air as Al Clark stepped from his car. Engine Number 7, located near the Municipal Auditorium, was the first to arrive for what was initially listed as a one-alarm fire with three fire engines, one ladder truck and a district chief. It was soon elevated to a two-alarm, with a second engine company responding. The Fire Department investigation team and the Police Department fire investigation team, able to walk through without breathing apparatus, had completed their preliminary work. Other firemen were busy "overhauling," hitting hot spots, clearing out equipment and putting it away, and picking up fifty-foot hoses and returning them to the pumps.

A shitload of people were already on the scene in addition to the firemen: detectives, FBI, ATF, uniformed officers, and of course, the news media. Curiosity seekers and heavy-hearted church members, some weeping while others tried to comfort them, were standing nearby.

A second church fire had set the detective's mind racing anyway, but when a body was found in the debris, they called Homicide. Even though he was already handling the Jammison case, Clark wanted to eyeball this one for himself. The black mayor's daughter kidnapped, her boyfriend murdered, and two black churches burned: maybe there was a connection.

The coroner's officer had not yet placed the remains into the meat wagon, so reluctantly the detective stopped the attendants. Clark hated the nauseous, sickening smell of burned flesh almost as much as he hated seeing it. He unzipped the black body bag for a quick look. Instantly his stomach started to churn, but of course that was a tough cop secret. The old man was burned so badly that a body search probably would not turn up anything.

Church fires in Louisiana, especially in New Orleans, were unusual. People generally got along. After all, this was the City that

Care Forgot. Everybody was so mixed up ethnically that half the time you could not tell who was white or who was black anyway.

Sure, there was racism. Even though it didn't seem like it, New Orleans was still part of the good old USA, and David Duke lived only fifteen minutes away in Metairie.

Suspects in other hate crimes across the country ran the full gamut from Neo-Nazi skinheads to the Ku Klux Klan, from murdering a white boy who was only walking with two black friends, to the three white men who dragged James Byrd to his death behind a pickup truck in Texas. Even New York City police officers had beaten and sodomized Haitian immigrant Abouda Louima with a toilet plunger, calling him a stupid nigger, invoking their mayor's name, shouting "It's Giuliani time."

"Hey, Al. You're in the wrong place, podner. The mayor's house is thataway," plainclothes detective St. Cyr pointed with a broad grin, dressed as usual in a suit that matched his expensive fedora hat.

You could always pick Ferdinand out in a crowd, Clark was thinking. If anybody else ever really wanted to find him, they could, too.

"Yeah," chuckled Meyer, Ferdinand's partner. "What's the problem? Tired of Dom Perignon and caviar?"

"Maid's day off, I'm slumming."

Up ahead, a man dressed in a black jacket with the letters ATF in white on the back moved through the rubbish holding a spotlight in one hand, the leash for his arson dog held firmly in the other.

"Any luck?" asked Clark, flipping his badge. "Clark, homicide."

"Zanich, ATF," the man nodded. "This is my partner, Sparky." The dog, a huge, German Shepherd, turned sharply, barking once. "One John Doe, so far. Hope that's it. The fire investigators cleared already."

"It's a good thing it happened between services," the detective added. "This could have been a catastrophe."

"Yeah. Tell that to the guy in the bag." The agent kept on moving. "Most churches have automatic alarms," he said. "Whenever one goes off, especially on Sunday, the rescue squad starts moving. The more they burn, the harder it is to find anything. We've got two hundred and fifty Federal agents investigating fires, including U.S. Marshals and the Treasury Department."

"So I've heard," Clark prodded. "I hear you're catching a lot of heat, too, for strong-arming black church members. Doing things like forcing preachers and deacons to take lie detector tests, showing up unannounced on people's jobs to question them. No way to make friends."

The agent turned slowly. "You're out here. You know the drill. Sometimes it takes years to close the books on a case, and that's after spending $190,000 a week."

"Well, you know what they say," the detective sneered. "If you can't stand the heat, get the hell outta the kitchen."

Clark knew that the murders, kidnapping the mayor's daughter and the church burnings might lead to violence, but there was little evidence to suggest that it was a national or even a regional conspiracy. That would be the Federal Bureau of Alcohol, Tobacco and Firearms' position, too.

President Clinton had asked Congress for an extra twelve million dollars for investigations, and legislation had been overwhelmingly approved, making it a federal offense to damage religious property.

Even the governor of Louisiana, Mike Foster, had signed bills into law that made it a crime to burglarize, firebomb, burn, or destroy a religious structure.

In spite of the dirt and the caustic odors, Clark's mind remained focused on the facts. Hotheaded young punks, drunk or high on drugs and poorly educated, not hard-core hate mongers, had committed most of the church fires. Sometimes they were looking for money. If they didn't find any, they might torch the church; or they might start a fire to cover their tracks. Then there were copycat crimes.

Still, this was not the kind of thing that happened in his city. Most of the churches that were burned down were easy targets, isolated or empty, like the four in the north Baton Rouge communities of Baker and Zachary in 1996. That was fueled by racial hatred and alcohol, and one of the men, Frankie New, had even been caught. Ten years in prison and a $250,000 fine still didn't seem like enough.

Walking through the ruins, Clark was searching for a clue, and finally there it was outside, sprayed on the part of the building that had not been completely engulfed. In red spray paint, it was the same message that had been left at the first church burning: "Burn Nigger Burn" and "KKK." There was a big red swastika there, too.

When Clark walked back outside, a metallic green Saab convertible was temporarily blocked in by the coroner's meat wagon that was pulling off with the old man's remains. Ordinarily, there would have been nothing special about the car, but the conspicuous driver and the detective made eye contact. He was a spike-haired young man in his early twenties, black leather jacket, wearing a studded dog collar. His face was pale, with black lipstick and black eyeliner. A crucifix was tattooed on the clean-shaven left side of his head above the ear.

* * *

An hour later Al Clark pulled up and parked in front of the New Orleans Drop-In Center, where gutter punks frequently washed up and sometimes stashed their bundles.

PLAYING FOR KEEPS

"Hey, buddy, can you spare some change so my girlfriend can get drunk and I can get laid?" asked a young punk puffing on a GPC cigarette, the cheapest cigarette sold. Some people even called them Gutter Punk Cigarettes.

"If you take that blunt outta your hand you could lay yourself and get the fuck outta my face," Clark answered sharply, not even breaking his stride.

"I don't need you or your fuckin' money, man!" the punk shouted. "I don't need your fuckin' money! I don't need it!"

The punks inside were just as confused as the ones he had left outside, some with camping bags or knapsacks, others sitting around on the floor in little groups.

"Hi," he said, flipping his badge and identification card. "I'm Detective Clark. I need your help. I'm trying to find somebody."

"Sure, if I can," answered the attractive young attendant, dressed much like a gypsy, including the headpiece, with a ring in her nose. "It's a madhouse around here this time of year."

"I'm looking for a gutter punk, a gothic, spiked hair, a crucifix on the left side of his head."

"I don't know, Officer," the young woman answered apologetically, shrugging her small shoulders. "There are so many of them, and after a while, they all start to look alike."

"Well, where else would he go if he didn't come here?"

"Maybe Covenant House on North Rampart Street, if you're lucky. They can grab a meal and a bed, but most of 'em don't stay—too many rules. Usually, they live in squats, you know, abandoned houses, empty cars, vacant doorways. You can check out Hippie Hill, too, across from Jackson Square. He could be anywhere: the French Quarter, Bourbon Street, Café Joel, oh yeah, and the Moonwalk. Gutter punks, as a rule, don't come out until after noon. Some Gothics don't even come out in daylight."

"Why do they do it?" Clark asked, toying with the absurdity.

"Why do they live like this? Maybe I'm too old, but I just don't get it."

"Some of them are bored, some of them believe they've been abused, whatever that means—maybe not a big enough allowance. I'm sure some of them were abused. It's kind of a con game, though, because after you're twenty-five years old, you're too old to be a punk. Drinking or doing drugs to black out doesn't make any sense to me, either. Why do college kids binge drink until they pass out?"

"I can't imagine my kids out here living like this," Clark told the young woman.

"Three hundred thousand kids sixteen or younger are working as prostitutes right here in the good old U.S.A. For girls, it's even worse," the young woman added. "They leave home, fall prey to pimps or pornographers. They're too embarrassed to call home, too scared to go to the police. Most of them aren't prostitutes, not in the strictest sense. They participate in what we call 'survival sex,' for food, shelter, drugs, and yes, sometimes money.

"A pimp will meet a girl through another girl, 'deep quiz' her, find out why she left home, then exploit her weakness. The girl is looking for a boyfriend, the pimp turns her out, telling her they need money and that it's only going to take a few dates. She's history after that."

"Here's my card. Give me a call if you see this guy, or if you hear anything. It's real important."

"Sure," said the attendant, taking the card.

"Got a restroom?"

"Down the hall, and turn right."

The bathroom walls were filled with graffiti, a gutter punk message board. Clark couldn't make heads or tails of most of it, but there was one thing he did know: he had to get some sleep, but he had one more stop to make first.

PLAYING FOR KEEPS

Al Clark walked casually along the levee of the wide, muddy Mississippi River near the Moonwalk, glancing occasionally at shadowy freighters, tugboats and barges pushing water out of the way as they moved in the darkness. The lights were twinkling in the city of Algiers on the other side, a replica of many of the other sleepy towns along the river, less than a mile away, but a world apart.

Al Clark was hoping that the Gothic had not taken off for one of the other gutter punk cities of choice: New York, Washington, DC, Seattle, Key West, Berkeley....

After about an hour, across the street, not far from the bright downtown streetlights, he spotted a most unusual couple talking, a tattooed skinhead with swastikas sewn on the front of a worn blue jeans jacket, and a Gothic wearing a black cape, spiked hair, with a crucifix over his left ear, laughing, with fangs in his mouth. In that same instant, the gutter punk glanced across the street, seeing the plainclothes detective's face in the crowd.

Without saying another word to the skinhead he was talking to, the Gothic turned and darted away. With New Orleans jazz and Cajun zydeco music echoing in the air, the detective chased the suspect past Planet Hollywood, across the train tracks, around the Jax Brewery and across Decatur to St. Louis Street. On Royal Street, he commandeered a tourist carriage, pulled the driver to the ground, taking his seat and grabbing the reins.

Whipping the reins frantically, the carriage sped up the street as Al Clark chased on foot, past antique shops and the Montaleon Hotel, forced to come to a halt because of traffic up ahead, one block from Canal Street.

Al Clark approached the carriage cautiously from behind, his gun held in two hands raised next to his head. Flat against the back of the carriage, he spun around, his gun aimed. Panic-stricken, an elderly man and woman huddled tightly, shuddering, but the Gothic had vanished.

CHAPTER 31

"Where's my daughter, Cintenni?" growled the mayor, storming into the mobster's study. One of Sal's men was right behind him, his right hand resting on the revolver in his waist holster.

"What makes you think I got your daughter?" asked Cintenni, mildly. "Temper, temper, Sam. Cool down, then we can talk calmly like two adults. And how the fuck did you lose that security team covering your ass?"

"You seem to be forgetting one very important detail, Sal. I'm my own man. I make my own rules. I walked out, got in my car. And here I am. On your ass. I want my daughter!"

Sam stared at the mobster with contempt, his eyes lingering on the automatic lying on the desk next to his right hand. He judged his chances, then rejected the idea of attack. Cintenni was right, he had to cool down; anger and his ego were giving his slippery adversary the edge.

Trying to overcome and control his rage, he quietly prowled the large room, Cintenni's pig eyes following him. The room was furnished in a combination of Italian provincial and Scandinavian modern: a large Bokhara carpet on the floor of polished oak, Impressionist paintings on the walls. He spotted two Van Goghs, one that had been stolen from the Van Gogh Museum in Amsterdam three years previously. There was a Degas, a Cezanne landscape, and a pointillist painting by an artist he could not identify. All stolen, he thought.

He walked to the glass-front case, set into the wall, housing Cintenni's gun collection. On the left were the weapons of the Old West: Remington, Sharps, Henry and Winchester rifles and carbines, Smith & Wesson handguns, Colt revolvers; the Peacemaker, a large cavalry saddle pistol, an Army Colt .44, and a single-action Navy Colt—John Wesley Hardin's favorite weapon. Hardin had killed more than forty men with that weapon and died of old age in Mississippi. Hardin knew the creed of the western gunfighter: "Never give a sucker an even break." Barnum might have said it; the gunfighters lived and died by it.

The mayor would hold onto that thought until he had his chance. Sal Cintenni had to pay for kidnapping his precious child, but in a time and place of Sam's choosing. He took a deep breath to calm himself, then eased into the Eames chair of black leather and molded rosewood that sat in front of Cintenni's huge oak desk.

"Bobby, you can leave us alone now," Cintenni told his bodyguard. "My guest here seems to have calmed himself down."

"Like I said," Cintenni repeated, toying with Sam, "what makes you think I got your kid?"

"Let's cut all the bullshit, Sal. Why did you do this?"

"We've been good to you, Sam. I'd even like to think that we were friends for a bunch of years."

"Why?" asked the mayor, his patience wearing thin. "Why the fuck have you done this?"

"Insurance."

"What?"

"Insurance," Cintenni repeated coolly. "You're a businessman, among other things. Let's call it collateral, or maybe security. Take your pick, whatever floats your boat. Know what I mean?"

Samuel Jammison lost control and shouted out his rage, the rage he had been trying to suppress, anger lines in his face deepening.

"What? What do you want, you repugnant sonofabitch?"

"You know what I want," Sal snapped, his voice rising too as he moved forward in his chair, both elbows resting on the desktop. "The casino, Sam, the casino. Jazzville. And the airport expansion contract, plus the Convention Center and Dryades Street. I want back in. They were my deals, anyway."

"That's what this is all about?"

"It's enough, don't you think?" Cintenni answered. "That money is mine. You know we're your friends and you try to fuck us. The port is booming, all that steel going to Japan. Jazzville's gonna kick ass when it's really up and runnin'. Dryades Street and that whole uptown neighborhood is gonna be worth a fortune once the white people take it back from you spooks and develop it. But you, you had to be fuckin' greedy. You wanted it all."

Cintenni paused and took a belt from a nearby brandy snifter.

"Peach brandy, straight up, nothin' like it. Now, where were we? Oh, yeah. Well, we think that holdin' your kid is gonna help you see things our way. How you call it? Clear up your perspective."

Jammison's blood boiled. Cintenni was deliberately antagonizing him. His opponent was a very dangerous man, and he had no choice but to play along with the game if he ever hoped to see Debbie alive again.

The mob boss continued his histrionics, the blood in the veins of his temples gorged and swelling. "You know," he yelled, "Bobby Kennedy may have fucked over Sam Giancanna and doublecrossed the Chicago mob after they helped put his big brother in the motherfuckin' White House, but you ain't no fuckin' Kennedy, and I ain't Giancanna. After Joe Kennedy got Sinatra to hook his son up with people he couldn't afford to be seen with in public they sold Giancanna out and stabbed him in the back. Giancanna fuckin' sent people around with suitcases full of money to buy votes, even broke a few legs when they had to… Payback's a motherfucker, ain't it. I saw on the news that all hell's about to break loose," Cintenni continued sarcastically. "Too bad. Lotta innocent people could get hurt for nothin'. I'll tell you. Hate to have a thing like that on my conscience."

"You know you're crazy, Sal," said the mayor.

"No, fuck me!" Sal shouted angrily, beginning to turn red, hatred in his dark eyes. "How soon we forget. When the federal prosecutors started bustin' heads for racketeerin' and video poker payoffs, your name never came up, not once. When the fuckin' FBI was probin' some of them fuckin' shady land deals we hooked up, again, nobody heard nothin', not a word about the Honorable Mayor Sam Jammison, did they? And this is how you pay me back. This is how you show your gratitude."

Cintenni took a cigar from the box on his spotless desk, took his time cutting it, lighting it.

"How's my daughter?" asked the mayor, still forcing himself to try to remain calm. It was a good thing the goddamn dago could not read his mind, or it all would have been over with, right then. The blood inside his head surged to the point that he was starting to think about his high blood pressure, and the possibility of a stroke. Cintenni would have realized instantly that there was never going to be any deal and shot him on the spot.

Sam sat at ease, legs crossed. He wore a two-button Brooks Brothers blazer of dark blue flannel, an open neck, button-down sport shirt of red checks, and cavalry twill trousers over black half boots.

"Just fine. Tough little lady. You oughta be proud," Cintenni answered, as both men calmed themselves to move forward. "My sons, now, they're weak as overcooked spaghetti. Take after their Anglo-Saxon princess mother."

"My folks warned me. Marry a good peasant woman from the Old Country, they said. Give you strong Sicilian sons. But no, from the time she walked into my club, all blonde and cool, I had to have her. Wipe that superior smile off her fuckin' face. I did, but she got the last laugh. Gave me three punk sons without a pair of balls between 'em."

"Look at you. You didn't do so bad, Sam. Creole society girl." Cintenni's diamond pinkie ring caught the light as he scratched his chest with fat, blunt fingers.

"Creole society girl, all right. Her great-grandmother took her grandmother to a quadroon ball at the Orleans Ballroom and hooked her up with some Frenchman. Got her a big house on Esplanade, some black servants and a matched team of black horses to boot. She had three children by the sonofabitch, then he got married. Of course, she kept everything."

Cintenni slid the box of Havana cigars across the desk to the mayor, keeping his right hand near the bone-handled, gold engraved Sig Collector Classic nine-millimeter automatic on his desk. He'd had to pull it out when the mayor came storming in. "Drink?" The mayor nodded yes, as he pulled out his own Portofino cigar.

"Thanks. I've got my own."

Cintenni slid the pistol into his waistband and crossed to the bar, keeping his eyes on the mayor in the mirror at his back.

"Glenfiddich, right? Neat," Cintenni said confidently, as he played the nerves game with Jammison.

He poured the mayor a drink, replenished his own brandy snifter, and returned to his desk, carefully keeping out of Sam's reach. He slid the heavy crystal old-fashioned glass across the desk and resumed his seat, putting the gun back on the desktop.

They sipped their drinks, puffed on their cigars while regarding one another somberly. Sam drank single-malt scotch for show, hated its pale weak flavor. Privately, he preferred bourbon, a man's drink: bourbon, with a splash of branch water.

"You been playin' footsies with the Vegas boys about the casino. Now, is that loyalty? I've backed every campaign you ever won with my own money and my organization. Kept the unions cool..."

"Not the police union," the mayor reminded him.

"That's the New York mob. Gambino's boys. I might be able to work something out. Mardi Gras is a billion dollar sure thing. That's a lotta cake to piss away," Cintenni answered.

"Who do you have inside my organization?"

"You don't expect me to answer that, do you? Safe to say that I know every fart you make. Tell me something, Sam. Why would you want to cut me outta the casino?"

"You wouldn't meet my price. They will."

"What's their offer?"

"Your snitch didn't tell you?"

"Of course."

"Mistake admitting that, Sal. That narrows it down."

"No need for you to know," said Cintenni. "You'll know who it is when they find him floatin' face down in a ditch somewhere. He's the reason your kid's boyfriend got wasted. I'm really sorry about that, Sam. Couldn't be avoided."

"Shee-it," said the mayor.

"No, really. I believe in a clean operation. Blood only when absolutely necessary. The Machiavellian way. Not like the old days."

Sam threw back his head and laughed. Cintenni joined in.

"You think you're a fucking Medici, Sal?"

"Naw," said Cintenni honestly. "I live in a modern mansion, collect Impressionist paintings, drink good Tuscan wine, but I know what I am: a Sicilian peasant in a twelve hundred dollar suit.

And you're a descendant of a bunch of slaves from Africa."

"That's all right, Sal. None of your relatives owned any of mine. Your father didn't get here until the late twenties. On the contrary, maybe one of my ancestors ruled yours."

"What do you mean by that?" asked Cintenni, puzzled.

He ran his hand over his heavy jaw. Sam could hear the scrape of stubble. Probably had to shave three times a day, Sam thought. Cintenni's massive arms were covered with thick hair. He wore a short-sleeved shirt of silk, open at the collar, thicker hair curling from its top.

"Perhaps when Hannibal's army retreated to Sicily from the Italian boot. Or more recently, when the Pan Islamic army ruled Sicily for eight hundred years. When we kicked your guinea wop asses."

"I keep forgettin' that you're a history fanatic, too. Educated black man."

"We might even be distant relatives," said Sam with a wry smile. Cintenni roared.

"Now, wouldn't that be somethin', huh, cuz?"

"The reason y'all hate us so much. You know you're part nigger. Hell, you're darker than my wife," said Sam.

"How'd your in-laws feel about you marryin' your wife? Maybe you could pass the paper bag and the comb test, but your old man had dark skin, kinky hair, and he was a dyed-in-the-wool baptist from out in the sticks."

"The LeBlancs pretended it was all right, but they weren't crazy about the idea. Anyway, my mother was creole, light enough to pass, and I'm not exactly black. But they were happy enough when Debbie came out light. And me being mayor gives them bragging rights."

Why the fuck am I talking to this ignorant Dago motherfucker like an equal? Jammison thought to himself.

"Enough of this family tree shit, Sal. Let's get down to business. But first, turn down the damn air conditioner. It's freezing in here."

Cintenni walked to the wall and switched off the air conditioner. Its soft hum stilled, they could hear the rain coming down steadily outside that had begun shortly after the mayor's arrival.

Keeping his eye on Sam, Cintenni slid open the heavy glass door leading to the balcony just a crack, and resumed his seat. A heady aroma came in from the rose garden below, the sound of the night birds and insects stilled by the earlier downpour.

"All right," Sal said, turning slowly to face the mayor. "I'll match the Las Vegas offer. Fifteen million up front."

"Their deal is twenty million."

"Just testing. Twenty million cash, up front, plus one percent of the gross for twenty years. Right?"

"Right, but I want another ten percent up front. Twenty-two million, total."

"For what?"

"For snatching my kid. For pain and suffering, that's for what, motherfucker!"

Sam slid forward in his seat. Cintenni held up his left hand in warning, slid his right hand closer to the Sig until Sam relaxed.

"You got it."

"Just one more thing. Keep the Vegas boys off my back."

"No sweat. Just a matter of business. I'll even give them a small cut of the action for their trouble. I'd rather have them as friends than as enemies. Lucky thing for you you didn't try to fuck with the Russian Mafia. I hear they laundered about $10 billion through the Bank of New York last year. Those motherfuckers are worse than the fuckin' Colombians. Your friends would be diggin' your tongue outta your ass by now. Tell me, did you contact my friends in Vegas or did they contact you?"

"That's confidential."

"Yeah. What I like about you, you can keep your mouth shut. Your wife know about your under the table deals?"

"As long as she has enough money to spend, she doesn't care where it comes from. Doesn't want to know," said Sam.

"Smart woman. I don't apologize often, but I'm sorry I underestimated you; then none of this needed to happen. I admire the way you're takin' it. Instead of stupid revenge, which wouldn't work anyway, you cut a deal."

"I'm a politician. You're a businessman. Making deals is what we do."

"Wonder what your constituents would think if they knew the real you: knight in shining armor of the Rampart Street War; decorated veteran of World War II; civil rights hero; on the take and rippin' off millions," said Cintenni sarcastically.

For a moment Sam Jammison's mind drifted as he sat there listening to Sal's bullshit, remembering June 6, 1944, D-Day in France, the day the Allied troops stormed the beaches in Normandy. He was part of the Quartermaster Battalion from Louisiana who had trained at Camp Claiborne, one of 1.2 million African-Americans who had served in the European and Pacific theaters. The Quartermaster Corps was a gigantic department store with thousands of branches that provided quarters, clothing, fuel and transportation. Only Colored boys and men served in the 351 Field Artillery Battalion, the 320 Barrage Balloon Battalion, the 679, 827, 828 and 846 Tank Destroyer Battalion and the Tuskegee Airmen, bomber escorts who never lost a plane to enemy fighters with over 15,000 missions, including bomber escorts to Berlin.

They hit the beaches in 40,000 Higgins boats, LCMs, built in New Orleans by black men and white men and by women, not paid by race or sex, but based on the work they did, even back in the '40's.

PLAYING FOR KEEPS

A frightened teenager, only sixteen at the time, Jammison remembered hearing the sound of German bullets hitting the side of the boat and being in the water, looking back, seeing friends dead behind him and on the sandy beach ahead.

The strong swirling tide pulled bodies out, then swept them back in, with personal gear belonging to dead GI's strewn for miles, soldiers' packs, bibles, paper for writing letters back home, burned tanks half-covered by water and wrecked jeeps.

One of his Louisiana homeboys, Jesse Powell, from Port Allen, didn't even make it to the LCM. He and three other soldiers carrying 80-pound packs and rifles were coming down the ropes from the Liberty ship to be transported to shore. Rough seas lifted the Higgins boat ten feet, then dropped it back down, slamming it against the side of the ship, crushing the men between the two boats.

The boat next to the one he was on sank when they were loading a tank onto the rear, and four men inside the tank died without being seen again.

The three-man crew on the landing craft was ordered to cover their faces and hands with grease. If they were not protected, once the battlewagons started firing heavy shells over their heads, it would be so hot that their skin would actually blister.

War was hell on earth, and it was not too much better for him and the other black troops on base than it was back in the States. They lived on one side of the base, the whites on the other. He and the others were not allowed to use the white PX, the cafeteria or the lunch counter, they had only a little building or canteen for their needs. They couldn't even use the swimming pools for recreational purposes, while German prisoners could. The Army also believed that southern white army officers could better deal with colored soldiers than northern army officers because they were the ones who knew how to handle niggers. The officers always told

Sam and the other colored soldiers from the south to stay away from those boys from up north, who would get them into trouble because they had been around those communist jews. Most of the colored soldiers didn't even know what a communist was.

Some of the white soldiers had never seen a live black person before and only believed what they had heard, that all colored people shot craps, carried straight razors, and that they were either from the south or from Harlem, where all black people lived. One thing hadn't changed, though, the white man's insecurity. The white soldiers were telling all the European women to stay away from the colored soldiers, who had tails.

Whenever a white woman accused a black soldier of rape, which happened from time to time, every colored soldier on the base was called out into formation. Sam remembered one cold morning at two a.m. when a white woman, escorted by civilian law enforcement and MPs carrying flashlights, walked through the ranks to identify a soldier. If you were picked, whether you were in town or not, unless someone said you did not have a pass that night or you had a detail, that was your ass.

At the bus depot there were buses for white soldiers and buses for black soldiers. If you did not have an overnight pass, you had to be back on base by midnight. If you missed curfew, the MPs could write you up AWOL, and you could be disciplined. Sometimes when more white soldiers or even-steven would go into town, the white soldiers would take the black buses and the black soldiers would get back late. Sam laughed, remembering one night that the black soldiers took all the buses, including the white ones, then turned them over, making the white soldiers late.

Even when they were guarding German prisoners, the Germans could sometimes eat a hot meal in a restaurant with white soldiers, while he and the other colored soldiers guarding them either waited outside, went around back for a cold sandwich, or hoped that the mess hall would still be open when they got back.

Another old friend, Medgar Evers, served in the all-black 93rd Infantry in the South Pacific, Guadalcanal, New Guinea, and the Philippines. Hoping that things would get better when he got back home, Medgar got involved in a grassroots effort of what would later become the civil rights movement. A klansman's bullet in the back did what the Japs could not.

Sam remembered the siege at Bastogne in December of 1944, when Eisenhower, desperate and short of infantry troops, asked black soldiers to volunteer as riflemen, but there was one big catch. Noncommissioned officers like sergeants had to take their stripes off, temporarily becoming "slick sleeves," privates. This was so they could not outrank the white noncommissioned officers and embarrass them by being in charge. Led by General George Patton and his Third Army, Sam Jammison and the other colored soldiers kept Hitler from pushing the Americans back.

"Mayor Sam Jammison pulled himself up by his bootstraps," Sal went on. "Well, we know who gave you those bootstraps, don't we, right from the beginning."

"And ripping off my people, among others, provided your bootstraps, Sal. Dope, gambling, prostitution... stealing their homes."

"You're judging me?" asked Cintenni, staring at the mayor as if he had been insulted.

"Not hardly," Sam replied. "We're two of a kind. Pragmatists."

"Machiavellians?"

"Machiavellians. Besides, I look out for my people," said Sam stiffly, taking another puff on the cigar and blowing smoke in the air.

"Sure you do. Right after you look out for yourself. Most of the money being pumped into that casino is coming from your people," Cintenni exaggerated. "Three hundred million; not bad. And that Superport that's gonna be built near the mouth of the river oughtta make you as rich as me once you get your cut," Sal laughed. "You're doin' a real good job of lookin' out for your people, poor suckers usin' what little money they got tryin' to strike it rich. Tell me something else, Sam. Did you know Brazzi was an uncle of mine?" It was something Sal had wondered about for a long time.

"Did you know I'm the one who dropped him? He was the first to go down. I'd just turned twenty. Threw up my guts when the shooting was over. Brazzi had the right idea. He just couldn't pull it off."

"Forty-five slug right between the eyes, I heard. Had the back of his head blown away. Lucky shot?"

"Two-hand grip at ten feet? Nothing lucky about it."

"Tell me your father was quite a man, as honest as you are bent."

"Leave my father out of this. He worked for nigger wages all his life. Not me."

"Me, neither. Watched my old man work himself to death on a shrimp boat he never even owned. Was workin' on it for somebody else until the day he died. Fuck that."

"They say that the fruit doesn't fall far from the tree. Our trees must have been on a mountainside," said Sam, with a wry smile. "When do we get Debbie back?"

"Soon. You raised the bread?"

"How much are you asking?"

"Two mil."

"That's tip money for you, Sal. Chump change."

"Exactly. That's why they'll look elsewhere. Where you gettin' it?"

"Independent donations. Not a dime out of my own pocket."

"Good. I'll split the take down the middle with you. Call it a peace offering. Make sure they're unmarked bills."

"Think I'm a fool?"

"Not any more. I'm not gonna make that mistake again. You gotta understand, I never knew any coloreds with both balls and brains, like you. The nig... uh, blacks I deal with just wag their tails and take whatever crumbs I throw down. Wish it didn't have to go down this way."

"It wouldn't have, if you'd met my original price on the casino."

"I know, I know. Won't happen again, I swear."

"If Debbie comes back harmed in any way, all bets are off, and I'll come at you with everything I have."

"Then we'll go down together," Sal answered, no longer smiling.

"So what? Nobody fucks with my family, understand? Not even you!"

"All right, all right, just cool down. I said I'm sorry, and I'll make it up to you. We made a pretty good team before this shit went down. Between us, we can tie this town up tight as a virgin asshole."

Cintenni looked away quickly, afraid he'd made a slip. He had. The mayor had noted his comment, but hooded his eyes as he took a sip of his drink. He'd have to check Sal out. If Cintenni was in the closet it would give him leverage. Mobsters hated homosexuals, although they ran most of the gay bars and clubs.

"Usual bag lady for the bread?"

"Yes. I'll have her contact you for the drop."

"You got a nice little stash in that numbered account in the Grand Caymans," Cintenni smiled.

"You fishin?"

"Nope. Know what you got down to the penny. Shit, I own

the fuckin' bank. Launder my dope and gamblin' money there."

"Then you know I'm not ripping you off."

"If you were, you'd be dead. Remember that. Nowhere in the world you could go without me findin' you. Capice?"

"Enough of this shit," Sam said sternly. "When will we get the ransom call?"

"Exactly two hours after you get home. I got somebody on your security team, too."

"Yeah. I know who that is. I'm not a complete fool, you know. Turner. The prick who had one man working security at my house and gave your men a clean shot at Debbie. You needn't put him in any ditch. I'll take care of him myself. And your inside man, too, if I blow his cover before you get to him," Sam said grimly.

Cintenni narrowed his eyes and regarded Sam closely. He'd forgotten how deadly this man was. He wouldn't make that mistake again.

Sam finished his drink, put out his cigar in the large marble ashtray and rose smoothly, extending his hand. Cintenni just smiled and shook his head.

"Well, can't blame a man for trying, right?"

"Just don't try too hard."

"Never," said Sam over his shoulder, as he strode to the door.

CHAPTER 32

Gino emerged from the bedroom, walked to the bar, poured himself a scotch, took the seat recently vacated by the mayor, shook out a cigarette and lit up.

"You hear all that?"

Gino nodded. "I thought you handled it well, Sal," he said, taking a sip, letting the good scotch linger in his mouth before swallowing.

"Yeah, I did, didn't I? Dumb fuck! Uppity nigger! Thinks he can put one over on me, huh? Well, when I buy somebody, they stay bought. If he really thinks he can play me off against the Vegas mob he's got another thought comin'. He'll wish it was the fuckin' Russians."

"What do you mean?" asked Gino, suddenly alarmed.

"I mean I'm gonna show him who really runs this town. Put him in his fuckin' place. Black motherfucker, tellin' me I'm part nigger. Sicilians part nigger! Damn that snooty, overeducated cunt motherfucker. It was all I could do not to blow his fuckin' brains out, sittin' there all high and mighty, givin' me a fuckin' history lesson. Shoulda never let niggers go to school. Let 'em get a fuckin' college degree, they think they're good as white people. Thinks he's good as me. I'll show his black ass."

Cintenni rose, turned to the window behind the desk and stared into the floodlit flower garden below.

"I still don't understand, Sal," said Gino, but he did understand, and it chilled his blood.

"When you get the money, I want you to whack his kid."

"Sal, maybe you should cool down."

"Fuck that, Gino. Give niggers an inch and they take a mile. I been too good to that fuck. Comin' in here cool as you please, bargainin' with me like I'm some pushcart peddler from the Old Country can hardly speak English. Wearin' clothes and drivin' a car he bought with my fuckin' money. I'll show him, then when I say jump, he'll just ask how high."

Gino gulped down the rest of his drink, walked to the bar and poured himself another scotch, a peach brandy for Cintenni. What Sal planned would be disastrous. Jammison was no pussy; he'd attack the mob with everything at his command, bring in the feds, close down everything in sight. Jammison might even turn state's evidence just to get back at Sal.

Cintenni and his damn color prejudice. He hadn't played football with blacks the way Gino had, hung out with them after games. Sal believed the stereotypes: niggers had no balls, no brains. Shit, when you pissed them off, nobody kicked ass the way they did. Gino thought about those big offensive tackles coming his way, fast and big as tanks, the way they hit, the way they couldn't be discouraged, their total lack of fear.

The mayor was no exception, he'd come at them hard and fast and never let up if they killed his daughter. Gino took Sal his drink, waited until he took a sip, then lit a cigar.

"Maybe you ought to sleep on this, Sal," Gino said carefully. "Whacking the girl could really stir things up. Knocking off our own kind from time to time, that's one thing. Killing the girl... "

"Who the fuck asked you!" shouted Sal, banging his fist on

the desk. "I want the cunt dead. Yeah, after you get the dough. Let's see. Make him sweat for a couple of days, then kill her and deliver her head to him, like that fuckin' horse in 'The Godfather.' That'll teach him."

"Sal... "

"Shut the fuck up! I told you what I want, now do as you're told."

"Right, Sal." They drank in silence, Cintenni smiling to himself, enjoying the cigar and brandy.

"I'd better get back to the safe house," said Gino, rising.

"Right. Treat her like the fuckin' princess she thinks she is. Tell her she's going home soon, back to papa. Two days after you get the money, kill her."

"Whatever you say, Sal."

"And remember when you make the first ransom call."

"In about two hours."

"Okay. Now, get outta here."

CHAPTER 33

It was getting late afternoon, almost time to leave. By now, Shannon was convinced that Debbie was inside. The guards were on twelve-hour shifts; four outside, three inside, including one who had come in several hours before.

Gino had appeared one Sunday afternoon to check the guards outside, and Nick zeroed in on the well-dressed man who was obviously too sophisticated to be just one of the boys. Again, his camera had gone to work. He recognized Gino instantly, walking with the slight limp Miss Peabody described. Boutte had come out several times since then, carrying water, beer, and sandwiches. Shannon would need an assault team of at least six. Eight would be better, but at such short notice he would take what he could get. He was sure he knew where he could find the combat-trained men he would need.

A twelve-hour shift was stupid, he thought, checking his watch again for probably the hundredth time. Four hours on, eight hours off would have been ideal, although it would require more manpower in order to keep the guards from becoming slack and careless, their reflexes dulled by boredom and fatigue. It would work to his assault team's advantage.

The long shifts indicated they thought the caper would end

soon; probably within the next twenty-four to forty-eight hours. Shannon would lead his team a little bit before dawn when the guards were the least likely to be alert, just as he and Joe had planned.

He sat back from the window, his Japanese binoculars in his lap. Out on the water sat a bearded fisherman in a skiff, with a small outboard at the stern. He'd appeared about five that morning and had pulled in at least ten good-sized fish, throwing the smaller ones back into the water.

A Louisiana sportsman himself, Shannon may as well have been in the boat beside the other man. Each time the fisherman's line jackknifed violently from a hard strike, Shannon's keen eyes became fixed, his curiosity piqued.

That's a big "red," he thought, as the line cut sharp to the right and ran. Fishing was one of the few things Shannon truly enjoyed. This scene reminded him that he was working too hard, because he hadn't had a fishing line in his hands in almost six months.

Shannon mopped his face with a towel from the upstairs bathroom. In the damp cold of the closed house, he snuggled deep into his jacket. He hadn't dared to light the fireplace, and the room had become icy and dark during the night. He took a sip of beer, which was still cold, threw a handful of peanuts into his mouth, and checked once more through his binoculars. His cell phone rang.

"Shannon," he said.

"Nick, this is Sue."

"Yeah, baby. I was just thinking about you. I miss you."

"Nick, we have to talk. I've been thinking about the ring."

"Can't it wait, honey? I'm on a case."

"No, it can't, Nick," she insisted. "We have to talk. About us."

"All right. I'll stop by later," he said placatingly.

"We need to talk right now!" rebutted Sue.

"Shannon sighed. "All right, Sue. What's up?"

"Your job offer is what's up."

"Job offer?"

"You know what I'm talking about, Nick. The job the mayor offered you last week. Head of security at the new casino."

"How'd you hear about that?"

"That's not important. One hundred thousand dollars a year, plus perks," she said.

"I told him I'd think about it. That's why I haven't said anything."

He watched the guard in the bushes to the left of the house stand and stretch. They were getting careless, as he knew they would.

"What's to think about?" she asked. "It's the opportunity of a lifetime, darling. Between us, we could do so much."

"I'm not sure I want to wear a suit and tie every day. Be anchored to a desk, busting dealers for skimming. Handling rowdy drunks. Sue, I like what I do; we've been through all this before."

"Barely being able to make ends meet? Hanging out with low lifes all the time. You're so talented. Surely you want more than that."

"It's what I do, Sue. You knew that when we met."

He wiped his face with the cold towel again, trying to still his growing disappointment. He loved this woman.

"Nick, I make more money at the hospital than you do." It was true; Sue was director of nursing at the hospital, pulling down more than seventy thousand dollars a year.

"That bothers you?"

"No, but I know it bothers you, Nick," she answered honestly.

"You gonna judge me by the size of my paycheck?"

"Nick, I'll be thirty-three this year. My biological clock is ticking." Her voice softened. "I want to have your babies. I want us to be a family."

"Then let's get married, the way we planned. Whenever you're ready."

"I can't, Nick, not until you come to your senses. Being in love is wonderful, but I've got to think about Kevin, too... And I do love you so much. So much, Nick," she sobbed.

"Sue..."

"I'm a nurse. I see tragedy every single day of my life. Life is so fragile and security is important to me. You've got to take this job, sweetheart!"

"I don't like ultimatums, Sue," he frowned. In the back of his mind he was telling himself that he really did want to be fair to her, to give her what she wanted to be happy. But, he had to be honest with himself, too.

"The hell with what you don't like! Grow up, Nick. You can't always have it your way. Either take that job or forget about marrying me. I mean it, Nick. There won't be any wedding, no matter how I feel about you!"

"Sue..." She'd hung up.

Shannon pressed the end button, then flipped the cover closed. He stood, stretched, and began cleaning up. Carefully wiping every surface he might have touched, he packed the remnants of his lunch, returned the chair to its original place and covered it with the white sheet, closed the drapes, then scanned the room. It looked all right. The owners of the house would notice nothing.

Shannon took a quick shower, replacing the towel on the shower curtain rod where he'd found it. He dressed, took one more careful look around the room, then went downstairs.

He peered out through the slightly open door, slipped outside, then locked the door behind him with his set of lock picks.

He walked back to the Firebird, got in, turned on the heat, then drove away. Shannon slipped an Alabama tape into the dash and began planning his assault on the safe house. He'd leave the cops and the FBI out of it. By the time they got set up, surrounding the house with an army-sized unit, Debbie would be long dead. They had to use a combination of stealth and surprise: hit them as the Cong would hit an outpost on the Mekong Delta. He'd learned a lot out there, and it was time to put his combat training to use one more time.

On the lake, the man who had been fishing raised his anchor, started the motor, and steered his boat slowly away toward the shore.

CHAPTER 34

It was a little bit past three in the afternoon, temperature in the mid sixties, the warming sun still high in the sky. It was the kind of day Al Clark loved, mild winds, a picture-perfect day for being out on his boat. The fact that it was officially his day off and he was still trying to follow up on the church burnings did not bother him at all. But the pace was beginning to take its toll: bags under his red eyes, and being tired all the time. He had not slept past noon in almost ten years, and would not again until the Jammison case was solved.

Like most veteran police officers in any big city, Clark bitched about the long hours, low pay, low morale, and the shit lowlifes he had to deal with day after day after day. For almost twenty-two years he would tell just about anyone who would stand still long enough how much he hated being a cop. It was true, he did, but with Al it was a love-hate thing, because he loved it, too. Being out there, being a cop, bumping a few heads, and hassling assholes. Damn, it felt good, and then there was all the uniform groupie pussy he had copped as a young officer.

Hurriedly reaching into a small paper bag and raising his hand to his mouth, Clark bit down into a warm beignet. With white powdered sugar on his lips and the fingertips of his right hand, he balanced the bag of beignets in the left with a hot cup of coffee. Standing beside the police car, after tossing a second bag of coffee in the back seat, he finished off the tasty snack that just might be supper, too, his sharp eyes on the lookout.

Crossing Decatur Street when the green light flashed on, he headed toward Jackson Square. Daylight quickly fading, the regulars were still out - the mime dressed in a colorful red, white and blue Uncle Sam costume complete with top hat and makeup, the three shoddy black youngsters who tap-danced for tips in front of La Madeline, the tarot card and palm readers, and artists painting everything from colorful caricatures to still life.

Up ahead, Clark could see what he had come for, gutter punks, panhandling and taunting the tourists.

"Hey man," the seedy young punk called to Clark, gleeful smile, orange hair. He was no more than eighteen or nineteen years old, tattoos encircling both arms, bare chested, his lips and nipples pierced, a black studded leather dog collar around his neck.

"How about a buck so I can get my old lady drunk and get laid?" said the teenage crusty punk. Crusty punk was what they called gutter punks who refused to bathe, and this kid definitely had not seen soap or water for some time. "If you got a couple of extra bucks, I just might be able to get you laid, too."

Don't they ever come up with anything original? Clark was thinking to himself. That tired line had been around for years.

"I'm looking for somebody," the detective answered flatly.

"So, everybody's looking for somebody. Do I get the bread or not?"

"I'm looking for a gutter punk, a gothic. I don't know his name. Got a crucifix tattooed over his left ear, spiked hair, black paint job. The whole ball of wax. He might be wearing a cape."

"Fuck you, man," he snapped, his youthful face twisted, filled with indignation. "I don't need nothin'. Fuck you and your dough!" He reached into the pockets of his smelly, dingy, once-blue jeans, pulled out some loose change and a few bills, then threw it all at the detective.

"Here, you need this more than I do. I live off America's waste, man. And there's plenty more where that came from."

The punk was right, and Clark knew it. Tourists were all over the place. Easy pickings, especially during Mardi Gras, drunk, ready to party, maybe even rowdy themselves, especially the ones under thirty and eager to turn the city out.

The truth was that gutter punks were lousy when it came to hustling. Compared to the "home bums," the resident winos and break-dancers, gutter punks were mere amateurs. On a good day, a punk might score a couple of dollars, but that was about it.

Ironically, because they were white, schooled, and generally from good homes, they still felt superior to everyday street hustlers. If cash was really tight, there were always dishwashing jobs, shoplifting, and for some, prostitution.

Instinctively Clark reached out, grabbing the boy by the black collar, pulling him closer.

"Listen up, you little scrungy rat-face motherfucker. I don't give a good goddamn about you or any of your other little pissant friends. And I hate repeating myself, but like I said, I'm looking for somebody. So, have you seen him or not?"

Passersby looked on curiously, but no one interfered. A second punk started toward Clark, turning sharply when the detective's snarling face stopped him dead in his tracks.

"Don't even think about it."

A uniformed police officer mounted on horseback spied the commotion, but seeing that Al Clark, whom he recognized, had everything under control, observed at a distance behind dark sunglasses.

"I don't know nothin'!" the punk squealed, eyes bulging, his face red and flushed with blood.

"I oughtta haul your puny ass in for panhandling."

"Prove it," coughed the punk. "I can do ninety days standing on my head."

"Well, guess what, asshole. Soliciting for prostitution will get you a lot more than ninety days."

Clark relaxed his grip, releasing the boy with a slight nudge. He turned and left Jackson Square, crossed Decatur Street walking past Café Du Monde, stopping to make sure there was still no orange parking ticket on his unmarked car. He walked about one hundred yards past the stone-stepped amphitheater the punks called Hippie Hill, crossing the railroad tracks to the rear.

His hunch was right. There they were, dozens of members of the tribe on the Moonwalk, facing the river. Most of them were "ground scoring," rummaging anything from trash cans to table tops for food that had been left behind, drinking half-full cups of booze or beer picked up along the way. For less than seven dollars, a gutter punk could buy a fifth of cheap vodka and a liter of orange soda.

Tribe was a good name, Clark thought to himself. These kids looked like a bunch of misguided palefaces trying to be new-age Indians. They all looked like psychopaths or sociopaths stoned on shit they can't even pronounce.

A brunette no more than sixteen years old walked up to Clark holding out a yellow balloon animal that looked a little like an elephant. She might have been pretty, he thought, if she had not tried so hard to be hard-looking. Red and blue paint was streaked in her hair, there was a silver ring in her left eyebrow and another one in the left side of her nose.

"Wanna buy a balloon, mister?" a warm smile highlighting her face.

"Yeah, sure, how much?"

"Two dollars. It's only two dollars," she politely answered.

"Give me one of 'em." Clark removed the money from his wallet. "Maybe you can help me. I'm trying to find somebody. A gutter punk."

"Do you know his name?" she asked, still smiling. "His street name, I mean. Everybody's got a name when they're on the road."

"No, I don't know that. But he's a gothic, with a crucifix tattooed on the side of his head over his left ear."

"I don't know any gothics," she answered. "Most of them don't come out until late, and some you don't even see until after dark."

"Do you know where I can find any of them?"

"I think I remember hearing something about some of them living in a squat on Frenchman Street right off North Rampart. Maybe the person you're looking for is there."

"Thank you. Thank you very much," Clark smiled.

CHAPTER 35

Clark cautiously walked into an abandoned two-story house on Frenchman Street, abandoned but not unoccupied, even though a blighted property sign was posted next to the front door. He had had no trouble finding the right building because of the other gutter punks he saw coming and going, squatting in parked cars, and the gothic sleeping in the doorway.

Cautiously he made his way from room to room holding a high-powered Coleman lantern in his left hand. Candles burned in dreary rooms without furniture, white sheets draped over the windows, sleeping bags, pallets, and old mattresses spotted the floor. Occupants, both gutter punks and gothics, looked up at the man with the big flashlight, but some paid little attention. One group sat in a circle smoking and drinking. In another room three young paintheads "huffed" spray paint, inhaling it, getting a buzz, then throwing up. Clark had read somewhere that the latest youth trend in Malaysia was sniffing cow dung to get high. They would find fresh cow droppings, put a large tin can over it, and sniff through it. Thanks to the Internet, it would only be a matter of time before US kids would be trying it, too.

"What's up, dude?" slurred one of the young men, his eyes

rolling in his head, laughing riotously. "Wanna take a huff?" taking the container from the girl next to him and reaching toward the detective, who kept walking.

Usually gutter punks were rebellious and anarchistic, even angry, but not violent. Generally, they were polite, except for the Agros, the aggressive ones who got their kicks scaring the hell out of the tourists. More than a few Agros had been arrested for mugging and Clark, a seasoned veteran, was making sure his right hand was free. Still, he found it hard to believe that kids from good homes could live in squalor like that, sleeping wherever they found a spot to lay their heads.

Ascending the creaky wooden stairs, which were missing spindles and floorboards, he opened the door to the first bedroom. There were more punks, tubing, cooking, shooting and smoking heroin.

Several of the people in the room were already tripping. Others were waiting for their turn to shoot up. Clark quickly unholstered and drew his weapon. Two punks pushed and shoved each other, one yelling to the other that he was trying to kill him. Others were drinking and shooting something directly into their feet, probably because they could not use veins any more. He figured it was crystal meth, the most dangerous drug available, because crystal meth made the user delusional, often thinking everybody was out to kill them. Two of the punks darted toward the door.

"Hold it! I said hold it! Police! Everybody freeze! Nice and easy. Nobody moves until we do a little talking." He had whipped his H&K out and was holding it firmly with a two-handed grip, his eyes flashing as they scanned the room.

"Now, I'm not here to rain on anybody's parade, at least not this time."

"So what's the fuckin' deal, man? If you're not here to bust us, what are you here for? Oh, now I get it. It's the dope. You want our shit, you fuckin' parasite."

"And they claimed they cleaned up the fuckin' police force," laughed another punk.

"I want a man. A gothic, crucifix over his left ear, drives a green convertible Saab."

"And that's it? That's all you want? And you leave us alone?"

"You can go back to your little party."

The punk paused for a second, whispered a few words to someone else, then answered.

"His name's Vamp."

"Vamp. What kind of name is Vamp?"

They all started laughing, then they laughed harder.

"So, where do I find this—this Vamp?"

"Vamp's what you'd call a high roller. Got himself a sugar mama. Saab belongs to her."

"That's still not answering my question," Clark threatened.

"He's been squatting with her in one of those luxury condos in the Warehouse District. That's all I can tell you."

Clark went back down to his car, where he radioed his partner, Burke.

"Yeah, James. Al. I need a favor. I want you to run a make on a 1999 green Saab convertible. I'm looking for a Warehouse District address. Then meet me at the mayor's house."

CHAPTER 36

Shannon parked in front of a large warehouse near the waterfront docks. It was dingy and gray, the windows opaque from years of soot and dirt. He entered a door of bright cardinal red next to the large double doors, and walked into a cacophony of sound: hammering, power saws, automatic hammers, and voices attempting to be heard over the din.

There were several Mardi Gras floats in various stages of readiness, the one closest almost finished. Six women, wearing skimpy bathing suits, struck pompous model poses on a van that was painted purple and gold with green accents. A long fringe of glittering red fell from the platform almost to the ground.

Shannon walked to the tall figure taking pictures and directing the models, and touched him on the shoulder. The man turned and smiled.

"Nicky, Nicky, Nicky. How you doing, man?" They shook hands then embraced. The girls, all in their late teens, watched them stoically.

"Fine, Barry," said Shannon with a big grin. "I see you're doing great, as usual," inclining his head toward the girls, who ranged in color from deep brown to almost lily white. The one thing they had in common were voluptuous bodies —deep chests, large firm buttocks, and gorgeous legs.

"See anything up there you like, cousin?" asked Barry. "Every one's a gofer. Go for anything if you got a few bucks."

Barry looked a lot like James Dean, and he loved it, late twenties, sideburns, hair combed back, and a smile filled with mischief that could melt steel.

They were now all regarding Shannon with some interest. If he knew Barry, perhaps he was a promoter or a talent agent. He looked up into the full wattage of their practiced smiles. One licked her lips seductively; another let her hand trail lightly across her breasts; a third turned and pretended to adjust something on the floor of the platform behind her, offering a clear view of the best-looking rear end on the float.

"That's Sylvia. Knows her best assets, don't she?" said Barry with a laugh. "Want me to introduce you?"

"No, thanks, man. I'm trying a new scene these days."

"What's that?"

"Monogamy," said Shannon. "Haven't had any outside action since Sue and I hooked up." Barry burst out laughing.

"You, being faithful? Bullshit. Man, you score more poontang than I do! Being a hot-shot private dick 'n' all."

"Not any more," Shannon answered, tearing his eyes away from Ms. Rear End, who regarded him over her shoulder with a come-hither look, hands on her ample hips, with a rear end on which you could set a coffee cup.

"This is business, Barry. Anywhere we can talk?"

"Serious business, huh, Nicky?"

"Real serious."

"All right, girls," said Barry, grabbing Sylvia's rear end and squeezing it tight, then slapping it. "Take ten. Come on, Nick."

Shannon followed him to a small office next to the entrance, with waist-high windows. Barry seated himself behind the desk, motioning Shannon to a nearby seat.

"All right," said Barry. "What's so serious?"

"I've found Debbie Jammison. In Lafitte."

"How many got her?"

"I counted eight."

"What kinda shifts the guards on?"

"Twelve hours. This is a tough one."

"When you going in?"

"Tomorrow at dawn. From the water. You with me?"

"Wouldn't miss it for the world. How many in the team?"

"So far, me, you, and Injun Joe Malveaux."

"Joe's a good man. Wouldn't want him mad at me. That sonofabitch is fuckin' crazy. Saw him take on four men by himself one time. Fucked 'em up bad."

"We're using his boat. He fishes in the area every night, so we won't arouse suspicion when we anchor there. We'll all stay below until just before dawn."

"That's a small team to attack eight armed men," said Barry.

"You seen the Robinson brothers?"

"My scuba diving cousins, work on the oil rigs in the Gulf?"

"Right."

"Yeah, they're in town. Want me to bring them in? They'll make a team of five. Much better odds."

"Think they'll go for it?"

"Shit, man, they were Navy SEALS in 'Nam; remember, they love action. Sure, they'll come. Hold on," said Barry.

He lifted the phone and dialed.

Shannon was tired. A good meal and a long, hot soak in the tub, followed by a few hours' sleep, and he would be fine. He motioned to Barry.

"Hold on a minute, Thad," said Barry into the phone. He covered the mouthpiece with his hand.

"Tell them to bring their gear and whatever weapons they'll need."

Barry nodded and spoke into the phone.

Shannon looked through the window. Sylvia smiled broadly, offering a lewd wink. She was definitely a piece of work.

"What about Billy?" asked Barry after he'd hung up.

"Billy!" said Shannon. "Shee-it!"

"I know y'all haven't been on the best of terms since you had that fight, but we can use him. He was a fuckin' sniper in Nam, man. Billy smuggled out a nine millimeter bolt action Mauser, with a twenty-four inch barrel. That mothafucker can hit anything with that piece. And you know he can get help, if we need it."

"I don't know, man."

"For you, fuck, no. For the mayor's kid, maybe. What have you got to lose? For once in your cocky ass life, Nick, swallow your damn pride and ask him. I'm telling you, I think he'd do it if you step to him right."

"Yeah, we could use a sniper to take out the guard on the waterfront side before we go in," said Shannon. He paused, looking at Sylvia again, then said, "All right, I'll ask him. Can't hurt, I guess."

"Good. What time?"

"Meet at my place at eight tonight. That'll give us plenty of time for the briefing, a light meal, maybe a nap before we move out. We meet Injun Joe at four. Let's synchronize our watches. I have six forty-five," said Shannon, checking his timepiece. Barry adjusted his own watch.

"Where you going now?" asked Barry.

"Check out Billy," replied Shannon, still skeptical.

"What was that fight about, anyway?"

"Remember Selma?"

"Yeah. Billy married her."

"He thought I was hitting on her."

"Were you?"

Shannon grinned. "No, but he swore I was."

"That was a helluva fight, Nick. Blood all over the two of you." Shannon fingered a scar on his chin.

"It sure was," said Shannon, remembering. "Sucker's so fast, you couldn't hit him solid."

"Wasn't he a martial arts instructor one time?" asked Barry.

"One of the best. He probably could have killed me with it, too. Somebody asked him about not using karate on me. Know what the sonofabitch said?"

"No."

"Said he didn't need no karate to kick my jive ass. Damn near told the truth, too." They laughed.

"Sylvia was giving you the eye out there, and she don't play. Sure you don't wanna use my back room?"

"Naw, man. I'm being true to Sue. It's hard sometimes," said Shannon with a wince. Barry threw his head back and laughed.

"Man, I never thought I'd see the day you'd turn down a piece of ass. Your dick must be fallin' off or some shit."

"Neither did I," Shannon said wryly. They both laughed until their sides ached.

CHAPTER 37

Billy was seated in front of his restaurant calmly watching his world go by. He truly loved the neighborhood he'd grown up in, although it had been going downhill for years. All of the middle class professionals had moved out years before, as well as most of the skilled workers who had worked the docks and factories.

Most of the people in the neighborhood were young, poor, on welfare, Section 8 or hustling the streets. The old people remained behind tightly closed doors, triple-locked, venturing out only during daylight hours, then returning to the security of their lifetime homes. Their children, safely removed to overpriced condominiums and new houses, seldom visited.

The potential riot had fizzled several hours before. The bars and liquor stores had reopened and the crowd had slowly drifted to their homes.

It was still warm, although the wind was expected to shift to the northwest, bringing in a cold front, and rain.

Billy looked up lazily as Shannon approached his table.

"Mind if I sit down?"

"Yeah," Billy answered. "I do mind."

Shannon sat anyway. Before Billy could react, Selma appeared in the doorway.

"Hello, Nick. How you doing?" She leaned over and kissed Shannon on the cheek as Billy glared.

"I'll bring y'all a pot of coffee. And, Billy, you two done had your fight, so be good. You hear?" Shannon grinned.

"What the fuck you want this time, Shannon?" growled Billy. "I just cut you some slack, didn't I?"

"I need your help, Billy."

"You need my help," he sneered.

"Can't we just let bygones be bygones, Billy?"

"You a sellout punk, like all the rest, split the neighborhood like rats from a sinking ship. "You wear clothes like you buckin' to become a model. You think you the fuckin' Lone Ranger, and you wouldn't even make a good Tonto."

"Tai Eee, kemosabe, motherfucker," said Shannon with a smile.

In spite of himself, Billy had to laugh. Selma returned with a tray laden with coffeepot, mugs and doughnuts.

"Y'all laughin'? That's good. You two make up, now, you hear me? It's been long enough." She turned and went back inside.

"You ever wonder how many kids listening to that show, seeing the television series, ever knew that Tonto means stupid in Spanish?" asked Shannon.

"Latino kids musta known," replied Billy.

"Remember when we were kids playing cowboys and Indians, nobody wanted to be an Indian because they were always losin'!"

"Until we saw the show the convicts put on from Angola prison, where the Indians won, then everybody wanted to be an Indian," said Billy with a smile.

"Native American," Shannon corrected.

"See there, politically correct! You think you're white, nigger. How come Native American is better than Indian?"

"Because they're not Indians."

"They fuckin' ain't 'Americans,' either," said Billy. "Not the way they've been fucked over."

"Have it your way, man," said Shannon.

"Fuck you, Shannon. Don't patronize me."

"Well, man, maybe I'd better go." Shannon started to rise.

"Hold on," said Billy. "I want to know what Superman needs help with. How you change into them faggot tights since everybody's usin' cell phones and they got rid of phone booths?"

Shannon laughed again, imagining Superman looking around the streets in frustration, unable to change from Clark Kent to the Man of Steel in private.

Billy poured the coffee after Nick resumed his seat. Across the street, a man and a woman were engaged in an argument, their lowered voices barely reaching Shannon's ears. The soft murmur of the customers' voices came from inside the restaurant, a Muddy Waters tune coming from the jukebox.

"Heard you smuggled a sniper rifle from the Nam," said Shannon, a smile slowly crossing his face.

"Yeah, nine millimeter Mauser, twenty-four inch barrel, Canon scope. Used it awhile for deer, but it was too easy knockin' down an unsuspecting animal from five hundred yards. Man, they couldn't even smell you if the wind was right. Just there munchin' on somethin' and you'd knock them down like on the firing range. No sport to it. Been using a bow and arrow. You got to stalk, get in close."

Across the street, the man was touching the woman lightly on her arm and she was letting him do it, although she was still angry. They watched him try to gentle her with his hands as you might do with an animal. Her body language was slowly beginning to change although there was still anger in her low voice, soft pleading in his.

"How'd you get busted down to PFC from staff sergeant, Billy?"

"Kicked a West Point Green Beret captain's ass."

"And you didn't wind up in the stockade? How'd that happen?"

"I was assigned to this Green Beret unit as a sniper. All them motherfuckers are gung ho crazy. We'd go out, captain would spot the target, I'd take 'em down. Never less than five hundred yards. I had fourteen kills in less than a year."

"So what happened?" asked Shannon.

"Went out one time after a Cong colonel. Twelve miles deep into the delta, just before the Tet offensive. Got the target in my scope, and the target was a woman! Fine as she could be. I told the captain I hadn't come all that way to shoot a female. He like to went crazy. Crazy any damn way. RA West Point fanatic motherfucker. Gave me a direct order, and when I refused again, the fool swung on me. So, I kicked his ass."

"You got away with that?"

"He'd been heavyweight boxing champ at the Point. Couldn't admit a nigger like me kicked his ass. Besides, I never left a mark on him. Used aikido and jiu jitsu on him. Pressure points, nerve endings, no bruises, no contusions, but man, that shit hurts. Had him crawlin' and cryin' like a baby," said Billy with a chuckle.

Further down the other side of the street, they watched little girls jumping double dutch, the slap of the clothesline in sharp counterpoint to the sound of their dancing feet on the pavement, their high, joyous voices calling the cadence in rhymed couplets.

"I made it on back to base, told them we'd been separated. Captain came in three days later, got lost out there, dumb motherfucker. They knew somethin' had gone wrong, but the captain couldn't say anything without lookin' like a fool. So they busted me on some bullshit and transferred me way out in the boonies. Got my stripes back in less than a year."

"Always wondered what happened."

They watched the girls jumping rope for a while.

"Ever seen white girls jumping double dutch, Shannon?"

"Come to think of it, no. Always one rope."

"Rhythm must be too complicated," said Billy. "Got to count it out sometime. Two ropes, two feet hittin' out the rhythm. Must be about eleven against fourteen."

Billy had been playing congas for years from time to time in Louis Armstrong Park on Rampart Street, formerly known as Congo Square.

"Cut to the chase, Shannon. What the fuck you want?"

"We're going in for Debbie tomorrow morning and we need a marksman," Shannon said finally.

"You know where she is?"

"Yeah. Lafitte, on the bayou in one of those upscale summer homes."

"I will say one thing, man; you good at what you do, even if you are a self-serving punk."

Shannon smiled. "You in, Billy?"

"Yeah, I'm in. Who else you got?"

"Barry Barrett, the Robinson brothers, and Injun Joe Malveaux. He spotted them when they took Debbie in on the night of the snatch. Me, and now you."

"Good men, but five goin' in, Joe givin' us cover from the boat? I don't know. How many we goin' up against?"

"Eight. Four outside on the perimeter, four inside."

"Damn," said Billy. "What kind of shifts?"

"Twelve hours."

"That'll help some," Billy answered, somewhat relieved.

"We come in from the water on Joe's boat. Everybody knows he fishes that bank."

"That's even better."

"If we lose the element of surprise, forget it," said Shannon.

"Know who they are?"

"You were right. Gino's running the show, probably for Sal Cintenni."

"Not good. Gino's no fool. I knew he was in it somehow. I told you Gino never misses the strippers." Billy frowned, sipped his coffee. "When do we go in?"

"Tomorrow morning, just before dawn," said Shannon.

"When do we brief?"

"Tonight, eight sharp," said Shannon.

"Billy refilled their coffee cups. "So run it down for me," said Billy.

Across the street, the man had the woman in his arms, murmuring softly into her ear. She finally put her arms around his neck. They kissed, then walked slowly away, arm in arm, smiling.

Selma sat inside behind the counter smiling to herself, as the two men slowly and reluctantly overcame their differences, two old friends getting it together again.

She then walked outside and joined the two men to bask in their affectionate attention. They had bonded long enough, she thought.

CHAPTER 38

Debbie heard the key turn in the lock. She hurried to the bed, lay down and closed her eyes as Boutte entered.

"Pretendin' to be all asleep won't help, darlin', 'cause I'm gonna fuck you anyway," he drawled, smiling as he locked the door and slowly approached the bed.

Debbie opened her eyes and watched in horror as Boutte unzipped his pants and stroked himself to erection.

"Wait," she said. "You don't have to take it. Just don't hurt me." She stood and began to slowly undress. "I'm a big girl. I've been around the block before. Besides, it's been a long time since I've had a good fuck."

Boutte licked his lips as he watched her sliding her dress over her head. She wore no bra, her firm, heavy breasts needing none. Underneath, she wore a thong bikini of black lace. She slowly slid it down her legs, watching him. She was five seven, one hundred and thirty solid pounds. Strong legs, wide hips, a marvelous hand-sculpted ass. He moved toward her.

"Wait," she said, and lay on the bed on one elbow, the other playing with the thick black bush between her legs.

"I can be so good to you, if you'll just help me," she told Boutte.

Boutte knelt before her, his eyes on her busy left hand, sweat breaking out on his face, mouth open, breathing hard. Debbie removed her hand, and took his balls gently in her left hand, then squeezed as hard as she could. As he threw back his head, she judo chopped him across his Adam's apple with the side of her extended right hand. He rolled off the bed, choking, trying to force air past his bruised throat. Debbie stood over him, raised her foot over his head, and stomped hard. Once, twice, three times, looking at his swollen face and remembering what they had done to Ray.

Terrified and trembling, she took the Walther P-38 automatic from Boutte's shoulder holster, and dressed, except for her high-heeled pumps, took his keys, unlocked the door, locked him inside, then moved slowly down the hallway, gun extended.

Gino entered the living room of the safe house, walked into the kitchen and placed Debbie's food on the table.

"Where's Boutte, Mario?" he said to the short, rat-faced man playing solitaire at the end of the table. Mario motioned with his head toward the door down the hallway.

"He's in there with the kid," said Mario.

"Shit!" said Gino. "Cover me."

He drew his weapon as Mario rose and did the same. Gino slowly opened the door and stared directly into Debbie's wide eyes, only a few feet away. He swung to the side and the gun roared as Debbie squeezed the trigger, firing twice, knocking Mario backwards and killing him instantly. Gino kicked the gun out of her hand when it swung his way and subdued her in a matter of seconds, forcing her, struggling and screaming, back down the hallway.

Holding her in an armlock with one hand, he unlocked the door with the other, pushing her inside.

"Yell all you want," he hollered back, his eyes piercing and filled with rage. "Nobody can hear you out here! Get over in the corner and stay there!"

Holding her covered with his automatic, he grasped the unconscious Boutte by the collar and dragged him roughly from the room, locking the door.

He pulled Boutte into the living room and dropped his body in front of the couch. Four armed men, who had been on guard outside, and Renzo, the man from upstairs, rushed in, guns drawn. Three had Uzis, the fourth a Mac-10 machine pistol, the fifth an M-16 assault rifle.

"It's okay! It's okay!" Gino shouted. "Bitch almost got out. Cajun fuck," he said, kicking Boutte hard in the ribs, causing him to stir slightly. "Check on Mario in the kitchen, Renzo. She shot him and almost got me."

Renzo entered the kitchen, came back hysterical. "He's dead, Gino! He's dead! She killed him! The fuckin' bitch killed my brother, Gino!"

"Okay," Gino answered. "Okay!"

"She killed my brother!" Renzo yelled again, his face filled with hate, tears streaming down his cheeks. Gino slapped Renzo across the face. "Renzo! Renzo! Pull yourself together. We still got a job to do for Sal."

"I'm gonna kill her, Gino!" Renzo shouted. "Let me kill the bitch!"

"You know I can't do that," Gino answered. "Put Mario in the bathtub, cover him with ice cubes from the big freezer, and we'll move him out of here before daybreak."

Hunching his shoulders and spitting as he yelled, Renzo was about to argue more, but the tone of Gino's voice stopped him. Instantly he remembered who he was dealing with. If he pursued his present course, Gino would shoot him, too.

"Right, Gino," said J.D., motioning to one of the men for help. They moved into the kitchen, returned with Mario's limp body between them, and moved toward the nearby bathroom.

"Upstairs," said Gino. They moved slowly upstairs.

Gino turned to the two remaining men. "What time does your relief come on, Renzo?"

"Two hours, Gino," he squeaked, his eyes riveted to the two men carrying his brother's body.

"Call and tell them we need two men to replace you and Mario, then get back to your posts."

"Okay, Gino. Okay," said Renzo, who headed toward the phone in the kitchen, his shoulders drooped, still sniffling.

Gino sat down, gun on his knee, and contemplated whether to kill Boutte or not. Getting rid of two bodies would complicate things, he thought. Also, Boutte, damn his ass, was a combat veteran, the best man he had in case of an assault. Boutte could hold off an army while he got away with Debbie in the speedboat behind the house, if they were raided.

But he's got an ass kicking coming, Gino thought to himself, crossing the room, slipping on a set of brass knuckles and waiting for Boutte to wake up.

Gino picked up the phone and called The Man. He got The Man's voice mail, entered a coded message, and hung up. He was going to enjoy working Boutte over.

CHAPTER 39

The phone rang. Callahan nodded, and Sam picked up the receiver with a sweating hand.

"Yes? This is the mayor speaking."

A strange sounding, disembodied voice responded, "You know what this is about, so I won't repeat myself. We want two million dollars cash, in unmarked small bills. No beepers in the stash, no exploding paint packs. Understand? And no cops or FBI. Try to get cute and your daughter dies."

"How do I know that she's unharmed?"

"Shut the fuck up, because I got a time watch going and in three minutes I stop talking."

The mayor looked toward Callahan, who smiled. His equipment, filling the large van in which they sat, parked behind the mayor's house, winked, blinked, beeped, and whirled. The strange voice came through overhead speakers.

"We'll let you talk to your daughter tomorrow when you get instructions where to drop the stash. Is that clear?"

"Yes," said the mayor. "I understand."

"No funny business, and you get your daughter back unharmed. Otherwise, you get her back in pieces. You'll get another call at noon tomorrow."

"Wait," said the mayor urgently. The caller rang off.

"Electronic voice scrambler," Callahan replied. "No way to get a voice print. But he's seen too many movies. Like I said, the three-minute rule on tracing a call no longer applies."

The mayor started to speak. Callahan held up his hand.

"Get it?" he asked the technician seated at the large console at the end of the van.

"Cellular phone," said the technician.

"What does that mean?" asked the mayor.

"We can't make a fix based on a phone number," replied Callahan. "The call could have come from anywhere in the area—even hundreds of miles away. Don't worry, we're running a satellite fix on the radio signal. We'll have it in a few minutes."

The mayor rose, tried to pace in the limited space, then resumed his seat.

One of the computers lining the wall next to the technician became active. After a few minutes, a printout began to emerge from one of the laser printers. When it stopped, the technician took the paper, glanced at it, then handed it to Callahan.

"What's that?" asked the mayor.

"The map coordinates of the signal's location," replied Callahan somberly. He walked to a large map of the New Orleans area against the back wall of the van, tracing first the longitude, then latitude on the map. His forefinger wound up on a spot in the Gulf of Mexico.

"Got it. They made the call from a boat."

The mayor joined him at the map, and studied it for a moment. He shook his head sadly.

"Afraid not, Agent Callahan," the mayor responded. "That's a prime fishing area. There are at least twenty boats out there about now."

Clark exchanged looks with Callahan. "They've probably

thrown the phone overboard by now," said Clark.

"And Debbie won't be aboard, even if we do luck up on the boat they called from," added Burke.

"Doesn't matter. The location is more evidence that they're probably somewhere in Lafitte. We'll continue the search there," said Callahan.

"My men are still on the job," Clark interrupted. "Doing a house to house from north to south. If she's down there, we'll find her."

"Anything we can do to help?" asked Callahan.

"Don't think so," replied Clark.

"How about a copter to take you to your command post in Lafitte?"

"Thanks, but I've got a stop to make first."

"Gentlemen, finally I'm beginning to think we're on the right track. That we're going to get Debbie back and find out who's behind this."

When Al Clark got outside, Burke walked up to him wearing green army fatigues and a plaid flannel shirt under a down vest, with a floppy weather-beaten fishing hat.

"He found her," Burke said excitedly, keeping his voice low.

"Shannon?"

"Yeah."

"Sure?"

"Pretty sure. Didn't see the girl, but the setup's right."

"Where?"

"Lafitte. He watched them from a house across the street. I checked them out from a fishing skiff offshore."

"How many guarding her?"

"Looks like eight. Four outside, at least three or four inside."

"Where's Shannon?"

"My guess is he's out recruiting a strike team."

"You still got the beeper on his car?"

"Yeah, otherwise he would have lost me twice."

"Still got his apartment staked out?"

"Yeah."

"Let's go, then."

Clark and Burke hurried away through the police cordon.

"We'll wait and see what Shannon's next move is. If he tries to double-cross us, we'll fuck him. Take a ride with me."

CHAPTER 40

Clark and Burke pulled up and parked a few doors away from the mask shop on Royal Street near Esplanade. The green Saab convertible was parked outside. Burke was still wearing his fishing outfit.

"That's his girlfriend's shop, and that's her car. Our man just might be inside, too." Al Clark turned to face his partner, stress obvious in his voice, which was just above whispering "You keep your eyes peeled out here. I'll go in."

When Clark attempted to enter the store, the door was locked. Not to be outdone by a little technicality, he picked the lock and went inside.

The small room was filled with colorful masks of every description, surreal and mysterious in some offbeat way. Nobody was minding the store.

Clark moved toward another door, then slowly turned the knob. He opened it and saw a long room, obviously a workshop, filled with tools and partially completed masks. A light was coming from beneath the door ahead of him, and he could hear what sounded like muffled voices chanting.

Clark drew his gun, then turned the knob, pushing the door open, stunned for a moment by what he saw. Hundreds of candles burned around the room. The carcass of a large dog, probably a black Labrador Retriever, rested on some type of altar, its blood draining into a silver chalice. At least twenty men, women, and children were wearing ritualistic black robes and chanting. A woman wearing a hooded robe and holding a bloody eight-inch hunting knife turned, rage in her eyes, blood on her mouth.

"What the fuck!" Clark mumbled. At that moment, someone rapped him sharply on the back of the head from his blind side, grabbed him from behind, growling ferociously, fangs piercing the side of the detective's neck. Screaming and twisting violently, trying to free himself, he could hazily make out Vamp crashing through a back window.

Hearing the glass break, Burke raced into the building where he found Clark on the floor in the back room fighting for his life. Using the butt end of his gun, Burke struck one man's head, pulling him off Clark. It was then, as he turned, that he saw the woman with the hunting knife about to stab him in the back. Firing once, he shot her right through the heart. He struck the other man fighting Clark, then trained his gun on the room, freezing everyone.

Clark and Burke talked outside as the last of the vampire cult were being loaded into the wagon. Vamp's girlfriend, the high priestess, was dead. Burke was bandaging Clark's neck.

"How do I write this one up? That I was attacked by some fool who wanted my blood?"

"You'd better get that taken care of," Burke cautioned.

"Yeah, a rabies shot. What the hell can somebody get out of drinking blood, or sucking on somebody's neck?"

"It's called Renfield's syndrome. They just like the taste, at least that's what they say. It starts off as auto vampirism, then a little zoophagia—animal blood. After that it's you and me."

"Yeah, I remember reading somewhere that a guy named Haig killed nine of his friends, shot them in the head so he could have cocktails."

"You probably saved my life tonight, Burke. I owe you one. I would have been on that table next. Thanks."

"You're lucky she didn't kiss you," Burke smiled.

"Yeah, yeah," Clark laughed.

"We missed Vamp, but we've got the car. Post a guard around it. I want it dusted and searched from top to bottom. Maybe it will tell us why Vamp is still hanging around."

About half an hour later, Clark and Burke were searching Vamp's girlfriend's luxurious Warehouse District loft. Like her mask shop on Decatur Street, dozens of candles burned in every room.

In a closet of one of the bedrooms, the detectives found men's clothes, all black and neatly arranged. Safely tucked away inside a large, tattered cloth suitcase, they found a scrapbook filled with newspaper clippings, magazine articles, and photographs of Timothy McVeigh, the Oklahoma City bomber. McVeigh was considered America's most notorious terrorist, and the worst mass murderer in U.S. history.

In the bathroom which was part of the bedroom suite, Burke found black lipstick, lip liner, eyeliner, and other makeup.

"Looks like Vamp's got a hero," Clark sighed regretfully, turning to show Burke some photos.

"Yeah, I guess he's one of the nuts who thinks the government made McVeigh do it," Burke added sarcastically. "They've got to blame somebody."

"Yeah, but what kind of hero blows up innocent kids and calls it collateral damage?" Clark found two more things inside the suitcase, a copy of the Anarchist Handbook, which he knew contained bomb making instructions, and an edition of the Turner Diaries.

The massacre at Waco made McVeigh believe that no American gun owner was safe in his own home, that the government was intent on disarming American citizens and making them defenseless.

"One hundred and sixty-eight people died in that explosion. I hope this guy isn't making any plans of his own."

CHAPTER 41

"How's the campaign war chest look, Chauncey?" asked the mayor.

Chauncey Williams III checked his clipboard before answering. "We have a bit more than two million, Chief," he replied. "With another million or so in pledges."

"What do we still owe?"

"The largest outstanding debt is for television advertising in the last campaign, but that can wait awhile. Comes to a bit more than four hundred thousand. Full balance of debts is a bit less than seven hundred thousand dollars."

"Good. I want you to start planning for a fundraising banquet in, say, six weeks from now. But no announcement until we get Debbie back. All right?"

"Right, Chief. I'll just be so glad when she's back home, safe again."

Sam took a sip from his coffee cup and studied Williams carefully over its rim. He wondered if Williams was the source of the inside leak to Cintenni. Closet queens were always a risk because they were open to blackmail in the way that open homosexuals were not, plus there was that little slip Sal had made about a virgin asshole.

The mayor, in the name of equal opportunity, had hired homosexuals and lesbians to solidify the gay vote. In return, his gay staff rewarded him with intense loyalty. Mayor Jammison, a consummate politician, did nothing without his eye on his constituency.

Closet queens were good actors by definition, thought the mayor—an excellent actor himself, who had been successfully putting people on for decades. Williams, for instance, never appeared in public without a good-looking woman on his arm. Takes a phony to know one, the mayor was thinking to himself.

"Has the next press release been prepared, Chauncey?"

"Doreen's working on it now, Chief. Should be ready as soon as I've had a chance to review it."

"Where have you scheduled it?"

"The conference room in City Hall. Six tomorrow, Tuesday morning, so it can make the early morning news in this time zone, the late morning news on the east coast," replied Williams. "The networks have set up a satellite hookup, so you'll be going out live."

"Excellent. Have you prepared an exclusive for Channel 6?"

"Right after the press conference ends," Chauncey told the mayor. He rose and refilled their cups from an antique silver service, a wedding gift from Morrow's parents. He spooned in a teaspoon of honey in the mayor's cup—no cream—and three spoons of sugar and cream into his own cup, unaware that behind his back the mayor was eyeing him suspiciously.

It was not quite seven in the afternoon. They were seated in the mayor's study, with the bank of three television sets going, with the sound off. The television control sat on the mayor's desk in case of something being broadcast on the kidnapping or the police strike. The shows were also being taped on the recorders hidden in the cabinets on which the television sets rested.

"At the risk of being crass, Chief, I believe there will be an outpouring of sympathy regarding the kidnapping that we can take advantage of," said Williams, "once Debbie's back."

Crass is your middle name, motherfucker, thought Sam Jammison to himself. It's one of the reasons I hired your faggot ass.

"I believe we can raise ticket prices for the banquet from seven hundred and fifty dollars a plate to an even one thousand."

Sam pretended to think about it, then said, "Perhaps so. I'll let you know. In the meantime, you can begin organizing the event. No leaks. At this point, we don't want people to think we're trying to cash in on this tragedy."

Right, Chief," said Williams.

Yeah, right, thought Sam. Cintenni should have the news as soon as you get to a phone. By now, the mayor was convinced that Williams was the leak. He was determined to set some kind of a trap for little Chauncey, and once he was sure, Williams would have an untimely accident.

"Anything else?"

I've postponed your appearance with the gay rights delegation for next week. They were very understanding and offered their condolences. Also..."

There was a knock on the door, and Morrow entered. "Sam, I need to see you," she said.

"Hello, Chauncey," she said.

"Mrs. Jammison," Williams replied. They roundly hated one another and were fiercely polite, in a mutually female way.

"Can't it wait, honey? I'm busy right now," said Sam.

"Now, Sam," she said, turned and left the room, closing the door softly behind her.

"Give me a few minutes, Chauncey, I won't be long."

Chauncey rose, and paused at the door. "Don't forget," the

mayor said. "I want to see the draft of the press release and my statement to the media as soon as Doreen's finished."

"Right, Chief," said Williams. "I'll get right on it."

The mayor hated that phony "Chief" label, although he'd never corrected Williams. But Chauncey would be gone soon. He'd replace him with his press secretary Doreen.

Doreen could be trusted, and she always took care of business. She had a long-standing lesbian relationship with a woman who was prominent in media, a serious advantage, and she was completely loyal to Jammison, an even better advantage.

The mayor studied Williams for a long moment. I'm not going to miss you at all, little Chauncey, he thought fancifully, as he turned to leave the room.

Before Williams could close the door behind himself, white city councilman David Greenberger and three of the mayor's creole associates entered brashly, closing it for him.

"Sam, I know this is a bad time," apologized the milky white leader of the delegation, "but we've got to talk. That big black sonofabitch is going too far now. He's trying to squeeze us on that landfill deal. He wants ten percent. That's ten million dollars... For what?"

"Yeah, that sonofabitch has lost his mind."

"David Duke was right," the first man continued.

Sam Jammison, Jr. was visibly upset, his voice loud and ringing through the next room. "Motherfucker," he said. "Give a nigger an inch, he wants the whole yard. Fuckin' black baboon. We set that deal up. What makes him think he deserves jack shit?"

"He's threatening to block the deal," said the third man.

Jammison calmed himself to think.

"Does he have the votes on the council to pull it off?"

"It'll be close," the third man answered. "We know he has three. But the attention is what will kill the deal, whether he has the votes or not."

"Fuckin' nigger," the mayor exclaimed angrily.

Greenberger, the only white man in the room, started chuckling. "You know life's a bitch. You can call Hunter a fuckin' nigger, a black nigger bastard or whatever all day long, and it's no problem. But, if I say it once, I'm a racist."

The mayor moved toward the councilman wearing a devious smile. "You can call him anything you want to, David, as long as you're behind closed doors with friends. It's a black thing." They all laughed.

"He already fucked us at the Convention Center. Take care of it, Victor. Tell him we'll give him what he wants, but this is the last straw. You know what to do."

CHAPTER 42

Morrow was seated in the den in her favorite armchair, with a glass of white wine in one hand, a filter tip cigarette in the other. She seldom smoked, except when angry or upset. Sam was immediately on guard.

Barely speaking above a whisper, she said, "I could hear you shouting, you and your pas-en-blanc wannabees. And you'd better be careful with that 'N' word. Someone just might overhear you. You're calling somebody else crazy. I think you're the ones losing your minds! You're still nothing but a bunch of uppity niggers, except for Greenberger. But then he's one, too, isn't he?"

Samuel Jammison Jr. knew his wife only too well. He had to remain calm and pretend to be interested.

Morrow went on. "At least Hunter is so black and his hair is so kinky that no matter how much he might want to be white, he still couldn't forget who he is."

"And those crooked-ass black preachers you've got in your back pocket with their first ladies... That's a real joke. Been nobodies all their lives, now all of a sudden they are royalty. I've got half a mind to buy a big box of those little plastic crowns and give them out as Christmas gifts... Them too, niggers. All the money they've stolen and all the clothes, the diamonds, the weaves, and the false nails still won't give them education or class. Now if they ever found out how you really felt about them, you could kiss about one hundred thousand votes goodbye. I thought..."

"Morrow, what's gotten into you?" Sam interrupted.

"Thank goodness you're Catholic. We know no preacher will ever see your W-2 form, don't we." She paused, then spoke again. "What happened, Sam? When did it all change? Larry Shannon and your parents would be turning over in their graves if they knew how far you've sunk."

Sam walked to the liquor cabinet, poured himself a cognac, then seated himself across from his wife.

"What's the problem, Morrow? What's really on your mind?"

"I want you to get Debbie back, unharmed," she said evenly, her emerald green eyes riveted to his.

"Honey, we're already doing everything humanly possible. I'm sure..."

"Not we, Sam. You!" she interrupted.

Sam took a sip of brandy before replying. "What do you mean?"

"I mean I'm holding you personally responsible for her safe return." She lit another cigarette from the first, another sign of her anxiety.

Cold bitch, thought Sam. Nevertheless, she looked properly distraught about Debbie when on camera. Otherwise, she was her normal self. It had been years since Sam could strip her of her façade in bed. She had been a screamer when first married, he remembered. Nowadays, she couldn't even come unless she was on top and in charge.

"How much are they asking? Two million dollars," she said, answering her own question. "Peanuts! You know that professionals would demand several times that amount."

"Perhaps they're not professionals, dear," replied Sam.

"Don't patronize me, Sam. I've spoken with Special Agent Callahan, and he's convinced that it's professionals at work. He's puzzled by the small amount too, but I know why they don't want more."

A Bach quartet was coming softly from the stereo speakers, but the mayor could not recognize the composer, though both Debbie and his wife could. He'd never gotten into classical music, although he did a pretty good job of faking it. He much preferred blues, jazz, even zydeco. His secret passion was doo-wop records from the fifties through the sixties: Marvin Gaye, Stevie Wonder, Jerry Butler, the Supremes, the Temptations, Martha and the Vandellas.

Sam took time to light a cigarette of his own, watching her closely as he did so, trying to figure out where this conversation was going. With Morrow, cigars were off limits, except in the confines of Sam's own study.

"What are you driving at, Morrow? There's no hidden agenda here."

"The heil there isn't! Do you think that I'm a complete fool because I play the role of the dutiful political wife? Whatever they want, I want you to give them! I fucking mean it."

Morrow almost never cursed unless she was extremely angry, except in the early days during some of their heated sexual bouts. At the top of her voice, she would yell, "Fuck me, Sam! Fuck me! Oh, shit. Fuck me hard!" The next day Sam would be too embarrassed to go outside, wondering what the neighbors were thinking and saying. Morrow would simply smile, say good morning, and get into the car as if nothing had happened.

"They?" asked Sam.

"Yes, they! Whoever they are. Give in on the police strike. Drop your plans to run for a third term. Peddle your ass, as you have already. Whatever it takes, Sam, and I'm not asking. Get Debbie back!"

"I don't know what you're getting at, Morrow."

"Save the innocent act for the voters, dear," said Morrow caustically. "I'm your wife, remember. I know you inside and out. Mayor Sam Jammison, 'man of the people'. Civil rights hero. Bullshit! You didn't get involved in the movement until you realized it could further your political ambitions. Then you cut your precious long curly hair and tried to grow an afro. How long did you last doing voter registration in Mississippi?"

"They needed my legal skills in Washington," Sam answered indignantly.

"Don't make me laugh. You scurried back to Washington the day after one of your team got killed. You never went back into the field. You never run from a fight. You never run to one, either. And the Rampart Street War, you had no choice."

She rose and strode to the liquor cabinet in that regal way she had, and poured herself another glass of wine.

"Everything you've done since choosing me as your trophy wife has been with an eye on what's best for you, Samuel Jammison. Everything!"

"I loved you," Sam protested.

"Nonsense! You just wanted a high yella, straight-hair wife like your mother to look good on your arm, to validate you. Your mother and Debbie are the only two women you've ever really loved. The rest of us are just whores and bitches, there to be used."

"Morrow, what's gotten into you?"

"My mother warned me about you. Said you were a narcissistic mama's boy who could never truly love another woman. She told me I should have married Conrad."

Sam laughed. "That little ugly black nigger?"

"Like I said. I wonder how many of your voters would

admire you if they really knew how you felt about them. You even held your father in contempt because he was dark-skinned and a nobody, by your standards. Told everyone at Howard Law School that he was an 'entrepreneur' when he was breaking his back keeping you in Brooks Brother's clothes, and that convertible you drove. You tried to figure every way you could to keep him from your graduation."

She walked to the window and looked out toward the swimming pool, but the FBI communications van blocked her view.

"That's a lie, and you know it!" uttered Sam furiously.

"Really?" Morrow smirked. "Tell me, Mr. Mayor, when did you ever openly date a woman who couldn't pass a paper bag or the comb test? If she was darker than the bag and a comb wouldn't glide through her hair, there was no way you'd be seen with her in public. Oh, you don't mind sneaking a little dark-skin, back-door pussy on the side from time to time. You know, 'the blacker the berry, the sweeter the juice'. But you keep the sweet juice carefully hidden on the back shelf. It wouldn't surprise me, not one bit, if you didn't have a little white sugar stashed on the side, too."

"You got your damn nerve, Morrow! If that's the way you felt, then why didn't you marry little black Conrad?"

"I should have. My mother urged me to. She said that men like you were all pampered and spoiled, too into themselves to ever truly love anybody else. I asked her: 'What about my children?' If I married Conrad, what would they look like? Do you know what she did?"

"No, what?" he answered, looking down at his hand as he rubbed the arm of the chair.

"Slapped the shit out of me. The only time in my life she ever struck me. But she made me realize that I was color-struck, too."

"So why did you marry me, then?" said Sam evenly.

"I couldn't marry anybody Conrad's complexion, could I? It

took me years to realize that when my mother talked about red men, she was not only describing you, but my father as well: a discreet and highly successful womanizer. Just like you."

Morrow had gotten over being color-struck during the heady days of the civil rights movement; about the only time when dark-skinned blacks had come into their own. 'Black is beautiful' was the motto, and even the jungle-fever white liberal women would pass over Sam, much to his chagrin, for an African-looking brother wearing a dashiki and a big bush.

Morrow remembered those chocolate, slim-limbed brothers she'd had on the sneak while Sam was out chasing white pussy. She would arrange a mirror so that she could see their muscular dark buttocks flexing between her creamy thighs. She felt herself growing weak thinking about them.

She thought about third grade at Corpus Christi when a little black boy wanted to play with her. Her creole playmates immediately rushed and told her, "You can't talk to him, he's too ugly."

"Are you saying that I don't love Debbie?" Sam protested as he poured himself another drink, this time a good stiff Jack Daniels.

"Oh, no. Your love for Debbie is one of your few redeeming qualities. Thank God for her that she inherited your mother's creole coloring. If she'd come out your father's color..."

"Morrow, I've heard enough!" said Sam in his most authoritative voice.

The CD player had switched to another disk, a symphony that Sam could not recognize. Beethoven, Mozart? But he couldn't care less. It was one of the reasons he kept the 'Ice Queen' around. Cold bitch couldn't even give good head, but she was marvelous at social gatherings and political rallies. Her parents' money in that fancy finishing school in Paris had not been wasted. Her French was impeccable, as was her knowledge of classical music, opera, fine wines, and gourmet food. She was right about one thing, she did make a fine trophy wife.

Morrow walked to her chair, sat and crossed her elegant legs, and took a sip of wine, a look of defiance on her beautiful face.

Why, wondered Sam, was standing the power position for men, but the opposite for women? He could usually win any argument with his wife, but tonight she had him on the run. Had she been faking him out all these years? He took a deep swallow of his drink, welcoming the burning sensation as it moved down his throat.

"All right, Sam," she said sweetly. "Let me leave you with this final word. If Debbie comes back harmed in any way, then you'd better not fall asleep in my bed, you sonofabitch! Now, go on back to being the damn mayor. Get the hell out of my sight!"

Sam stared at her for a long moment, as if seeing her for the first time. She returned his gaze with a cat-like smile that never reached her eyes.

He stood outside her closed door, finished his drink, and one by one, wiped his sweaty palms on his trousers. He walked back down the hall to his study, then closed the door. He crossed the floor to the bar, poured himself another drink, then quickly gulped it down. He was more than a little bit confused. Until Debbie's kidnapping and Morrow's comment about Larry Shannon turning over in his grave, he hadn't even thought about him in months.

He nodded, solemnly thinking to himself, "she's right." Larry really would have been turning over in his grave if he knew some of the treacherous things he had done and how far he had gone astray. So would his mother and father. All the people who had ever meant anything to him were sincere, hard-working, decent human beings.

What was it that had changed him and when did it happen? He didn't start out trying to selfishly get all he could get. In the beginning, no matter what Morrow thought, he really did want to do a good job. Maybe he wasn't perfect, but he wasn't a crook either.

It had just happened slowly. All the attention, the under-the-table deals, a few thousand dollars here and there, until there was never enough. Because of their lavish lifestyle, like any doctor or lawyer, they were living above their means. He had been swept from being able to live comfortably on fifty thousand dollars a year to actually needing more than one hundred and fifty thousand. And of course he had to make sure he would always live that way because he could never go back to doing without again, or being a nobody.

And this business with Morrow and little black Conrad. Had she secretly been sneaking around behind his back fucking darkies with long, black dicks?

CHAPTER 43

Nick Shannon had just arrived at his office, after stopping to buy a newspaper and picking up his mail. He sat at his desk, glancing from time to time at a five-by-seven photograph of Sue and Kevin, wondering if he should call her. Sure, he was a little rough around the edges, and yes, a family would mean more responsibility, but he still wasn't sure he was ready for a steady job. And suppose Sam really was dirty.

Why did he have to make the first move, Shannon thought. If Sue loved him as much as she said she did, why couldn't she call him? Why were men and women always playing power games with each other, and why did women always think that the man was the one who needed to change?

Shannon picked up the remote control and clicked on the nineteen-inch color television set mounted in the corner. Slot machines in the background, uniformed officers were leading an average-looking, forty-year-old white male away in handcuffs. Dale Warren, an attractive brunette, was interviewing another officer.

"As you can see, police officers have just made an arrest in what they hope will bring to an end a spree of robberies and murders in the area. The suspect, Romalis Charles, is suspected of having committed as many as five murders to support his gambling addiction. Ironically, Charles had just picked up a check for winnings totaling twenty-one thousand dollars. Joining us is Lieutenant Martin Stringer, information officer for the New Orleans Police Department. Lieutenant, I suppose the police department can breathe a sigh of relief now that you have the suspect in custody?" Miss Warren asked.

"Well, yes and no, Dale. We've apprehended one, but there are others out there following in his footsteps, obsessed with gambling, housewives becoming prostitutes, and yes, even murder."

"That's right," the reporter added. "Sandra Grimes shot her parents to death to feed her video poker habit, and Barbara Ballard left a three-year-old that she was babysitting in a scorching car for five hours while she played the tables."

"And that's just the tip of the iceberg," the officer continued. "To keep her husband from finding out that she had lost thousands of dollars playing blackjack, another woman reported that she had been robbed by two men at gunpoint, and on and on and on. We've got eleven-year-old kids, fifth and sixth graders, skipping class to gamble away their lunch money. There's a tremendous amount of denial. People really don't want to see it as a problem."

"Money really does make people do some crazy things." That was what Nick Shannon was thinking as he listened.

Suddenly his eyes caught the bold black heading on the front page of the Times Picayune.

"MAYOR'S DAUGHTER MISSING - RACIAL TENSION BUILDS." Further down the page, another article was headed "SECOND BLACK CHURCH BURNS."

Shannon picked up the telephone, continuing to read as he dialed.

"Yeah, ah, Chet Henry in the crime lab, please."

The connection was made by the operator.

"Chet Henry, police lab."

"Hello, Chet. Nick Shannon."

"Hey, how are you, Nick? How is everything?"

"Not too bad," Shannon answered, propping his feet on his desk as he continued reading the article. "Anything on the Jammison case?"

"No, sorry, Nick. Nothing. But you'd better watch your back. Detective Clark wants this case and I think you're in the way."

"Yeah, I know," sighed Shannon, frustration on his face. "We've been down that road. Thanks anyway, Chet. I'll keep in touch."

Shannon hung up, picked up the Federal Express envelope that was with his mail, tore it open and removed several newspaper clippings. He quickly read, studying the photographs carefully, then folded the articles and tucked them back into the folder. He left the office and drove downtown to Sherif's headquarters on St. Bernard Avenue in the Seventh Ward, the core of the black creole community.

Half the people in the Seventh Ward still looked white, with names like Desdunes, Carriere, St. Julien, and Gonzales. It was Nick Shannon's old neighborhood, too. He had gone to church at Corpus Christi, the largest black Catholic Parish in America, and graduated from St. Augustine High School, a Catholic school for black males.

Sherif was speaking to a group of young people when Shannon entered the room.

"There's an old adage that you may have heard your parents use," said Sherif. "To thine own self be true. Another way of putting it is, know who you are. If you don't, the odds are stacked against you from the start. You also need to know who your enemies are."

"Do you really think there's a conspiracy to destroy black people?" asked one boy, about fourteen years old.

"Thomas Jefferson once said that nothing in politics happens by accident. If it happened, it was planned that way. President Jefferson was a very wise man. He also believed that we should tear the government down every fifty years and started over again. Term limits. We're in the twenty-first century, and every day we're hearing more and more about globalization and the New World Order instead of democracy. Figure it out for yourselves. By two thousand ten, one-third of the people in the United States are going to be people of color. The hispanic population in California, Texas and Florida is already growing like crazy. By two thousand fifty, the majority in America will be non-white, and we're running out of natural resources. In order to survive, you young people are going to have to be prepared. That's the bottom line."

"Why is it that black people are always the ones on the bottom?" asked the boy. "Do you think my generation has any chance?"

"That depends," Sherif answered. "It depends on whether we get our act together or not, and I do mean together. Take gun control legislation, for example. If your parents give up their guns, legally registered of course, how can they protect themselves or defend their property? Every day in this country five hundred farmers lose their farms. They're foreclosed on. That means that not only does the farmer lose his business, he loses his home, too, because farmers live where? On their farms. Without a means to fairly defend themselves, if somebody wanted to steal their land or their animals, what could they do?

"What about Ron Brown's plane crash? Do you think that was an accident? Black people have been down so long, most of them don't even know which end is up. I don't blame white people for that. We've got to handle our own business. That's why we're here. White people, who understand that each day we're losing more of the rights, guaranteed by the Constitution, they have different militia organizations. We have the Posse, a pro-active way to take care of our own problems."

"But why are we so far behind everybody else?" asked the same youngster. "Even the Vietnamese."

"Because we don't know our own history, for one thing," Sherif answered. "Because we don't read. You know what they say," he continued. "If you want to hide something from a black person, put it in a book. And when we do take the time to think, we think about the wrong thing. Everybody's dressed up to go to church and show how much money they can put in the collection plate but nobody knows where the library is."

Sherif paused, taking a sip of water from the pitcher on his desk. Shannon noticed that three of Sherif's favorite books were still there, between two sculptured wooden bookends: "The Miseducation of the Negro" by Carter G. Woodson, "The Isis Paper" by Dr. Frances Cress Welsing, and "In Search of Goodpussy" by Don Spears.

"It's all about population control," he continued. "Before you know it, we're going to have too many people and not enough resources. That's what this is all about."

Sherif's eyes panned the room. Every eye was glued to him. These young people wanted to hear the truth because their future depended on it and they knew it. If only the adults were as wise, he thought.

"In 1712, a slave holder named Willie Lynch, that's where the term lynching came from, you know," he continued, "like lynching niggers... Well, anyway, he came up with a blueprint for maintaining a slave. He told the other plantation owners to turn the old slaves against the young ones, the light ones against the dark ones, turn the black woman against the black man and the black man

against the black woman. Willie Lynch told them that if they did what he said, they could control their slaves for three hundred years or more. We're too dumb to realize if we don't make it together, we won't make it at all. Mr. Lynch was right." Sherif picked up the books on his desk. "Remember what these three books say. Know your history. Know who you are. And think for yourself."
"Because we've got to do what?"
"Kick butt," the group said in unison, smiling.
"Why?" asked Sherif.
"Because this is real life and not make-believe."
"And..."
"And We're Playing For Keeps!" they all yelled together.
"That'll be all for today," Sherif told them. "Be safe, and I'll see you next week."

Nick Shannon was impressed. Sherif really had a way about him, but why shouldn't he? He was a product of the streets: pimp, hustler, former drug dealer. He had even done some time in Angola Prison. Now Sherif was a Muslim, a self-made man, and like Malcolm X, he was trying to make a difference.

"Nick Shannon," said Sherif, "it's not often that the mountain comes to Mohammed. I could guess, of course, but why don't you just tell me why we've been honored with a visit from someone as illustrious as you."

"All work and no play. You know the drill," said Shannon.

Shannon hesitated, the two men eyeing each other with mutual respect.

"You know what's happened to the mayor's daughter. I need your help."

"Thought you'd never ask," said Sherif confidently, with a smile. "Like I was telling the kids, nothing in politics happens by accident... Nothing," Sherif repeated. "This city is coming back, and there's a helluva lot of cash being passed around. And just like the days of Reconstruction after the Civil War, history is repeating itself. Those half-white creoles are stealing everything that ain't nailed down. Them and the preachers. Damn near every black man you see riding around in a new Benz, or a new Lexus is either a pimp, a dope pusher, a politician or a preacher. Churches on every corner. Thought about one myself, but the idea of burning in hell scares the shit outta me. Honest black man ain't got a chance. That's the trouble with this city now. No new blood.... Personally, I think the mayor knew who kidnapped his daughter all along. Can't prove it."

Just then one of Sherif's club members entered with two strangely dressed characters, one wearing a curly blonde wig and a red spandex dress at least three sizes too small. The other was a short, bald man who was obviously gay, wearing tight black leather pants and a silver studded black leather jacket with a matching leather shoulder bag. Actually, the woman wasn't too bad, Shannon thought, if she would just do something with her hair and take off a few layers of that thick makeup.

"Peaches, Julius. What's up?" asked Sherif, smiling, relaxed, unlike his usual combat mode.

"Now you know what's up, Sherif, cutie. And if it ain't up, Peaches can sho' nuf' get it up," pouted the woman with a lewd smile. Peaches had a lot to say with her eyes as they slowly roamed over Nick Shannon.

"Well, well, well. What have we here, and where have you been all my life, sweetness?" she said, grabbing Shannon's hand, then caressing it with her own hand. "You must be the man who's been asking all the questions. We've been looking for you."

Sherif was about to crack his sides laughing, but somehow managed to hold it in.

"Nick Shannon, say hello to the lovely Peaches," said Sherif with a wave of his hand, as if he were presenting royalty, "and this is Julius," his eyes moving toward the plump little man.

"Isn't this a pleasant surprise?" said Peaches. "He looks like loads of fun."

Julius still hadn't said anything, Peaches was doing all the talking. Peaches was good, but Shannon had already made her, or rather him, for what he was. Imagine some guy ready to lay him and getting all the way to the hotel, Shannon mused.

"Lay off, Peaches," said Sherif, coming to Shannon's defense, a sly grin on his face. "I don't think you're his type."

"Can't win 'em all," snapped Peaches, "but never say never," she smiled, giving Julius the high-five.

Peaches was confident, but so was Shannon. He was very sure he would never find himself in bed with anybody else with as much hair on his chest—or on his behind—as he had on his. But he had to admit, some of the women on Bourbon Street could fool anybody, and many of the men who had been tricked probably felt the same way.

"What a waste," replied Julius faggishly, giving Shannon the eye.

He would not admit it, but Nick Shannon was actually amused. If you've got it, you've got it, he thought. There was no getting around it. If they didn't like what they saw, he would have been disappointed. Well, less complimented, at least.

Looking at Peaches and Julius, Shannon thought about all the theories people had about men and women who were gay. Were these two born that way, or was it their choice? How could anybody choose to look like that? And how about Butch? What was her story? When she said that she loved pussy too much, Nick knew she wasn't lying. Butch really did love pussy, and tits, and ass, and everything else about women.

"Do you believe that some men make better mistresses and lovers than some women?" It was more a statement than a question.

"I'd like to hear you answer that one myself," Sherif told Shannon, smiling, instigating.

"I hadn't really given it any thought," Shannon answered, thinking that he wouldn't touch a question like that for all the tea in China.

"We don't have to play the silly little games you so-called 'straight people' play," said Julius fastidiously. "When I want to control somebody, I just break out the whip and chains. I let it all hang out."

"Speaking of hanging out," said Sherif, "you still haven't told us why you're here."

"It's about the mayor's daughter, Debbie. We want to help out."

"How's that, Peaches?" asked Sherif.

Shannon's curiosity was instantly aroused. What did Peaches and Julius know? What were they about to say? All the leads he had tried to run down, nothing. Now, his best lead might be coming from two flaming fairies.

"This girlfriend of mine, Stephanie, has been, shall we say, providing certain services for a real creep. Says he's been shooting off his mouth about how much money he's going to have after he finishes this little job."

"A real freak," Julius interrupted.

"Sam Jammison's all right in my book," Peaches added. "This young cop busted me one night for soliciting. The bully busted my lip, too. Well, the mayor heard about it before they booked me. Gave him two choices: fill out a report and lock me up, including his improper use of force, or let me go. Like I said, we want to help."

CHAPTER 44

Shannon stood flat against the wall beside the door, motionless, his gun raised to his shoulder, while Peaches waited quietly down the hall. Sherif was standing to the other side anxiously holding a .38. Julius knocked softly.

"Who's there?" said a woman's voice from the other side of the door.

"It's me, Julius. Open up."

They heard footsteps, then a lock clicking. When the door opened, Sherif grabbed the woman as Shannon bolted forward, carefully fanning the room with his gun, then checked the bathroom.

"Where is he?" asked Sherif, still holding the woman who was trying to free herself.

"There's nobody here!" she shouted. "Let me go!"

"She's right," said Shannon, sliding his revolver back into his holster. Sherif did likewise after releasing the angry woman. "There's nobody here."

"Where is he?" asked Shannon, disgusted, his breathing heavy because of the rush.

"Where is who?" the woman whined. "I don't know what you're talkin' about. And who the hell do you think you are anyway, breakin' in here like this? What the fuck is up with this, Julius?"

"Your john, the one bragging about all the money he's gonna have. That's who we want," Julius answered.

"I don't know nothin' about nobody with no money," she snarled. "So all of you can just turn around and get the fuck out of my apartment before I call the police."

"Stephanie, a young woman's life is at stake, for god's sake."

"One minute, that's all I'm givin' you," she growled repulsively, as if she hated their guts for exercising bad taste in bothering her.

Shannon knew the type. He didn't see the pipe, but he could still smell the crack. The woman was on the edge, probably anxious for them to leave so she could light up again.

The four left the apartment, stopping downstairs to talk.

"She's lying," Shannon told the others. "She knows something."

"I'll send somebody back to keep an eye on her," Sherif said.

They had driven two blocks in Sherif's van when Shannon spotted the red pickup. They turned around and raced back to the apartment building. Nick jumped out.

When Shannon reached the top of the stairs he heard a woman screaming and what sounded like someone being knocked around. The noise was coming from the apartment they had just left.

Busting the door in, Nick found a large man wearing a cowboy hat and a pair of snakeskin boots, brutally beating the hooker with his fist. It was Boutte, and he looked even worse now than he had at the safe house.

"Freeze, or I'll send your ass straight to hell," said Shannon evenly, his gun held comfortably like an old friend, with a tight two-handed grip.

Boutte lunged forward anyway, and in the same instant blood gushed from his mouth where the barrel of Nick's gun slammed against his face.

"Don't fuck with me!" Nick shouted. "I'm not here to play games with you. I want some answers and I want them now."

Boutte seemed more irritated than anything else as he raised his arm, using his shirtsleeve to wipe away the blood, spitting some of it on the floor. They missed him the first time because he had ducked into another apartment. One of his lookouts, a twelve year old boy, had alerted him the minute Sherif's van had pulled up.

"Up yours, mothafucka," said Boutte coolly. "You want fuckin' answers, talk to Ann Landers. I ain't got nothing to say."

Nick's fist slammed into Boutte's stomach. Curled up on the floor and wincing with pain, Shannon's blow had done little to soften him.

"I don't think this is going to get us anywhere," Sherif told Shannon, standing in the doorway.

Peaches and Julius were busy trying to help the woman.

"What about your place, Sherif?" asked Nick. "We've got to get him somewhere where we can work on him. We can't stay here all night."

"We'll take real good care of him," Sherif answered, a mischievous smile framing his face.

Shannon reached down and grabbed Boutte by the collar.

"Come on. Get up. Get up!" Fighting and kicking, his hands held in place behind his back by a nickel-plated pair of police handcuffs, Boutte continued to struggle as he was partially thrown down a rear stairway and hurled into Sherif's van.

CHAPTER 45

They were still trying to get answers from Boutte. The little room in the back of Sherif's headquarters was painted brown, and clean like the rest of the building. There was only one thing: it had no heat, and Shannon was cold even with his jacket zipped up. The walls were bare, except for a plaque with an inscription that read ...AMERICA... OUR COUNTRY, RIGHT OR WRONG. WHEN RIGHT TO BE KEPT RIGHT. WHEN WRONG TO BE PUT RIGHT.

Shannon knew Sherif, but they had never really been much more than polite acquaintances. Sherif was like the head of some giant corporation, omnipotent and incorruptible.

Shannon looked up at the plaque again, remembering a documentary he had seen about the Nazis exterminating the Jews. He remembered the gas chambers Hitler used, hills of human remains, the heads on one pile, the bodies on another, and mountains of hair, stacked, to be used as clothes.

He had known so-called activists before, some out to help the cause, most of them out to help themselves. He could see that Sherif was dedicated, that he wanted to make sure black people in this country didn't get shafted again.

Don't worry about your friend," smiled Sherif, taking

Shannon's attention away from the plaque. "We'll treat him just like one of the family. Before you know it, we'll be talking about old times... Still think the girl's all right?"

"Probably," Nick answered. "But Boutte's not the sharpest knife in the drawer."

The Cajun was too confident, like he had an ace up his sleeve. The only logical explanation was that Debbie was still alive and he thought that he still had something to bargain with. Shannon had Boutte and the kidnappers had Debbie, but the advantage was theirs because the kidnappers didn't know Boutte was missing. They had to make him talk and time was running out.

A round-faced clock on Sherif's desk ticked away the minutes, but Boutte remained mean-spirited and tight-lipped.

Tip, one of Sherif's men, rushed in and whispered something in his ear. Sherif's eyes flashed, and springing to his feet, he rattled off orders to his anguished comrade.

"Get everybody downtown."

Sherif turned to Nick, troubled but decisive.

"Well, it finally happened. Two young punks tried to knock over Abe's liquor store and got busted."

From a locked compartment in his desk, Sherif took out a magnum .45.

"Seems that Tyke was around and finally got what he wanted. I'll leave a couple of men behind to keep working on our friend."

They all left the building together, but Sherif was picked up at the curb by a van loaded with young black men, a conspicuous blue light flashing on the dash.

The dark sky was now a brilliant orange, fires springing up everywhere, mostly from automobiles that were being burned. Sirens screamed and wailed as the fire department, police department and emergency services tried to move in.

A few blocks away, Sue had not yet made it home, eager to check on Kevin, who was at a classmate's house after school. She had been forced to follow the main streets because of the destruction and chaos on side streets. Traffic had virtually come to a standstill because the looting was so out of control that people flooded the streets, darting wildly in the path of oncoming cars.

She sat in her red 5.0 Mustang ready to move at the first sign of a break, her hands firmly gripping the steering wheel and the stick shift, her eyes alert, registering any activity. People were running by the car with sticks, bricks, pipes, and some were carrying guns. Sue extinguished her headlights and killed her motor, trying to be less conspicuous. The car was not even a week old and still had the window sticker on it.

Sue had served as a nurse during the Persian Gulf War, but as she sat listening to the upheaval, the wailing sirens, and the screams, she remembered that it was nothing like this.

When the traffic started to move again, she noticed that some of the cars had been abandoned, and that she was pretty well blocked in. Sue also saw that a group of young thugs had moved in and were vandalizing cars and antagonizing drivers.

Three men pulled an elderly couple from a new Saturn, beating them with their fists and kicking them. They broke the windows, smashing them with bricks, scratched the car with metal pipes, then jumped up and down, running on the hood and top.

Next to it was a burgundy colored mini-van with a middle-aged white woman behind the steering wheel. She screamed hysterically when two men shattered the window on the driver's side, raised the lock, opened the door, and forced their way in, then dragged her from the front seat to the back of the car. Her cries were drowned out as they pulled her down and out of sight.

By now, Sue was seriously beginning to worry, but she kept a cool head. She reached into the glove compartment, removed a nickel-plated revolver, and placed it on the seat beside her. She could still take care of herself and she knew it. She remembered that was one of the things Nick loved most about her, but she was really getting scared. She was trapped. If she got out of the car, she would have to take her chances on foot. If she stayed there, the rabble would eventually see her.

The traffic moved slowly but she was still blocked in by an abandoned Monte Carlo in front of her and a Ford pickup truck to her left. Two men were standing by the front fender, but luckily they were looking the other way. They turned when the driver behind her started honking his horn, cursing and yelling for her to move, but there was nowhere to go. She was still boxed in.

The two men approached the car, faintly seeing her pretty face through the tinted windshield. They walked past her to the car in back. In her rearview mirror, Sue could see them having words with the other driver, then one of the men hit him across the face with a gun and the man slumped in his seat. The two men had that look in their eyes when they started walking back toward her car, like they had the same thing on their minds, and she unfortunately was it.

Sue put her hand on the gun, then quickly moved it to the key. She turned it, bringing the motor back to life, then slammed the shifter into reverse. She couldn't go forward, she couldn't go to the left, and there was still a car behind her. All there was was a narrow sidewalk on her right, but she would have to settle for that.

The tires smoked as she stomped down on the accelerator and skidded backward, smashing into the other car. The way the two men were trying to get out of the way, she was sure they were thinking 'this bitch must be crazy!' Cutting hard to the right, Sue screeched forward for two feet, but still not enough to be clear. Back to reverse again, cutting hard to the left, then a sharp right and onto the sidewalk, jumping the curb. Hitting some debris and a lamp post, she spun around the Monte Carlo in front, banged the rear quarter panel of her spotless Mustang and lost the rear rubber bumper, but she was clear. Sue maneuvered through the confusion, driving over bricks and broken glass, and watched the two men grow dim in her mirror.

* * *

The mayor's telephone rang at 8:00 p.m. sharp. The FBI electronic audio surveillance equipment clicked on once more. Because of the terror and maddening confusion surrounding the riot, communications had come to a grinding halt. The mayor's telephone had been ringing off the hook all evening, and after pushing most of the furniture back against the wall, a mini command center was set up in the den for Sam Jammison's staff. The FBI had become part of the communications center.

The police superintendent, Chief Taylor, was in charge, with all of the other departments answering directly to him. Overwhelmed, the chief's staff held down the conference room at police headquarters and relayed incoming information to him. The mayor had left the house briefly with Chief Taylor and Officer Boyd, his bodyguard, in a National Guard helicopter to personally survey the chaos for himself.

The men in the mayor's study were alert even though they had previously been told that the next call would be made on Tuesday at noon. Agent Callahan raised his hand to silence everyone in the room.

"Jammison," the mayor answered anxiously, tension in his voice, after snatching the receiver up from its cradle. "Hello... hello."

"This is it, Mr. Mayor," croacked the voice at the other end of the line. "There's been a change of plans. You're to put the money into a suitcase, I'm sure you have a good one around somewhere, then put the suitcase into two extra strength trash bags, and tape them. Your wife is to..."

"My wife!" the mayor frowned, rising to his feet behind the huge desk and making eye contact with the others around the room. "You must be out of your mind. We're in the middle of an emergency. I can't send my wife out there!"

"You're wasting valuable time," the voice continued deliberately. "Mrs. Jammison is to come alone. She's to take Carrollton Avenue to Wisner Boulevard, then turn right at Robert E. Lee. When she gets to the top of the Judge Seiber Bridge she stops the car, walks to the rail, and drops the bag over the side. She gets back into the car and drives away. And again, let me remind you... No tricks. You've got twenty-five minutes, starting now."

"How do I know my wife won't be..." Jammison started, but the caller had hung up.

Quickly, one of the agents rounded up Morrow, who was upstairs in her bedroom watching a newscast. Callahan and the others hustled the money, which was already in the suitcase, into the trash bags, then tied and taped them. The agents had suspected that the ransom might be moved up because of the chaos, but still, there was little that they could do in twenty-five minutes without jeopardizing the mayor's daughter, and now his wife.

Agent Callahan loaded the trash bag into Morrow's silver Lexus as Sam Jammison gave his wife a tight hug. She slid behind the wheel and started the engine as he slammed the door shut and stepped back. Sam and Morrow made eye contact one last time and she drove off.

On the other side of the action, Sherif and his men were trying to help the few policemen who were on the job, the State Police, and the Louisiana National Guard. Nick Shannon was with them, working side by side to protect innocent people. Even the fire department had done its job. In a couple of hours, thanks to reinforcements from surrounding parishes, much of the brutality had subsided, but some of the vandalism continued. People raided clothing stores. Others were stealing small appliances and jewelry. Several men struggled down a side street with a home entertainment center that weighed at least three hundred pounds.

Things were just about back to normal when a single shot rang out, and one of Sherif's men fell to the ground. Shannon and Sherif rushed over to him while more of Sherif's men and several police officers ran over to check the area that the shot had come from.

"It was an accident! It was an accident! I didn't mean to do it!" cried a rookie officer, on his knees in tears. One of Sherif's men and a brother officer helped him to his feet and brought him out.

For a moment it looked like the fury might kick off again. Everyone stood frozen, waiting to see what the next move would be, and who would make it. Sherif's men watched for some hint of what they should do. O'Malley's men waited for orders from him. Both sides were pent up, waiting in hopeful silence.

"He's still alive," Train announced after examining the wounded officer. "But he's losin' a lot of blood. We gotta get him to the hospital on the double."

Sherif and Shannon helped Train place the injured man onto the stretcher while everyone else looked on. After the ambulance pulled off, Detective Clark approached Sherif.

"I'm sorry about this," said Clark, in his most sincere voice. "Of course, there will be an investigation. I'm hoping your man pulls through."

"That's mighty black of you, detective," Sherif rebutted.

"Look, accidents happen!"

"One of my men made a mistake," said a flustered O'Malley.

"What do you want us to do? Hang him?"

Sherif's eyes rolled.

"Accidents happen. If Leon doesn't make it, how do I tell his wife and his kids that he's dead because some jumpy cop fucked up?"

Frustrated, Clark snapped back. "It was an accident, okay? An accident! We're all sorry it happened. That's the best we can do."

Santos, one of Sherif's men, lunged for Clark, connecting solidly with his left jaw. Seconds later, the battling had begun again, Sherif's men, bystanders, and O'Malley's riot squad. Clark fired twice into the air and everyone froze.

The detective was thinking about his record. How would it look if there was a second riot? Even worse, suppose one of his squad or O'Malley's squad had caused it by a bad shooting.

Clark was thinking about the Watts riot in August of 1965, that started with a police beating on 116th and San Pedro. Because of police brutality, L.A. had become a pressure cooker, the burning and looting lasted for forty-five days while the National Guard stood by watching.

After the Rodney King verdict, it happened again in South Central L.A. Clark didn't want to see the same thing happen in New Orleans, and if it did he sure didn't want it to be his fault.

"Why don't we all just break this up," said Clark. "This kind of thing isn't going to help any of us. Everybody needs to just cool off!"

"You know I'm really glad you're doing your job, officer," said Sherif, "protecting us. But we can take care of our own."

Sherif whistled, and more young men appeared in the shadows, all heavily armed.

"We're leaving," said Sherif coolly, the cold wind biting his eyes, smooth and self-confident.

Sherif's men began to disband, walking conspicuously past Clark, O'Malley and the other officers, still holding weapons in plain view. His van screeched up, the unauthorized blue light on the dash still flashing, but who was going to tell him anything? Shannon got into the van with Sherif and the other men, and they drove away, disappearing into the darkness.

Clark, Burke and O'Malley walked through the rubble. A contingency of officers was directed to stay behind to guard the stores against more vandalism. The detective lit a cigarette, puffing slowly.

"It will take a month to clean this mess up," said Detective Burke bleakly.

"Yeah, but it could have been a helluva lot worse," Clark answered.

"You still think we're going to crack the Jammison case, don't you?"

"I haven't busted my ass all these years to retire on a detective's pay. Somebody's behind it. All we've got to do is find him."

Clark stopped walking and turned to face his partner, placing his hand on Burke's shoulder, while O'Malley kept walking.

"You and I are good cops, James. We're the best. Between the two of us, there's no way we won't get to the bottom of this. The next move is still Nick Shannon's, but he'd better make it quick."

* * *

In the meantime, Morrow Jammison had done exactly as instructed. Arriving at the top of the Judge Seiber Bridge, she stopped her car, walked to the railing, then threw the bag over the side. Below, a speedboat awaited her delivery.

CHAPTER 46

A white Lincoln Town Car pulled up and parked next to a new black Mercedes 600 sedan at an abandoned shipyard on Chef Menteur Highway, at Bayou Savage. A man wearing a hat, with the collar on his coat turned up, exited the Lincoln and got into the back seat of the Mercedes. In the darkness, inky black water rushed just twenty feet ahead of the two cars.

"Glad you could make it," smiled Sal Cintenni warmly. "Any trouble gettin' here?"

"Are you kidding?" said the other man.

Light from a passing eighteen wheeler briefly revealed the face of Lawrence Daniels, Samuel Jammison's friend.

"Things cool down yet?" asked Cintenni.

"Everything's come to a standstill. NOPD and the State Police have taken over. The governor had to call in the National Guard. The mayor has imposed a curfew until six tomorrow morning. But if you know what you're doing, you can still pick your way around the roadblocks. Looks like he'll have to cancel Mardi Gras, too."

"Yeah. Too bad. That's gonna piss a lotta people off. Probably fuck up his chance for a third term. Know what I mean?"

"Probably," Daniels smirked.

"That's what happens when you fuckin' forget who you're workin' for. You won't forget, will you, Lawrence, that you're workin' for me?"

"Sam's a fool, Sal. I'm not. He's been lying so long he's starting to believe his own bullshit."

"And that won't happen to you, right?"

"No way. You bought me. Who knows how many others are on your payroll?"

"What I like about you, Lawrence. Respect, that's what it's all about. Know what I mean? And you ain't gonna forget where you came from, not like that black mothafucker Jammison."

Sal Cintenni was forgetting something, however. Lawrence Daniels owed much of his success to the mayor. When he was ready for college, it was Sam Jammison who pulled a few strings to get him admitted to Tulane instead of some obscure college no one had ever heard of in the middle of nowhere.

"Told me he was glad I wasn't going to run against him so he could go after that third term. He said the people wouldn't know which one of us to vote for," laughed Daniels, clearing his throat. "I told that egotistical sonofabitch that I was learning the tricks of the trade, but he's so busy thinking about how great he is that he didn't even catch on."

"We're both gonna show that dumb mothafucker who to fuck with," said Sal contemptuously, staring out the window into the blackness. "This time next year, you'll be mayor and Sam Jammison's gonna be fertilizer. Fuckin' plant food."

"It's pretty damn nice of him to give us all this help," Daniels continued, becoming more serious. "But we do have a problem, a private detective named Nick Shannon. Old friend of the mayor. Been doing a lot of snooping."

"You worry too much, Lawrence. Probably just tryin' to get his name in the papers. Don't let it get to you. The only way he can find out anything is through Sam, and I don't think he'd do anything that stupid.. Maybe you're right, though. Maybe the mayor's a little slicker than we think."

"I just don't like it. And he's already tried to fuck you once, Sal. Just think about it, okay?"

"I'll mention it to Gino. About this Nick Shannon, too. He'll handle it."

Daniels looked at his watch. "I'd better get back." He pulled the hat down on his head, turned up his collar again, got out of the Mercedes and into the Lincoln.

CHAPTER 47

Shannon was exhausted and angry. Trying to get Boutte to talk, Sherif's men had still gotten nowhere. Time was running out, and Nick knew he had to do something. He grabbed Boutte by the hair, pressing his gun barrel to his right eye.

"Time's up, Cowboy. There was a riot tonight. People got hurt, some may die. Guess what. Your turn."

When Nick cocked the gun, Sherif and his men didn't really know what Shannon might do, either. His eyes were blazing.

"You got sixty seconds to decide whether you want to keep living or not," Nick said calmly, looking at his watch.

"Fifteen seconds."

A few more seconds ticked by.

"Okay, okay, I'll talk!" Boutte yelled. "I'll tell you what you want to know."

Boutte hesitated for a moment, sweating.

"And just what the fuck do you think this is, a picnic?" asked Shannon, still flashing the revolver.

Boutte's eyes searched the room for sympathy, but there was none. To the contrary, he saw only hate and resentment.

"You've got my word. If you tell us what we need to know, without forgetting any important details, you'll live."

"Your word," Boutte chuckled. "And who the fuck are you? Why the fuck should I believe you? Why, huh? Why?"

"Because I'm the only chance you got, asshole. Take it or leave it."

Boutte was a killer himself. He could see clearly that these men had no second thoughts about taking his life. They had reason enough already. Besides, they wanted to kill him, especially if he lied at this point.

"Where are they holding Debbie?" Shannon pressed, with an odd coldness, his tight face only an inch away from Boutte's, so close that they looked like they would kiss.

"She's in Lafitte at a safe house."

"Lafitte? Why Lafitte?" asked Shannon evenly, the gun barrel again pressed against Boutte's eye.

"We run drugs outta there," Boutte uttered nervously. "No cops down there. Only a sheriff and a deputy."

The gun clicked as Shannon removed the safety.

"I'm tellin' you the fuckin' truth!" Boutte shouted, perspiration beading on his forehead.

All Boutte wanted to do now was stay alive, save his own neck. They could see that. And he had already answered the first two questions right.

"I ain't got to lie to you. I know you'll kill me! You fuckin' bastards!"

"How is she?"

"She's okay. She's okay."

Boutte's free eye darted wildly from one man to the next.

"Nobody laid a finger on her! I swear, boss's orders. Nobody touched her."

Boutte was perspiring feverishly, stirring in the chair.

"And you always follow orders, don't you?"

"I didn't touch her! I'm tellin' you! I swear!"

"Kill that mothafucker," shouted one of Sherif's men. "He's fuckin' lyin'!"

"Bang!" The tip of the gun barrel flashed. Boutte lurched, yelling hysterically, blood squirting from the side of his head.

"I can't hear! I can't hear. You fuckin' mothafucker. You shot my fuckin' ear off. I can't hear!"

Shannon remained cool and collected, blood running down Boutte's head onto his shirt.

"Don't lie to me. And don't waste any more of my time."

"You're fuckin' crazy! You sonofabitch! Mothafucker! Mothafucker!"

Boutte couldn't hear, but he could still see. Nick had put the barrel of the gun back over his eye.

"Okay! Okay!" he shouted. "I come clean! I'll fuckin' come clean!" he cried, tears streaming down his face.

"It was an accident!" he shouted. "An accident!"

"What was an accident?" Nick asked, his expression as frigid as hot ice.

It had happened after Gino beat him with the brass knuckles. Fuckin' Ivy League punk. It was all his fault. If Gino hadn't beaten him up, none of this would ever have happened, and he would be back at the safe house. But it was too late now. He had fucked up, and he knew it. That's why he had left the safe house, that's why they had found him at Stephanie's apartment whipping her ass. Because he had fucked up, and it was too late.

Gino had put a good ass whipping on him with the brass knuckles, knocked him out. Then he left, probably gone back to kiss Sal's ass, Boutte thought, when he came to. Well, he wasn't going to let them get away with it, not beating him like a dog. He hated Gino, but it was Sal, too. Gino wouldn't have done it if it wasn't okay with Sal. They had underestimated him if they thought for a minute that he would just sit back and take some foul shit like that. He was going to pay them back, and he knew how. Did Gino and Sal believe that he wouldn't want revenge? That he was too scared? J.D. was sitting outside Debbie's door guarding her. Boutte approached him, holding a damp cloth to the left side of his face.

"Hey, J.D. What's up, man?"

J.D. winced when he saw Boutte's scarred, swollen face: eyes black, lower lip cut and purple from bruised blood.

"Damn!" said J.D., frowning. "Look at your fuckin' face! Gino do that to you?"

"Brass knuckles," Boutte answered bitterly. "Sonofabitch busted me up pretty good, huh?"

"Fuck!" said J.D., his own face twisted and contorted with disgust. "Gino didn't have to do that, man. That mothafucker didn't hafta fuck you up like that. Whatcha gonna do?"

"Pay him back, what else?" Boutte said, striking J.D. across the face with the blackjack he was holding in his right hand. He toppled to the floor unconscious.

"Sorry about that, J.D.," said Boutte, slipping the blackjack into his jacket pocket.

Boutte turned the doorknob, stepped over J.D.'s body, and entered the room where Debbie was being held. She was lying on the bed, her legs and hands apart, each tied to a different corner of the metal bed frame. This is gonna be easy, Boutte thought. Gino intended to make sure the girl did not try to escape again.

Debbie's eyes followed Boutte as he moved over to the bed. His stare was unfeeling, like that of a hawk who had spied a defenseless rabbit. He looked down at Debbie, helpless, completely at his mercy. "No! No!" She twisted and jerked, trying to avoid him, but it was no use.

Boutte raised her dress, took the knife from his boot, and cut off her bikini panties with one stroke. Debbie could feel his hand brushing against her pubic hairs, the pulling, and the pain as he forced his fat finger inside her, feeling the moisture and hearing her own wetness as he played with her.

One by one he took off his boots, dropped his jeans and underwear to the floor, his organ erect and throbbing. He got into the bed beside her, breathing hard, his stiff penis pressed against her leg. Boutte crawled on top of her, gripping her head in his powerful hands, squeezing, then forcing his putrid tongue into her mouth. She tried to resist, but the pressure was too great.

"You might as well relax and enjoy this," Boutte said, "'cause ain't nobody gonna help you now."

Boutte raised up, straddled her, then started punching her face, again and again and again, until she was nearly unconscious, delirious with pain. He slid up, knees planted on her shoulders, grabbed her hair, then forced his swollen penis into her mouth.

"Suck it, bitch! Suck that fuckin' dick," he said, thrusting himself deeper into her warm mouth. He plucked it out, shoved his tongue into her mouth again, slid down between her legs and thrust his tongue into her vagina, savagely sucking her clitoris, biting, her wetness all over Boutte's face. He slid up again, guided his penis with his right hand, then rammed it into Debbie. She bolted again as he pushed himself deeper into her and again his fist slammed into her ribs. Debbie groaned painfully, between her legs and the bedding wet with perspiration and semen.

When it was over, through blurred eyes, she could hazily see Boutte zipping up his pants, putting on his cowboy hat, holstering his gun, and leaving.

"What was an accident? What happened to her?" Nick repeated, yanking at Boutte's collar.

"I'll tell you!" Boutte answered. "But you promised me you wouldn't kill me. You promised! It was Renzo," Boutte explained anxiously. "I didn't have nothin' to do with it."

"To do with what?" Nick asked, but Boutte paused for a

moment before speaking.

"He raped her. Renzo raped her!"

Shannon lunged toward Boutte, striking him along the side of his left jaw, blood gushing from his mouth.

Sherif and two of his men struggled to restrain Shannon.

"Let him talk, Nick! Let him talk!"

They struggled for a moment longer, then Nick relaxed, his eyes burning.

"Okay! Okay! I'll be all right." Shannon turned to face Boutte. "Talk, mister. And this time, you'd better get it right!"

"You said you wouldn't kill me!" Boutte said, his shirt red with blood. He paused again and then continued.

"Renzo raped her. I tried to stop him, but I couldn't. I felt sorry for her, but what could I do? He was like a fuckin' wild man. I was scared! You woulda done the same thing."

Again the room was quiet, then Shannon responded, emotionally.

"And you just sat there and watched? You weigh over two hundred pounds, and you want me to believe you were scared? I'll fuckin' cut your heart out and shove it down your throat. You raped her too, didn't you?"

"No! No!" Boutte shouted. "I didn't have nothin' to do with it. I'm tellin' you, Renzo did it!"

"As much as you like pussy," Shannon responded, "you'd probably fuck your own mother."

Shannon twisted Boutte's ear, stomping his boot in his groin.

"Ahhh!" Boutte shrieked painfully, as Nick twisted his ear tighter, making the pain unbearable.

"I raped her! I raped her, too!" Boutte shouted. "I did it! I did it!"

In a flash Shannon's hands were clutching Boutte's throat. Again, Sherif and his men tried, and finally separated the two.

"This bastard deserves to die," said Sherif passionately. "But we don't want to waste him here. We'd only be asking for trouble. And we still need to know who else is in on this."

Precisely at that moment, two gunshots rang through the room from the window that opened to the alley. One of the bullets struck Boutte in the heart. He slumped forward dead, rich red blood saturating his shirt.

Shannon, Sherif and the others raced out of the building as a late-model Mercedes swung from the alley, almost hitting them.

Shannon and Sherif got into the Trans Am, just as the van Sherif was in earlier pulled up. All of them gave chase to the Mercedes. They didn't know it, but Clark and Burke had staked out Sherif's building and were in on the chase, too, after hearing the gunshots.

On Gentilly Boulevard the Mercedes struck two parked cars, but the driver maintained control, continuing his escape. They were on his bumper when he decided to cut sharp off DeSaix, speeding toward Esplanade Avenue. Shannon skidded, barely missing a street light, then continued with the van, and the police car's siren and flashing red and blue lights following close behind.

The Mercedes turned left on Esplanade, headed toward the French Quarter.

But on St. Claude he turned right and headed back toward Canal Street. They were only about ten car lengths back when a police car pulled out from behind the Saenger Theater on Iberville Street.

They swerved around the car, jumping the neutral ground, driving against traffic on St. Claude to Canal, then turned left, headed to the river. The van had spun around to avoid the police car, and stalled in back of the Woolworth store. Clark and Burke weren't so lucky. Shannon smiled to himself, thinking about the two cops, running into one of their own cars.

Magazine Street was deserted. Shannon fired at the suspect car. One of his shots struck the right rear wheel as the car careened into a brick building. Shannon and Sherif screeched to a half, then approached slowly, guns drawn. The engine of the Mercedes was pushed into the front seat, the hood had come through the front windshield, the tires were blown, the rims bent and the doors swung open, with the suspect bleeding and pinned behind the steering wheel.

Looking into the driver's bloody face, they were shocked to find out that the man who had killed Boutte, in the car they had been chasing so recklessly, was none other than Gene Kennedy, the mayor's right-hand man.

They pulled him from the car, which had started to burn, and laid him on the ground a short distance away.

Kennedy was coughing up blood, his breathing difficult.

"Nick," he said, "never know where you'll turn up."

"Gene, what the hell's going on?" asked Shannon.

Kennedy coughed, trying to smile.

"All in a day's work. The world is full of surprises, isn't it? You should know that by now," blood pouring from Kennedy's mouth. "A man will do almost anything for the right price, and some of us will even do a little more."

"But what about Sam?" Shannon asked. "He's been good to you. How could you sell him out at any price? How could you do it?"

"Don't fool yourself," Kennedy laughed. "Sam Jammison never did anything for nothing. Had to be something in it for him."

Kennedy's breathing was becoming even more strained.

He laughed. "You don't know how funny that is. You're a fool, Nick. So full of Girl Scout cookies."

Kennedy raised his arm and wiped some of the blood from his mouth.

"Don't feel too bad, though. You've been had by one of the best. You know, Nick, I think a good salesman could sell you your own house. Sure, Sam did a lot for me, but I did a lot for him, too, things he couldn't talk about. He had the personality and the drive. I supplied the brains..."

"Why did you shoot Boutte?" Shannon asked, still looking for the real connection.

"He was going to tell you about me and Sal Cintenni. I had to kill him. Boutte was a coward. I knew he would talk if it meant saving his own neck. I was going to pop him at his girlfriend's apartment, but you got to him first."

Kennedy started coughing again and choking on the blood. There was a horrible gurgle, his head fell to the side, and he never said another word.

"What do you make of that?" asked Shannon, even more puzzled than before.

Sherif leaned over Kennedy and closed his eyes.

"Something I've been telling you all along," Sherif answered. "That nothing in politics happens by accident. It was a scam. Jammison knew all along who kidnapped his daughter... just like I said."

Nick Shannon's face registered the intense pressure he was under as he made eye contact with Sherif. He paused for a moment, then said, "We've got two dead bodies on our hands. Boutte, who worked for Sal Cintenni, was murdered by Gene Kennedy, who was working for Cintenni and double-crossing Sam Jammison, who according to Kennedy is conning everybody. We've got to get some answers fast, and we've still got to get Debbie out alive."

CHAPTER 48

Back at Sherif's headquarters, Boutte's body had already been disposed of. Explaining what a white man was doing there and why he had two bullet holes in his chest would not have been easy. Nick and Sherif were left alone brainstorming.

"So, what do we do now, Big Brother?" asked Sherif, diplomatically feeling Nick out. "It's the same old game, Nick. Greed. It always is. Black people misuse black people every day of the week. White people ain't got no monopoly on that. Just like the Rampart Street War back in the forties. It's all about the money. Economics. Business."

"Yeah, I know," Shannon answered. He threw the Federal Express envelope on the desk in front of Sherif.

"Absolute power corrupts absolutely. I just got those," he said, glancing at Sherif, who was reading the clippings. "Had some of my contacts in Chicago do some digging."

The articles had been clipped from the "Chicago Tribune" and the "Chicago Sun Times." Sal Cintenni was a high roller. Ordinarily, pictures of a mob boss out celebrating would have meant nothing, but these particular photographs were very significant. Unknowingly, the photographs had captured Mayor Samuel Jammison, Jr. in the background, broad smile, a luscious brunette in his arms.

Shannon was thinking about what he had to do. It was a position he had hoped he wouldn't find himself in. After all, Sam Jammison had been like a father to him. Life's a bitch, he thought, and unlike Burger King, you don't always have it your way.

"Looks to me like Jammison forgot who he was shacking up with," Sherif answered, raising his arms and stretching.

"I have an idea," Nick said, taking out his cell phone, then dialing. It was the mayor's untapped private line. It was the fifth ring, and he was about to hang up when the mayor answered.

"Hello, Sam. Nick."

"Nick," Jammison answered anxiously.

"Can you talk?"

"Yes, I'm alone. You have some news."

"Gene Kennedy's been killed."

"What?!" exclaimed the mayor, shocked. "Killed!" But who... why? Why would anybody want to kill Gene?"

"It's a long story. I'll tell you more about it when I see you. But I think you need to meet me at his house. He might have something incriminating lying around that you don't want found."

"Yes, I think you're right," the mayor answered, checking his watch.

"It's about ten now," said Shannon, as his eyes met Sherif's, watching him lie to his old friend.

"Let's say, four a.m. before the cops show up in the morning."

"Four... I'll be there. And Nick, thanks."

Half an hour later Shannon and Sherif waited, their van parked on a side street facing Kennedy's Garden District cottage. Clark and Burke waited in the detective's banged-up, unmarked Crown Vic down the street. They had only been there for a few minutes when a white Toyota Camry pulled up, drove half a block past the house, turned around, then parked. They could see a flicker of light and the orange glow of a cigarette tip. It may have been a coincidence but it looked a lot like Debbie's car, Shannon thought.

CHAPTER 49

Sherif and Shannon watched as their suspect smoked several cigarettes. He was probably staking out the house himself before making a move. Shannon pressed the END button on his cellular telephone.

"No answer," he said, flipping the lid. "That's funny. Sue's not at home."

"Maybe she's still at the hospital."

"Yeah, maybe. I'll call back in a few minutes, then I'll try there."

Clark and Burke waited and watched, too. Clark was thinking about his kids again, about how much they needed him, and about Celeste, his slob of a wife. He just had to solve this case. There would be newspaper and magazine articles written about him, maybe even a series of them, about the cop who rescued the mayor's daughter, maybe even a book or a movie.

He hadn't worked all these years, only to end up with a small retirement check every month. He remembered how his father would go to work even when he was too sick to be there because he felt obligated. As a black man, he had worked long and hard to get where he was, not to mention being fucked over, and he intended to go even farther. He took out his cell phone and punched in a number.

Burke was thinking, too, about what Miss Peabody had said about blacks and Irish working together, but he doubted that he would consider it progress. His father David had been a policeman, too, walking a beat for nearly twenty-five years. Every day of his life, his father had complained about how much he hated niggers. His mother Kathleen worked the cosmetics counter at Godchaux's on Canal Street. He thought about the crowded market on Rousseau Street, where small Irish businessmen would try to make an honest living.

As a boy in the Channel, he remembered all the fights he had had with niggers, how much the Irish had suffered like the blacks, and how there was no Affirmative Action for him. His ancestors had come to America penniless, too.

He was ten times smarter than Clark, but Clark was the one who had a slight advantage because of court rulings and a black police superintendent. Blacks and the Irish had competed before. They still did. This case meant just as much to him as it did to Clark, he thought. It could put him exactly where he wanted to be. Nothing was going to get in his way, especially Nick Shannon, or even Al Clark.

They watched the man finally get out of the car. Silhouetted by a street light he appeared to be about Jammison's height and build, wearing a wide-brimmed hat pulled down low on his head, with the collar of his coat turned up around his neck.

He was behaving very suspiciously, and there was little doubt that he was up to something. If it wasn't Sam Jammison it was somebody who had been sent by him. The man took another draw on his cigarette, looked around to see if anybody else was around, flicked the butt to the ground, then turned and walked briskly through the white picket gate and up the landscaped walkway. Looking around once more he reached behind a flower pot, then used a key to unlock the door and entered the house.

Shannon picked up the cell phone that he had laid on the dash, punching Sue's number in again. He loved hearing her voice, even when it was only a recording. He smiled for a moment, remembering how much he loved her, but his expression quickly changed.

"Still no answer." When he called the hospital, she wasn't there either.

"We can swing by there on our way back," Sherif told him.

"Make sure somebody stays with that car," Clark told the person at the other end of the phone before hanging up. "That was Chet," he told Burke. "They lifted several sets of prints from the Saab, but we struck gold on two of them. Cross matching with the FBI computer, Chet came up with two brothers, Delbert and Rory Pike. It seems that they grew up in Denver and their father Roger is a white separatist. Their old man's doing time in a Texas jail for blowing up a church and killing three innocent Sunday school kids. According to their rap sheet, they were both skinheads at one time."

"Following in papa's footsteps," Burke added.

"The FBI and the ATF are looking for Rory, the younger one, for blowing up a church in Danville, Illinois. Nobody was killed, but about thirty people got messed up pretty bad. They were arrested in a drug sting in Houston in 1998, but it was a bad bust, so they walked. Chet saw that and a red flag went up. Found three kilos of top grade coke hidden in the gas tank."

"You can buy a lot of machine guns, silencers, bulletproof vests, night vision equipment and explosives with that much uncut coke."

"A Timothy McVeigh copycat and a pyromaniac. Some pair."

"Well, you know how it is," Burke added. "Ever since the FBI killed Randy Weaver's wife at Ruby Ridge and those seventy

Branch Davidians in Waco, they've been coming out of the woodwork."

The man inside closed the door and turned on the lights as his shadowy image moved from room to room. Fifteen minutes later, the lights went off, the door opened and he came back out. As he passed under the streetlight, they could see that the suspect was carrying the same yellow envelope Nick had stuffed the Chicago newspaper clippings into.

The suspect got back into the Camry, started the engine, turned on the lights, and sped off down the block. Burke radioed ahead to several units that had been stationed in the vicinity, instructing one of them to intercept the car for violating the curfew, but what they really wanted was a positive ID of the driver. After allowing the man to go about his business, the officer radioed Burke, telling him that the Camry was registered to Debra Allain Jammison on Audubon Place, and that the driver was Mayor Samuel Jammison, Jr.

Jammison was furious, pounding the steering wheel. He snarled as he watched the police officer getting back into his car fade in his rearview mirror.

How could he have been so careless? Someone had seen him. No problem, he thought. After all. He was the mayor. Who would question him?

But now he had another problem, an even bigger one. He still didn't know any details, who had murdered Kennedy, and why? Had he been wrong about Chauncey, the little fairy, all along? Had his hatred of gays blinded him? And what about Turner, his security chief?

Maybe it was Gene Kennedy all along, after all these years. With Kennedy he had broken one of his own rules. NEVER TRUST ANYONE WHO IS TOO HELPFUL, because they're up to something. No wonder Sal Cintenni knew every move he made.

Cintenni still had Debbie, but he wouldn't hurt her as long as he played along with him. He hated that ignorant sonofabitch, but Cintenni had outsmarted him, at least for a minute. How could he have been so stupid?

He touched the envelope confidently. At least he had the evidence now.

Back at Kennedy's house, Sherif and Shannon walked over to where the Toyota had been parked. Using flashlights, they searched for discarded cigarette butts, but instead found cigar butts and several Portofino cylinders, which Shannon carefully collected and placed into a white handkerchief.

"Don't be a litterbug," said Sherif with a sly smile.

CHAPTER 50

Not far away, Tony and Georgio had forced a window open at Sue's Fountainbleu Drive apartment and were waiting in the dark for her to come home.

"This waitin' around is startin' to get to me," Tony complained. "I hate to wait for anything."

"Yeah, me too," Georgio agreed. "Nothin' pisses me off more than sittin' around . . . What do you think the boss is gonna do with this one?"

"Fuck if I know. Might let us have her when he's done with her."

"Yeah, how about that," Georgio smiled. "This fuckin' job keeps gettin' better and better. You get paid pretty good, and you get to bust your nuts at the same time."

"Yeah, but Boutte fucked up. The boss said not to touch the girl. You know Sal. Where the fuck can he hide? Big mistake."

"I hope this broad brings her ass home soon," Georgio said, picking up a photo and moving to the window for light.

"Hey, not bad. This must be her kid and her old man," acknowledging the other two people in the snapshot.

"They look real happy. I hope she makes me happy, too."

He dropped the picture to the floor, then stepped on it, breaking the glass.

"She ain't no virgin, but she'll do."

"If some coon's been puttin' it on her, you might as well forget about it and save your little short dick for some white girl, and you better pray that no nigger ain't been fuckin' her, too. You better give it your best shot. Eat that pussy first and hope she likes it."

"Bullshit!" Georgio snapped. "Fuckin' bullshit!"

"Bullshit, my ass. I was in Nam with them mothafuckers. Yeah, some of 'em was normal, but some of them niggers shoulda been studdin' horses and cows."

"Man, that's just a myth. A bunch of hype."

"Yeah, sure, hype," said Tony emotionally. "Well, I seen this hype with my own two eyes. I remember this one guy in our platoon, Ozz Mose, straight outta the sticks. You know, one of them cornbread and collard greens-eatin' niggers from Alabama. Big and stupid. Mama used to keep tabs on him so he wouldn't get into no trouble. Well, anyway, Ozz hadn't never got no pussy, something about breakin' the Ten Commandments, and we believed him. He was too dumb to lie. We was just havin' some fun, so we asked him to show us what he did to feel good. I'm tellin' you, that nigger unzipped his pants and yanked out a club as big as my arm, with a head like a tomato, only it was black. I kind of looked around at the others, too, and let me tell you, they hadn't never seen nothin' like that either. I couldn't even sleep that night," he continued, "and I hated that sonofabitch until I got out of the service."

Tony was still bitter, moving anxiously toward Georgio at the window.

At that moment they heard voices coming down the brick walkway, a child laughing and a woman's voice.

"Be quiet," Georgio snapped. "I think it's them."

The two men hid in the dark apartment, one on each side of the door. The footsteps stopped outside, they could hear the lock turning. Swinging the door open, the two figures were silhouetted by the light from the outside.

Flicking the wall light on as she was closing the door, Georgio grabbed the woman, putting his hand tightly over her mouth to muffle her screams. She fought desperately to get loose, while Kevin tugged at Georgio's pants leg. When he pushed the child, he fell, knocking his head against one of the end tables. Seeing her tiny son lying helpless on the floor, Sue struggled even harder. Tony struck her with his gun, knocking her out, then packed her over his shoulder and carried her out.

The room was quiet, furniture overturned, a lamp and other accessories broken. Kevin was lying on the floor unconscious. The telephone was ringing, but there was no one to answer it.

CHAPTER 51

"Something's wrong," Shannon said to Sherif, turning the knob and pushing. "Sue never leaves her door unlocked."

Again, he and Sherif drew their weapons. Shannon reached for the light switch next to the door, then flicked it on. Entering slowly, the two men could see that the living room was in shambles. Obviously, there had been a struggle.

Nick moved in first, calling for Sue, then spotted Kevin lying motionless on the floor. Sherif searched the rest of the apartment. Kevin was still breathing, but his pulse was weak. Shannon gently picked him up, rushed back to the van, then they raced him to Touro Hospital Emergency.

As Sherif expertly maneuvered the van, Shannon sat holding Kevin in his arms, ironically remembering a Touro television commercial, "Where Babies Come From."

"If anything's happened to Sue, or if Kevin doesn't make it, I'm gonna kill Sam and Sal Cintenni myself," Shannon murmured.

At the safe house, Sue was thrown into the same room with the mayor's daughter, who was sitting dazed on the side of the bed. Her abductors had untied her when they found her beaten and raped by Boutte, but nobody had done anything to help her. She was weak and disoriented.

The two women tearfully embraced each other. Debbie's face and eyes were swollen, arms scratched black and blue, her white dress soiled and spotted with blood. Sue tore a small piece of material from her own dress and tried to freshen Debbie up, using her nursing skills as best she could. Sue banged on the door.

"Hello! Hello! Is anybody out there? Can you hear me?"

She kept banging.

"Is anybody out there? We need to get this girl to a hospital! Can anybody hear me? What kind of animals are you?"

J.D. was sitting at his post by the door, his face bandaged where Boutte had hit him with the blackjack. He was in excruciating pain himself, too much to care about anybody else. He had messed up once. It wasn't going to happen again. Gino even put on four extra men. Sal had already given the order anyway. The girl was going to die, and so was her friend. Cintenni intended to make sure there were no witnesses.

It was getting late. After leaving Kevin in good hands at the hospital, Sherif and Shannon had gone back to pick up Nick's car before going on to meet the assault team. When they pulled up and parked, they could see two men inside the Trans Am trying to start it. Nick and Sherif ran toward the car, guns drawn, but when one of the men hot-wired the switch, the car exploded, knocking Sherif and Shannon to the ground.

CHAPTER 52

It was almost midnight when Nick and Sherif arrived, but because of the rioting everybody else was late too. They sat in the large living room of Shannon's house. There was a stone fireplace; a large white sofa; several matching chairs; a nude painting on one wall; a framed, elaborate mirror on another; a marble cocktail table in front of the sofa; and wall-to-wall carpeting.

The house was of brick, one story, three bedrooms, a medium-sized kidney-shaped swimming pool in the backyard, and a large den in back that they'd used for the two intense briefings. One more briefing and they would be ready for the raid.

Between the first two briefings, Injun Joe had fixed a light meal of fried seafood: oysters, clams, shrimp, trout; and cornbread that did not come out of a box, made from scratch. Barry Barrett had fixed a large mixed green salad. Nothing heavy to dull the mind.

They were mostly silent, controlling the adrenaline so that it would not peak before the raid and leave them tense and tired. Unreleased adrenaline was mildly toxic, they knew.

The Robinson brothers sat on the sofa, sipping fresh orange juice. They did not drink or smoke. Thad was the tallest of the two—five-eleven to his brother, Calvin's, five-eight. Thad was a sleek, flat-bellied one hundred and forty-five pounds. His brother, stockier at one sixty-five. Barry Barrett was the tallest of the group at six five, and had been an offensive guard when he was all-conference at LSU. He'd played three years of pro ball in Italy, where he had learned the art of float building. In addition to designing and building Mardi Gras floats, he did work ranging from designing advertising campaigns to decorating topless bars. Barry had gained his combat experience during Operation Desert Storm.

Sherif, legs crossed in front of the fireplace, was reading "The Unseen Hand." Billy, sitting relaxed with a rum and coke in his hand, made up the final member of the seven. He was looking at the safe house pictures Shannon had taken.

Seven was all right for the strike team, especially these seven, even though Joe would be on the boat providing cover for their escape route; skilled combat veterans to a man, almost a dozen combat decorations among them, and not one Purple Heart. They were not only good, they were careful, and in combat, the terms were synonymous.

Shannon was about to bring them into the back room for the final briefing when the doorbell rang.

Billy slipped his piece from the shoulder holster lying next to him on the floor, a Colt Woodsman .22 target pistol with an eight-inch barrel. He jacked a round into the chamber, stood next to the back door, the gun hidden behind his right thigh, and nodded to Shannon, who opened the door a crack.

Clark shouldered his way through the door, followed by Burke. Clark took one look at Billy's hidden hand, and his right hand flashed to his hip, drawing a Heckler & Koch nine-millimeter automatic. Burke drew his Beretta, beating Clark by a hair.

"Let's see your hand, Billy. Slow," said Clark.

Billy slowly withdrew his hand, carefully lying the pistol on the floor by his right foot.

"Now move it away," ordered Clark.

Billy slid the piece away with his foot.

"Further," said Clark. Billy complied.

"Is this a bust?" said Shannon. "We're just having dinner. Is that against the law?"

Clark and Burke relaxed, but kept their weapons drawn, down against their right legs.

"At midnight. We know what you're doing," said Clark.

"Doing what?" asked Billy.

"Going in for Debbie. Don't handle me like that, Billy."

"We had a tail on Shannon since the night of the snatch. Burke's been on you around the clock . . . Aren't you going to introduce your dinner guests?"

"You think I'm some amateur? Nobody followed me," Shannon answered indignantly.

"Had an electronic beeper on the top of the transmission in your car before it blew up," said Clark. "Better buy yourself a scanner, Shannon."

The men watched, tense and ready. Hopefully there were only these two.

"Now what?" asked Shannon.

"We're going in with you."

"What?"

"You heard me. There are eight armed men in the house. Four on the perimeter, four inside," Clark responded. "You need us to hedge the odds."

"That was Burke out there in the skiff."

Burke nodded his head.

"Well, Shannon, it seems that you ain't Superman after all," said Billy with a grin.

"We can use 'em," said Injun Joe. "Let 'em in."

Joe was like E.F. Hutton: when he spoke, people listened.

Shannon scanned the room; the men nodded their approval.

"All right," said Shannon, "you're in."

Clark and Burke holstered their weapons and sat in the remaining chairs. Billy sat back down on the floor.

Shannon and Sherif went into one of the bedrooms that had been converted to a home office, making several trips with supplies that did not include computer paper or paper clip—ordnance, concussion and flash grenades, M-16s, an AK-47 and two-way radios tuned to the frequency on Joe's boat. Nobody wanted gas masks. Barry said that he hated them because they restricted both vision and breathing.

"How about Uzis, Mac-10s?" asked Burke.

"No way," Shannon answered. "Machine pistols spray all over the place. What if Debbie's close? We want the rounds to go where they're aimed."

"You got an infrared night scope?" asked Sherif.

"And a sniper rifle, too," said Clark, turning his head toward Billy.

"No," said Billy, shaking his head. "No time to zero it in. I'll use my own piece. International fitting on my scope. I'll have my handgun too."

"Yeah," said Clark.

"Flak jackets?"

They all shook their heads no; they needed mobility more than protection, and the jackets were cumbersome. They were roundly hated in Nam, even by the troops who routinely wore them.

"Anything else?"

"That's it, then," said Shannon. "We'll go in just before dawn."

"And now we are nine," said Billy in his best Yul Brynner imitation, passing the pictures to the detectives. Everybody cracked up, except Burke, who seldom smiled.

CHAPTER 53

The strike team assembled at two on the dot, drove the short distance in two vans. Shortly after four they were on their way, the boat moving at a steady eight knots.

A light rain had been forecast, its smell a hint on the western breeze. It would help that the outside guards would be sleepy, cold, and wet, dulling their reflexes.

The surface of the water was flat and calm, barely rippled by the soft breeze. Inside the pilothouse, Shannon stood next to Injun Joe at the wheel, peering out into the darkness, the radarscope between them, sweeping the water ahead.

"Bring back old memories, Joe?" asked Shannon.

"Yeah," replied Joe. "I always did prefer night attacks. Cut down on casualties, if you knew what you were doing."

"What was your outfit?"

"First Infantry Division. The Big Red One," Joe replied. "They didn't segregate us Injuns, like the blacks. I tried to get a transfer into the Ninety-Second Division, but no luck."

"Buffalo Division?"

"Yeah. All black, except for the officers," said Joe. "They went overseas combat ready, then they took their weapons and had them loadin' and unloadin' ships in North Africa, under fire at Anzio. The southern brass thought it wouldn't be a good thing for blacks to be killin' white Italians and Germans. Might give them ideas when they got back home."

"Then, when the Allied drive stalled at Monte Cassino, they threw the Ninety-Second into the line with no refresher trainin' against a crack SS unit. Ninety-Second took thirty percent casualties in less than ten days, but they broke the line. After the war, General Clark badmouthed the colored troops. Spoke against integratin' the Army before Congress."

"So did Eisenhower," said Shannon.

"Yeah," said Joe. "Patton was about the only colorblind American general in that damn war," said Joe. "He demanded that colored tank battalion. Said he didn't care if they were green as long as they killed Germans."

"How'd they treat you in your outfit?" asked Shannon, taking a sip of the strong coffee from a paper cup.

"Not bad," said Joe, puffing on his corncob pipe, "except for three east Texas rednecks in my company. Ran into them in an alley in Rome right after we took the city. Tried to jump me, and I killed all three with my paratrooper's knife. Army figured they'd been mugged," said Joe.

The Robinson brothers were silent, leaning against the bulkhead in the fantail of the boat.

Barry Barrett practiced field stripping his AK-47 with his eyes closed— placing the parts before him from left to right, replacing the parts on the stripped-down carbine in reverse order. Satisfied after six tries, he reassembled the piece for the last time, wiping each part with an oily rag. When he'd finished, he put on the safety, and slapped the thirty-round banana clip firmly in place. He leaned back against the bulkhead.

Burke sat apart from the group, relaxed, rocking with the

motion of the boat, staring straight ahead.
Billy and Clark sat on the port side, near the stern, talking softly.
"Feels like the night before a big football game, Billy. With you and me trying to keep cool until kickoff."
"Yeah. Had us some times, didn't we? Talkin' about makin' the NFL," Billy answered.
"Yeah. You had the speed, I had the size; but I was a half step too slow to play safety for the pros. Almost made the final cut with the Giants, though."
"What might have been," said Billy. "Theme song of the aging jock."
"Got that right," said Al.
"How the kids doing, Al?"
"Not good, Billy. Al, Jr. has been fucking around with drugs."
"I know," Billy answered. "I caught him trying to score some reefer."
"What did you do?" Clark asked softly.
"Took his little jive ass back in the alley and slapped the shit out of him. He hasn't been back," said Billy.
"So that's how he got that black eye," said Clark with a grin.
"What about the girl?"
"Running with a wild crowd. They got no parental supervision, Billy. You know how their mother is. I'm trying to get custody, but she won't agree. Man, the other day I was fantasizing about killing the bitch myself. Can you imagine that? Thinking about the insurance policy. With the double indemnity clause, it's worth five hundred grand."
"Why don't you ice the no-good, drunk ass bitch?" asked Billy.
"No way I could kill the mother of my children, no matter

how fucked up she is, Billy."

Al had never been good with women, thought Billy—shy, reserved, placing them on a pedestal when they wanted to freak out in bed. Billy had known Celeste would be no good for him, but how do you tell that to a man in love? Celeste had fucked like a rabbit since the age of fourteen; even at that age, she'd worn a B cup bra. Billy had tapped that pussy on a regular basis, among dozens of others, but his buddy had been stone blind in love, and when Celeste announced she was pregnant, even an army could not have prevented him from doing the right thing. Fortunately, the boy had come out a spitting image of his daddy. Billy felt truly sorry for his long-time friend.

"You know, life is funny," Clark went on, changing the subject. "Earlier this year I went to Blackwater Lodge for SWAT officers in North Carolina. We used to have to worry about bank robbers holding hostages, or the angry husband or boyfriend with a gun. Even with drive-bys the shooters had their targets. When ordinary kids are the ones doing the shooting we can't tell who the good guys are anymore, and all the victims are bystanders."

"What about the militia movement?" Billy reminded Clark. "They say the government has turned on us. Big Brother is everywhere, like George Orwell said in "1984." They're ready to go to war. And they may be right. You know, like Hitler's plan to disarm everybody. They say that what happened at Waco was a wake-up call. If the government can burn out a church full of kids, what's next?"

"Well, I'm not giving up my gun either," Clark said. "If I wake up one morning and they say give up the guns, I'm going to war, too. I'm tellin you, it's these kids blowing my mind. You know, during World War II in a one-on-one, 80 to 85 percent of the riflemen wouldn't shoot at the enemy. They would run and hide first. But in Vietnam, 95 percent would rock and roll. You know what the difference was? In Vietnam they were trained to shoot at people, using silhouette pop-ups. That's what happened with video games. We've taught kids how to shoot at people."

"So now big bad cops have to kill kids who kill kids," Billy responded.

"I'm tellin' you it's fucked up. Chaos, confusion, noise, you don't know who the shooter is . . . blood all over the place. And at Blackwater it's kick-in-the-door and start pulling the trigger."

'Yeah, just like we're gonna do in about half an hour. You know, Selma's pregnant."

"Great, man. Congratulations. When's she due?"

"July. Gonna have a Cancer child, like you. We want you to be the godfather."

"I'd be honored, Billy."

"Too bad you're so honorable, man," said Billy. "If your wife was dead, it would solve all your problems."

"No way I could do it, man."

"I know," Billy answered.

As Nick Shannon looked out over the water he remembered all the times he and his father Larry had spent fishing early in the morning with his uncles Francois and Rene, his mother's big brothers in Vacherie, Louisiana. Leontine De Breaux, his mother, could easily have passed for Injun Joe's little sister, smooth almost jet-black skin with Caucasian features, gray eyes and long black wavy hair that fell to her waist. They had grown up in a house on the River Road about half a mile away from the Humel Post Office and the sugar refinery in St. James Parish. His grandmother Maribel, who was Haitian and Indian, was married to Debroid Chaisson, a Frenchman whose father had come to Louisiana from Marseilles.

His father Larry was half Irish. His grandfather Michael had come to America in the 1930's and fallen in love with a black woman from Baton Rouge named Viola Brenner. Nick was also thinking about what an honorable man his father was and how much he loved his friend Sam Jammison.

CHAPTER 54

It was time. Joe had pulled the boat into its usual spot, anchored fore and aft, and begun fishing from the stern, keeping his eye on the shore. An hour before, a fine, cool, misty rain had begun. Joe, snug in his slickers, knew the guards would be tired, wet and miserable.

Behind him, the Robinson brothers struggled into their wet suits and scuba diving gear, carefully checking one another's tanks.

The balance of the team slid a large rubber pontoon boat over the side away from the shore, and attached an electric outboard motor at its stern. The electric motor would make much less noise than an internal combustion engine.

The Robinson brothers adjusted their face masks, put in their mouthpieces leading from their scuba tanks, gave a thumbs-up sign, slid into the cold water, slipping below the surface, leaving a brief trail of phosphorescent bubbles trailing up from below.

The balance of the team, except Billy, silently descended into the pontoon boat. Billy turned on the night vision scope and waited for it to warm up.

Thad Robinson rose to the surface until only his head was above water. Less than twenty yards away, the guard in the rear of the house was soundly asleep, a pump action Browning shotgun cradled in his arms. Thad turned toward the boat, and signaled with three blinks of a waterproof flashlight, before submerging quietly.

"All right, Billy," said Joe. "That's the signal. Do your job."

Billy rose, made an adjustment to the scope, put his arm through the strap, and gazed at his target, asleep beneath the covered verandah at the rear of the house. Billy took careful aim, took in a full breath, let out half, then squeezed off the round, catching his target square in the chest, the silencer on the end of the long barrel of the Mauser making no more sound than a light cough.

Billy continued to watch the shore through the scope. Thad rose again, gave another three blinks with the flashlight.

"Answer them, Joe. The dude is dead," said Billy.

Joe responded with three blinks from his own flashlight, and the Robinson brothers went into action.

The brothers silently crawled onto the bank, took off their tanks, face masks and flippers, took a handgun each from the waterproof bag at Thad's back, placed the pieces in shoulder holsters and moved silently to each side of the house, K-Bar knives in hand. Billy watched them move away.

"Won't be long now, Joe," said Billy.

Moving with stealthy ease, Thad maneuvered behind the guard, placed a hand over his mouth, reached around and stabbed him from the front, the blade entering just below the ribcage, and moving upward to the heart. The guard was dead in an instant.

On the other side, Calvin slit the other guard's throat, then moved to the front of the building, crouching at its corner. He waited until his brother signaled with an owl hoot, looked around the corner and said, "Hey, motherfucker," ducking back out of the line of fire.

The guard rose, turned toward the voice, and Thad placed two rounds from a silenced pistol between the guard's shoulder blades.

After scanning the first floor of the house quickly, the brothers retreated to the shore and gave three blinks on their flashlights, then took their assault rifles from the waterproof duffel bag, jacked a round into the chamber, set the safety, and waited for the rest of the team to arrive.

"That did it," said Billy. He turned off the scope, wiped off the rainwater, and returned the weapon and scope to a waterproof duffel bag.

As Billy went over the side into the pontoon boat, Joe whispered, "Good huntin', y'all."

Shannon turned on the motor, and the pontoon boat moved almost silently around the stern of Joe's fishing vessel, the electric motor emitting no more than a low hum.

They beached the boat, split into two teams of three each—the first moving to the back porch, taking position next to the back door.

The second team, Thad Robinson in the lead, moved to the front of the house. Shannon pulled the pins on both grenades, holding down the safety levers, and nodded to Barry, who fired directly into the picture window at the front of the house. The glass shattered, and Shannon threw both grenades inside. They kept their eyes tightly shut so as not to be blinded by the flash grenade. When the grenades exploded, the team vaulted into the living room and moved immediately to their left.

Clark kicked in the back door, and his team moved in, fanning out to the right of the door, leaving a free field of fire for both groups. They took an extra moment to be sure that Debbie was not in the room before opening fire.

Two stunned, half blinded guards went down in a hail of gunfire. Three others put up a good fight, but it was over in a matter of minutes. Another guard came from upstairs, shotgun at the ready. Before he could get off one round, drawing quickly, both Nick and Sherif dropped him, each simultaneously firing three shots. Sherif turned to face Shannon. "Eight, plus two freebies," he said. "That's a pretty good clean-up for one day's work." He raised the barrel tip of the M-16 almost to his lips, puffing away a stream of gray smoke.

"Come on," said Shannon. "Debbie must be in here." He kicked down the door to the hallway leading from the kitchen to the room where Debbie was, then kicked in that door.

Debbie and Sue were crouched in a corner.

"Debbie, Sue! It's me, Nick."

"Thank God!" Sue cried, and fell into Shannon's arms, sobbing wildly. All three hugged.

"Thought there was supposed to be eight of them," said Barry.

Sherif nodded his head. The room was filled with the smell of cordite, and the rising odor of blood. "Yeah. We'd better check the rest of the house."

They all looked toward the stairs. Billy and Sherif moved to the foot of the stairs, nodded to one another, and began to climb. There was the roar of a powerful motor from the front of the house, and they all poured through the smashed picture window to see a rapidly receding black BMW moving down the road.

"Shit," said Billy. "Gino. Musta dropped from the window up there."

They moved back inside to see Shannon coming into the kitchen with Debbie in his arms, Sue tugging his jacket.

"They all right?" asked Clark.

"Yeah," said Shannon.

"Looka here," said Billy, placing a duffel bag on the kitchen table. He held up several bundles of cash.

"The ransom money," Clark sighed. "Leave it."

"Leave it?" Billy snapped. "Man, you got to be kiddin'."

"Nobody's going to worry too much about a bunch of dead

thugs; but if the money is missing, they'll track us down like dogs. Leave it, Billy."

"He's right," said Barry.

Shannon carried Debbie through the back door toward the pontoon boat. Sherif helped Sue.

"Maybe one got greedy and took a taste," said Billy.

Clark looked at Burke, who nodded his head.

"All right, Billy, take five packs."

"Five?" said Billy.

"Burke and I are out of it. Okay, Tim?" Again, Burke nodded.

Billy stuffed five bundles in his shirtfront and left the duffel bag on the kitchen table.

"Now, let's get the hell outta' here," Clark ordered. "Our car's parked down the road in a stand of trees. We stashed it earlier. Working another case."

The team moved swiftly away. Minutes later, Burke and Clark were back at their car, the balance of the strike team were on the boat, and Joe was weighing anchor.

CHAPTER 55

Debbie sat in Shannon's lap, refusing to relinquish her grip around his neck. She squirmed her firm buttocks into his groin. Sue's head rested on his shoulder.

Billy watched the scene with great amusement. When Shannon looked his way, Billy winked.

The Robinson brothers checked their equipment. Sherif was standing beside Joe, who kept the boat at a steady eight knots, humming a soft blues beneath his breath. The rain had ended, and overhead the full moon turned the lake into a shimmering beauty.

Clark and Burke pulled up and parked behind a police car near the city auto pound. Two detectives in an unmarked unit were on stakeout.

"Nothing yet," said one of the officers who had walked over to the car.

"We'll take it from here. It's only another hour or so before sunup."

Half an hour later, two men walked up Claiborne Avenue, looked around, then used wire cutters to get into the pound.

Before emerging from the car, Burke radioed for a back-up. Easing up quietly, they could see the two suspects tampering with the Saab, one man with a clean-shaven head, the other one with spiked gothic hair.

"Police, don't move," Clark yelled. The suspects turned, swinging out Uzis, and started firing. Clark and Burke, both expert marksmen, fired back. A moment later, it was all over, with the two brothers lying near each other, dead.

CHAPTER 56

8:00 a.m. – the morning after the riot

"We interrupt this regularly scheduled programming for an important news story. We join Alexis Gardner live from Blaine Kern Floatbuilders.

"Norman, something almost unprecedented is about to happen. Only once before in the history of Mardi Gas has it been canceled, back in 1979. Today, twenty years later, it looks like it's about to happen again. The Captains of twenty-one Carnival organizations have gathered here to make an announcement." One of the captains moved toward a microphone as the others filed in behind him.

"First, I would like to thank you all for coming," he said. "The captains you see behind me and the members of their organizations, sadly and reluctantly, have decided that we are not going to parade this Carnival season. We will not let Mardi Gras be held hostage by the Teamsters. Nothing but harm can come to the spirit of New Orleans Mardi Gras the way things are proceeding. It is wrong to use Mardi Gras as blackmail in this dispute. The same thing can happen next year, and we are not going to let our organizations be puppets in such a plan," he continued. The camera returns to the reporter. "There you have it, Norman. It's official. Twenty-one parades have been canceled in New Orleans."

"Are there any options?" Norman asked. "Like parading in Jefferson or St. Bernard Parish?"

"Nobody has said anything so far," the reporter answered, "but I'm sure they're keeping their options open."

"Alexis, the atmosphere in the city is like a timebomb just waiting to go off, the vandalism; police using tear gas and firing rubber bullets to break up unruly crowds. How big a part do you think that played in the captains' decision?"

"Well, naturally it was a consideration," she answered, "because of course public safety is the most important thing. But overwhelmingly they said that they just refuse to be manipulated."

"Thank you, Alexis." Across town, reporter Hugh Kerry talks to Carmine Gambino, the police union chief.

"Hugh," said Norman, "as you know by now, twenty-one of the Carnival organizations have decided to cancel their parades. Can you tell us what's the sentiment at police headquarters?" Surrounded by 120 Louisiana National Guardsmen carrying M-16s, hundreds of screaming, clenched fist policemen shouted and waved signs—"Crime doesn't pay, and neither does police work" and "Take this job and shove it." Two officers sprayed blue police shirts with lighter fluid and burned them, shouting "Strike! Strike! Strike!"

"I ain't got nothing now, so why should I worry about being fired?" shouted one policeman.

One officer was standing atop a parked police car, telling the others to remain calm, while angry officers turned on sirens and honked horns. The strikers had arrived in vans and pickup trucks from every district station in the city to participate in the rally. Some carried booze. Others had revolvers.

"Anybody who gets in my way is gonna get run over,"

bragged one man.

"Norman, I'm here with Captain Carmine Gambino, head of P.A.N.O., the police union. Captain Gambino, can you tell our viewers how your membership feels about this latest turn of events?" The police captain is visibly upset.

"It's a disappointment," he answered. "The city is just trying to make us look bad. The way things are going, though, they might have to cancel it next year, too."

"But in all fairness, Captain Gambino, the City didn't make the clubs cancel their parades," the reporter answered.

"It's a disappointment. We love Mardi Gras, too, just as much as anybody else. We didn't want to strike, but the mayor's refusal to bargain with the majority of the policemen in good faith has left us no alternative. I'll tell you this much, though, if the mayor tries to fire any of the striking policemen, this is a declaration of war. And we've warned our rank and file not to harass any National Guardsmen or state troopers because they're only trying to do their jobs. Only the policemen know what's good for the policemen. We don't condone any act of vigilantism and anyone who commits any will be forced out of the union."

The noise was building so much that the reporter had to yell to be heard above it.

"But isn't it true that Mafia boss Sal Cintenni would increase his influence in New Orleans if the Teamsters succeed in taking control of the police department? That's a fear shared by politicians, law enforcement officers, and business and civic leaders."

"That's a lot of bull," the officer snapped belligerently.

"But Captain Gambino, when questioned by the state Attorney General's office, didn't you admit that you have family and quasi-business ties to the Mafia chief? They've even seen your blue-and-white New Orleans police car parked in front of Cintenni's home."

"I don't have a 'police association' with Sal Cintenni. Yes, I do. Yes, I do. I have a quasi-business association with him. When I need doors opened, I call him. He's very influential. You know, if you have a rich uncle or cousin, you'd go to him for help. He helps me and I help him."

Alexis turned with the microphone and faced the camera. "Norman, back to you."

Norman turned, nodding his head. "Incredible. We also have an interview with Mayor Samuel Jammison Jr. Mr. Mayor, we talked to the Carnival captains and the police union president. Now it's your turn."

The screen switched to the mayor at Touro Infirmary Hospital. "As you know by now, Norman, my daughter was rescued early this morning, and I just want to thank everyone for their prayers." The mayor was very emotional. "You know, Norman, they say you take two steps forward and one backward. I have my daughter back, and the police have also solved the mystery of church burnings in New Orleans. But the Carnival captains are right. No city should be kept under siege by anybody, especially the police. It's regrettable. In spite of their substantial investments, the krewes acted in the interest of public safety and security of our citizens. This strike is illegal, Norman, that's the bottom line. And it's a terrible thing when the police don't obey the law. They have been duped and deceived. The union is only thinking about one thing: we're going to get ours."

"What about the lootings and the fires, Mayor Jammison?"

"Norman, racial tension permeates this country, from racial profiling to unarmed African-American males being fatally wounded by white police officers. In many cases it is true that officers are firing their weapons with no evidence that fellow officers or the public is in imminent danger. Police work is hard and dangerous, we all know that, but there is never a good excuse for violence and lawlessness, no matter who it is. Anyone caught breaking the law will be arrested and prosecuted to the fullest extent of the law. The rioting last night resulted in two hundred arrests and the dusk-to-dawn curfew will be in effect again tonight."

The camera switched back to the studio. "Mr. Mayor as I drove in to work today everywhere I looked store owners were busy boarding up windows, trying to protect their property. In light of recent events is there anything you'd like to say to them?"

"Norman, we're on high alert," the Mayor answered. "I just want to assure them . . . I want to assure everyone, that the arson, the vandalism, the uncontrolled violence on our streets and attacks on any of our citizen's cannot and will not be tolerated. What started out as peaceful demonstrations sadly became an opportunity for young thugs and troublemakers to set fires and beat people up, running wild and breaking store windows, stealing whatever they wanted to. I've been contacted by the President and he's asked the Attorney General to look into this situation. But I need to make one thing absolutely clear. There is no room for hate here, for any reason, and it's just not going to happen. The violence and the craziness is going to stop, and it's not going to stop a month from now, or even a week from now. It's going to stop today!"

"Thank you, Mr. Mayor," Norman said empathetically. "And I know I speak for everyone in expressing how happy I am that your daughter is safe again."

Norman turned back to the camera, "And what about you, the man in the street? How do you feel about the police strike and Mardi Gras being canceled? For answers from the man on the street, we go live to Barbara July."

"Yes, Norman. With me is Clifton Smith, a man with a definite opinion."

"Yeah," said the man eagerly. "In the past whenever there was a strike, who was it who broke it up? The police, that's who.

And I'm not talkin' about people making 1500 a month. I'm talking about people just trying to make a living and feed their families. No pensions, no hospitalization, no paid vacation . . . Now it's the cops' turn. If it's good for the goose, it's good for the gander."

Norman comes back on the camera, smiling. "We wanted one man's opinion, and that's exactly what we got."

During the weeks that followed, there were many volatile confrontations between police officers who were striking and those who were not, and between angry policemen and angry citizens. Eventually, the strike ended with compromises being made on both sides.

PLAYING FOR KEEPS

PART 2

CHAPTER 57

"That double-crossin', two-timin', yella nigger bastard! Tryin' to put one over on me, huh? Sittin' in that fuckin' chair, all calm and superior, playin' with me, the motherfucker. When a deal is made, a deal is made. He got the fuckin' dough, didn't he? A deal is a deal, then he goes and makes a raid! Sonofabitch," shouted Cintenni, angrily, the veins in his temples gorged and throbbing.

Gino kept his mouth shut. He didn't remind Sal that he was the one who had planned a double-cross when he ordered Debbie's murder. When Sal was like this it was better to let him vent his anger.

Luckily, Gino had been taking a nap in the upstairs bedroom when the raiders hit. By the time he'd roused himself, everything was over. He'd dropped from the second floor window onto the sand at the rear of the house, performing a gymnastic roll-out, and in the same motion darted for his car. He was lucky all right, he knew, because whoever it was on that raid had been damn good.

Gino had insisted on a larger number of guards, three shifts that would have four hours on, eight hours off, but he'd been overruled by Sal, who was long on enforcing loyalty but short on organizational skills. It was the reason he'd moved Gino up to his right-hand man, but Sal kept fucking with Gino's plan. A boss who couldn't delegate authority was a nuisance wherever he reigned, thought Gino.

"Sal, we have no definite proof that the mayor had anything to do with the raid," Gino said, realizing what Sal was thinking was absolutely crazy. "I know damn well it wasn't the police or the FBI; it was a military operation. A damn commando raid, quick hit and out."

"Who else could it be but that fuckin' Jammison? Pretending to Tom, but really thinkin' he's superior to me. Laughin' behind my fuckin' back. Nothin' worse than an uppity nigger, Gino. Remember that."

Sal was pacing the carpet in his large study next to his bedroom, cigar in one hand, a large glass of brandy in the other, red-faced and furious. He stopped in the middle of the room, took a sip of his drink, a long puff on his cigar. His eyes narrowed and he seemed calmer.

"I want that nigger dead. Call The Man. I want him whacked. The sooner the better."

The Man was their top hit man. Fourteen kills and never a hitch. The Man preferred guns, but it didn't really matter to him: piano wire garrot, explosives, knives, bare hands, whatever. He would make it look like an accident, or make it a dirty kill. He was quiet, efficient, and never left a clue. He wasn't cheap, fifty thousand dollars plus expenses, but worth every dime.

"Sal," said Gino, "maybe you ought to calm down and think this over. Knocking off a man as popular as the mayor may not be a good idea, especially after the kidnapping. They'll come down on us like a ton of bricks. Police, FBI, ATF, every damn body. The Attorney General's office might even get involved and investigate the murders as hate crimes."

"Bullshit," Sal exploded, his booming voice echoing throughout the house. "The fuckin' police hate his guts because of that Mardi Gras fiasco and he's still stonewallin' 'em on their demands for better pay. And the fuckin' Feebies couldn't find their own ass with two hands. I want the fucker whacked, so the next one jumps when I say jump. Got that?"

Sal's gone off his rocker, Gino thought. He had never been particularly intelligent, but he did have the shrewdness and cunning of any Sicilian peasant. The town would go wild, and the impact on the organization's operations—dope, prostitution, gambling, bars and restaurants might ruin them in the short run and cost millions. Decades of effort by Sal's predecessors could be shattered, Gino was thinking; but he knew that Cintenni was unmovable in his present state of mind.

"Call The Man right now," Sal growled, still yelling loud enough to be heard down the hall. In all the years Gino had known the mob boss until recently he had never spoken to him so harshly.

"Sal..."

Cintenni slid the phone toward Gino.

"That black sonofabitch'll be fuckin' maggot food before he knows what hit him! Right now, I said, Gino. Do what I say!"

Gino dialed. "You know who this is," said Gino into the phone. "Got a job for you, big one. Double your usual fee." He looked at Cintenni, who nodded his confirmation.

"Meet me tomorrow night at eight. Usual place." Gino hung up the phone with a sigh. It was a dumb move, he knew, but Sal just smiled.

CHAPTER 58

Chauncey Williams III stood naked, legs spread, bracing himself with his arms on the dresser, smiling into the large mirror at Sal while he plowed his ass with his thick dick, slow and deep. Chauncey groaned and Sal knew he was ready to come.

Sal reached into the right-hand pocket of his open silk robe and withdrew a white silk scarf. Chauncey's smile broadened as Sal wrapped the scarf around his neck. As he tightened the scarf, his motion quickened and Chauncey threw his head back in ecstasy, but when he came, feeling Sal's own ejaculation in his widespread anus, Sal pulled tighter. Chauncey's eyes bulged, and his tongue came out as he frantically reached for Sal's hands, then clawed wildly at the scarf wound tightly around his neck. Too late, in his final moments, he knew this was no foray into the rough love he desired: it was the end.

Sal held on for at least a minute more, holding the body up by the scarf wound tightly around his fists. Then he let it slump to the floor, his stout penis sliding out, dripping cum.

That was fucking great, though Sal, coming while his partner was dying. Shit, he'd have to try that again. When he got tired of a lover, he'd just snuff him. But he hadn't tired of Chauncey, and for a moment Sal was truly saddened. Had to do it, he thought, the little faggot had fucked up on his information about the kidnapping, and he'd been careless lately, calling him at home during the daytime, even writing him love notes. Shit, he thought, if anybody knew about me and men, I'd be finished.

Not that he was gay, Sal told himself. He just liked some round eye from time to time, and had ever since he'd been turned out at nineteen when he was doing short time in prison for assault and battery, the only time he had ever done.

Sal thought with fondness about the sweet little faggot cellmate and how he'd been seduced. They'd had a discreet affair for years until Thomas had gotten strung out on blow, and Sal had to whack him one night after he threatened to snitch on him when Sal denied him his beloved drugs. Never fuck around with a pothead, or any other kind of addict, Cintenni remembered.

Sal walked toward his marble-lined bathroom to wash himself off. He took one last look at Chauncey's beautiful, almost hairless body, face bloated and blackened by strangulation, sighed regretfully, and entered the bathroom.

CHAPTER 59

Downstairs, The Man inserted the key into the small vial of oil, slid it silently into the lock and let himself in. He moved to the alarm box, punched numbers into the code panel to quiet the alarm, and stood in the dark hall, like a predatory beast sniffing the air for food. He knew that Sal always dismissed his staff and bodyguards on the nights of his homosexual trysts. The Man knew almost everything about Sal.

The Man slid his feet out of his soft loafers, and silently crept up the stairs, carefully placing his feet next to the wall to cancel any possible creak.

He entered Sal's study, went to the large desk and took the nine-millimeter Sig from the right-hand drawer, walked to the half-open bedroom door and paused to listen.

He moved into the bedroom and silently regarded the body at the foot of the dresser, the automatic hidden behind his right thigh.

Sal entered from the bathroom and stopped short, startled. "What the fuck you doin' here?" Cintenni asked. "I told you never to come to my house."

At once, Sal realized that he had been caught. Embarrassed by Chauncey's naked body on his bedroom floor, he quickly tried to recover by playing it off. "I guess you can see I had to take care of a little business myself." Sal waved his hand. "Guess it's all right this time. You got the mayor set up?"

The Man nodded, then moved swiftly across the room and shot Sal twice in the stomach at point-blank range. Sal staggered and went down, his feet twitching just short of Chauncey's head.

The man regarded his work. Good, he thought. It will look like two faggots fell out, a double murder. Cintenni got too rough, Chauncey realized what was happening and shot him. There would be powder burns on Cintenni's stomach, and he would place the weapon in the right-hand drawer, long enough to leave oil marks.

The Man returned to the study and poured himself a stiff drink of Sal's good twenty-year-old bourbon. He went back into the bedroom, sat in a chair next to the massive bed, cut the end of a cigar, placing the cut end in his pocket, lit the cigar, took a drink of the bourbon, and waited for Cintenni to die.

"Why?" Sal demanded. "Why?" a stream of blood running from the corner of his mouth.

"You were getting out of hand, Sal," The Man answered. "Whacking the mayor was a crazy idea."

"Gino?"

"Who else?"

"Ungrateful fuck," said Cintenni. "Never shoulda trusted that damn college boy."

His breath was coming in short gasps. It wouldn't be long, now, thought The Man. Two hollow-point nine-millimeter slugs would have done massive damage. Cintenni was a damn bull. Most men would have croaked from the shock. The Man sat in silence, enjoying the good Havana cigars, the smooth bourbon.

With a last gasp, the mob boss died. The Man watched him for a while, taking in the scene, photographing in his mind what the Homicide Squad would see. It looked good: double murder of two homosexuals, one of them a mob boss. The police would make a cursory investigation and close the case.

The Man finished his drink, put out the cigar and placed it in his pocket. He walked across the room and placed the pistol next to Chauncey's right hand, after opening the dresser drawer and lying the gun on one of Sal's shorts for a moment.

The Man took one last look around the room, then walked into Sal's study. He took a handful of cigars from the humidor, considered taking the bottle of bourbon, decided against it, and walked downstairs.

He slid his feet into the loafers, walked into the kitchen, broke the glass into the garbage disposal in the sink, turned on the motor, and ground and flushed the glass fragments down the sink. He left the kitchen, punched the code into the panel at the front door, and let himself out. Less than an hour later, The Man sat in his bedroom watching "Little Caesar," an old Edward G. Robinson movie, on television. He savored the good cigar as well as his own bourbon. Not as smooth as Sal's but good, nevertheless.

He waited patiently for his favorite part in the movie: when Edward G. Robinson, riddled with bullets, staggered to the church steps, collapsed and lay there dying. The part came, and The Man leaned forward in anticipation.

"Mother of God," said Edward G. Robinson, "Is this the end of Rico?"

The Man threw back his head and laughed joyously.

CHAPTER 60

"How's the investigation going, Pat?" asked Clark.

Callahan took a sip of beer straight from his bottle of Heineken before replying. "We're just going through the motions, Al. The mayor's daughter is back safely, we recovered most of the money, and some predatory scum are no longer walking the streets. Not a bad deal, I'd say."

They were seated outside at concrete tables in front of Castnet Seafood, a joint that sold fresh fish, and cooked it for you on the spot. The fish store and small restaurant was divided into two rooms. The one to the left had glass cases featuring fresh fish and shellfish displayed on a bed of cracked ice. The room to the right of the entrance sold condiments: sauces, mixtures of herbs for curries, gumbo, sandwiches, Cajun and Creole cooking, and various kinds of fish and shellfish in cans and jars.

It had turned warm again, and they sat in their shirtsleeves, enjoying the sun and sharing a plate of fresh oysters. The sky was cloudless, except for a towering cumulus on the far horizon. The levee, just across the street, blocked their view of the lake.

"Who do you think made the raid?" asked Clark, as he speared a fresh oyster, then dipped it into a spicy red, peppery sauce.

"The raid was done with military precision, from the evidence, what little they left. Almost as if at least one of the raiders had some police experience," said Callahan as he observed a gull high overhead, riding the thermal currents. Not for the first time, Callahan wondered how a bird that was so ugly and awkward on land could be so graceful in flight. Divine compensation, he thought.

The sun was warm on their faces, and Callahan's beefy face was turning red.

"Military Police, maybe?" prompted Clark, as he took a sip of Beck's.

"Might be," Callahan replied. He took another sip of beer, his eyes still on the gull. "You were military police in Nam, weren't you, Al?"

"So were you, Pat. At least, that's what I heard."

"True," replied Callahan. "It's one reason why I decided to join the FBI when I was discharged. That, and the fact that my family goes back three generations on the Chicago police force."

"Why are you certain it was a military type operation?" asked Clark, taking a bite from a saltine cracker.

"The man at the rear was hit at long range. By the nature of the wound, he was probably hit by a round from a nine millimeter rifle of German make, perhaps a Mauser sniper's rifle."

Callahan turned to Clark and began counting off on the fingers of his large right hand. "Second, the two guards on the flanks were killed by large knives. K-Bar type, with a serrated edge. Third, forensics indicated that at least one concussion and one flash grenade was used before the team moved in. Fourth, the cartridges inside were from M-16s and at least one AK-47."

"Most of that stuff can be ordered by mail or bought on the open market," Clark answered. "You could even find a sniper rifle, if you tried hard enough."

"True," replied Callahan. "But when you add the weaponry

to the tactics involved, it bears the unmistakable stamp of military training. A team of combat veterans who haven't lost their skills. Most probably Nam vets, and probably black."

"Why do you say that?"

"That part is speculation. Who else would have that kind of motive to rescue the mayor's daughter? Mayor Jammison is a community icon. Plus there is that little matter of the missing five hundred thousand dollars."

"I think you make a good case, Pat," said Clark. He gathered their paper plates. "Another beer?" Callahan nodded.

Clark disappeared into the restaurant. He returned with two steaming bowls of shrimp gumbo and two more bottles of beer.

They crumbled round crackers into the gumbo, and sipped beer while waiting for it to cool.

"Why does beer taste so good straight out of the bottle?" asked Callahan.

"I dunno. Maybe it's a macho thing," said Clark.

They were similar physical types, Clark tall, broad-shouldered and thick, Callahan bulky but square built, whose bulk belied his six-four height. He stayed in shape with regular workouts at a gym: Nautilus weight machines for muscle tone and handball for aerobics.

Clark, a strong safety at Grambling, had maintained his playing weight of one ninety-five. He ran two miles a day, worked with free weights, played racquetball, and swam. They were two well-conditioned, middle-aged ex-jocks, except for the bulge around Clark's midsection.

They dug into the gumbo and ate in silence, two men who enjoyed good food more than ambiance. They both preferred small, funky restaurants over the fancier and overpriced restaurants in the French Quarter. They finished the gumbo, sat back, and sipped beer.

"I think you were in on the raid, Al," Callahan said finally.

"Really?"

"As I said, speculation. It's not in my report. Ever think about joining the FBI, Al?"

Clark frowned. "You know how black people feel about the FBI, Pat."

"Yeah, I know. COINTELPRO, the civil rights movement. Too bad, you'd make a good agent. You play it by the book, with the exception of the raid. Even then, you covered your tracks well."

"I don't know what you're talking about," said Clark, with a poker face.

"Sure."

"Great day, huh," said Clark, with a smile.

"Why don't we fly up to Chicago and catch some jazz sometime? Von Freeman does a jam session on Seventy-Fifth and Eberhart every Tuesday night. Chicago and New Orleans, two of my favorite places."

"Sounds good to me," said Clark.

"But not until the weather breaks. Colder than whale shit up there about now," said Callahan.

"Man, you grew up in Chicago. I thought you white folks dug cold weather."

"Hell, I was cold all the time I was in Chicago. Why I busted my ass to get this assignment. You got me confused with the Scandinavians. I'm Irish, remember?"

* * *

It was a Saturday, a month after the raid. They were off duty, and their beepers had not called them back for an emergency. They each lit a cigarette and sat in easy silence, two men becoming friends and enjoying the trip.

Clark checked his watch. "My boat's docked not far from here. Let's go check the Bulls game."

"Right," said Callahan. "Who are they playing?"

"Detroit, in the Stadium."

"Yeah. Let's go," said Callahan.

"We'd better pick up a six-pack of Heineken for you on the way."

"Sounds good to me."

Clark gathered the empty bowls and went inside to pay the check.

CHAPTER 61

Debbie figured that the time had come. It was three months after she'd been rescued by Shannon and the others, and as she'd promised, she swore that she had no idea who they were. They all wore ski masks, she'd said, which was true, but Nick had taken his off when he found her and Sue

However, as she'd planned, Debbie told the shrink who was treating her for post traumatic stress disorder that Shannon had rescued her, and the shrink indicated that since she had fixated on Shannon, it might be good therapy for her to see him regularly until she got better.

Debbie knew that shrinks believed that their patients never got better. How else could they milk them for years at such prices?

The truth was that Debbie had stopped having bad dreams within a couple of weeks and was really just fine, but she told the shrink what she wanted to hear so that she could spend more time with Shannon. Even though she missed Ray very, very much, there was a certain comfort and security she felt whenever Nick was around. The shrink, who was not a bad-looking white woman, decided that she should meet Shannon shortly after Debbie described him in detail. She had him sit in on the sessions at least once a month because it was obvious by the way she dressed and looked at Shannon during the sessions that she was interested in him, too. He was trying hard, resisting the advances of the shrink, who showed more cleavage and leg at every meeting.

Debbie would drop by Shannon's house at least twice a week, making herself useful. Shannon, like many bachelors, was an excellent housekeeper, but he hated washing dishes and was a lousy cook. Debbie always washed the dishes and would cook them something to eat when she dropped by. She had learned Creole cooking from her grandmother, Genevieve, and French cuisine from her mother.

She made sure that she read the kinds of books that Shannon liked, mysteries mainly, as well as history books.

They would sit in front of the fire before it turned warm and discuss the books; but Debbie always left before Shannon could become bored with her. She always left just after Sue might arrive, acting very sweet toward the jealous girlfriend, who obviously did not trust her, and knew exactly what she had on her mind, which was to seduce Shannon. Women always knew those things, but the more jealous Sue acted, the more she annoyed Shannon, who was trying very hard to be faithful to a woman who was becoming increasingly more frustrated.

Debbie would clean the swimming pool in the back yard at least once a week, stripping to a bikini or one-piece suit that showed off her body, but she never obviously posed, and knew that at times Shannon couldn't take his eyes off her when he thought she didn't know that he was looking.

Today, she hadn't taken a swim after cleaning the pool, but a shower instead, in Shannon's bathroom. When she came out of the shower, she stopped at the foot of the bed with a towel wrapped around her, then asked Shannon to come into the room.

When he stopped at the door Debbie let the towel drop. Shannon's mouth dropped open, too.

"Debbie, uh, look, now. You gotta put that towel back on. Cut this out!" said Shannon, his voice cracking and sweat breaking out on his face.

Debbie walked slowly up to him, took his limp hands in hers and placed them on her full breasts. Then she put her arms around his neck and kissed him tenderly, full on the mouth. When he opened his mouth to her tongue, then shifted his hands to her hard, high buttocks, she knew she had him.

They kissed gently at first, their tongues exploring the wetness of each other's mouths, and then their passion exploded. The more they tasted each other, the more intoxicated they became. She slowly lowered herself to the bed, using her powerful legs to smoothly push herself forward.

Her girlfriend, Chantal, had been having a secret affair with her father's best friend since she was sixteen, and she assured Debbie that older men knew just how to please a girl, especially one like Nick.

Debbie could hardly wait for Shannon to enter her, but instead he stood at the foot of the bed and slowly undressed. He crawled onto the bed, spread her legs apart, then slowly lowered his head between her smooth, rock-hard limbs. He stiffened his tongue and ran it along the inside of her thigh, kissing and licking it affectionately. He softly blew his warm breath over the silky black hairs hiding her vagina, crossed to the other side and repeated the action.

Using his tongue, gently twirling it around like a spinning top to circle her clitoris, he artfully titillated the supple lips of her labia, shooting electric streams of pleasure throughout her body. He flattened his tongue, dragged it over her clitoris, then sucked, nibbled and bit it lovingly.

Wow, Debbie thought. For a moment she felt guilty about Ray. Before she knew it, she began to shudder and felt her orgasm on the way. It was going to be a big one, she could tell, as she thrust her fist against her mouth. She then remembered that no one could hear her, withdrew her hand, then thew back her head and howled.

He lifted himself then slid forward, grabbing his throbbing penis firmly and holding it just above her mouth, then lightly rubbed the pink head back and forth across her lips. In his excitement, he had started to leak. She opened her eyes, staring into his, then extended the tip of her tongue. She teased and licked the wet tip of the head of his penis, then opened wide and sucked it deep into her soft warm mouth. She tilted her head slightly and it slipped out. She held it gently as she quickly flicked her tongue back and forth along the underside of the shaft, then started licking and lightly sucking his scrotum.

Nick Shannon basically practiced only two kinds of sex, what he called utility sex and the deluxe. Utility sex was generally what everybody else referred to as fucking, a skill he had tactilely mastered, like most men attempted to do by playing a sport like golf, or playing a musical instrument like a saxophone or a trumpet.

As a teenager, while the other boys his age were trying to impress the opposite sex with their prowess at football and basketball, he was busy trying to cut straight to the chase, to figure out what really made little girls tick. He spent hours at a time reading books like "The Art of Love," "The Act of Love," "Human Sexual Response," "Kama Sutra" and anything else he could get his hands on, then working out. With the deluxe he pulled out all the stops. He had always chuckled at the fact that when a woman was being artfully seduced, she so often misguidedly assumed it was love.

Debbie was so young and so beautiful that he actually found himself going beyond the deluxe to a state of euphoric lovemaking where he allowed himself to drift into a dream-like easiness. He sucked her perfect breast, then licked and nibbled, first on one erect nipple and then the other. He put his fingers between her legs, then gently played with her. Discreetly placing his head on her chest over her heart, he could hear it pounding loudly while he skillfully manipulated her.

He raised up, turned her over, then pulled her perfectly rounded ass toward him. He pushed his penis inside her. On her knees and her elbows, she looked over her shoulder at Shannon, thinking that she had a few tricks of her own. She pulled her body forward, arching her back downward, relaxing and controlling her breathing, stroking his penis rhythmically. She backed up, arching her back upward, tightening then relaxing her vaginal walls, moving faster and faster, squeezing and massaging the shaft.

Over and over she sensuously moved forward, smoothly, like an ocean wave on a clear day with blue skies, then backed up with the fury of white breakers crashing against a mountain cliff.

He had started out easily controlling her, but suddenly found himself hanging back and just trying to hold on.

"Ahhhhhh!" he screamed, as his body spasmed automatically. His eyes were squeezed tight, his face contorted in painful ecstasy, soaking wet with perspiration, his legs wobbling. His mind was so far gone that he did not realize how deeply his fingers were dug into Debbie's delicate flesh.

"I think I've bitten off more than I can chew," he gasped, lying on his back after collapsing next to her.

With a big smile on her face, she stared deep into his eyes and answered, "It's called a vise grip. I read a lot."

Later, they lay in the bed, the perspiration cooling on their bodies, with Debbie's head on his shoulder, when the portable phone rang.

"Hello."

"Hello, Nick. How are you?" Sue asked.

Debbie stuck out her tongue, and Shannon almost laughed.

"I'm glad you called, Sue..."

"Baby, I wanted to apologize for being so bitchy the other

night. Of course, I'm not really jealous of that child. I just think she should spend more time with young men her own age."

"Sue, I've made a decision. I'm not going to take that job with the casino. I just can't see becoming a suit, and... "

"You what? Nick, you promised!"

"I promised to think it over," Shannon answered calmly as Debbie eyed him playfully, seductively sucking his thumb. But he had decided before the raid that he could never work for Sam Jammison. He felt guilty not telling Debbie about her father.

"Do you remember what I said, Nick?" said Sue evenly.

"Yeah, I remember, and I'm going to miss you. Anyway, I think that lawyer you've been spending time with would be much better for you than I would."

"How did you know?"

"I'm a detective, remember?"

"Nick, you're a damn fool. Besides, he's only a friend."

"Well, we all need friends, don't we. Look, I'm really tired."

Shannon looked down to see Debbie grinning around his growing penis. She remembered that Chantal said that she should use her hand near the base of the man's dick. She tried it and felt him getting harder in her mouth.

"Sorry, I gotta run. Something's just come up."

Shannon rang off, reached for Debbie's hips and guided her toward his face. She straddled his head and lowered herself toward his talented tongue. Anxious after the rape, her two HIV tests had come back negative.

Shit, thought Debbie, sixty-nine. I wonder what else we're going to do today. She wondered what it would taste like when he came in her mouth. She worked harder so that she could find out, as her own orgasm took her.

CHAPTER 62

"I'm so glad you could stop by, Detective Clark," said Miss Peabody. "Please do sit. Would you care for coffee, or are you off duty? Perhaps you'd prefer something just a wee bit stronger."

Miss Peabody stood silhouetted by the large window in the living room, her backlit blonde hair glowing halo-like, the light shining through her sheer white Egyptian cotton dress, giving a full-shadowed view of her gorgeous legs. He could smell the faint aroma of her perfume.

Clark wondered how old she was. She must be well into her sixties, he thought; however, she had a body a thirty-year-old woman would have killed for, and a face not much older than that. Plastic surgery, good diet, and regular exercise had done wonders for this still-gorgeous woman.

"Thank you, Miss Peabody. Bourbon, maybe?"

"Of course, Detective Clark. May I call you by your first name?"

"Please do. It's Al. I've been trying to get back to personally thank you for your help, but there's never a free moment."

"Please call me Florence," she said, with a cat-like smile. "How thoughtful of you."

Miss Peabody sank gracefully into a chair across the low

table from Clark, reached over, revealing a gorgeous pair of breasts and no bra, and rang a silver bell. Her house servant appeared immediately.

If she's trying to seduce me, Clark was thinking, she's doing a damn good job so far. Go with the flow, he thought, and leaned back into the chair.

"Bourbon, you said, Al?"

"Please," said Clark.

"Two bourbons, please, Edna," said Miss Peabody with a smile. "Edna's been around since I was a child. My father was district manager for an oil company. We had servants, free Cadillacs, our house was free. People think I'm rich because I have a housekeeper and I live in this big house."

"Is that your Infiniti in the driveway?" Clark joked.

"You see these, Al," she said, playing with two strands of necklaces dangling from her neck. "This pair is real crystal, see how they pick up the light, and these," as she touched the other pair which were pink, "they're real plastic, but who would know?"

Surprised at Miss Peabody's sense of humor, Clark started laughing.

"You're a beautiful lady, Miss Peabody."

"Thank you, Al," she blushed. "My contractor saw me an hour before I got all dressed up, then he saw me afterwards and said he couldn't believe the difference. I told him you know the difference a little paint can make. Well, I told him he paints my house and makes it beautiful. I'm an excellent painter, too. I paint my face and make it beautiful."

"You're right, Florence. You're one helluva painter."

"I'm so glad that Debbie's back safely, Al. She stops in at least once a week. It gladdens an old woman's heart to be cared for by such a well-bred young woman. Do you have children, Al?"

"A boy and a girl."

"I would imagine you'd be a devoted father," said Miss Peabody.

"I try," said Clark.

Edna returned and served the drinks, giving Clark a measured look as well as a peek at her own massive cleavage. As she stood, she gave Clark a lewd wink, before leaving the room like a stalking lioness.

What the fuck is going on? Clark asked himself.

"Cheers, Al," said Miss Peabody, raising her drink in toast.

"It's a shame to put water in this kind of bourbon," he said. "Smooth as silk. What is it?"

"My daddy's private stock. He owned part interest in a small distillery in Kentucky. Twenty years old, I believe. Daddy used to say that his moonshining ancestors would kill for liquor this good. Don't you agree?"

"Yes, ma'am - uh, Florence, I sure do." Clark took a sip of the smooth whiskey, held it in his mouth a moment, then let it slide slowly down his throat. Nectar, he thought. Must be a bitch to be rich, even when you say you're not.

"I believe that I mentioned that I knew your father, Al. In fact, I knew him quite well. Intimately, you might say." She smiled that cat-like smile. She leaned back in her chair and slowly stroked her thigh with her free hand.

Clark nearly choked on his drink. Florence grinned. She took another sip of her drink, regarding him over the rim of her glass with her clear blue eyes.

"He was a good friend. To be honest, Al, we were lovers for years."

This time, Clark did choke. He wiped his mouth and his brow with his handkerchief and took a deep swallow of his drink.

"Did I shock you, Al? Of course, you know all the clichés about aristocratic Bourbon women and their colored retainers.

"Historically, the term 'jody' came from those colored bucks who serviced their white slave mistresses while their husbands were off fighting for the Confederacy. 'Gone With the Wind' would have been more historically correct if Rhett Butler had been colored," said Miss Peabody.

"You may smoke, if you like."

Al took out his cigarettes and lit up. The way this was going, he wished he had a joint of good reefer.

"Served those slave owners right, I do believe," she continued. "Just revenge for enslavement, and for their tendencies to neglect their poor wives on behalf of their slave mistresses and colored concubines, don't you think?" She took a dainty sip of her drink. Her breasts were well shaped and pointed. He wondered if she had implants. "Well, I'm afraid that your daddy and I were just that kind of cliché. I guess you might call him my jody. You remind me of your daddy a great deal."

"Coming from an elegant lady like you, and considering how well you knew Daddy, I consider that quite a compliment." He finished his drink in one big gulp, then nervously looked at his watch. "I guess I'd better be on my way. Thanks again, Florence. And I'll make sure I mention you to Daddy next time I see him."

"The pleasure was mine, Al," she answered, giving him a lewd smile as she reached for his hand. "And don't be a stranger."

"Uh, I won't. I won't," the detective stuttered. "Goodbye."

"Goodbye, Al."

CHAPTER 63

He picked the lock in a matter of minutes and entered through the back door. He knew that she was in because he had seen her Bonneville parked at the curb, and that she was probably passed out because he'd called on the cellular phone from the van, and there had been no answer.

Celeste was on the living room couch slumped against the back, looking like a beached whale, grossly fat, triple-chinned, face mottled, mouth open, snoring loudly. The room was filled with the stench of booze and stale cigarette smoke, her stale breath, and an unwashed body and hair. There was a half-empty fifth of cheap vodka on the cocktail table in front of her.

She wore a dirty housecoat, half-open, partially revealing her large flabby breasts. He shook his head, remembering how fine she had been, parading at the beauty contests, filling the one-piece bathing suits to overflow, her smile bright and artificial, the finest thing on the stage. Now, she was an alcoholic wreck, old before her time.

He went into the bedroom and took the gun from the bedside table: a nickel-plated .32 Colt revolver. He broke it open and checked the rounds. They were clean and new enough to do the job.

He returned to the living room and pondered the job. If he

made it look like suicide, it would probably make the insurance policy invalid. An apparent robbery would probably be best. She discovered the burglar, and in the struggle, he'd shot her at close range.

He moved closer and raised the gun, then his eyes fell on the open bottle of sleeping pills. An accidental overdose, a fatal combination of booze and barbiturates, was even better because it would invoke the double indemnity clause of the policy.

He returned the gun to its place in the bedside table and returned to the living room. He pried back one eyelid and looked at the dilated pupil. She was already heavily sedated. It wouldn't take many more. He poured six pills into his open palm, not worrying about fingerprints because he wore surgeon's gloves, then dropped the pills into her open mouth and held her nose until she automatically swallowed.

He stood there for a few minutes regarding his handiwork. If she doesn't throw them up, they should do the job. Even then, he thought, she might choke on her own vomit. Her breathing was already slowing.

He returned to the kitchen, checked his surroundings, through the partially open door, then moved into the backyard and walked the short distance to the van.

It was a warm Tuesday in a district of working professionals, and no one was around. He'd counted on that; but just to be sure, he'd stolen the van an hour before.

He entered the van and drove slowly away. Parking it in a supermarket parking lot, he discarded the gloves in a dumpster and walked the short distance to his own vehicle.

He slid a tape into the dashboard deck and listened to Gladys Knight singing "Midnight Train to Georgia." *I need a drink,* he thought, and stopped in a bar near his home and ordered a Southern Comfort and Coke.

Even after all these years, thought Billy, *I still can't feel right*

about killing a woman.
    He finished his drink and ordered another.

CHAPTER 64

"I believe it's time to retire from politics, Mr. Mayor," said Gino. "You've had a good run. The people adore you, at least the blacks—even most of the white voters, in spite of the fact that you canceled Mardi Gras and the police went on strike. There's not been a hint of scandal during your regime, so... "

"If I don't?" asked Jammison, taking a sip of scotch.

"Then I can't be responsible for what might happen. Giuseppe, J.D.'s cousin, is foaming at the mouth. He's sure you were behind the raid that rescued your daughter. Family honor. Been wanting to take you out."

"I see," said the mayor.

"In our business, we don't like political assassinations."

"President Kennedy?" asked the mayor, raising his eyebrows.

"We learned from that mistake," Gino answered. "The heat was on for years after that hit. It's still on. The old heads, the Mustache Petes, are being phased out of the Organization. A more corporate type is slowly moving into the top echelon nowadays."

"Like you?"

"Like me. We're even moving out of drugs here in New Orleans. The price of cocaine is one-quarter its price five years ago because the South Americans have overloaded the market. Plus, the overhead in bribes to Immigration authorities to smuggle it in and to local police and DEA cops is enormous. Smaller profits."

Gino took a drag on one of Sal's cigars, a sip of his twenty-year-old cognac, before continuing. Opera emanated from hidden speakers.

"Those Colombians have no business sense, really," said Gino, with a shake of his head. "They haven't got a clue."

"So if I don't retire, I might meet with some untimely mishap."

"Precisely. Like I said, you've had a good run. Built a good stash in our Grand Caymans bank. You'll do all right."

"I'll miss the action," the mayor responded, looking down at the half-filled, peach colored glass held firmly in his hand. "You know, I really enjoyed running this town. Did a good job, I think. It wasn't only the money. You know, power is one helluvan aphrodisiac."

"Like becoming governor. Nobody gets it all. I'm curious. Did you order the raid?" asked Gino.

They were seated in Cintenni's former study. The house belonged to a dummy corporation, and Gino, now capo di tutti of the New Orleans mob, had moved in a month after Sal's funeral, one of the biggest in history. Five bands had played "Didn't He Ramble" on the way back from the St. Louis cemetery on Esplanade Avenue. Sal had been laid to rest in a massive marble mausoleum, hundreds in attendance at the funeral, including politicians, civic leaders, and corporate executives. Cintenni had always been lavish with charitable donations.

"Would you believe me if I said no?" said Jammison.

"Maybe," said Gino.

"Well, I haven't a clue. It sounded like a group of military veterans, according to what little evidence they left. A smooth commando raid. Actually, I'd relied on Sal's word after we closed the deal." Of course, the mayor knew that it was Nick Shannon, but he would never let Gino know that.

"That was a mistake, Sam. Sal ordered your daughter's murder."

"Fucking bastard. Is that why Cintenni met an untimely demise?"

Gino lit another Corona before replying, then pushed the humidor and cigar cutter across the desk toward the mayor. "Exactly. Sal was losing control, becoming egomaniacal. Dangerous in our business. I never shared his hang-ups."

The mayor took his time cutting and lighting the cigar, his mind racing.

"How much time do I have before I announce my retirement from politics?" asked the mayor.

"I'll leave the timing up to you," Gino answered.

"Have you chosen my replacement yet?"

"Your friend Daniels," replied Gino.

"New recruit, or has he been on your payroll all along?"

"Since we recruited you," was Gino's reply. "Don't worry, we never used him as a snitch. Just told him to bide his time and back you up."

"I'm relieved. He's been a friend for years. Damn good man. A bit cold, but a good man. I believe he'll make a good mayor."

"Not as good as you," Gino answered.

Gino rose to replenish the mayor's drink.

"Bourbon this time, Gino. I don't need to drink scotch anymore to appear trendy."

They smoked and drank in silence, listening to the songs of the night birds coming from the rose garden through the open window. The mayor breathed deeply of the rose-scented warm air.

"Pavarotti?" guessed the mayor.

"Yes," smiled Gino. "Don Giovanni."

"I always liked that one... I'll announce my retirement a month before the election. That way Daniels can ride on the momentum of my campaign until that point. I'll claim failing health. All right?"

"That sounds fine," Gino said. "I admire the way you're taking this, Mr. Mayor. I really wish it could be different, believe me."

"Know when to hold them, know when to fold them," uttered the mayor. "And as you say, I had a good run. Now I can enjoy my ill-gotten gains with no need to live within artificial means in fear that some ambitious reporter might become curious. I really hate the media."

"You worked them like a champ," said Gino.

"Stroke their little egos, make them feel important. Remember their first names. Childish motherfuckers. Petty gossips posing as profound journalists. Most of them can't even spell."

They both laughed.

"What will you do?" asked Gino.

"Travel a bit, at first; then take positions on various boards, engage in charitable work," lied the mayor. He hadn't believed Gino for a minute. As a graft-taking mayor, he was a loose end, thought Sam, and Gino is a careful and cautious man. Gino might wait a year or so, and then the mayor emeritus would have a fatal accident.

Sam knew just what he would do: work a few careful moneymaking scams while he was still mayor, then disappear with his fortune forever; and he wouldn't take that cold bitch wife of his, either. He'd miss Debbie, but nothing else. But she had moved out and distanced herself anyway.

The mayor stubbed out his cigar, finished his drink, and rose. Gino got up and held out his hand. The mayor grinned and shook it. They both laughed heartily.

CHAPTER 65

"Well, Inga, I believe it's time to move on to that villa in the hills of Rio," said Jammison.

"When do you announce your retirement from politics, honey?" asked Inga.

"Next Friday," said the mayor.

Mayor Jammison and Inga Sorenson were leaning back on pillows against the headboard of Inga's king-sized bed.

Inga was a Wisconsin Swede, five-ten, one hundred and thirty pounds of gorgeous blonde woman. They had been lovers for most of the mayor's tenure, a well-kept secret.

"What then?" she asked.

"We quietly disappear as planned."

"You've decided against faking your death, then?"

Inga was a vice president at one of New Orleans' most prominent investment banks. A graduate of the University of Wisconsin, Madison, Inga had an MBA from the business school at MIT. The daughter of a prosperous dairy farmer in upstate Wisconsin, Inga was worldly, urbane, well read and well traveled. She was also a total sexual freak, a gofer who would try anything in bed and often did.

"Yes," said the mayor, taking a sip of Dom Perignon from a

crystal flute glass. "Too risky. I'd have to find a body the right size and age; even then, there are my dental records for identification, as well as those damn DNA tests. No, baby, we'll just quietly fade away."

Inga was not so much a bisexual as a sexual omnivore. "No holds barred in bed," she often said. Inga frequently surprised the mayor with another woman, a wide variety of racial and ethnic types from all walks of life.

"Well, I've liquidated most of your investments, stocks, bonds, CDs, interest bearing accounts. We still have some cash plus bearer bonds in the safe deposit box in the bank here."

"Good. I want you to clear out the box three days after I announce, then leave for Grand Cayman right away. I'll join you within a week," said Sam.

Inga had carefully invested the mayor's graft over the years and was the only person, including the mayor's wife, who knew his true wealth. She served as Jammison's bag lady, making trips several times a year to deposit that cash not invested in the numbered account in the bank in the Grand Caymans.

"What's the total?" asked the mayor.

"A bit less than fifteen million," replied Inga, "not including the bonds and cash in the safe deposit box. All told, more than fifteen million."

"Not bad," said Jammison. He sighed and stretched.

Inga left the bed with their glasses and refilled them from the bottle resting in the silver ice bucket on her large teakwood dresser.

The mayor ran his eyes over her lush body, the hard high buttocks, long dancer's legs. She'd plaited her long hair into a single ponytail that stopped just short of the crack of her ass.

She returned with a smile, her large, firm breasts slightly swaying. She handed the mayor his glass and got back into bed.

"You made the final payment on the villa in Brazil?" asked the mayor.

"Last week, Sam."

"Good. Then we're all ready."

"Right. Once we reinvest the cash at a conservative ten percent, we should have an annual income of more than one and a half million. That will go a long way in Brazil, and think about how many lovelies it will buy us from Ipanema Beach."

"My mouth waters," the mayor answered. They clinked their glasses in toast.

"You're sure that Gino won't try to hunt you down? The Mafia have global connections, you know."

"No, he'll take my disappearance as a sign that I intend no blackmail or double-cross. Gino's more of a corporate executive than a thug."

"I've never been able to tell the difference," Inga said with a smile.

"The former have college degrees; otherwise, they're the same breed."

"And politicians?"

"The worst of them all."

"And you?"

"The champion of sleaze. Watching my mother and father working themselves to death, putting in fourteen-hour days, six days a week in that grocery store, I finally decided I'd get mine any way I could."

"Is that an alibi, Sam?" asked Inga, looking at their reflection in the plate glass mirror overhead. She reached over with her free hand and began playing with Jammison's penis.

"Not at all," said the mayor. "I would have become a greedy thief no matter what my background. Scoundrels are born, not made, baby."

"That's what I like about you, Sam; you're a total sociopath. No conscience whatever."
"Takes one to know one."
"It does, doesn't it," laughed Inga.

CHAPTER 66

It was late evening and the large window leading to the balcony was open slightly, admitting a cool breeze from outside. They'd made love only once, and after a short nap he was about ready for another bout. Jogging five miles a day, working out at the gym three times a week, and eating the right foods had worked miracles. At the age of seventy-two, the mayor's sex drive was little short of amazing. Inga had always enjoyed sex, but the mayor had fully opened her up to an amazing variety of sexual activity. Brought out the maxi-freak in her, as he often said.

"I'll miss Debbie," said the mayor, "but not that frigid bitch Morrow."

"You're sure she's frigid?" asked Inga, taking a sip of champagne.

"For years everything was great. Then she just seemed to lose interest in sex. Haven't touched her hardly in years."

"About when did that happen?"

"Shortly after we began our affair," said the mayor. "Good thing for me you came along."

"Perhaps she has a lover," Inga responded, stroking the mayor's chest and gently biting his nipple.

"Frankly, I don't give a damn. Morrow's a good hostess and

a great first lady and mother. That's good enough for me."

"Do you think she knows about us?"

"Definitely not. After all, she's only met you at official functions."

"It's a shame that she's not into sex. She's absolutely gorgeous," said Inga. "We could have made a wonderful threesome."

Soft music wafted from the stereo across the room, the air lightly scented with sandalwood incense and Inga's perfume. The mayor gave a deep sigh. Life was sweet.

"Too bad I couldn't have had another term in office," said Jammison. "I could double our stash."

"Darling, didn't you warn me about the dangers of uncontrolled greed?" said Inga.

"Just dreaming, baby. Conservative theft is the watchword. Everyone, except you and Gino, thinks I'm a paragon of virtue, living well within my limited means. That's why there will be no concerted search for me. I'll just vanish and be missed for years by the multitude. You know, like 'Hollywood Insider' or 'Entertainment Tonight'… 'Whatever happened to Sam Jammison?'"

Inga watched Sam's penis slowly stiffening in her free hand in the overhead mirror. Sam reached over and began playing with her pussy, feeling the juices flow over his inserted finger, watching her nipples stiffen, as he gazed at her marvelous body in the mirror.

Inga closed her eyes as he began to slowly stroke her erect clitoris, while she continued to stroke his now fully erect penis with her right hand.

Her breathing quickened, she dropped her empty glass on the carpeted floor next to the bed and began playing with her left breast, as the mayor leaned over and began sucking the other.

Her toes curled and uncurled as she began that soft moan that always announced her impending orgasm. With a shudder and a soft cry, she came. The mayor moved as if to mount her.

"Wait, honey," she said, and walked to the dresser, opened the drawer and returned to the bed with a small vial of cocaine, with a small spoon attached to its top by a tiny chain.

"This is fabulous blow, Sam. Take it easy, now."

She took a small amount from the vial and held it to the mayor's left nostril. He inhaled deeply, then she repeated the process twice, sat back on her haunches and awaited the rush.

"Damn!" said the mayor once the coke hit. "That is dynamite shit!"

Inga laughed and took a quick two on two. She capped the vial carefully and placed it in the drawer of the bedside table, then began sucking the mayor's erect penis. After a short while, she moved to straddle his face. Sixty-nine was one of her favorite positions, whether with a male or female partner. Inga loved to have Sam's tongue on her while she sucked him off.

She came again, much stronger this time, but when the mayor reached for her, she withdrew.

"Not yet, Sam," she said. "I have a surprise for you in the other room. Just a minute."

She returned shortly with a doll-like woman, not quite five feet in height, her size and golden brown skin in sharp contrast to Inga's Viking girth.

"This is Hartini, Sam," said Inga, with a wide grin. "Hartini is a student from the island of Java in Indonesia. Of course, I've checked her out, and she's great in bed, honey." Inga slowly slipped the white silk kimono from Hartini's perfectly formed tiny frame. Hartini raised her downcast eyes, then smiled at the size of Sam's erect penis.

Hartini crossed to the bed, kneeling at the mayor's feet, and took his large penis into her small mouth as Inga ate her from behind. He groaned and watched the tableau reflected in the overhead mirror through slitted eyes.

After a short while, Sam crossed to a large armchair across the room and watched them sixty-nine, Hartini on top waving her small, tight buttocks in ecstasy. Through half-closed eyes, he watched the two of them at play, while slowly stroking himself.

After fifteen minutes or so, and several orgasms from the tightly entwined female bodies, he slowly crossed the room and joined them.

CHAPTER 67

"Al," said Pat Callahan, "there's a contract out on Mayor Jammison. He's on the run, and we want you to bring him back because he'll trust you."

"Contract? Who?"

"Gino Provenzano."

"Why?"

"The mayor's been on the take throughout his political career. Sal Cintenni backed every campaign he had, from councilman on up to the mayor's office," said Callahan. They were seated in Callahan's unmarked car at New Orleans International Airport, outside the gate that led to the field for private aircraft.

Clark waited until a 727 took off, its sound receding in distance as it rose swiftly toward cruising altitude.

"Shit! On the take? The sleazy motherfucker! You sure?" asked Clark, pretending to be surprised.

"We're certain. We've been on to him for some time, but lying in wait to get at his mob connections. Gino took the mayor off the payroll after he took over the job, and now he's afraid that the mayor might turn state's evidence."

Clark calmly lit a cigarette, his anger tightly tamped down. I've been waiting for a chance to kill that lying, hypocritical motherfucking mayor, he thought.

"How'd you find this out?" Clark asked.

"Giuseppe Di Marco. His brother J.D. died in the raid and he's pissed that Gino was the only survivor. Also, he wanted to be capo di tutti. Jealousy and revenge are a potent combination. We've got him in the witness protection program, and he's singing like a bird," Callahan answered, looking into the rearview mirror.

"Where's the mayor?"

"In the Grand Caymans. He has a numbered account there, according to a source at his bank. I think he intends to make a run for either Spain or Brazil. Probably Brazil, because it has no extradition treaty with the United States, and we know that he has property there."

"Who's on his tail? The hit man?"

"The Man."

"Shit, Jammison's as good as dead already."

"That's not all," said Callahan. "We believe he's responsible for more than fifty hits throughout the country. Stay away from him, Al."

"Do you know who he is?"

"Finally. A tip from Interpol."

Two stunning flight attendants passed by, pulling their wheeled luggage behind them. Clark and Callahan gave them hardly a glance; although the women checked out the two of them, two good-looking men deep in conversation.

"Who is he?" asked Clark.

"You'll know when you see him, but avoid him at all costs. We've got a tail on him, and we'll pick him up when he returns to the States. In Miami. It's already set up."

"What do you want me to do?" asked Clark.

"Convince the mayor that he'll be safe if he returns. Here." Callahan handed Clark an envelope.

"What's this?"

"An immunity agreement. If the mayor testifies, he won't be prosecuted and we'll put him in the witness protection program."

Clark studied the document, then replaced it in the envelope.

"You have any idea what kind of impact this thing will have on the black community? Black folks idolize that asshole."

"We'll claim the mayor was working undercover for the government. He'll emerge a hero. Come out smelling like a rose."

"He oughta emerge with a good ass-kickin'," said Clark angrily, stamping out his cigarette butt in the dashboard ashtray.

"I agree, but we don't want another incident like the one we had with Mayor Barry in Washington, do we?"

"No, I guess not," said Clark. "But the idea of that asshole looking like a hero."

"There are people in Washington who wanted to expose Jammison, but we looked bad in setting up Mayor Barry, and we don't want this thing to backfire on us. Gino Provenzano and the mob are our primary targets. Fuck the mayor!"

"Damn!" said Clark, pounding his fist against the dashboard.

"Look, Al. I can sympathize with how you feel. Jammison betrayed your people, and your own personal loyalty toward him. But we can't let personal feelings get in the way. This is the best way to do it," added Callahan.

Clark sat in silence for a while, his mind racing. He lit another cigarette, took a deep drag.

"I guess you're right," Clark said finally.

"If you don't want to do this, Al, I'll understand."

"No, I'm a pro, and the best man for the job. What do you want me to do?"

"There's a Lear jet parked outside this gate, ready to go. They'll take you into Grand Cayman."

Callahan handed Clark another envelope. "Your instructions

are in there. You have a hotel reservation, and our tail on The Man will contact you and let you know the mayor's whereabouts. Get to him before The Man does, and get him out of there. You should be back by tomorrow night, or the day after that, at the latest."

"Who's the contact?"

"She's undercover as a stew on The Man's plane. She'll tail him to wherever the mayor is staying, then contact you. The Man always does reconnaissance before he makes the hit. That will give you time to snatch the mayor from under his nose."

"How will I know the contact?"

"She'll contact you. The password is Robin..."

"And the countersign is Hood," Clark chuckled.

Callahan grinned sheepishly. "Yeah, I know. Mickey Mouse shit. But you know the Bureau."

"And you think I could make it in a chickenshit outfit that uses Robin Hood as an identification sign?"

In spite of themselves, they had to laugh, reducing the tension. "No, I guess not," said Callahan. "Even so, you'd be a good one."

"I'd rather be a good cop. I'm up for a promotion next year."

"And the homicide chief retires in two years. Think you might get that?"

"I was counting on Jammison for that boost. Who knows with a new administration?"

"I'll do what I can to help out. We have good connections with the New Orleans police force, not to mention a few more friends in the right places."

"We'll see," said Clark.

"They know you're good at what you do and won't snitch, even though you're not bent yourself. Even New Orleans needs a few honest cops."

"Oh, yeah? Sometimes I wonder."

"Trust me," said Callahan.
"What else can I do?"
"Any questions?"
"Naw. Piece of cake. Go in, bring him back. I'm not looking forward to flying that many hours with that fucking dirtbag."
"No fuckin' shit," Callahan frowned.
"You hang out with a lot of the brothers in Chicago, Pat? You're starting to sound like us."
"Growing up on the South Side? Football at De La Salle High School and Notre Dame? Hell, yeah."
They watched a tan Bentley pull up to the curb. The black chauffeur got out, skirted the back bumper, and opened the rear door.
A tall, muscular man, an obvious bodyguard, emerged from the front passenger seat. He wore shades. There was a large bulge under his left armpit. He stood next to the front door, his head swiveling like a Rottweiler guard dog.
A short, plump man emerged from the back seat, followed by a tall, elegant redhead. He strode toward the gate, two hundred dollar shades, five hundred dollar attaché case, benchmade shoes, and wearing an Armani suit worth a month's lieutenant's pay, the suit doing little to camouflage his soft, Pillsbury doughboy body.
"Big dude's carrying," said Clark.
"Yeah. Forty-four magnum, by the looks of that bulge in his jacket."
"Think the chick can type?"
"No, but I bet she gives great shorthand," Callahan said with a grin.
"Must be great to be rich," said Clark, thinking about Miss Peabody again.
"Not if you have to look like that," Callahan sneered.
"Almost worth it for a chick like that," responded Clark.

The party strode past the security guard, who greeted the little man with a wide smile. Shorty never gave him a glance. The chauffeur followed with the expensive Louis Vuitton pigskin luggage.

"I think there's everything you need on the plane. You're carrying, of course."

"H & K nine millimeter."

"You're not going to need it," Callahan said.

"Beretta on board for you - nine millimeter, seven-inch barrel, thirteen shot clip. No way to trace it."

"Good piece. You got a Kevlar jacket on board, too?"

"Yeah, thought you might want one."

"Don't usually wear one, but if I have to go up against The Man..."

A man motioned toward the car from the gate.

"That's Smith," said Callahan. "He'll show you on board and be your backup, if you need one in Grand Cayman. There's booze, beer, and food on the plane."

"Oh, man."

"No," said Callahan. "He's a good man. Not a robotic bureaucrat like most of the Bureau. You'll get along."

"Okay, I'll take your word for it," said Clark, as he got out of the car.

"Good luck. And watch your back."

"Don't I always?"

Clark walked through the gate, automatically checking his surroundings as he went.

CHAPTER 68

"I'm truly sorry, Mr. Johnson; however, your, uh, friend, Miss Jensen, had the entirety of your funds transferred to a numbered account in Zurich, only three days ago. She did have the right to make such a transfer, as it was a joint account."

"Yes, yes, uh, of course she did," said Sam Jammison, alias Stanley Johnson.

"Of course, I'm not allowed to offer the number of that Zurich account. You understand, of course," said Ian Garrison.

Sam Jammison recovered quickly, although he felt as if someone had kicked him very hard in the pit of his stomach.

The rotten bitch has cleaned me out, thought Sam. Never trust a woman. I'm just one more pussy-whipped sucker. She must have been waiting for this moment for years, watching the bread mount until the faucet turned off, and off to wherever.

Probably the south of France, he thought; she doesn't have much imagination, except in bed. Well, she had enough imagination to set me up for the double-cross of my life. I'll give her that.

Back in New Orleans, it was thought that he was on a quiet vacation, so he had time. Only Inga knew where he was. Even Morrow thought he was incognito in Nassau. He had connections with the French Surete; he could locate her in a matter of hours once he reached France. Then, he'd torture the account number out of the bitch and kill her slowly.

"No," said Sam, "of course not. I just thought she'd left enough to clear up some local bills. Just a simple matter of missed signals."

They were seated in Garrison's paneled office in Grand Cayman. Sam had been puzzled to find his rented villa empty when he'd arrived the evening before. Now he knew why.

Damn freak ass bitch, he thought; and briefly imagined cutting her throat. Fuck it, though Sam, get on the run and save your own black ass. He would go underground in Brazil, establish a new identity, then hunt the bitch down. He was a patient man. Inga could wait.

"Yes. However, we could arrange a small signature loan, if that will help," said Mr. Garrison, president of the bank, who wished to please a depositor of very large funds, even an ex-depositor. One never knew when they might return with hugh amounts of cash to be deposited in rigid secrecy.

Garrison spoke with a phony, fruity Oxbridge accent, although he'd been born in Liverpool and had attended a red brick university.

"No, that won't be necessary," Sam answered confidently. "I will need access to my safe deposit box."

"Certainly, Mr. Johnson. I'll tell them you're on the way to the vault. Can I be of service in any other way?"

"No, thank you. It's been a pleasure doing business with you over the years."

"Indeed," said Garrison, as they rose to shake hands.

Good thing I never told her about this box, thought Sam, as he checked its contents. It held three different sets of identification: passports, driver's licenses, photo identification, all in three different names, as well as more than four hundred thousand dollars in bearer bonds, and a bit more than one hundred thousand dollars in cash.

He transferred the items into his attaché case and left the bank without a backward look. He did not notice the man in the sunglasses, wearing a garish Hawaiian shirt, watching him carefully from across the street; nor did The Man notice the attractive black woman who was watching his reflection in the plate glass window just down the street from the bank. The three of them moved down the street in parade formation.

Sam had an additional four hundred thousand in the carefully hidden safe at the house. He'd checked the night before shortly after arriving on the evening plane. At least she hadn't found the safe. He might have been a sucker for the bitch, but not a complete fool. He had seed money, and he was a survivor.

I have about a million dollars, he thought. A long way from fifteen million, but at least he wasn't broke. He'd still make it to Brazil. First to Miami, then Mexico City, and on to Rio, using different ID to cover his trail.

He wouldn't be able to live as lavishly as planned, but high on the hog nevertheless. The villa in Rio was paid for, he'd made sure of that.

Sam thought he might open a small restaurant in Rio for modest income and invest the balance of the money carefully. He'd always wanted to be a restaurateur. Feature New Orleans style food: Black, Cajun, Creole, pull in the tourists and eventually the moneyed Brazilians, who were as faddish as their kind throughout the world.

High yella went a long way in Brazil, although the Brazilians pretended a lack of racism that was absurd. He'd let his hair grow, not too long, just enough to bring back the curls the women loved. He'd hated to cut it years ago when he'd gone into politics, but it had worked to bond his identification with dark-skinned New

Orleanians, while assuring the high yella creole vote. He'd make sure that he never became more than lightly tanned. He might even marry into one of the nouveau riche families in Rio.

He would hire a valet to look out for himself—take care of his carefully built wardrobe in Rio; give him a professional shave daily; shine his expensive shoes; look out for the ex Sam Jammison. He might even grow a beard.

He'd hire a good-looking Swedish housekeeper to supervise the Brazilian staff and take care of his sexual needs when he wasn't copping tail from the beaches, both tourist and local. No, thought Sam, I'll do all right, I'm a survivor.

Sam strolled to an expensive restaurant on the beach, just off George Town Harbor. He took a table on the verandah overlooking the sea and sat in the warm, bright sun - the temperature in the low eighties - and ordered an expensive meal.

He started with a bourbon on the rocks, then had a shrimp cocktail as an appetizer, followed by a bowl of turtle soup, and an entrée of grouper menuire with asparagus tips and boiled new potatoes, with a half-bottle of Piper Hiedsek champagne. Can't afford Dom Perignon nowadays, thought Sam, and briefly thought of that bitch, Inga.

He finished the meal with a crème caramel, lit a Portofino to smoke with his café filtre and Martell cognac, the sun warm on his face.

A short distance away, The Man had a seafood platter, but he did not drink an alcoholic beverage. He never drank until he'd finished a job.

Inside at the bar, the attractive black woman watched the two of them over a chef's salad because she was watching her weight. Every man in the bar watched her weight as well.

CHAPTER 69

Clark picked up the phone. "Yes?" he said.
"Robin," she said.
"Hood," Clark replied.
"I'll be right up."
"Right."
Shortly, there was a knock on the door. Clark stood to the side, listening.
"Robin," she said.
"Hood."
Nevertheless, he opened the door a crack before letting her in, then searched the hallway with his eyes.
He holstered his pistol and turned to her, who was regarding him through amused eyes. She reached into her large shoulder bag and Clark put his hand on the holstered pistol beneath the shirttails of his black linen shirt.
"Easy," he said.
She smiled as she slowly removed her identification wallet and passed it to Clark, who studied it carefully. Careful and cautious, she thought; not bad for a cop off his own turf.
"Special Agent Robin Carter, Detective. At your service."
She could look Clark straight in the eye, even in sandals. An

Amazon, thought Clark: broad shoulders, hefty hips, breasts to match. She wore an unfashionable short 'fro, large hoop earrings dangled from her well-shaped ears. Her face was round with a gently pointed chin, high cheekbones, and almond eyes, her skin the color of bittersweet chocolate. She must be six foot or more, thought Clark.

"I'm an even six feet, " she said, reading his mind. "I weigh one hundred and fifty-two pounds, and yes, I played high school basketball."

"Have a seat," said Clark. "Drink?"

"Whatever you're having," she said.

"Mineral water, or fresh orange juice," said Clark.

"You don't drink?"

"Not when I'm going into a scene."

"I thought the troops in Viet Nam usually got high before they went into combat."

"Yeah, and most of them are dead."

He poured two glasses of orange juice from the thermos. A soft, salt-scented breeze blew gently through the open window. They were in a hotel on the beach just off High Street, the main drag.

"You don't like air conditioning?"

"No," said Clark.

She loosened two buttons on her silk blouse, showing some cleavage, judging his reaction over the rim of her glass. Clark realized she was wearing no bra. He felt himself stirring.

"Run it down," said Clark, motioning with his hand.

"Smith and I have been on them all day, switching off and on. The mayor had a leisurely lunch, took some sun, then went into the gym at the hotel for a workout. They seem to know him here. The Man's been on him all the way. He changes shirts and hats, fades into the background."

"Has he made you yet?"

"I don't think so. We give them both a wide berth," she said. She crossed her long legs and began gently moving her foot back and forth.

"Where are they now?"

"In the bar downstairs. Jammison is trying to pick up a woman. A blonde," she said with some distaste.

Like that, thought Clark. She's probably a feminist as well.

"How do you feel about working with a woman?" she asked.

Clark ignored the question. "Where's The Man staying?"

"Four-oh-six."

"You?"

"Three-oh-two."

Clark was on five; they had him bracketed.

"Smith will phone if there's any change. What time are you going for the mayor?"

"Just after dark. The Man won't move before then. I'll call the mayor on the cellular phone. I think he'll let me in without a fuss. He trusts me," said Clark, and for a moment, his feelings flashed across his face. He looked away to hide them.

And you trusted him, she thought, and he not only betrayed you, but your people. She could feel the pain he was attempting to hide. A sensitive macho man, she thought. Isn't that an oxymoron?

"The Man?" she asked.

"He's not our job. We take the mayor back on the jet, and they pick up The Man in Miami."

"Now what?"

"How far is the mayor's house?"

"Ten-minute drive," she said.

"Come on, I want to check it out. Tell Smith he can contact us on the portable phone."

Clark finished his orange juice and moved to the elevator

while she was on the phone.

She held out the keys to the rental car.

"You drive," said Clark. "You know the road."

Again, she was slightly amused. A man who doesn't want to drive?

She drove the way she did most things, with smooth efficiency.

"You race?" said Clark.

"Used to. Georgia, mainly. Stockers."

They arrived in less than five minutes.

"Park near that hill," said Clark.

He took a pair of binoculars and climbed the short rise, then studied the beach house and area with great care.

She lit a cigarette, standing back in the shade of the pines, and studied him. Six-two or three, she thought. A little loose around the middle, but good muscle tone, must work out. Probably about fifty, but looks to be in his early forties, even with a touch of gray in his close-cropped hair.

He's in a zone, she thought, and except for a brief once-over, and when she'd unbuttoned her shirt, he'd been all business, and she knew how fine she was.

I wonder how big he is, she thought, then dismissed the thought as she felt her nipples begin to harden. It's not him, she thought; everyone gets horny before the deal goes down. I hate macho men.

Clark moved to several vantage points, then put the glasses back into the case.

"Tell Smith we're on the way back," he said.

She watched his pantherish grace as he moved down the hill. She dialed the number.

"Mind if I take a shower?" she asked, when they got back to Clark's room. "I have a change of clothes in my bag."

"Help yourself," he answered, as he poured himself a glass of mineral water.

She moved to the bathroom door, stopped and turned, one hand on the knob, the other on her hip.

"Why don't you join me?" she asked.

CHAPTER 70

She was riding him, hips moving gently, stringing it out, when the phone rang. She picked up the phone without missing a stroke.

"Yes? Be right down."

Clark had found that spot. Her movements quickened; he wet his fingers and stroked her clitoris, timing it. In seconds they came simultaneously. It had been a long flight and he was a bit more uptight than he had expected. The release was good, relieved tension.

She rose and began to dress, as did Clark.

"The mayor has just left," she said.

"The Man?"

"Went up to his room fifteen minutes ago."

"Call his room, make up a story when he answers," said Clark.

She rang The Man's room. "No answer," she said.

"Shit!" said Clark. "Tell Smith to meet us at his room."

He moved swiftly to the stairs, as she followed.

They moved slowly toward four-oh-six, guns drawn. She was packing a forty-four magnum, the most powerful handgun in the world. Dirty Harry's piece —and she looked like she knew how to use it.

Smith moved from the elevator, a gadget in his hand that looked like a television control.

"What the fuck is that?" said Clark.

"Infrared scan. It will read his heat, if he's in there."

Clark raised his right foot and kicked the locked door open. The Man was gone.

"Come on!" said Clark. They raced down the stairs for the car.

CHAPTER 71

The mayor was sitting in the dark, smoking a cigar, drinking bourbon, when he heard the car drive up. He picked up his pistol and peeked through the window, as the figure approached, gun drawn.

He jacked a round into the chamber, cocked the piece, and without hesitation, opened the door and fired twice.

The Man went down on his face. The mayor moved to the right of the door and searched the area carefully. Two shots smashed him against the wall. He slid down slowly, trying to raise the automatic that had somehow become too heavy.

The Man slowly approached, gun in both hands and trained on the mayor.

"You," said the mayor.
"Yeah, me."
"Gino?"
"Taking out insurance," said The Man.
"I wasn't going to snitch."
"I know. But you know the way they are."
"You jive motherfucker. How'd you know where I was?"
"Phone call. Woman's voice."
"Inga," said the mayor. "Double-crossing bitch." His voice

was weaker, his breath coming in gasps. It wouldn't be long now.

"You always were a sucker for a piece of ass," he said.

"What the fuck?" said the mayor. "I know I hit you twice."

"I always wear my vest, Mr. Mayor," said The Man.

"I should have gone for the head," the mayor answered, coughing.

"Shit happens," said The Man, but the mayor never heard him.

The Man slid his piece into a shoulder holster, moved into the house, and began searching it carefully.

CHAPTER 72

They heard the shots as they moved toward the house; first two, then shortly, another. They began to run.

When they reached the house, Clark said, "Robin, take the right flank, Smith the left. Get down and stay in the shadows. Don't do anything until I give a signal. This is my play."

They moved away as Clark attempted to slow his breathing.

Inside, The Man finished his search. No papers or tapes. Jammison's luggage held nothing more than clothing and personal belongings.

He searched the mayor's body for the key, then unlocked and unzipped the nylon carry-on bag. Bingo! He swiftly looked through the cash and bearer bonds. Must be about five hundred grand, he thought. Good score. Gino would never see the money. He relocked the bag and put the key into his pocket.

He opened the door, switched the bag to his right hand, and wiped the knob of fingerprints with his handkerchief.

"Hold it," said Clark. "Turn around slow."

"Hello, Al," said The Man.

"Burke," said Clark, stunned. "You sonofabitch!"

"How'd you find me?"

"You were followed."

"Bullshit. Nobody followed me," Burke snapped confidently.

"Yes, she did," said Clark. Clark was wearing black against the dark sea behind him. Burke was silhouetted by the light from behind, framed in the doorway.

Need every edge I can get, thought Clark. I know just how good he is with that piece.

"Lotta dough in this bag. Why don't we split it, and I'll be on my way," Burke told his partner.

"No way."

"Now what?" asked Burke. "You gonna try and take me in?"

"No," said Clark.

"Like that, huh?"

"Like that," answered Clark.

"You really think you can take me, partner?"

"Yeah."

"You gonna die trying," said Burke.

"You were the leak to the Mob."

"Yeah. Until we were transferred to Homicide."

"You killed Cintenni?"

"Sure," said Burke. "I've done forty-two hits for the Mob over the years."

"Just one thing," said Clark. "Why?"

"Two reasons. First, I like to kill. Took down my first man when I was sixteen. Bastard dishonored my sister. Knocked her up, then refused to marry her. Six-inch blade in the gut. Loved the look on his face when he knew he was gonna die.

"Lied about my age and joined the Corps. Korea, three stints in the Nam. Never even a scratch. Did my twenty, then joined the force. Been killing all that time. Killing's what I do."

"Second reason?"

"Money. Need a lot for the Lady," said Burke.

"Bullshit. You never had a woman. You're a classic whoremonger. When you want some, you buy it."

"A boat."

"That fucking fiberglass sloop you got at the marina?"

"Naw, the General's Lady. Forty-two foot motor cruiser. Hatteras. Mahogany hull, teak deck, ketch rigged, custom sails, Perkins diesel, satellite navigation system, automatic depth finder. The works. Got it docked in Bimini. Gonna take it on a cruise of the South Sea Islands when I retire in December."

"You're gonna retire tonight, motherfucker!" said Clark.

Burke sighed, turned his head to distract Clark, dropped the bag and moved his hand toward his holstered piece.

Clark hadn't been fooled. You don't watch a man's eyes, because the eyes can lie. As a boxer does, you focus on a point on the chest just below the chin. The hands can lie, but not the shoulders. When they began to shift, Clark brought his gun up smoothly, ignoring the flashing hand, ignoring Burke's rapid draw, ignoring his left hand moving up for the two-handed grip Burke favored, ignoring everything except the target, taking that extra instant to be sure before he gently squeezed off the shot.

The reports blended into one another, and both men went down.

Robin ran swiftly to Clark's supine figure, as Smith slowly approached Burke, his Mac-10 machine pistol held steady on him.

"Clark!" she said.

"I'm all right. I'm wearing a vest, remember? I was counting on that, because he knows I hate these damn things."

He felt his chest. Two shots to the heart, he knew. He'd have a heavy bruise tomorrow, because of Burke's attitude the bullets would hurt more. Clark had seen what he could do on the firing range and in the shoot-outs they'd engaged in as a team. Team, he thought, the thought bitter. All these years, and both Burke and

Jammison putting him on. Clark felt like a prize sucker.

"You dumb sonofabitch!" said Robin. "What the fuck do you think this is, some Hollywood western? You should have used your backup!"

"Naw. Something I had to do myself."

He rose on unsteady legs, she helping him. They approached the two bodies.

"Both dead," said Smith. "Why'd you go for the head in this kind of light?" asked Smith.

"Only chance I had," said Clark with a sigh of relief. "I knew he always wore a vest, and he knew I hated 'em. Robin, get a branch and rub out all the footprints except Burke's."

"Yeah," said Robin, "the woman does the housework."

"If you'd rather carry Burke..."

"Think I can't? I can bench press..."

"Woman, would you shut the fuck up?" said Clark.

"Yassuh, boss." She grinned and moved toward a nearby pine. "Nobody knows the troubles I'se seed," she sang.

Smith and Clark grinned at one another.

"We'll move Burke back to where he fell the first time." They did, Burke's blocky body was heavy.

"Let's see," said Clark. "He fired two rounds to kill the mayor. The rounds should have gone through his body and fragmented on the wall, so there will be no ballistics match. But just in case, let's leave the right piece."

Clark fired another round from his weapon toward the sea. Carefully wiping the drop gun Callahan had provided, he placed the mayor's prints on it, then placed it near his right hand. Looks good, Clark thought. "The Man got the drop on the mayor. The mayor shot him, but he didn't know The Man was wearing a bulletproof vest. The Man gets the drop on the mayor, makes him get rid of the piece, but the mayor has a second gun. They had a shoot-out and both went down. Okay?"

"Looks good to me," said Smith. "I'll give Robin a hand."

Clark quickly searched the Man's pockets for the key to the lock of the carry-on. Inside he found the cash and the bearer bonds. Nobody alive knew what was in that bag but him. Looking out the window, he could see beams from the flashlights in the blackness as Robin and Smith wiped out footprints. He quickly searched for a hidden safe and found it. What the hell, he thought. He had to see if he still had it. Minutes later the safe was open. He removed four hundred thousand dollars in cash, plus over one hundred thousand dollars from the bag, concealing some of it in his Kevlar jacket and some in his pants waistband under the shirttail he was wearing outside his pants. He relocked the safe and the bag, wiping away any fingerprints, putting the key for the bag into his pocket. Clark took another look around the area.

He walked to the covered verandah and regarded Jammison's body for a long moment. "Motherfucker," he said softly. "It's about time." He picked up the nylon bag and walked back toward the car. Robin and Smith wiped out all the footprints except those of Jammison and Burke.

They entered the car and headed back to the hotel.

"Okay, Smith," said Clark. "Did you report in with the local police?"

"Yes," said Smith.

"Robin?"

"No," said Robin. "They think I'm a stew who worked her way here for a vacation."

"Good," said Clark. "We'll check out of the hotel together. They'll think I picked you up and we're going someplace else. When we check out, Robin, make it look like we're new lovers."

"That won't be difficult," said Robin. Smith snickered in the back seat.

"Smith, call the Lear and say we'll be leaving in an hour."

Clark waited until he'd made the call. "Now, here's your story, Smith: You followed Burke to the mayor's house but got there too late. Let them take it from there. You take the car back to the house, give us a half hour after takeoff, then phone the locals from Jammison's house. Okay?"

"Right," said Smith.

He can't even call him the mayor anymore, thought Robin. That bastard really hurt him. She wanted to reach out and hold his head to her breasts. There will be time for that, Robin, she thought.

What am I ever going to do with this man? she thought. He's not my type. Not at all my type.

She'd figure out something, she was sure.

CHAPTER 73

"Mano y mano! I hate macho men. If it had been me, the sucker would have gone down as soon as he came through that door," said Robin.

"Well, it wasn't you," Clark responded evenly. "I did it my way. The way it had to go down. He was my partner, and he'd been messing me around for years. Both of them! Burke understood."

They were high above the Caribbean, moving swiftly on the way back to New Orleans, sipping rum and Coke, slowly coming down from the adrenaline high.

"I'll never understand men!" she said in exasperation.

"Sure you do. All women do - from infancy on. It's what gives you the edge."

"Then why aren't we ruling the world?"

"Because y'all compete with one another, while men work as a team. If women ever got together, y'all could take over in a year."

"Well, look who's talking like a feminist," she said with a wry smile.

She lit a cigarette and looked out at the sea far below. The moon had come out, full and bright, striking pale fire off the water's surface.

"Why were you sure you could take him?" she asked. "You said he was faster."

"Overconfidence gave me the edge. He was faster, but not by that much. On the range, I used to let him win. Not always, but enough to keep him cool."

"Keep him cool?"

"Yeah. He hated to lose. Whenever I won, he'd pout for days. I didn't want a crybaby watching my back." He took a sip of his drink. "Besides, in a strange kinda way, I really liked Burke," he said sourly. "Even saved my life a couple of times."

"You think he felt the same way about you?"

"Who knows, but I sure as hell wanted to kill him once I found out he was the fuckin' assassin we've been after." He did some shoulder rolls, trying to work the stress stiffness out.

"Turn around," she said. "I can take care of that."

He turned, and she began digging deep into the trapezoid muscles with strong yet gentle fingers.

"You married?" she said. "I guess it's a little late to be asking."

"No. My wife died not long ago. Accidental. Overdosed on sleeping pills and booze."

"I'm sorry," she said.

"It's all right. We'd been divorced for some time. Still..."

"If it was ever right once, that feeling never completely dies." She looked out the window, remembering.

"Yes, that's true, I guess," he said.

"You have any children?"

"Two. Boy and girl. Boy's at Howe Military Academy. Girl's in boarding school. Good kids. Ummm, that feels good." He could feel the stiffness easing, blood rushing into blocked tissues.

"I'll bet you're a sucker for the girl."

He grinned. "You know it. That's my baby."

"How old are you?" she asked.

He looked at her over his shoulder, smiling slightly, before replying, "Fifty-two."

"I'm thirty-four, and my biological clock is ticking. I want to have some babies."

"So, have some babies."

"I intend to."

"Picked out the father yet?"

"Oh, somebody about fifty-two, strong, a dedicated father."

"Baby, slow your roll. Ouch! I don't know where you're headed, but my kids are almost grown. I've been down that road already."

"You didn't tell me to slow my roll this afternoon, Mr. Kama Sutra." They laughed.

"You're a whole lot of woman, Robin. Why would you want to get mixed up with a broken-down ex-jock, living on a cop's salary?"

"Maybe I like what's in your genes," she answered with a smile.

She finished the massage, and he sat back with a sigh. "You're good."

"That's only a sample," she said. "I studied Shiatsu and acupressure. I can walk on your back, too."

"Big as you are? No, thanks."

"I'm going to spend a few days in New Orleans. Want to show me your town?"

"Sure," he said. "I've got some vacation time. I'll take a couple of days off. Where you staying?"

"I have a suite at The Fairmont."

"The Bureau paid for that?"

"No, I upgraded."

"On your salary?"

"You could do worse," she said. "My father owns three very successful businesses in Atlanta, including one of the largest construction companies. You see, I'm rich and fine."

And I'm not exactly poor, he thought. Double indemnity on a quarter million insurance policy, plus my share of Jammison's stash. This time, he'd take his share; he'd earned it. He'd split it with the nine raiders, eight now that Burke was dead.

He levered the seat back and closed his eyes. He was tired.

She watched his face for a long while, sipping her drink. Yes, she was sure; she'd been looking for this man for a long time.

She sat for a while, deep in thought, then rummaged through her large shoulder bag. She took out her birth control pills and slipped them into the pouch on the back of the seat in front of her.

Clark observed this through half-closed eyes. She did not miss the fleeting smile that crossed his face as he slid into deep sleep.

Something kept nagging her: Why would a cop of his experience and talent not check for the freight elevator that The Man had used as an escape route?

The question puzzled her until she dropped off to sleep.

CHAPTER 74

Finally, it looked like the time had come. Nick Shannon had even planted an electronic bug under his prey's car, but there was never a payoff, at least not the one he wanted. If there really was such a thing as a sex addict, Lawrence Daniels must have been president of the club. Everywhere he went he was trying to pick up women. College girls, high school girls, prostitutes, friends' wives, it made little difference. Using his favorite toy again, the 35 millimeter Contax camera, Nick had hundreds of damaging photos of the man who was sure to become New Orleans' next mayor, but blackmail was nowhere in the cards.

Tonight something different was going down. Daniels had pulled up in front of the Meridien Hotel on Canal Street and picked up one of the finest ebony-colored black women Shannon had ever seen. Exquisitely shaped, with a face like Halle Berry, well dressed and wearing a broad smile, she slipped into the seat beside Daniels, closing the door behind her. The Lincoln pulled off and Nick followed.

In a couple of minutes, they were on I-10 headed east toward Slidell. Traffic was steady, so Nick had no problem blending into the flow, but this time he had an idea that he knew exactly where they were going.

PLAYING FOR KEEPS

Those on the inside knew of Lawrence Daniels' reputation for discreetly providing both drugs and girls for the well-heeled before he got involved in politics. It was funny, Nick thought, that once a person got enough money or enough power, nobody seemed to care about what they had done or how they got the money. Everybody knew how Gino felt about black women, and Daniels intended to score big with this one.

His hunch was right. Lawrence Daniels and his companion drove straight to Uncle Sal's mansion on Highway 90 near the Rigolets. Gino was not as paranoid as his predecessor and usually kept only three guards. Nick had done his recon homework already, just waiting for the right opportunity, hoping it would come.

So many people had been hurt. How could Gino or Daniels possibly have overlooked their own vulnerability? How could either one of them have forgotten that Debbie Jammison had been beaten and raped by Boutte? Had her rescue been enough? Would no one avenge her pain and suffering?

Nick pulled over and parked on the side of the road about a half mile away from the house, grabbing his binoculars.

He spotted the guard at the front of the house as he inched his way forward, putting the silencer on his Beretta. One shot, one hit, the dog beside the guard. A second later, as the guard rose reaching for the shoulder holster inside his coat, a second shot, and he fell to the ground.

Nick Shannon made his way around to the water side of the house, where a second guard was seated on a bench beside the dock smoking. He took a long draw, plucked the cigarette into the water, stood up, then stretched. A third shot and the guard fell into the water with a loud splash.

Using a sling and hook, he clamped onto the iron rail of the upstairs balcony and pulled himself up. Between the plants he could see Daniels, Gino, and the woman laughing, drinking and snorting lines of cocaine, Gino's hand stroking her ass. The woman dropped to her knees, unzipped Gino's pants, pulled out his penis, then sucked it to erection.

Nick entered the room, gun drawn. Daniels flung the mirror with the cocaine at Nick, hitting the barrel of his gun, deflecting it as it discharged. Daniels reached for a gun in his belt holster, getting off one wild shot. An instant later, Nick fired twice, two shots to Daniels' chest, as he crashed into the coffee table.

As the woman screamed hysterically, a third guard burst into the room, firing at Nick and spraying the room with his machine pistol. Nick lunged for the floor, as Gino darted toward the greenhouse. Nick returned fire and the third guard went down, the woman standing in the center of the room still screaming.

Gino ran across the greenhouse, climbed the rail and dropped to the ground. He ran the short distance to the dock, untied one of the speedboats, boarded, turned the key, then hit the throttle.

Nick was only a couple of minutes behind Gino. As the speedboat pulled away, Nick made a desperate leap and landed in the boat. Gino and Shannon fought as the boat sped out of control. As the fighting raged, Gino drew a knife. Finally, Nick overpowered Gino, driving the knife deep into his abdomen. Nick recovered, jumping overboard seconds before the boat collided with a trawler in the darkness and exploded.

CHAPTER 75

"Why'd a cop with your experience not cover the back exit?" asked Callahan.

"Fucked up, I guess," replied Clark.

They were sitting on the back verandah of Injun Joe's restaurant, cooled by a slight breeze off the bayou, sipping Beck's and Heineken from the bottle.

Clark regarded Callahan from half-closed eyes. Injun Joe sat a short distance away, puffing on his corncob pipe, sipping Martell, pretending not to hear.

Joe hears every word, thought Clark. He's got ears like a cat.

I wonder if he's wired, thought Joe.

As if reading Joe's mind, Callahan stood and slowly unbuttoned his short-sleeved khaki bush jacket, revealing his massive chest, a thick layer of hard fat covering his big muscles. He turned around and held up the back of the jacket.

"I'm not wired," he said. "Okay?"

"You gonna turn me in?" asked Clark.

Callahan sat back down, took a sip from his bottle. "Hell, no," he answered. "I knew you wouldn't bring him back. That's why I sent you. We both know damn well Washington was lying. There would have been the inevitable leak, and another black hero down the tubes."

"You used me?"

"I put the ferret down the hole, and the ferret did what ferrets do. Five hundred thousand in bearer bonds was in that carry-on you lifted from Jammison. Funny thing, though. The authorities found less than one hundred dollars on him. I wonder what happened to all that cash he stole?"

"Guess we'll never know, will we?"

"Like I said before, Al. You're a damn good cop," said Callahan with a smile.

"Thanks," Clark answered. "You, too."

"I'll drink to that." They clinked bottles.

Overhead, they could hear the raucous cry of flying gulls, as waves lapped against the sandy beach.

"I'm going up to Chicago next week. Check out the free Blues Festival in Grant Park. Why don't you come along?" said Callahan.

"Why not?" said Clark. "I can bring my son over from Indiana. He needs to hear where hip-hop came from."

"Blues. Yeah, Chicago's a blues town. Buddy Guy's joint on South Wabash," said Callahan with a grin.

"Checkerboard Lounge on Muddy Waters Drive on the South Side," added Clark.

"Unleaded Blues on South Chicago Avenue."

"Don't forget the jazz," said Callahan. "Von Freeman at the New Apartment. Hanah John Taylor at the Other Place."

"Soul food!"

"Gladys."

"H & A."

"Army & Lou's."

"Fried catfish."

"Corn on the cob."

"Homemade biscuits!"

"Yeah, man!"

They sat back, mouths watering.

"Black people cook almost as well in Chicago as in New Orleans," said Callahan.

"Plenty of folks from Louisiana up there," said Clark. "My cousin's a lieutenant on the force. We can stay with him. Got a three bedroom condo in Lake Point Towers."

"On a lieutenant's pay? He bent?" asked Callahan.

"Naw, plays the stock market. Has an MBA from the University of Chicago. Put my own portfolio together. You got to talk to him; let him put your bread to work."

"Yeah," said Callahan. "You'll get a chance to meet my girl. Mary O'Keefe. Met her a couple of years ago at a family reunion. She's assistant principal at St. Anselm's. We can stay at her place, too." "Maybe you, me, Mary and Robin can have a double wedding," Callahan laughed.

Clark laughed back. "What makes you think I wanna get married?"

"She asked for a transfer to New Orleans. I approved it. Probably be here in a month. Watch out; she's like the Canadian Mounties: always gets her man."

"Already got this one."

Callahan looked out toward Joe's anchored boat, riding light on the slight swell. He clapped his big hand on the table, almost knocking over the beer bottles.

"You came in from the water when you rescued the mayor's daughter!" he said. "No wonder the roadblocks didn't turn anything up."

"Don't know what you're talking about," Clark said with a broad grin.

Across the way, Joe grinned also. White boy's not as dumb

as he looks, thought Joe.

"Hey, Joe," said Clark, "stop pretending you don't hear. Bring that bottle over here. We got to celebrate, man. Agent Callahan's gonna get married."

"I'm getting married in the morning . . ." sang Callahan.

Clark joined in, as did Joe when he came over with the bottle. He poured them two stiff drinks in their unused glasses.

"Get me to the church, get me to the church, please get me to the church on time . . ." they all sang.

They clinked glasses and drank deeply.

"Hey, Marie . . ." Joe shouted.

"Shut up, Joe," said Marie. "I'll bring the food when it's ready."

They all laughed.

CHAPTER 76

It was a week later. They were flying at supersonic speed at sixty thousand feet toward Paris in the Air France Concorde.

"Here's to us, baby," said Inga. They clinked their glasses of Dom Perignon.

"I love you, Inga," said Morrow Jammison, holding the other woman's hand tightly. "Tell me about the boutique again, honey."

"It's in the square just off the marina in the old quarter in Antibes. Not too small, and I've not redecorated. That's your job. You pick out the clothing, decide on the décor, I handle the business end and recruit the sales force. It's less than a half-hour's drive from St. Paul du Vence, where we'll be living. "We'll go to Paris three times a year to do the buying, and find some seamstresses to carry out your own designs."

"The villa?"

"On a hill in St. Paul du Vence. You'll love the village. Are you having second thoughts about us?" asked Inga. "After all, we've been in the closet for years. I'll understand."

"No, not that. I'm glad we can let the world know how we feel about each other. It's Debbie who worries me. She's been through so much—the kidnapping, Ray's death, her father's murder. What will she think when she discovers her mother's gay?"

Inga fixed them caviar on small points of bread, squeezed fresh lemon juice, handed Morrow one, and took a small bite from her own before answering.

"She might already suspect. Anyway, young people are very broad-minded these days; homosexuality doesn't frighten them at all. Besides, she might have experimented at that convent school you had her in, in Paris."

"Inga!" Morrow said, shocked.

"Well, didn't you tell me you had your first sexual experience at the same school years ago?"

Morrow blushed. "Yes," she said, smiling slightly. "Little Catherine. Took her three patient months before she seduced me. Hot little thing. Wonder what happened to her?"

"Probably married a rich provincial banker. Had a slew of children, and thinks about you when she masturbates." They laughed.

"I don't know," said Morrow. "Debbie?"

"Calm down, honey. There's nothing queer about Debbie."

"Do you think Nick Shannon's too old for her?"

"He's not too old for me. That's one sexy man."

"Look, Inga. You promised no more playing around. I was married to one player, and I don't need another one in you."

"All right, sweetheart. I promise. But there's nothing wrong with a little three-way party now and then, is there? Tell me you didn't enjoy Hartini."

Morrow looked at the window to hide her smile. They'd spent almost two weeks in New York, in an expensive East Side hotel, going to theaters, dining in fine restaurants, checking out the latest fashions, and making wild love celebrating their mutual freedom from Samuel Jammison Jr.

Now they were on their way to a new and open life in France. Morrow was a bit frightened.

"Scared?" asked Inga, reading Morrow's mind and stroking her arm delicately.

"A bit. You don't mind, do you?"

"No," said Inga. "Being in love is new to me, too."

"You do love me, Inga?"

"Oh, yes, baby," she said. She leaned over and kissed Morrow. At first she hesitated, then returned the kiss passionately.

Inga turned to see the couple across the aisle. The man gave a classic Gallic shrug; the woman seated behind him next to the window gave Inga a broad smile and a wink. When the man returned his attention to Paris Match, Inga returned the wink.

As they were standing in the aisle waiting to deplane, the woman sneaked a card into Inga's hand. She glanced at it briefly: Monique Nostrand, a fashion critic. She might be a good contact.

Two afternoons later, Inga, Morrow, and Monique had a wild and happy session in the King George V Hotel, while across the city on the left bank, Monique's husband was fucking his mistress.

EPILOGUE

Robin transferred to New Orleans and moved in with Al Clark. Later that year, he and Robin and Callahan and Mary were married in a double wedding in St. Anselm's Catholic Church on Sixty-First and Michigan Avenue on Chicago's South Side.

The Robinson brothers invested their part of the mayor's stash plus investments from the money from the raid, and bought a hotel in St. Thomas that they ran as a resort and school for scuba divers. The silent brothers married two talkative St. Thomian sisters, who supervised the kitchen and housekeeping staff, respectively.

Barry Barrett continued his freewheeling lifestyle, taking flying lessons, and buying a six passenger, twin engine Cessena.

A year later, Debbie and Shannon were married in a small church in St. Paul du Vence, where Morrow and Inga had a large villa, just after Debbie received her master's degree in finance. Selma was matron of honor and Billy the best man.

As a honeymoon, Debbie and Shannon rented a yacht, and with Joe at the helm and Marie in the galley, took a two-week cruise of the Greek islands.

Debbie opened a day care center on South Rampart Street with Selma as her assistant, specializing in taking care of children whose mothers were addicts or had AIDS.

Robin gave birth to a son, who was named Patrick Callahan Clark. After the birth of her son, Robin resigned from the FBI and formed a partnership with Shannon.

Sherif, a freedom fighting pragmatist till the end, was elected to the New Orleans City Council from District B. He represented the area where the Rampart Street War was staged. New businesses, beautiful hotels and fine homes were being built there, just as Theo Brazzi had predicted.

After Samuel Jammison Jr.'s retirement, then murder, and Lawrence Daniels' death, several popular New Orleans city council members and the hard working Chief of Police threw their hats into the ring to run for mayor.

At least twice a year, everyone and their respective families, plus the Callahans, joined the Robinson brothers in St. Thomas, with children everywhere, telling lies and reminiscing about the raid to save Debbie. The lies grew every year.

Inga and Morrow lived happily ever after.

BOOK AVAILABLE THROUGH
Milligan Books, Inc.
An Imprint Of Professional Business
Consulting Service

Playing For Keeps $14.95

Order Form

Milligan Books
1425 West Manchester, Suite B,
Los Angeles, California 90047
(323) 750-3592

Mail Check or Money Order to:
Milligan Books

Name _____ Date _____
Address _____
City _____ State _____ Zip Code _____
Day telephone _____
Evening telephone _____
Book title _____

Number of books ordered ___ Total cost .... $ _____
Sales Taxes (CA Add 8.25%) .... $ _____
Shipping & Handling $4.50 per book .... $ _____
Total Amount Due .... $ _____

_ Check   _ Money Order   Other Cards _____
_ Visa   _ Master Card   Expiration Date _____
Credit Card No. _____
Driver's License No. _____

Signature _____   Date _____